THE REUNION

ALSO BY SAMANTHA HAYES

In Too Deep
You Belong to Me
Before You Die
No Way Out
Until You're Mine

THE REUNION

SAMANTHA HAYES

bookouture

Published by Bookouture in 2018

An imprint of StoryFire Ltd.
Carmelite House
50 Victoria Embankment
London EC4Y 0DZ

www.bookouture.com

ISBN: 978-1-78681-305-3
eBook ISBN: 978-1-78681-304-6

For Ben, Polly and Lucy,
with all my love

PROLOGUE

August 1996

'It's not your fault.'

That's what the police officer told me as I sat shaking under a blanket. 'Little girls go missing,' she said, as if it happened every day. I felt as though I was underwater – her words fizzy bubbles, popped one by one by my mother's piercing screams.

I'd lost my little sister.

'Mrs Lucas,' she said. 'We need you to keep calm…'

The rest of the officer's words floated, unheard, between me and my panicking mother as the horror of not having little Lenni in the kitchen hacking up chunks of crumbly cake or sloshing milk from the carton settled between us.

Of course it was my fault.

They asked me what she was wearing but my mind was on fire, wouldn't work. Then my younger brother, Jason, came in, tripping on the step, wide-eyed, grabbing the door frame, panting. He looked around – his gaze a slow swirl of realisation. Everything was in slow motion.

'Is she back?' His hair was the colour of tandoori spice as the curls brushed his tanned cheeks.

I shook my head, then tried to focus. I knew what I wanted to say, but it wouldn't come out… a swimsuit, plastic beach shoes… My teeth clamped together. The gritty sand between my toes felt like rocks. 'Or maybe a dress…' I heard myself saying. The lightness of that perfect summer's day – a day when things should have been special for Nick and me – had transformed into a crumpled photograph of horrific possibilities.

'No, she's not back yet,' the police officer told Jason. One of the two entrenched in our kitchen, she was young, kind and patient. Their uniforms made everything seem so badly serious.

'*Yet?*' My mother stopped crying, scoring her nails into the table top. Her face was ferocious, splitting at the seams in a way I'd never seen before.

'I'm sure we'll find her very soon,' the officer said, as if we were discussing the chance of rain later. 'Most are just runaways or get a bit lost.'

'She's only thirteen,' Jason said. 'But she acts much younger,' he added for some reason. He glanced at me, swallowing several times. I stared at my feet.

The officer spoke into her radio, turning away from us as the crackled message fed back.

Think, think, think…

'Please, Claire, *please?* Pretty please with cherries on top and fairy dust and icing sugar from angels' wings?' Lenni's feet had scuffed the hot sand. She was so impatient. So determined to be independent.

I laughed. She seemed tiny with the ocean behind her. Her hair was ratty, dripping and dark from the salty water, not the usual flyaway red-gold. She jumped about in the one-piece bathing suit I'd lent her – sloppy at the legs and loose at the shoulders because she insisted on wearing a grown-up swimsuit. She hated those stupid ones for younger kids that Mum always bought. Her protests would be terminated with a pout – a delicious little-sister pout that I couldn't resist.

Lenni hadn't matured much since she was eight.

'I'll be quick. Lightning quick. So quick I'll be back before I've even gone.'

'Then you must have been and come back already, Lenni, so sit down and wait for the others to finish their swim. We can all go and get ice cream then.'

She jumped and stamped and went red with rage.

'Lenni, you're thirteen. Stop it.'

'Exactly. So let me go and get ice cream.'

'You know the rules. Mum says not to let you out of my sight.'

'Mum won't know.'

Poor Lenni. The baby of our family. The one Mum and Dad protected the most out of the three of us. She was driven to school every morning instead of taking the bus. She wasn't allowed into town on a Saturday to pick her way through racks of cheap earrings and nail varnish with the other girls. She wore flat shoes, all her skirts were below the knee and she'd never held hands with a boy. Accident-prone and without fear, Lenni had already got herself into enough scrapes to make our parents constantly concerned. Over the years, their anxiety spiked as Lenni's trusting and innocent nature became her vulnerability. Dad said she was easy prey. The kids at school joked she was simple.

I sighed. 'You promise you'll be quick as a fox?'

Lenni's face broke like a sunrise as a wave crashed and spilt around her ankles. I jumped up and we dragged the trampled-on beach towels and discarded clothes above the tideline. The air was humid and salty; the water cool and dangerous. We'd all dived straight in when we arrived.

'Here's a pound,' I said, pulling money from my purse. Lenni's eyes lit up. 'Go straight along the beach, up to the road and use the zebra crossing—'

'But that way takes for*ever*,' Lenni whined. She pulled on her shorts and wiggled her feet into her rubber beach sandals. The denim darkened at the hips where the water seeped through.

'Not the cliff path. Mum would have a fit.'

She pulled a face. 'OK.' She took the money and pushed it into her pocket. 'Hate you, sis.' She grinned cheekily over her bony shoulder.

'Hate you too, Len-monster,' and I lunged for a tickle, but she darted off down the beach, leaving a trail of footprints in the sand.

The police officer was talking to me, but I couldn't understand what she was saying. She was holding a notepad.

'Sorry…' It was an apology more than a question.

'I asked you who Lenni's friends are.'

I touched the side of my head, squinting as the room went blurry. Truth was, Lenni didn't really have any friends. The kids in her class were mean to her and she never had anyone back to play. 'Oh God…' I buried my face in my hands, hardly able to stand what I'd done. If I hadn't gone back into the sea, if only I'd watched her go down the beach, tracked her veering off inland to where the sandbank rose, dotted with gorse and marram grass, separating the dunes from the row of shops, counted down the minutes until I saw her again, perhaps I'd have somehow kept her safe.

But Nick had called out to me. He'd dived head first into the waves, beckoning me with his whole body – his tanned shoulders, his lean back, his long legs. He broke down my name into streamer-like syllables when he resurfaced.

Clai-*aire*…

It was my last try for Nick, part of the reason I'd got us all together that day for one final burst of fun before we went off to different universities and colleges where he would surely find someone else. It was as though I was still underwater with him. Suspended. Nothing real.

It had been three hours.

Three hours since I'd said *Hate you too, Len-monster.*

Three hours since the tide washed away her footprints.

CHAPTER ONE

June 2017

Claire looked up from her work. She hadn't noticed them come in.

'How about this one?' the man said. A couple were browsing the wall display.

Had he just called her Eleanor?

She put down her pen, watching them for a moment, focusing on the woman, giving her a slow look up and down.

'Morning…' Claire came out from behind her desk. They were in their late thirties, professional-looking, browsing the half-million-pound and above properties. 'How may I help you?'

The man turned, giving a polite smile. 'We'd like some more details on this one, please.' He pointed to a property.

'And this one too,' the woman added, smiling.

Claire hesitated before replying. Wondering, extrapolating, working out the age. Had she misheard the name? 'Are you looking for an older place?' she asked. 'Or would you consider something new as well?'

'Something with character,' the man replied. She decided to give them the details for Cliff Lodge anyway. On the surface it seemed old, with its reclaimed bricks and gnarled timberwork. The builder had done a great job, but buyers were generally savvy. They'd soon realise it was overpriced.

'This one has amazing views,' Claire told them, slipping the details inside a glossy brochure. 'You get the feel of an older property but with all the benefits of a new build. It scores top on energy ratings, has a media control panel for the entire house, underfloor heating, state-of-the-art security…'

'It looks interesting,' the woman said, glancing at her partner. 'Though we really were set on something original.' She smiled. Her hair was light brown, short and highlighted with flecks of red. Her skin was pale, slightly sun-kissed, and her height, Claire guessed, would be about right. Her breathing quickened.

'Well, take it anyway,' she said, handing over the brochures. She'd lost count of how many clients with fixed criteria would, three months later, be moving into somewhere entirely different.

'I can make a few calls now to arrange some viewings if you like.' She didn't usually go for the hard sell, but it had been a lean month, though she also wondered if it was her interest in the woman making her pushy. 'Would you like a coffee?'

The couple looked at each other and nodded, so Claire went into the back to pour the drinks. 'Have you a property to sell?' she asked, returning.

'Our London place is sold. We're renting down here,' the man replied, turning the brochure pages.

Claire's heart fluttered. With only ten days left in the month, she could do with a decent sale. 'I'm Claire, by the way,' she said, holding out her hand. 'Claire Rodway.'

They both smiled. 'I'm Gary and this is my wife, Eleanor.' Claire couldn't help gripping the woman's hand for a moment too long.

An hour and a half later they'd viewed two empty properties. Cliff Lodge, followed by what Claire thought would be the perfect property, not far from Rock. She'd questioned Eleanor about her past as much as she could, but it turned out she'd lived in Kent and

London all her life. As they stood outside the last house, gazing back at the façade, Claire's phone buzzed in her pocket.

'Excuse me,' she said, stepping aside. She overheard Gary and Eleanor whispering about furniture, the piano, kids' bedrooms and where they could put a vegetable plot. It sounded promising.

'Hello, Claire Rodway speaking.' There was silence on the line apart from background noise that either sounded like traffic or the tide rushing in. 'Hello? Who is this?'

The line went dead.

Claire stared at the screen. It was the second time that day – and each call had come up as number withheld. She shrugged and went back to the couple. 'So, what do you think?'

'It's certainly got potential,' Eleanor said. 'I'd just hoped for more of a project. Something I can put my mark on.' The couple nodded at each other, joining hands.

'We were wondering if you have any barns to convert or old farmhouses with potential, that sort of thing?' her partner said.

Claire stifled a sigh. 'Possibly,' she said in a way that would make them believe there was hope, even though she knew they didn't have anything like that on their books. 'I'll check the files and give you a call.'

If she'd known then what she found out later, she could have taken them straight to the perfect property and probably had an offer on the table by close of business.

CHAPTER TWO

'Mum, Dad, it's me…' Claire called from the back hall, letting herself in. She'd stopped by at her parents' farm next door to her own house to pick up the dress her mum had altered for Amy. There was no reply, so she went straight into the large flagstoned kitchen.

She stopped suddenly.

'Mum, what's wrong?' She glanced between her parents.

Her father was sitting at the kitchen table with the newspaper open in front of him but obviously not reading it. His glasses were lying beside him, his eyes looking as though they'd been glued, unfocused, to the same page for the last ten minutes. Her mother was making a point of banging pots and pans as she prepared their evening meal.

'Is anyone going to speak?' Whatever was going on, Claire didn't think it seemed fair on her father under the circumstances.

'Everything's fine, darling,' Shona said, glancing up. She wore a tight expression, one that gave her an instant facelift. But instead of making her appear younger – although Claire hoped she looked that good when she reached seventy-one – it made her seem weary, as though she'd had enough.

'Thanks for altering the dress,' Claire said, catching sight of it on the chair. 'Amy will love it. She has a party at the weekend and—'

'Your mother wants to split up the farm and sell it off to rich people from London, so they can bugger about with it and convert it into bloody holiday lets.'

Claire stared at her father. Surely he was confused again.

'And considering everything, is that not a sensible idea, Patrick?' Shona held a large knife inside a tea towel, her long fingers gripped around it. Only her mother could make drying up seem elegant.

'Mum, is this true?' Claire felt her heart grinding, as if trying to slow the inevitable. Neither of her parents answered directly.

'Oh, Patrick,' Shona said through a sigh. She went to her husband and clasped his shoulders, pulling him close to her chest. She kissed him on the head. 'We've talked about this already. Don't you remember? You said it was a *good* idea.' She returned to the worktop and snipped at a bunch of parsley growing in a pot on the windowsill. A strand of hair fell in front of her eyes like a grey brushstroke on a painting. Again, Claire noticed how tired she looked.

'It's *not* a good idea,' Patrick stated with a growl.

'You're really thinking of selling the farm?' She couldn't believe what she was hearing. She'd grown up here. Everything had happened at Trevellin Farm. The enormity of her mother's decision swooped through her.

Someone must always be here…

They'd made a promise.

'I don't believe I'm hearing this.' Claire was instantly on her father's side. And what did she mean, *We've talked about this already*?

'Your mother's lost her bloody mind,' her father said. He rose and went to the old dresser, reaching into the bottom cupboard. He pulled out a bottle of red wine, uncorked it and poured himself a large glass. The kitchen was swollen with silence. Claire felt her mother's stare, but she couldn't return the look. It was a relief to see her father so opinionated rather than vague and confused, but what he'd just said cut deep, even though he didn't realise it.

'Patrick, have some fruit juice instead.' Shona tried to remove the glass from her husband's hands, but he clung on to it, downing a large mouthful. 'Be sensible, darling. You know what the doctor said about your blood pressure.'

In the days before his diagnosis, Patrick had always enjoyed a glass or two while Shona prepared dinner. They would chat, reminisce, laugh and bind themselves up in the safety of over forty years of marriage. Now, though, alcohol was strictly off limits, and usually he complied. They'd been told that raised blood pressure could worsen his Alzheimer's, and Shona wanted to do everything she could to slow the disease.

'Are you certain about selling, Mum?' Claire ran her fingers over the perfect seam her mother had stitched on the dress.

'Yes, love.' Shona looked at her husband, a knot of concern tied between her brows. 'We won't leave the area, of course. We still want to be near you, Callum and the children.'

The subtext of this told Claire that her mother *needed* to be close, that she wouldn't be able to cope with Patrick alone wherever they lived.

'You know how much time and energy this place takes up.'

Claire heard her mother speaking but couldn't take it in. Her words blended into one big truth that she didn't want to hear – that her parents weren't the immortal beings she'd always believed them to be.

Her father was already ill, deteriorating, and that had been shock enough earlier in the year. But accepting that they would grow older still and one day both need taking care of was unthinkable. Why had she never considered this before? Why had she thought that her mother, whippet-like and capable, elegant and stoic, would remain fixed inside an unchanging body, as if Claire herself would catch up and die first?

'Pat, where are you going, love?' Shona called out.

'To the bloody toilet, if that's all right with you.' He banged the hallway door behind him.

'He's had a bad week,' Shona confided in a low voice. They both knew there was nothing wrong with Patrick's hearing. 'It's so very worrying. If we sell, then I can focus more on caring for Dad. Please try to understand, darling. It's not easy for me.'

At that moment, Claire felt both desperately sorry for her mother and like she wanted to lash out, scream at her for even contemplating selling the farm. She closed her eyes. Apart from the obvious – that someone would *always* be here, just in case – she couldn't begin to imagine not visiting her parents here. They were her closest neighbours, literally at the end of the long, shared drive, and she couldn't imagine her father ever getting used to living anywhere else. The farm had always been the family's home.

'He's been doing… odd things,' Shona said quietly. 'It's very upsetting.'

'What kind of odd things?' Claire wasn't sure she could stand to hear. Over the last eighteen months they'd all noticed changes in Patrick, and between them had discussed what it might be – stress, age, plain forgetfulness. In the end, they'd coaxed him to the doctor and a diagnosis wasn't far behind.

'He's been in Lenni's room a lot. Talking to her as if she's really there.'

Claire hung her head and sighed. The clear-minded man of her youth, the capable father who'd taken control when Lenni disappeared, searching tirelessly, organising and never giving up, seemed a million miles away from the man now being eaten up by this wretched disease. She hated how he sometimes believed she had never disappeared, that his youngest daughter might walk into the room at any moment.

'And yesterday he told me he saw her skipping down the street,' Shona continued.

'What was he doing out alone?'

'Love, keeping your father indoors would be the end for him. You know how stubborn he is. He might have Alzheimer's, but I refuse to let the disease have *him*. We do things our way.'

Claire folded the dress and placed it on her knee. She didn't like hearing any of this. Until recently, she hadn't wanted to accept her father as anything but the man she remembered when she was five. A kind-hearted, gentle giant, yet stoked with a reserve of seriousness if need be, Patrick was always up for a make-believe adventure with her and her friends out on the farm or ready to tell a good story. Hard-working, yet soft as butter in the sun, Patrick adored his family.

And Claire had taken delight in sharing him with her friends when growing up. He'd become a kind of surrogate father to them all, forming a special bond with her close-knit group. Her friends would be envious of the indomitable man as he gave them piggybacks up and down the beach, played cricket with them on the sand – *how they wished their fathers were like him* – yet occasionally they'd scamper home a touch frightened when he'd overreacted about inconsequential things. Sand in the porch, the fire not laid right, running through the house – any trigger that worked him into a mini rage, which would usually burn itself out after carting some bales or an afternoon's fishing.

'And what if she comes back?' Patrick's voice boomed. He was braced in the doorway, as if holding up the house.

'Pat, she's not coming back. You know that.' Shona's voice was as soft as she could make it. 'Come and sit down.'

Only Mum would ever dare say that, Claire thought. She began to fidget with the dress again but stopped herself from ruining it.

'Claire, I'd like someone from your office to come out and give us an opinion,' Shona said. 'I don't suppose it's fair to ask you to value the place personally, but we'd like to give your agency the business. You have such a good reputation round here.'

Claire had been working at Greene & Galloway for nearly a decade. Chris Greene and Jeff Galloway were away from the office more and more now they were approaching retirement. She virtually ran the place single-handedly.

'Take more time to decide, Mum,' Claire said, glancing at her father. 'It's Dad's decision too.' She watched her mother's eyes crystallise and harden. Claire put a hand on her arm. 'Thanks for doing this.' She held up the dress. 'I'll bring the kids down to see you at the weekend.'

She kissed both of her parents and went out to her car. The sea breeze smelt like a salty soup bubbling on the stove. The tide would be out, she guessed, remembering how, as a child, she would scamper over the rocks and sandy patches between the crystal-clear pools, marvelling at the intricate gifts left behind. If the tide was out, the sea-smell was in, her father used to say, excited as a kid himself at the prospect of an afternoon beachcombing with his daughter and her friends.

Her friends. How would they feel when she told them that Patrick had been diagnosed with Alzheimer's? So far, they'd kept the news amongst close family, and besides, she didn't get to see any of them as often as she'd have liked. And how would they react to the house sale? Patrick and the farm had been as much a part of their childhoods as it had hers. It was all heartbreaking.

Claire drove back down the long driveway, past the Old Stables where she lived, spotting that Callum wasn't home yet, and on into the village. It was time to fetch Amy from the childminder.

'Oh, Dad,' she said to herself as she parked the car on the quiet lane, her head tilted back against the seat. She couldn't bear to see her father deteriorate in such a short period of time and, since his diagnosis, she'd been desperate to do something helpful for him. Until now, she had no idea what that could be.

Behind all the worry and concern, Claire felt the first glimmer of a plan hatching. She smiled to herself as she locked the car. She'd read up on how this sort of thing could help, and she reckoned it would do him the world of good. Her mind was made up.

CHAPTER THREE

Callum knew Marcus must already be home as he unlocked the front door to the Old Stables. He felt the resonant thud-thud of the bass beat in the floor, the walls, even the air, before he actually heard his son's music.

The breakfast remains were still on the kitchen table – exactly how Claire had left it as she'd dashed out for the school run and then on to work, except now the cat had dragged a piece of toast onto the floor and licked off the butter. The ginger tom wound between Callum's feet as he poured a glass of water.

'Anyone else home?' he called out, swigging and wiping his mouth with the back of his hand. 'Claire?'

Nothing. He supposed she would be fetching Amy.

He went back to the hall and picked up the newspaper from the mat, settling down in his favourite armchair to have half-an-hour's read before the evening chaos began. But for some reason, he couldn't concentrate.

There was nothing specific worrying him. Work was interesting and challenging as ever – though it could not escape the usual NHS managerial stranglehold, he was grateful his department had avoided yet more funding cutbacks. The health scare he'd had earlier in the year had proved nothing more than a minor infection mimicking something more serious, and even his new secretary had surpassed all his expectations. He couldn't suppress the small smile at the thought of her as he skimmed the day's news.

Agitated, he rested his head back on the chair. Claire seemed happy enough, he supposed, and the kids were doing well at school even if Marcus's form tutor had found it necessary to telephone twice this term already about missed coursework. But that was Claire's department. She'd sort it out.

Why, then, these feelings – a sense of dissatisfaction, of *fear* almost? Why the aggravating peck-peck at the back of his mind that something wasn't right, that something was missing? He wondered if it was his age – he was approaching fifty, after all. Was it some kind of mid-life shift that, while it wasn't a full-blown crisis, made him feel that surely there must be more to life than work-sleep, work-sleep?

No, he thought, as he heard the front door unlock. It wasn't any of that. It was a far bigger thing, burning at the very core of him as it always had done, and he knew there wasn't a damn thing he could do about it.

'We're home,' Claire announced.

Then he heard the shrill voice of his six-year-old daughter telling off the cat for licking the toast and Claire's long sigh followed by the clatter of plates as she began clearing up.

'How are my two favourite ladies?' he asked, standing in the kitchen doorway. He flicked on the light. There was an eerie orange-pink glow outside, making it seem more like a nine o'clock summer sunset than the three hours earlier it really was. The red bricks of the barn across the yard looked on fire.

'Looks as though there's a thunderstorm on the way,' he said, reaching down to hug Amy. He paused, wondering if it was prophetic. 'How was school, little one?'

'One of the chicks died. Mrs Henry told us it would get better, but she lied.' Amy pouted.

'That's sad.' Callum gratefully took the glass of wine Claire offered. Judging by the ingredients she was unpacking, she was going to cook curry. A Friday night tradition in the Rodway household. Another regular occurrence in the steady beat of his life.

'It had been pecked to death,' Amy went on. 'It had blood and beaky marks all over its head.'

'That's called pecking order,' he explained, glancing at his wife.

Claire raised her eyebrows. He thought her hair looked stunning in the strange light. It didn't normally look quite so red, but tonight it was as if every strand had been dipped in a different shade of liquid copper.

'Why did Mrs Henry lie, then? Why didn't the mummy chicken look after the baby?'

Amy twirled the tassel on her cardigan around her finger. Callum knew it meant she was tired, that she'd had enough of school, the childminder, and wanted nothing more than supper, a warm bath, a story and bed. Claire would see to all that.

Callum sighed. What was he to do – tell her it was OK for adults to lie to children but not the other way around? Explain survival of the fittest in language a six-year-old wouldn't question?

He was too tired for all that right now. Instead, large hands dragged down his face and when he reappeared he offered up a playful *boo!* sending Amy squealing off and hurling herself onto the beanbag in the snug.

'Nicely avoided,' Claire said, pulling a face. He wasn't sure if she was being sarcastic.

'You want me to tell her the truth?' He desperately wanted to avoid a Friday night battle. He'd been longing for her all day. Then the new secretary was on his mind again.

'Mum wants to sell Trevellin,' Claire said out of the blue, stopping what she was doing.

'Because of Pat?' Callum helped her unpack the rest of the groceries.

Claire nodded and leant on the worktop, allowing her head to drop while he topped up her glass. She was so tense these days.

'Dad doesn't want to move, of course, but Mum won't be able to cope with the farm *and* his illness.'

'I agree with your mum. It's not just the house but the land and all the old buildings too. It's a lot to look after.'

'Dad still does what he can. He goes out and potters about most days.' Claire was defensive.

'It takes more than pottering to look after a place like that and you know it. They're in their seventies now, Claire.' Callum allowed his hands to settle on his wife's shoulders and drift down her arms. He held her hands.

'I know. You're right. It's just the end of an era, that's all.' She gave a small smile.

'Will you be selling it for them?'

Claire nodded. 'Mum's talking about offering it to developers. For holiday lets.'

'Shrewd,' Callum said, raising his eyebrows. 'All the barns, the cottage, the land… Perhaps a caravan park too.' He blew out through his teeth. 'And only half a mile from the beach.' He gently massaged her hands. He knew she liked that and reckoned he'd averted a blow-up.

'It seemed like ten miles when we kids, I stole walking it four times a day.' Claire softened at the memory.

Callum didn't want her to get maudlin, so he lowered his mouth onto hers, kissing her gently. She responded briefly, their fingers in a loose weave, but then she pulled away.

'I should get on with supper.'

'Yuk,' Marcus said, bending into the refrigerator after glancing at his parents. 'This milk's well off.' He emerged sloshing a carton which contained something verging on cottage cheese. His hair flopped over his eyes.

'Hi, love,' Claire said, pulling some fresh milk from the last of the shopping bags. 'Dad and I were just talking about how we used to walk to the beach as kids.' She took the old milk from him and washed it down the sink.

'Well, you lot did. Don't forget I'd just started at medical school while you were still playing with buckets and spades.' Callum winked at his son when Claire didn't respond.

'Marcus prefers surfing on his laptop than in the sea, don't you, love?' Claire said, chopping an onion. Secretly, she was glad he didn't go the beach often. She could never relax until he was home safely – the rip tides were strong – and she couldn't even contemplate the future when Amy would want more freedom.

It had taken her and Callum many years to conceive their daughter after they'd had Marcus. It was only after several rounds of IVF that their family was finally complete. But all the stress of having Amy had occasionally led Claire to wonder if her protective instincts were in danger of mirroring those of her parents, especially with Amy being a girl – who was all the more precious for the agonising suspense of her arrival.

She tried to put these thoughts from her mind, along with the memory of the tension that her infertility had caused between her and Callum at the time. When out as a family, Claire suspected that people thought Marcus was from a previous marriage, but now, aged eighteen, the freedom he enjoyed with his mates only spotlighted what the future held for her little girl. And after what happened to Lenni, she didn't think she could stand it.

'Not entirely true, Mum,' Marcus protested. 'I went—'

Callum shot him a look. He could see the entire evening going down the pan if an argument ensued. Marcus took the hint and skulked off upstairs again, while Claire cut up the chicken. Her movements were slow and laborious, showing Callum that something was still on her mind.

'I've had a crazy idea,' she said finally, putting down the knife.

'Go on.' Callum sat on a stool, resigning himself to an evening of serious discussion. Under the worktop, his leg jiggled on the bar of the stool.

'I want to organise a reunion.' She stared out of the window. The sky had turned an even more ominous orange-grey, Callum noticed, following her gaze. 'I want to get everyone back together for Dad. You know, all my childhood friends. The group.' Claire ran her hand down his arm. 'I think it'll do him the world of good, don't you?'

Callum immediately thought it was a terrible idea. 'Claire, your father's got a disease that won't get any—'

'My mind's already made up, Cal,' she said. 'I want everyone to come and stay at Trevellin, to spend time with Dad. It'll bring back memories for him, remind him of all the good times, help him feel like his old self again.' She paused, tears pooling. 'I want him to know how much everyone loves and cares for him. He's been such an amazing father, it's his turn now. The summer holidays aren't far away.' She wiped a finger under her eye. 'It's the onions,' she added.

Callum could tell she'd convinced herself it was a good plan, and, in many ways, she was right. Patrick would gain a temporary respite from his degenerating brain. But she needed to accept that some stupid reunion wouldn't halt the daily deterioration as his disease took hold. He decided that keeping quiet was best for now.

'It's a lovely idea,' he said, drawing close and wrapping his arms around her waist. But she didn't respond. She was staring out of the window again. Big drops of rain splatted against the glass and the magical light was gone. Claire's hair returned to its normal mousey-brown colour and the electric atmosphere in the kitchen fizzled out.

CHAPTER FOUR

Maggie was soaking in the bath when her phone rang. She'd swooned when she'd first seen the place with its sunken Italian marble tub, and had virtually melted at the luxury of the entire house when she'd moved in with Gino two months ago.

She stood up, sending a wave of water over the edge as she reached for a towel, drenching the floor when she ran to the bedroom.

'Hello?' She caught it just in time. 'Oh my God, oh my God, *oh… my… God…!*'

Both women were laughing hysterically.

'I know, right…' Claire said down the line. 'It's been so long. How *are* you?'

'How long have you got?' Maggie replied, suddenly feeling the need for a cigarette, even though smoking in the house wasn't allowed. 'You know better than to ask me that. Anyway, if you got yourself on Facebook, you'd know.'

The two women laughed again.

'I'm unemployed and living the life of Riley in Gino's – yes, Gino, I *know*! – amazing place.'

She heard Claire say something about never settling, about nothing changing. The line was bad but even through the humour and the crackles, it still stung deep.

'Rain's fifteen now, can you believe? She has the body of an adult woman with the common sense of a five-year-old. And there's me with an urgent need to travel the world on the back of a Harley with a man ten years younger than me and an even more desperate need for immediate sex, but my Italian lover is working late tonight.' Maggie lit a cigarette anyway, blowing out. 'And how are you, my darling, *darling* girl?' She giggled at the stupid accent she'd put on. There was a long pause. Maggie wondered if Claire had hung up, if her flippancy had overstepped the mark. Perhaps she was calling with bad news.

'I'm fine. Still working at the estate agency.'

'That's fantastic, Claire.' Maggie didn't think she sounded very enthusiastic. Drying off a little, she lay back on the bed, flicking ash into the wine glass she'd drained earlier.

'Marcus is doing his A levels and Amy is in her second year at primary school now.'

'How time flies.' She'd not seen Claire's youngest since she was a toddler. She'd always considered Claire her best friend, but as time drifted on, so had their lives, their loves, their jobs and regular contact. 'And how's that wonderful man of yours?'

Claire laughed. 'Callum's fine. He's a consultant now.'

'Mmm, a brain surgeon,' Maggie replied with a giggle.

'Sometimes it's brains,' Claire said, echoing the laugh. 'Listen, I was wondering…'

Maggie sat up. She knew there'd be a reason for the call.

'Are you free at all during the summer holidays? I thought it would be nice if…' Claire was hesitant.

'Spit it out, Claire, for God's sake. I'm going to say yes anyway.' Maggie plumped up her pillows, drawing in on her cigarette.

'I have some sad news first, I'm afraid. Dad's not been well.'

Maggie felt a chill run up her legs and back. She'd always adored Patrick. He'd been a second father to her – sometimes a *first* father.

'He was diagnosed with Alzheimer's six months ago.'

Maggie sighed heavily. 'Christ, I'm so sorry to hear that, Claire. How rotten for him. How rotten for you *all*.' She found it hard to imagine the workhorse of a man, the long-limbed climbing frame of a father she'd loved as her own, struck down by any illness, let alone this. 'If there's anything I can do...' She meant it.

'That's why I'm calling, actually.' She heard Claire swallow. 'I'm organising a reunion. Mum's decided to sell the farm. It's too much to cope with as well as looking after Dad. So I thought getting everyone together would be good for him. It'll be just like old times.'

There was silence.

'Oh, Claire...'

'Say you'll come, Mags. For Dad.'

Maggie could almost feel their hands clenching together as they used to do as inseparable teens. The passage of so much time so quickly made Maggie sad. 'Of *course* I'll come,' was her heartfelt reply. In reality, she was wondering how to tell her daughter that she'd be spending some of her precious summer holidays in Cornwall.

Later, Maggie woke to the sound of the front door banging shut.

'Rain?' She glanced at the clock. Eleven thirty. She'd not long dozed off. 'You're back early, love.'

Rain was silhouetted in the doorway by the landing light. 'That's because I only have one friend in this dump of a town and she's a loser. No reason to stay out.'

'Oh, love.' Maggie reached out to her, but Rain didn't respond. She stood stiffly, her arms clamped across her chest.

'Can I go back to school tomorrow? I don't want to come here at weekends again.' Rain shifted from one foot to the other.

Maggie knew how hard it was for her to get used to another potential stepfather, settling in a different town yet again. They'd moved around so much it was difficult for her to make local friends. But being a single mother was also hard. Deep down, Maggie knew

Rain hadn't exactly hit it off with Gino, and was best off back at her boarding school. At least she had friends there, even if they were from all over the world.

'Of course, love,' Maggie said, patting the bed. 'Come and sit. I've something to tell you.' The bed dipped slightly as Rain reluctantly planted herself on the mattress. Maggie flicked on the bedside lamp. 'Good heavens, what happened?' Rain's make-up was smudged from tears and her lips looked swollen, almost bruised.

'I just went to a bar…' She trailed off, running a finger over the duvet.

Maggie frowned, knowing that something more had happened, most likely to do with a boy. Rain was a troubled soul and she daren't risk an explosion by asking who or what had upset her. 'I had a call from an old school friend earlier,' she said, trying to sound casual. 'Do you remember Claire Lucas… or Rodway as she's called now?'

Rain shrugged.

'I haven't seen her in ages. She was my best friend.'

Something must have struck a chord with Rain because she looked up and listened.

'Four of us were great friends in Cornwall. We did everything together, but now Claire's dad is poorly. She wants us to have a reunion for him, to make him feel better.'

'Cool,' Rain said genuinely. 'You'll have fun.'

'It's down in Cornwall, where I grew up,' Maggie added. She hadn't visited for twenty years. No point in mixing old crap with the new. Even though it wouldn't be easy going back, she wanted to show Rain a piece of her past. The time finally seemed right.

'Where grandma and grandpa used to live?'

Maggie swallowed. 'Yes… yes, that's it.'

She was saddened that Rain had missed out on loving grand-parents. Taken at face value, her childhood sounded perfect – scampering around a big farmhouse, playing down at the beach all summer long, exploring caves, being part of such a close-knit group of friends. But that was Claire's childhood, not hers. Maggie had always left out telling anyone – let alone Rain – the truth about her mother and father, how they'd neglected her, how she'd lived a virtually feral existence on their council estate, fending for herself while they pleased themselves, mainly with fags, drugs and booze.

Thank God for Patrick and Shona.

Maggie's parents had died since she'd moved away, so now it was her turn not to care. She'd managed OK, hadn't she? Threading her way through life on the goodwill of whichever well-off bloke would take them on. 'So, you'll come?'

'Me?' Rain tucked her legs onto the bed, snorting. 'Come to Cornwall?'

It was the reaction Maggie was expecting. 'Of course. We've both been invited for a week. You'll get to meet everyone. Claire's got a little girl and a teenage son called Marcus.'

Maggie wondered if he looked anything like his father, which led her to wonder what Callum, not part of their original group, looked like now. He was a bit older than the rest of them, she recalled, although it had seemed like an entire generation back then.

Rain poked her mother.

'What?'

'You've got tears in your eyes.'

Maggie blinked furiously. Was it the news of Patrick's illness that had upset her or that she'd suddenly realised how far off-track her life really was?

'So, you'll come?' She gripped Rain's hands. 'There'll be picnics on the beach, silly games, stories that'll bore you stupid and lots of pub visits and walks. What do you say?' It was about time Rain met them all. It might help her understand.

'I say it sounds the worst way ever to spend a whole week of my summer holidays. But I don't suppose I have a choice, do I?'

'Is that a yes, then?'

Rain shrugged again.

'Good, because I've already told Claire we're coming.'

At last, Maggie thought, flopping back onto the pillow after her daughter had gone to bed. Something good was going to happen.

CHAPTER FIVE

'That's one,' Claire said.

Callum put his book on the bedside table. 'One what?'

'Maggie said she'll come to the reunion.' She'd sounded exactly the same – wild, crazy, passionate, kind. 'She's bringing her daughter too.'

'Great,' Callum replied. 'Let's hope she doesn't take after her mother.'

'Don't be mean, Cal.' She prodded his arm, scrolling through her phone's address book, angling the screen slightly away, searching for a particular name. But when she couldn't find it, she closed the list down. Anyway, she didn't want to talk to him yet, not until she'd spoken to Jason. She knew they'd been in touch once or twice over the years and she felt it would probably be wise to get the low-down first, though she doubted he was the type to broadcast his life on social media.

'You're not making more calls now, are you? It's late.' Callum rolled onto his side and pressed his face against Claire's stomach. 'Why don't you turn that thing off and get yourself out of this?' He tugged at the oversized T-shirt she was wearing.

'I need to call Jason,' she said, smoothing down her nightdress.

They usually spoke weekly, and if Claire ever went up to London they'd always meet for lunch to make it seem as if they didn't actually live several hundred miles apart. Their relationship was strong, unbreakable, forged silently over the years by the sense of culpability they shared. But inviting Jason back to Trevellin was another matter entirely. He never came to the farm. Time may have passed, but she wasn't sure it was long enough to heal the deep hurt he felt. It could do more damage than good, leaving her stuck in the middle.

Greta answered her call and the conversation flowed as easily as ever.

'Oh Claire, how lovely to hear from you. No, that's fine… we're still up. Sleep is hard now anyway… Yes, I'm huge! Work's fine, really busy. You? Yes, I'm looking forward to being off for a while though. Sure, hang on, I'll fetch him.'

There was a muffled sound as Greta called for Jason. A second later her brother's voice came on the line. 'Hey, sis.'

'Hi,' Claire said, sliding Callum's hand off her thigh. 'How are things?'

'Good. Greta's massive. You?'

Claire laughed fondly. 'Everyone's really well. I tried to call you earlier, but it went to voicemail.'

'Everything OK?'

'Kind of, yes. Mum's thinking of selling the farm, Jase. *Seriously* thinking about it. It's all her idea.' Claire knew that he would be thinking the same as her, as their father – the same as everyone except their mother it seemed.

'Christ, what's brought this on?'

Claire explained about how coping with the farm as well as Patrick was getting increasingly hard for their mother. She heard Jason swallowing heavily at the mention of their father. *Shame it's not your pride you're swallowing*, she thought so loudly she worried he'd hear. 'Anyway, how's work? Much on?'

'Zilch,' Jason replied, no doubt grateful for the reprieve, even if it was about his failed career. 'If it wasn't for Greta, we'd be living on the streets.'

'I'm sorry to hear that.'

'Pity isn't what I need.'

'Then maybe you need a holiday,' Claire said, trying to sound bright. She heard Callum groaning beside her, fully aware that he was on a hiding to nothing. He picked up his book again.

'Greta can't fly anywhere now. Doctor's orders. She's on maternity leave soon.'

'Then I have the perfect solution.' She waited, but Jason was silent. 'I'm organising a reunion. It's for Dad. I thought it would be good for him if we – you know, all the old group – got together at Trevellin for a few days. We could do all the things we used to as kids. The beach, the walks, the games, tell stories. I've done a bit of research and apparently it could really help his long-term memory.'

'You honestly think it's that simple?'

Claire sighed. 'I'm trying to make this all right, Jason. To do something good for Dad… for you too. Why are you always so against stuff like this?'

'I'm sorry, Claire. I didn't mean—'

'It's OK,' she added quickly. A disagreement could lead to him refusing and she didn't want that. But for the first time she was wondering who, exactly, the reunion was for. She pushed the answer from her mind.

Callum got out of bed and stretched into his robe. He walked into the bathroom, shaking his head, while Claire lay back on the pillows, closing her eyes. 'So, will you and Greta come to Trevellin?'

'No,' was his instant reply.

Claire's heart sank. Out of all of them, it was Jason she wanted there the most.

'I won't stay in his house. You know that.'

'But Jason, he's *ill*. You have to let this go.'

A pause. 'It's not that easy, Claire, and you know it.'

But Claire didn't know it. She simply couldn't understand how one misjudged incident had turned into years of bitter feelings.

'Then stay with us. We have room here. The others can stay at the farm.' It felt unfair pressing him, but she was determined to do this for Patrick.

'I'll speak to Greta,' was Jason's final response.

Claire knew not to push further, so she took a deep breath. Callum was still in the bathroom. 'By the way, I don't suppose you have Nick's number, do you?' There. She'd said his name.

'Yeah,' Jason replied. 'I'll text it to you.'

And the conversation was over.

CHAPTER SIX

Nick Malone stared at the wreckage. It was the same as his life: the insides all ripped out, a huge amount of vision required to see anything good in the future.

'You really think it'll only take a couple of months?'

'Sure,' the contractor said. 'Believe me, I've seen a lot worse.'

Nick was nodding but not seeing a kitchen at all. There were four walls and a floor, something resembling a ceiling above them, though the network of ancient wires and pipes made the space appear more like the aftermath of a multi-car pileup than a catering kitchen.

The restaurant area was no better. In fact, it was worse. A previous flood meant the floor had been ripped up, but not until the sodden plaster of the ceiling above had been dragged down.

'I have to be open by the end of September. I need to build a buzz in the run-up to Christmas.'

Trevor, his builder, unfolded his thick arms and swiped a hand across Nick's back. 'Mate, the plans are finalised, and I've got eight of my best men on the job. I've done dozens of restaurants, so relax. I'm talking with the architect on a daily basis, so you just need to get working on your menu, interview your staff and pick some wallpaper. OK?'

The décor. That would have been Jess's job. The furniture, the flooring, the lighting, the paint, right down to the colour of the soap in the toilets would have been her department. She'd have loved every minute of it.

'I'll need an interior designer. I don't have a clue about that sort of stuff.' Nick's mobile phone was vibrating in his pocket.

'I know someone,' Trevor said, turning to one of his builders.

'Hello, Nick speaking.' He didn't recognise the number. He walked up to the window that overlooked the small yard, wondering what was stirring inside him.

'Claire? Claire Lucas, how the hell are you? It's so good to hear from you.' He didn't think he conveyed how much he actually meant this.

In a daze, he stared out to where the industrial-sized dustbins were stored. The enormity of what he'd taken on still made him wake up at night in terror.

'I'm really well,' she said back. 'It's lovely to hear your voice, Nick. How are things with you?' She sounded bright and sweet and hardly any different to when they'd last spoken, which must be about five or six years ago.

'Things have been, you know, OK. Up and down.' He couldn't possibly tell her everything on the phone. It would be hard enough face-to-face. 'And I've finally bought my own restaurant. It looks more like a war zone at the moment though.' He attempted a laugh.

'That's great news,' Claire said, although he sensed she was holding something back.

Nick imagined her there with him – taking her hand and showing her around the empty space, telling her all about his crazy plans, how he'd only be serving organically grown and locally sourced food, all the dishes inspired by different times in his life. He was even sketching out a cookbook, had a vision of himself being interviewed on television, and the restaurant becoming a favourite with celebrities. And then the emptiness set in. Doing it all alone just wasn't any fun. If he thought too hard about what had happened, all he really wanted to do was burn the place down. With him trapped inside.

'Callum's fine, thanks,' she said in response to a question he hadn't realised he'd asked. 'Marcus went and got all grown up and Amy's six now.'

Nick's heart skipped. She'd been a baby last time he'd seen Claire. The child had broken his heart as well as melted it, drawing a line under what would never be his.

'How's the lovely Jess, then? And what about Isobel? She must be a teenager now.' Claire laughed so sweetly it almost made everything seem all right, as if none of it had happened.

Nick was aware of Trevor approaching, glancing at his watch. It was Saturday morning and the men had only come in for a couple of hours as a favour.

'Things have happened, Claire.' He hoped she wouldn't probe further.

'OK,' was her slow, tactful reply. She added a little cough as punctuation. 'I'm calling because I'm organising a reunion. It's for Dad.'

Nick listened as she explained everything. He mouthed 'two minutes' to his builder.

'So will you come to Trevellin in July?' She paused but then added, 'It'll be twenty-one years soon.'

'That long?'

'She'd be thirty-four.'

They were both silent for a moment.

'Claire, I've got someone with me. Can I call you later?'

'Sure. On this number though.'

'Right,' Nick said to Trevor, after adding her to his contacts and putting his phone back in his pocket. 'We've got a restaurant to open.' And for some reason – the first time in many months – a tiny smile lifted the side of his mouth. He felt scared admitting it, but it almost felt good.

CHAPTER SEVEN

Shona heard her granddaughter before she saw her. Perfect timing, she thought, smiling, as she dusted the cake with icing sugar. The kettle was simmering on the Aga as Claire and Amy gambolled with Russ across the farmyard towards the house. She watched as two of the dearest people to her in the world approached the back door, feeling love and warmth seep through her.

But she also couldn't help feeling that the welcome she was about to offer – the cake, the tea and the chit-chat – were a mask for reality. Inside, everything hurt.

'My darling Amy,' Shona said, going outside to greet them and scooping her grandchild under her arms. She was still just able to lift her and wouldn't consider herself old until she couldn't. 'You wait till you see what Grandma's got for you.'

'A present?' Amy dropped down, scurrying inside.

Claire laughed. 'Hi, Mum.' She gave her a kiss. 'Something smells good.'

'Just a sponge cake.' Shona left the door open so Russ, Callum's Labrador, could come and go as he pleased. 'And don't chase the chickens,' she told the old brown dog, though she didn't think he'd have the energy.

'It's so warm,' Claire said, fanning herself with her straw hat.

'Summer at last,' Shona replied. 'Earl Grey?'

'Thanks, Mum.'

'And all this, young lady, is for you.'

Amy's alert green eyes tracked Shona to the corner of the large kitchen. There seemed little point in ever using the rest of the house when this room had an open fire, the cooking range, comfy old sofas and the French doors leading out to the garden. No one ever called at the front door unless they were on official business, and countless dogs and kids and even chickens had tramped in and out for as long as Shona could remember. So far, everyone seemed to believe that selling up was what she actually wanted to do. It wasn't.

'This box,' Shona began, as Amy sat down cross-legged on the rug, 'is full of toys from a long time ago. You won't find any noisy electronic gadgets in here.'

Amy gasped with joy and Shona left her to delve inside the box. She turned to Claire, who was filling the teapot. 'I've been having a sort-out,' she said quietly. She knew there would be a reaction, she just wasn't sure what yet.

Claire glanced over to Amy as she pulled a pretty rag doll from the box. Her daughter squealed with delight. 'Mum, *no*.' She was wide-eyed.

'Yes, love,' Shona replied firmly although inside she didn't feel at all firm about her decision at all. 'It's long overdue.'

'But—'

'They've sat collecting dust in her room for over two decades.'

They both knew there was little hope now, even though they'd always tried to keep positive. Months after the police had found her shorts in a ditch, even the detective in charge of the case said the chances of finding her alive were slim.

'I just don't think it's right.' Claire went over to Amy. 'You'll have to put those back, I'm afraid, sweetie. Grandma made a mistake.'

'No, I didn't, Amy. You go right ahead and play with them.' Shona also loomed over the child until she realised what they were doing to her. 'I'm sorry, darling, you'd better do as Mummy says.' Shona backed off, clattering cups onto a tray. She cut up the cake and suggested they sit outside as the sun was still on the terrace. 'Why not take Russ for a run around the lawn, Amy? He looks as if he could do with the exercise.'

'He's not very good at running any more. Daddy says he's on his last legs and it'll be a blessing when he's gone.' Amy pulled the reluctant dog by its collar.

'It wasn't quite like that,' Claire assured her mother, as they sat at the flaking wrought iron table. 'The vet's bills have been pretty high recently and Callum—'

'You don't need to explain,' Shona said, pouring the tea. 'I didn't mean to upset you with the toys. But I have to sort things out ready for the move.'

Claire bowed her head. 'I know. It's just that I don't *want* you to move. I know looking after this place as well as Dad is a lot of work, but I could help out more. I could go part-time. What about a holiday to mull things over? Take Dad on a cruise?'

'Your father would hate a cruise.' Shona sipped her tea and watched as Amy tried to run with Russ. The dog lay down, panting.

'He was never big on holidays, was he?' Claire said. '"No one speaks bloody English and they all eat horse meat,"' she said in a deep, growling voice, mimicking her father. '"There are perfectly good beaches on our doorstep and all for free!"'

They laughed, knowing that Patrick was probably right. But even if they'd wanted a holiday, the bed and breakfast had always tied them to the farm during the summer. Looking back, Shona wondered how she coped with it all.

Claire took a deep breath. 'Mum, I've done something I hope I don't live to regret.'

Shona frowned. The sun was behind her daughter, so she squinted, raising her hand to her forehead. 'Go on.'

'I wanted to do something nice for Dad... so I wondered, I thought perhaps—'

'What, darling?'

'I'm organising a reunion.' Claire hesitated. 'I thought if I invited all the old group – Maggie, Nick, Jason, perhaps Uncle Angus and Aunt Jenny too – it would be really good for him. Like old times. And with partners and children too, there'd be so many of us to help that you wouldn't have to do a thing.'

Shona listened to her daughter tripping over her words, trying to make it sound appealing.

'I'd take care of everything. You wouldn't have to lift a finger. It would be stimulating for Dad, really help with his memory. I worry about him so much and…' Claire was rambling. 'I've already made some phone calls, actually.'

Shona's face gradually broke a smile. 'I think it's an excellent idea, darling. I would love nothing more.' Then the smile fell away. 'But what about Jason?'

'I'm not sure. I've said he can stay with me rather than here at the farm. I was hoping it might help repair things.'

Shona raised her eyebrows.

'I've called Maggie and Nick too, but nothing's completely firmed up yet. I should have run it past you first, I know, but…' she trailed off.

'But you knew you didn't have to, right?' Shona took her daughter's hand.

It was all going to be OK, Shona reassured herself as mother and daughter sat in the late afternoon sun. The light filtered through the twisting clematis onto the lawn, dancing like fleeting memories. She recalled Patrick buying the quivering purple-flowered plant, choosing the perfect spot for it. It had quickly flourished, spiralling up and along the pergola to form a thick canopy and flowering every summer with velvet blooms the size of saucers.

'I'm sure Dad will think it's a splendid idea,' Shona said. In truth, she wasn't sure. His reaction would depend on his mood and that hadn't been predicable for a while. It wasn't just his mind that was changing with the knotty, foreign weed that was invading his brain, but rather that his whole personality was shifting to accommodate the assault.

They spent the rest of the afternoon chatting about plans, which week in the summer would work best, what they would all do, and who would have which room. Shona decided not to say anything when Amy ducked back inside the kitchen and sneaked out the rag doll, riding it around on Russ's back as if it was finally having the time of its life.

CHAPTER EIGHT

Not So Long Ago

I'm awake but it's dark. The same tarry black as my empty sleep.

What do you dream about with when all your memories have gone?

The electricity is off again.

'Can you fix it?' I asked last time it happened, but I was told I should be more understanding, more grateful.

I feel my way to the tap, twisting it so it spews a trickle of water into my glass. Last week it came out brown and gritty, so I got bottled water again, though not enough. 'To tide you over,' I was told, which reminded me of something, some*where*. Fresh and free.

I try to make a note of every day that passes and wind my watch, but sometimes I forget. I could be out of kilter with the rest of the world by days or even months or years. I lost a whole season once. But I'm set straight with a smile, or I get a flower to show me it's summer, and one time I was taken out to see the snow. I'm thirty-three years old and today is the twelfth of February 2017.

Or maybe it's August and I'm only thirteen.

I sit in the chair, waiting. When the power has been off before, the food in the fridge went bad. I've paid the price of slimy ham and lumpy milk once too often. Hospitals aren't for people like me, I'm told.

Later, I wake with a jolt. I must have dozed off. There's a horrid smell. Everything stinks in here anyway, but this is worse. The walls stink. The floor stinks. The furniture stinks and I stink. It's a soup of mould and sweet yeast and sad, exhaled breath. But this time there's something else in the mix – a dog, wet and salty from the sea. Just your mind playing tricks and best forgotten, I'm told, when I complain that people keep visiting, talking to me.

Suddenly, the light comes back on. I screw up my eyes, opening them gradually as the glare from the bulb burns through my lids. There's an image scorched onto my eyes, which doesn't go away even when I blink – me on a long stretch of beach with a cobalt-blue sky and a bright umbrella straining in the breeze. Frothy green waves rush up the sand and there's a man walking his dog. It runs up and licks me. This memory tastes as delicious as ice cream, but when the wind whips up I'm all alone again, screaming, begging not to die.

Then I run at the wall. There's hardly any space in here, yet I manage a good speed, hurling myself against it. Usually, I just get a bruise, but sometimes I go nice and dizzy. Once, I prised off a couple of the wooden panels to see what was underneath, but all I found was yellow padded stuff that made me sneeze. It helps pass the time.

I put on a film. I've got loads. I've seen them all a thousand times and know all the words off by heart. It's summertime in this movie, which is why I like it. I imagine my room to be hot and bright, the sun beating down. My head throbs and so I pretend I'm wearing a hat. I slip on some sunglasses while my skin scorches, peeling and bubbling from the heat. Then, much later, a pair of gentle hands rubs cool cream on my shoulders.

'You've caught the sun, little one,' she says. I giggle up at her, crinkling my nose, imagining myself running about with my hands cupped, ready to catch the sun as it falls from the sky. Her voice is sweet, and she smells of roses. I don't know who she is.

Suddenly, a pain grips my side. No food for three days now. Then, as if my thoughts have sent out an emergency signal, the familiar clattering and clanking sound heralds what I hope will be a glorious feast. I get down on all fours and crouch behind the chair, sucking on my fingers, chewing and eating the peeling skin, waiting. When the door opens, a rush of cool, fresh air sweeps in.

'Hello,' I whisper. My voice is croaky.

The door locks again and the chair is shoved aside.

'What are you doing down there?' The face looms like a big pale moon – doughy and troughed. I can smell the outside.

'Hiding,' I giggle. 'What did you bring me? I'm *starving*.'

'Stew.' Two bags of food are unloaded onto the little table. I've had lots of tables. I smashed all the others. The stew is in a plastic bag and feels cold and sloppy. There's a huge bag of crisps and I pull it open immediately, shoving my face inside like a horse. They're delicious. The best crisps ever!

'Drink this orange juice,' I'm told, so I do. Over the rim of the glass I see ham and bread and more margarine being put on my table. I'm given some baked beans and a tin of frankfurters too, plus there's a can of mixed vegetables and some real potatoes still with the earth stuck in their eyes.

Then a vitamin pot is rattled under my nose. 'Make sure you take these.'

Later, after I'm alone again and my belly is cramping around the crisps, I decide to watch another film. I know it inside out and back to front, but it always makes me feel better. A woman gets into her car, strapping her two little children in the back. She drives off down a lonely road and the music gets loud and scary. At the junction, when she stops, a bad man forces his way into the car.

'You should have stayed inside! You should have stayed inside!' I scream out, like I've been taught. I tear at my hair, throwing my shoe at the screen.

Doesn't she know how dangerous it is out there? Why doesn't she ever listen to me?

I cover my eyes, and when I peek again, the children are dead and the man is on top of the woman. That's when I count my lucky stars that I'm locked up safe in here.

CHAPTER NINE

'Thanks for letting me know. That's excellent news,' Claire said, hanging up. She gave Jeff a thumbs up. 'Gary and Eleanor offered on Cliff Lodge. Guess how much?' She couldn't help the smile.

'Twenty grand under asking?'

'Nope.' Claire stood, hands on hips. '*Full* price,' she squealed, making a silly face.

She was well on target for an excellent month now, despite the slow start. Halfway through July and she'd streaked ahead of the others in what was usually a quiet time. 'They're cash buyers too. I must ring the owner.'

Claire settled back at her desk and made the necessary calls. Of course the vendor was delighted and solicitors were instructed to set the grinding wheels of paperwork in motion next week. Nothing else would happen this late on a Friday.

'Such a great start to what is going to be a fabulous few days,' she said to anyone who was listening. She stretched back in her chair, glancing at her watch. It was almost time to go.

'Sorry?' Jeff looked up from his computer.

'You haven't forgotten, haven't you?'

'Forgotten what?'

'My week off,' she said, rolling her eyes. 'I've got guests coming to stay, remember? I'll pop in for a couple of hours here and there if you need me, but that's all.'

'Yes, yes, of course I remember,' he replied.

'Don't let the place fall apart while I'm away,' she said, winking and scrolling through her inbox to answer a few emails.

'Don't worry, all is safe with me.' He gave her a wink back, tucking his shirt in and straightening his tie.

The agency was well respected locally. Located in one of the oldest buildings in Porthmarryn, it boasted an interior that would take even English Heritage's breath away. From the limewash colours to the original quarry tiles, the bent oak beams straddling the ceiling of what used to be the baker's shop, and the old oven where Claire kept a stash of handmade local chocolates to offer customers, they were one of the most prestigious agencies in the area.

'Hello, Greene & Galloway, Claire speaking.' She made a face, glancing at Jeff as he prised open the heavy cast iron door of the oven, taking out a truffle. He popped it in his mouth.

'Hello?' Claire frowned and held the handset away, staring at it. 'Hello, how may I help you?' She shrugged and hung up. 'That's the third one today,' she said, puzzled.

'We get those annoying spam calls at home. They make Marion hopping mad,' Jeff said with his mouth full. 'But really, you have fun next week, Claire. I've arranged for Janie to work extra hours, so we'll manage.'

'They're not spam calls,' Claire said thoughtfully. 'There's just no one there.' There'd been a lull for a couple of weeks, but in the last day or so they'd begun again. No one ever said anything, but occasionally she'd heard breathing, the sound of a car in the background and once, the wail of a child.

She wondered whether to call the police. Would they think them significant? She guessed they wouldn't, not after all this time.

'Everything's up to date,' Claire said an hour later. She double-checked a pile of papers, the draft sale particulars for Trevellin Farm included. Her parents would be sent a copy soon. She wasn't in any rush.

'Right, I'm off.' Jason and Greta were due at six and she wanted to get started on preparing dinner. She went through to the office's little kitchen and removed a package from the fridge. 'Fresh squid,' she said on the way out, holding up her purchase from the fishmonger's earlier. 'Jason's favourite.'

Jeff wrinkled his nose, giving her a brief hug.

'Remember the viewing tomorrow morning,' she said. 'It's important.' She slung her bag over her shoulder and left the office. Outside the air was humid and heavy with the scent of the harbour. It caused her heart to skip as she walked to her car, and as she drove off she made a mental checklist, ensuring she'd got everything for the meal. She didn't want to have to dash out later – tonight was important. She wanted to talk to Jason about reconciling with their father. It was time to let the past go.

By 4.45 p.m. Claire had picked up Amy, driven home, fed Russ and bribed Marcus to take him for a walk. She set out all the ingredients needed and made herself a cup of tea. When she saw the telephone answerphone light flashing, she pressed the button in passing. There were messages from the window cleaner, the local garage about an MOT, and Greta asking if there was anything she could pick up on the way. Then Claire stumbled back against the kitchen wall, shaking as she heard the final message. She covered her face with her hands, feeling sick and disgusted.

'What's up, love? You look as if you've seen a ghost.' Callum had just come in. He took her gently by the shoulders. 'Are you OK?'

'I'm fine,' she said quietly, gathering herself. She pushed past him, pressing the delete button over and over until the vile message had gone away. She instantly regretted doing so, although nothing could erase the words from her mind.

CHAPTER TEN

'Here, have some more wine,' Claire said, topping up Jason's glass. The evening was going well, and it was wonderful to see her brother and Greta, but by nine o'clock she was seriously considering calling the police. Initially, she'd convinced herself the message wasn't meant for her, or that it was just kids playing a prank or a wrong number. She wondered, too, if she'd misheard it, although she could still remember every sick word. But denying or distorting facts wasn't helping.

Greta was huge and glowing, just as Claire had imagined, and they'd discussed babies and birthing and even moved on to the subject of schools. She tried not to seem distracted but couldn't focus. The voice had been unfamiliar and there'd definitely been background noise on the crackly message – a lawnmower or engine, perhaps? Dialling 1471 was no use because a friend had called after the message was left. She'd been the target of a malicious call and she had no idea why.

'Claire, that was absolutely delicious. And *they* thoroughly approve.' Greta put down her knife and fork and smoothed her hands over her large belly.

Everyone fell silent, grins spreading.

'*They?*' Claire stared first at Greta, then at Jason.

'It's twins,' Jason announced. 'We've known for a while but thought we'd wait to tell you face-to-face.'

Claire clapped a hand over her mouth. 'That's wonderful! I'm going to be an aunty twice over.' It was exactly what she needed to help her forget.

'It came as a bit of a shock,' Greta said, laughing. 'But we're used to the idea now. In fact, we're delighted.'

Claire could see that pregnancy suited Greta. Her blonde hair was glossy and thick, and her skin radiant even with a minimum of make-up. With her well-paid job in the city, she was able to afford maternity clothes that made it seem chic to have a fifty-inch waist.

'That's why they don't want me to fly now. Twins often come early and I'm already thirty-five weeks. Chances are they'll be born within the next two or three weeks.'

'Perhaps I should bring home some scrubs and forceps,' Callum said with a laugh.

'Oh please have the babies here, Aunty Greta,' Amy piped up. 'They can sleep in my room. And make them girls. I want a little sister, but Mummy says I can't have one.' She pouted and smiled at the same time, squirming in her seat. A trick that usually won her what she wanted with her long lashes and rosebud lips.

'I don't know if they're boys or girls,' Greta told Amy. 'And I don't think you'd want them sleeping in your room, sweetie.'

'I do so.'

'Then you'll have to put up with changing their nappies and feeding them all night long.'

'Remember it well,' Callum said, groaning.

Claire raised her eyebrows, though didn't say anything. She was feeling the first flare of a headache. She'd only had two glasses of wine, but the damned message was still on her mind. For Jason's sake at least, she wanted to enjoy the evening. One of the conditions of him coming was that it would just be the four adults plus Amy and Marcus tonight, to ease him back into being at home, even if he wasn't staying at the farmhouse itself. He hadn't been up there yet, and Claire knew not to press the point. Coming to Trevellin was a huge deal for him. She had to play by his rules for now.

'We're going to draw up a contract about nappies and feeds, aren't we, darling?' Greta looked directly at Jason and smiled. Then she pressed a hand on her belly and pulled a face. 'Don't worry. Just a Braxton Hicks.' She relaxed again.

'How much time are you taking off?' Claire asked.

'As little as possible. In my business, if you're away from your desk too long, then you can expect some young hotshot to have taken it over when you get back. Probably two weeks. Less if I feel OK.'

Claire immediately sensed the tension between Jason and Greta. 'Good for you,' she said. 'I don't see why women should feel guilty about going back to work straight away if they want to. And it's perfect really, isn't it, Jase, with you being at home?'

'Unemployed, you mean,' he said, downing his wine.

'How is the thespian business these days?' Callum asked. Claire tried to nudge his foot but clipped the table leg instead.

'I got a walk-on, walk-off part in a fizzy pop advert last week.' Jason was deadpan.

'That's great,' Claire said.

'A forty-five second ad and my bit didn't make the final cut.'

No one said anything, so Claire cleared away the plates, insisting Greta stay seated when she tried to help. Jason followed her out to the kitchen, carrying a couple of serving dishes.

'That was a lovely meal, sis.' They faced each other, unable to deliver the hug they both felt was in order because of the stack of crockery between them. 'Sorry if I seemed a bit hacked off just then.'

'I understand,' she said. 'Just dump those over there.'

He put the dishes by the sink.

'Jase, someone left a really sick message for me today.' She wrapped her arms around her body. 'And I've had other calls too. I hear breathing and weird noises and then they just hang up.'

Jason frowned. 'What did the message say? Can you play it to me?' He looked concerned.

'Stupidly, I deleted it,' she said. 'It was a man. His voice was strange, like he was growling. He swore a couple of times and said stuff I couldn't understand. But then… then he said…' Claire let out a little sob. 'Then he said *I know where she is…*' Claire covered her face.

'Oh, Claire, that's awful. Come here.' Jason hugged her. 'Did you call the police?'

'No. Do you think I should?'

They gave each other a knowing look.

'What did Callum say?'

'I haven't told him. I didn't think there was any point worrying him.'

Jason nodded and made a thoughtful sound. 'If you get another one, don't delete it.' He eased her away, looking her in the eye. 'I can call the police for you if you like?'

Claire nodded. 'Thanks, but they'll probably say it was just a prank.'

In the early days, her parents had received a spate of calls ranging from fake bed and breakfast bookings made in Lenni's name, psychic cranks claiming to know where her body had been dumped, to menacing whispers in the dead of night telling them they'd burn in hell for losing their little girl.

The police investigated the calls as much as resources would allow, but none of them helped find Lenni. In the end, Patrick didn't bother to report them until they finally dwindled and burned themselves out. Until now.

'Let's try to put it out of our minds. Help me with dessert, would you?'

She put on a glove and slid the large dish from the oven while Jason carried the bowls. She headed for the dining room but stopped. 'It's really good to see you, Jase,' she said, unflinching as the heat scorched through the glove.

CHAPTER ELEVEN

Marcus lay on his bed. He was stuffed from all that food. It was good to see Uncle Jason, but he'd wanted to get back to his room to see if that girl was still online. He'd made his excuses at the table, but could tell his mum wasn't impressed.

He opened Messenger.

—*when u arriving?* he typed. He replied to three other conversations he was having with mates from school, bragging about the girl called Rain who was coming to stay, sending them a picture of her to prove he wasn't lying about how hot she was.

—*she'll be staying right next door to me*, he typed as fast as he could. He reckoned he was suddenly going to be very popular.

—*early AF* was Rain's reply. —*what's to do near you? sounds grim.*

She was right about that, Marcus thought, suddenly feeling different about the village he'd grown up in and always loved. But he wasn't about to confess that they lived in the middle of nowhere in case she changed her mind about coming.

—*cool stuff*, he typed, hoping that would convince her. They could go to Newquay, he supposed. And he could teach her to surf. He'd like to see her in a bikini. —*decent clubs, great beaches*.

More messages came in as his mates learnt of Rain's imminent arrival. There was a definite shortage of pretty girls in their year. Not only was Rain stunningly gorgeous, as he'd shown them all, but, even though they weren't Facebook friends yet and he couldn't see her birthday, she'd said she was his age. At least they'd all be able to get into the clubs. Marcus had looked at a couple of her pictures, but her privacy settings were strict, and he'd tried not to stalk her too much. He didn't want to feel creepy.

Suddenly, Rain was offline.

Marcus threw his phone down beside him. Only eight hours until he met her, he thought, sticking in his earphones, falling asleep in his clothes.

Greta had gone to bed. She'd thanked her hosts profusely, confessing to hardly being able to keep her eyes open much after nine o'clock these days, so making it to eleven was an achievement.

'Scary business, this having babies lark,' Callum said with a knowing laugh. He'd got out the whisky, which Claire didn't think was a terribly good idea seeing as Maggie and Rain were arriving in time for an early breakfast. Maggie had decided to leave at an ungodly hour to avoid the traffic.

'I think it would be scarier *not* having them.' Jason took the tumbler, swirling the liquid in the glass, thinking how grateful he was that he would soon be a dad.

Claire declined the whisky, sticking to tea. It was a mild night and the French doors were open. Insects darted about in the border between light and dark, while Claire breathed in the sea breeze. The evening had been a success despite the phone message. Several glasses of wine, a good meal and her thankfully waning headache had all served to make her conclude that the call was most likely a cruel prank.

'We didn't get to see much of Marcus tonight,' Jason said.

'Perfectly normal,' Claire replied. 'Once he hit thirteen, it was as if anyone outside his circle of friends didn't exist.' She laughed. 'And he's hard-wired into his phone.'

Callum muttered something about his son being a recluse as he settled down in the armchair with his drink. Claire knew he'd had a hard week. 'Personally, I don't see the appeal of all that social media stuff,' he went on, laying back his head. 'Give me a newspaper or a dog to walk and I'm happy.'

'You're just easy to please,' Claire said. 'Or getting old.' She patted his leg. Things had become so routine between them over the years that she only realised how much she loved all that when reminded of the simple things. She hoped he felt the same – contented, grateful, happy.

'Just so you know, I won't be around much next week. I have my clinics and operating schedule as normal.'

'I understand.' But Claire couldn't help the pang of regret wondering if Callum somehow felt sidelined. He'd not been part of their group when they were younger. 'When Maggie and Rain arrive in the morning, we'll have a lazy catch-up breakfast, then see what they feel like doing.'

'What kind of a name is Rain?' Callum said.

'A typical Maggie name,' Jason replied, smiling fondly.

'I was at medical school. I don't really know her.'

Claire thought how strange and impossible it would have seemed to her thirteen-year-old self to be dating a twenty-three-year-old man. Only when they met again in her late teens did the ten-year age difference suddenly seem less unacceptable. And Callum kept himself fit, running several times a week and always eating healthily. Plus, she couldn't have wished for a better father. He was as happy in the operating theatre as he was rolling about on the floor with his daughter or setting up her doll's house. They were content. The four of them. A family.

Why then, Claire wondered, did her stomach twist in knots when Jason asked about Nick's arrival?

'Is he bringing his wife?' Callum asked.

'I'm not actually sure.' She forced herself to sound casual, making a mental note to iron the sundress she'd bought earlier in the week. It had been on display in the boutique window on Monday morning and by lunchtime it was in a bag under her desk.

It was the truth – she didn't know if Nick was coming alone or with his family. Like the first, her second conversation with him had been curtailed. While he'd quickly agreed to the reunion, they hadn't had the time to discuss much about his life. All she knew was that he'd sounded a little tired, a little sad, and very grateful for the chance to take a break.

'I'm off to bed now. I need to get up early for Maggie.' She kissed her brother on the cheek and gave Callum a quick wave, indicating she'd say good night properly when he came up.

In the bathroom she removed her make-up, smoothing out the fine lines, wondering if Nick would think she'd aged much since he'd last seen her. She woke later when Callum finally got into bed beside her, but pretended to be asleep. She felt his warm breath on her neck as he kissed her, sensed the roughness of his stubble and smelt the sour tang of whisky mixed with toothpaste as he draped a hopeful arm across her waist.

Quietly, before sleep took over again, she opened the safekeeping box in her mind and locked up thoughts about the message, stashing them away along with everything else she kept secret in there.

CHAPTER TWELVE

When Lenni was five years old, she fell off a cliff. One moment she was scampering over the springy grass, her hair blowing in the onshore breeze and her little skirt flapping around her skinny legs, and the next moment she'd completely disappeared. They'd only looked away for a moment.

'Where did she go?' Patrick said, gripping onto Shona while frantically glancing around. He was trying to sound calm, but his insides had ignited.

'She was chasing gulls,' Shona replied, also scanning around for their daughter. Her hand slowly went up to her mouth as Patrick tore off towards the edge of the cliff, calling Lenni's name. She'd been drilled about going too close to the edge and they'd only stopped a moment to check the dog's paw because he'd been limping. When they looked up, Lenni had gone.

'*Lenni…*' Shona screamed. 'El–ea–nor, where are you?' Her heart thrashed inside her chest as she ran to join her husband. He was standing frozen at the cliff edge with his hands clawing at his head.

'Get help!' he yelled back at Shona. 'She's gone over.'

Shona could hardly bear to look down. Even if she'd survived the drop, she'd have landed on craggy rocks. Through narrowed eyes, Shona forced herself to lean over and look. She saw her little girl lying on her back in the only patch of soft sand within the expanse of barnacle-encrusted rocks. She was staring up at them, giggling.

'I was chasing the gulls,' she said with a croaky voice, but then her laughs turned to bubbling cries and she held out her arms to be picked up.

Somehow, Patrick scrambled down the rocks, dropping more than climbing. 'Lenni, oh my darling baby, what have you *done*?' He leapt over the rocks to get to the oasis of sand. He hurled himself onto his knees and ran his hands over her body. 'Does it hurt anywhere? Can you move your legs?' Then he saw the blood streaming from her head.

Lenni squinted up at her mother on the clifftop. She gave a little wave through her waning sobs, half sitting up. 'I'm OK, Daddy,' she said, allowing herself to be scooped up and cuddled, the blood dripping from behind her ear. 'I wanted to fly like the seagulls.'

'But you can't fly, darling. You don't have wings.'

Patrick realised that he was also crying. He buried his face in his daughter's sandy hair, breathing in the scent of her. It was the sweetest smell in the world, but he needed to get her to hospital. Meantime, Shona was running along the clifftop, scrambling down the shingle track to the beach. She was standing at the point where the rocks met the expanse of sand beyond.

'Bring her to me, Pat,' she called out, watching, barely able to breathe as he carried their precious little girl to her. When they finally reached her side, she took hold of Lenni, cradling her tight.

'I'm OK, Mummy. It was that bird's fault.' Lenni coughed and winced.

'We need to get her to hospital,' Patrick said, carrying her back to the house and the car.

Later, after Lenni had been given stitches in the zigzag gash behind her ear, they came home with a clean bill of health but a whole load of guilt for having taken their eyes off their daughter. Lenni was becoming more and more accident-prone, more fanciful and absent-minded, and far less aware of dangers than they thought normal. She was so different to Claire and Jason. Just last week Shona had found Lenni about to push a screwdriver into the plug socket because she was pretending to be a handyman. Days before that she was playing hospitals with her dolls and a packet of aspirin. She was about to crunch all the tablets up. So that evening Shona and Patrick made a pact. She would always be supervised by an adult.

Maggie was singing along to the radio to stay awake. Rain had long since fallen asleep, stretched out in the back of the campervan. She wasn't wearing a seat belt, but Maggie thought it would be worse to suffer a grouchy Rain for the whole of the next day if she didn't get any sleep at all.

She mumbled the words to some eighties song she vaguely remembered, no doubt from the village disco. She grinned at the memory of the weekly event that got them all so excited. Those two hours on a Friday night were certainly the highlight of her week. She and Claire would shuffle around the edge of the hall, eyeing up the boys who went to the posh school near Wadebridge, waiting for them to ask for a dance. Everyone was holding out for the slow tunes, hoping to get a snog.

She could almost smell the old village hall – a blend of dusty floors, ancient curtains and disinfectant in the grotty loos. Afterwards, she'd sleep over at the farm with Claire, gossiping until the early hours. But then they became too cool for the local disco, especially when the younger kids infiltrated. She'd heard from a friend that Lenni went once, though she could hardly believe she was allowed – such a shy little creature, who probably stood glued to the wall in terror all night.

Maggie approached Exeter and the end of the M5 with a smile on her face. The campervan stopped vibrating as she slowed, taking the exit for the A30. She'd had little sleep before they left – partly down to preparing for the trip, but also because Gino had got talking when he came home from the nightclub he owned.

Maggie's stomach clenched when she remembered his words. 'I'm not sure things are working out the way I want,' he'd said.

Working out between you and Rain, she'd thought bitterly, but didn't say. Subsequently, she'd loaded the camper with more possessions than she'd normally take away for a week, deciding not to say anything to Rain. She didn't want her to worry that they could be homeless and virtually penniless yet again.

Rain stirred. 'Are we nearly there?'

Maggie glanced in the rear-view mirror. 'Another hour and a half to go. Maybe two, depending on traffic. There's some water in the fridge.' She heard Rain shuffling about and then silence as she swigged from a bottle. Then she felt her daughter's warm breath on her ear as she climbed into the front.

'It's going to be all right this week, isn't it?'

'Of course,' Maggie replied, not used to hearing insecurity from Rain. 'You'll adore Claire, and she's got a teenage son too.'

'He's a dork.'

'That's a bit harsh.' Maggie's heart sank. She was hoping the holiday would do Rain good, perhaps strengthen their relationship which, she had to admit, hadn't been the best over the last few years. 'You haven't even met him yet.'

'We've messaged. He didn't have much to say for himself. I looked at his photos. Trust me, he's a dork.' Rain switched on to another radio station, turning it up loud, and Maggie couldn't help wishing that her daughter was still asleep.

CHAPTER THIRTEEN

Claire opened the back door and stepped out into the morning sun. It was a beautiful day and normally she'd have taken Russ for a walk already, but she'd been clearing up from last night and preparing breakfast. Amy stood beside her, clinging onto her legs as the pale-blue VW campervan trundled down the long drive.

'It's so wonderful to see you,' Claire said, as Maggie stretched out of the car.

There was a moment's pause, a moment of appraisal as each woman stood back and sized the other up without being obvious. Then they hugged fiercely, laughing into each other's hair about how crazy this all was, how they should have done it years ago, and how time flew by. Finally, they held each other at arm's length.

'You don't look a day older than when I last saw you,' Maggie said. Her hair was wild around her face.

'You neither,' Claire echoed.

They let go of each other as a groggy figure emerged from the other side of the van. The girl's long hair was highlighted with streaks of pale-copper and blonde, looking stylishly dishevelled. Slim tanned legs stuck out from beneath tiny ripped shorts and Claire noticed that she was already a few inches taller than her mother.

'Rain,' Claire said fondly, approaching her for a hug. 'You've certainly changed a bit!'

Rain stood rigid, so Claire just patted her on the shoulder, refusing to be fazed by the girl's lack of greeting or, indeed, the skimpy top that showed off much of her flat belly. She'd got her own teenager. She knew how things were. 'Last time I saw you, you were at primary school,' she said, but there was still no response. Maggie was fussing over Amy, who was bouncing up and down.

'And doesn't Amy look just like you?' Maggie said. 'Where's that big lad of yours?'

'I don't suppose we'll see anything of him before midday,' Claire replied.

'Lucky him,' Rain said, swishing her hair back off her face. She pulled a pair of huge sunglasses from an oversized shoulder bag and put them on.

'Good journey?' Claire asked, patting the campervan. 'Marcus would give a limb to own something like this. Some of the surfer lads around here have them.' Claire noticed Rain suddenly paying attention.

'It was a bit of an indulgence,' Maggie confessed. 'I was seeing this guy who—'

'Maggie,' Rain cut in. 'No one wants to know about all that.'

'Oh, but I do,' Claire said, taking Maggie's arm. 'I want to hear about it all, in *great* detail.' She whispered the last part. 'Come inside. Let's get coffee. There's bacon cooking and fresh bread. Jason and Greta arrived yesterday. I heard them moving about so they must be up by now...'

Claire chattered non-stop until Maggie and Rain were inside sipping on mugs of coffee. She busied about in the kitchen, feeling strangely self-conscious, extremely happy yet nervous all at the same time. After weeks of planning, the reunion was finally happening.

'I have lots in mind for the week,' Claire said. 'And I've dug out a ton of old photographs. I thought it might help Dad's memory if we all went through them together. I'd like us all to take him to the beach often, perhaps play some of the old games he taught us and...'

Claire heard herself reciting plans but was conscious of a sadness brewing inside her. This time next week it would be over. They would all go back to their own lives – her included – and get on with another decade or so. It was that last part that brought Claire down from the high she'd survived on these last few weeks. Didn't she *want* things to go back to normal?

'Is there any fat-free yoghurt?' Rain glanced disdainfully at the spread Claire had set out on the long table.

'Rain,' Maggie said, scowling, but then leapt to her feet. 'Oh my God, *Jason*!' She flung her arms around him as he came into the kitchen.

Claire smiled. Maggie the performer. Maggie the centre of attention. Maggie the one always up for taking a risk. Though she sensed that something had dulled her since they'd last met. Taken the shine off her just a touch.

'You feeling a bit ropey, bro?' Claire laughed as Jason ran his hands across his face.

'Callum's fault,' he confessed, before introducing himself to Rain.

She stared back. Her sunglasses were now forked on her head and her full lips sat in a pout, making her appear innocent and childish while giving off an undeniably sexy look at the same time.

'Yes, this is my mute daughter, Rain,' Maggie said. 'She clearly left her voice and her manners at the services three hours ago.'

'Thank you, Maggie, but I'm quite able to speak for myself.' Rain held out her hand, almost as if she expected him to kiss it. 'Delighted to meet you,' she said in a voice that revealed her boarding school background. 'You're Claire's brother, right?'

'Indeed,' Jason replied, not knowing what to make of the kid. He coughed, trying to clear his voice. Callum had got the cigars out late last night.

'Where's Greta?' Claire asked.

'Right here,' came a voice from the doorway. Greta radiated such a picture of glowing health that Claire heard Maggie catch her breath.

'Jason, you're married to an angel! A burgeoning angel, you lucky, lucky man!' Again, that over-the-top voice that had always been Maggie's trademark briefly resurfaced. It had often landed her in trouble.

'I'm not sure about the angel bit, but I'm definitely burgeoning.' The two women hugged lightly, and Maggie placed her hands on Greta's belly.

'Twins?' she asked. Bangles and chunky bracelets jangled at her wrists, under the floaty sleeves of her gypsy-style top. 'I think they're both boys.'

Greta laughed, eyeing Jason.

'They don't want to know the sexes,' Claire said, smiling and laying out the rest of the food. Callum joined them, and everyone sat around the table, soaking up Claire's hospitality. There was much chatter and laughter for the next hour or so, with none of the eggs, bacon, tomatoes and homebaked bread left when Claire cleared away. Even Rain had managed to down a few blackberries and a quarter of a piece of toast.

Claire offered to make something else for Rain, but Maggie insisted they all ignore her fussy daughter and her silly eating habits. 'She's always on some stupid fad diet or another just to be awkward.'

'It's good to watch what you eat,' Callum said. Rain gave him a small smile. 'Especially when you get to my age.'

'She's got a long way to go, darling,' Claire said. 'Don't worry, Rain. You won't end up looking like him.'

'How old are you, Mr Rodway?'

'Rain!' Maggie scolded.

'Let's just say I'm still in my forties,' he said.

'What he means is he's nudging fifty.' Claire grinned as he pushed back his shoulders and sucked in his stomach.

'You still have time, then,' Rain said.

'For what?' Callum leant forward on the table.

'For some fun, of course.' Rain stood, excusing herself from the table, lifting up her long legs as she stepped over the wooden bench.

'Right,' Claire said, after she'd gone, clearing her throat. 'Anyone want more coffee?'

CHAPTER FOURTEEN

Rain sat on the closed toilet seat and pulled her phone from her bag.

—*he def looks like a loser*, she tapped into WhatsApp after spotting Marcus coming down the stairs.

—*but he's male, right?* Katie, her best friend, replied seconds later.

Rain managed a smile despite her dismal mood.

—*haha not entirely sure.* She added a sticking-out-tongue emoji.

—*don't let the girls down.*

Rain deleted what she was typing, about how she really felt.

—*i won't*, she replied, adding a couple of cheeky aubergine emojis.

She put away her phone and rested her head in hands. *Don't let the girls down.* But what about letting herself down? Despite what all her friends thought, she wasn't really like *that*. She might act a certain way, but it wasn't really her. Not if she dared to look deep inside.

She remembered taking to heart something her mother had once said, a drunken comment that was probably more to do with Maggie than anything, but it had resonated with her own low mood at the time.

'You can't fall off the floor, sweetheart…' She'd passed out after that, but Rain had since wondered if it was Maggie's fault that she hated herself so much. Her friends' mums were different, always doing lunches and playing tennis and having people over and stuff.

Maggie never seemed to have time for her. Katie's mum took her shopping regularly, they went riding together, had spa days and did other cool things. Instead, Maggie was always off with some new man or other, far too busy for her own daughter.

'No, I won't let you down, Katie,' Rain whispered, feeling a sudden surge of defiance. She stood up, grimacing as she caught sight of herself in the toilet mirror.

She knew what to do to make things better, she thought, flipping open the toilet lid. She dropped to her knees, forcing her fingers down her throat, stroking the soft flesh until the first retch came. Soon, the tiny amount of food she'd just eaten was swirling in the water, ending with the dark purple of the fruit she'd swallowed first – an indicator it had all come up.

Rain sighed, staring into the pan. She heaved herself up off the floor, pulling a toothbrush and paste from her bag. She scrubbed out her mouth, staring into the mirror. She didn't hate herself quite so much now. Until next time.

She smeared a slick of gloss across her lips and rolled them together, pouting at her reflection. Then she flushed the toilet, slung her bag over her shoulder and headed out into the flagstoned hallway of the farmhouse. It was very different to anything she was used to. Sure, she'd lived in old houses before. She'd also had modern apartments with great expanses of glass overlooking city rivers and trendy eating areas. There'd been the houseboat on the Thames and the castle in Scotland, the Parisian apartment in the Marais over a gay nightclub where she'd never got to sleep before the early hours, and the stately home which had been open to the public during the summer. Maggie had a knack of rehoming them regularly.

But this place was different, and she wasn't quite sure why. It smelt of cut grass and bacon, of coffee and bread, and then there were the flowers and the fresh-smelling washing folded and left on the stairs… but there was another scent. Something she couldn't quite identify.

She snapped the elastic band around her wrist to make the tears go away.

Slowly, Rain put her bag on the polished hall table. A couple of letters addressed to Callum Rodway had been propped against a vase of lilies. There were some hooks on the wall beside the front door, each overloaded with a muddle of coats and scarves and a couple of bags. Below was a rack with a dozen different pairs of shoes, ranging from tiny black patent ones to men's walking boots with soles like tractor tyres.

On the wall opposite was a collection of framed photographs of the family. In the centre of the arrangement was a large black and white photo of the four of them lying on their fronts on a furry rug. Amy was very young, probably only about two or three, and her geek brother was posing next to her, wearing too-big glasses and with a crop of spots around his mouth. There were various other pictures, mostly of the kids with the dog or at the beach. She straightened a couple of crooked ones.

Rain peeked into the living room beyond. It was similarly decorated with slightly shabby yet once plush furniture: faded sofas with giant cushions, a wicker basket overflowing with toys that would once have set Rain's heart pattering, as well as several bookcases stuffed with paperbacks. There was a log burner and thick rugs on the wooden floor, heavy tapestry curtains and someone's magazine left open next to an empty coffee mug.

She gritted her teeth as the tears welled up again. Her breathing was short and shallow. She knew exactly what was different about Claire's house – a place she'd been in for only an hour. And she now realised exactly what the unfamiliar smell was too.

This place was a *home*. A proper, permanent home. It was comfortable, lived-in and brimming with memories. Rain fought the feelings of jealousy but couldn't prevent the tightness in her chest. She wondered if she should throw up again.

The smell was undeniably of love.

'Hey...'

Rain swung around and came face-to-face with Marcus. He was holding a half-eaten piece of toast in one hand and a mug of tea in the other.

'Oh, hi,' she said back.

He wasn't that bad-looking up close, she supposed, now that he wasn't wearing nerdy glasses and the spots had cleared up. His ripped jeans and that T-shirt with the name of a band she and her friends talked about non-stop were OK too.

'You a fan?' she asked, staring at his chest.

'Saw them at the O2 last year. They were awesome.'

'Sick.'

'I'm Marcus,' he said, flicking his long fringe from his eyes with a toss of his head. 'I would shake your hand but...' He glanced at the mug and toast.

'I'm Rain,' she replied. 'As in pissing down.'

'It's pretty.'

'Pretty weird,' she replied, despising herself for smiling.

'Are you weird, then?' Marcus's voice was deep and resonant, as if it belonged inside someone much older, more manly. Someone like his dad.

'Very,' she said, twirling her hair. God, this was going to be easy. Easy and boring. 'Maybe I'll get a chance to show you?'

She gave him her best selfie pout and Marcus's gaze followed the predictable route from her mouth, down her neck, settling on her breasts. The bra she wore hitched up her Cs into Ds. Some of her friends were seriously considering implants, but there was no way she needed them, especially as she was still developing.

'How long are you staying?' Marcus took a bite of his toast, forcing his gaze back up.

'A week. But it's going to feel like a year around here.' She squeezed past, retrieving her bag off the hall table.

'It's not so bad. I'll introduce you to my mates. There are some decent clubs in Newquay. You got your ID?'

'Of course.' She patted her bag.

'We could head down there tonight if you like. Plans are already afoot.'

Afoot, she thought incredulously. A geek, after all. But if nothing else, she could brag about him to the girls, big him up a bit, use some filters on Instagram. She couldn't let Katie down.

'Cool,' she said, sliding between him and the wall as she headed back to the kitchen. She made sure her body brushed against his.

CHAPTER FIFTEEN

Shona was waiting for Claire to bring Maggie and Rain down to the farm. She wanted to settle them into their rooms but was feeling agitated. She hadn't wanted to have the conversation with Patrick today of all days, but he'd brought it up out of nowhere and he wouldn't let it drop. And on top of that, he'd completely forgotten about the reunion, refusing to join everyone up at Claire's for breakfast.

'You're being more stubborn than usual, Pat,' Shona said, instantly regretting it. She didn't think he looked at all well, so she'd ended up making him breakfast at home. 'And don't put so much butter on your toast. You know what Dr Jenkins would say.'

'And you know what I'd say to Dr Jenkins.'

Shona sat down next to him. He wasn't going to get any better, she knew that, let alone change his ways. She also knew there was one thing and one thing only preventing him from agreeing to sell up – and that's what had been on his mind this morning.

'You know, it's OK for us to move house now, Pat. She's not coming back.' She hated herself for wishing that this was one thing he'd actually forget, but his brain stubbornly refused to let go.

Patrick put down his knife, staring at Shona through eyes she'd never seen look quite so sad. 'We made a promise, Shona...' He looked away, as if he couldn't recall what the promise was. Just that there was one.

Shona felt tears building. Each day he seemed to get a little worse.

'We promised her. And we promised each other,' he added.

Shona went to the window, squinting up the drive to see if Claire and the others were coming. Behind her she heard Patrick clear his plate, gather his stick and hat and leave the house without another word, shrugging away as she tried to catch his arm. Then she heard the Land Rover's engine start up and she knew it was too late to stop him.

She sighed, staring up the long drive. As long as he stayed local or on farm tracks, she wouldn't worry too much. He was still a good driver, but she wished he'd just cool off with a walk around the farm like he usually did. Suddenly, the back door opened, followed by chattering. She closed her eyes briefly.

'Mum, we're here.' Claire kissed her cheek. 'Where's Dad off to in such a hurry?'

Shona avoided answering. 'Oh, Maggie, how lovely to see you.' She gave her a hug. 'And you must be Rain?' Her welcoming nature kicked in. She was adept at making people feel as though they'd lived at Trevellin all their lives, a skill developed from bed and breakfast guests constantly coming and going as well as a houseful of children – hers and their friends. She hugged them both, finally giving her daughter a fond squeeze.

'Shona was like a second mother to me when I was a kid. I virtually lived at Trevellin,' Maggie explained to Rain.

'Thank you for having us, Mrs Lucas,' Rain said politely. 'You have a beautiful home.'

Shona was warmed by the girl's slightly old-fashioned manner, which her looks belied. 'It's my pleasure,' she replied, though the comment prompted another pang of regret about selling.

When she'd first walked through the front door of the derelict old farm nearly half a century ago, she'd fallen in love with the place immediately. A slate and stone farmhouse, Trevellin Farm was a failing old dairy business back then. Patrick worked it back to profitability while Shona took in bed and breakfast guests. One thing was for certain – when they first set eyes on the place, they knew it was their forever home where they would raise happy, healthy children on the Cornish coast just like they'd always dreamt.

How time had flown, she thought, catching her breath as she showed them up the creaky old staircase. She watched the trail of women in the big gilt mirror on the half landing, each one a different generation. She felt both proud and desperately sad.

'I thought you and Rain might like the attic bedrooms,' Shona said, leading them up the second staircase. 'It's cosy up here.'

When they'd moved in, the top floor had been nothing more than a draughty storage space crawling with birds and spiders. When they'd turned their first year's profit on the farm, Patrick had instructed an architect to plan the conversion, although he'd done most of the actual work himself. He was good with his hands. It became extra guest accommodation during busy summers but was hardly used nowadays.

'I thought you could have the lilac room, Maggie, and Rain, you're in here.' Shona was a little breathless as they reached the top floor. She swept back an errant strand of grey hair as it escaped the clip she always wore. 'I'll leave you to settle in.'

Back on the landing, Shona saw Claire slipping her phone back into her pocket. 'That was work,' she said. 'They need me to do a quick viewing.' She glanced at her watch.

'Really? Can't you say no?' Shona felt she should go out and look for Patrick, but it would be rude to leave Maggie and Rain alone.

Claire shook her head, pulling a face. 'Not really, though I'm not happy about it. One of the agents was meant to cover for me, but she's called in sick and Jeff's doing another viewing. He's desperate, but did say it won't take long.'

Shona sighed. There was no point arguing with her daughter any more than there was with Patrick. She went back downstairs, leaving Claire to explain to Maggie. She stood at the kitchen window again, watching out for her husband just as she used to for Lenni in the early days. When there was still hope.

CHAPTER SIXTEEN

Claire drove as fast as she dared along the narrow lanes. She knew all the passing places, the sharp bends, the blind corners and junctions, and was able to dash to the office in town to collect the keys and still make it to the property before the client arrived.

Whatever happened, she'd be back home within the hour.

'It's a man viewing on his own, Claire.' Even over the phone, she'd heard the guilt in Jeff's voice – partly because he knew she was on annual leave, and partly because he never usually sent female agents to view with male clients they didn't already know. He was old-fashioned like that. But he'd sounded desperate.

'He's a cash buyer,' Jeff had added, offering to swap viewings with her, though the alternative was much further to drive. Claire opted for the quick job close to home.

Galen Cottage was as derelict as they came and had been on their books for over a year. She'd be glad to see the back of it, but with only two bedrooms and a roof that had more holes than slates, the remote cottage wasn't getting any bites. She hoped this man wanted a project.

Claire parked up and unlocked the front door. Inside it smelt musty and damp, but that was to be expected; it hadn't been lived in for years. As she waited for the client, she wrestled with a couple of warped windows to let in some air, but they wouldn't budge. Years of paint and the salty sea air had made them stick fast.

'Oh, come *on*,' she said, glancing at her watch, pacing the small living room. 'Don't be late today of all days.'

She went upstairs and looked around. While she was up there, she thought she heard the crunch of gravel on the drive. She peered out of the tiny panes but saw nothing. She managed to force open the bathroom window, feeling slightly sick from the stench. The toilet wasn't exactly going to help the sale, even if it was obvious that the whole place needed gutting.

She heard a noise downstairs.

Finally, she thought. If it wasn't him, she'd call Jeff and ask for Mr Barrett's number. She'd been in such a rush that she'd forgotten to make a note of it, but when she felt in her pocket she realised that she'd left her phone in the car.

'Hello?' she called out, wondering if he'd let himself in. She'd left the door wide open. She trod carefully on the steep stairs, going down to greet the client.

The narrow hallway was dark and gloomy – the electricity had been cut off years ago – and she kicked aside all the old mail and flyers lying on the grimy tiles. But there was no sign of anyone.

She put a hand on the front door, tugging on the handle, convinced she'd left it open. Perhaps he'd come in and had a quick look, seen the state of the place and left immediately. She pulled harder on the handle, but it wouldn't move. 'Damn this stupid house,' she said, giving the door a kick.

'Hello,' she called out, her face close to the wood. 'Anyone out there? Can you give the door a shove?' She tried again, but when she bent down and peered through the gap, she could see it was more than stuck. It was locked.

'What the hell…?' She felt in her back pocket for the large, old-fashioned door key, but it wasn't there. She dashed back upstairs to see if she'd left it in the bathroom, but she hadn't. She froze in the bathroom doorway, staring at the window she'd opened only a couple of minutes before. It was now shut. The stench of drains was already building up again.

'Christ,' she whispered, hand over her mouth, slowly checking behind the door. She didn't believe in ghosts but was willing to if it meant she wasn't locked inside the cottage with a psycho.

Halfway down the stairs she stopped, suddenly remembering where the key was. She'd left it in the lock. On the *outside*. Back in the hallway, she glanced about nervously, wondering what to do. Habit made her reach into her pocket for her phone again – it was time to call Jeff – but of course, she'd left it in the car.

Then another noise. She couldn't be certain if it had come from inside or outside.

'You're being silly,' she tried to convince herself. The noise was most likely from a passer-by who had seen the door open and decided they should lock it. The locals looked out for one another around here, and she'd noticed the public footpath sign cutting across the driveway. No doubt loads of walkers came through. Claire almost burst with relief.

Then she heard a different noise – something that sounded too much like a floorboard creaking upstairs. Her skin prickled.

'Hello? Who's there?' She reached for an old poker lying beside the fireplace and approached the bottom of the stairs. Jeff would be ecstatic if she bludgeoned a potential buyer. 'Anyone up there?' Her voice was croaky, loaded with fear.

The floor creaked again, as if someone was on the landing. She trod on the first step, her throat pulsing in time with her racing heart. She'd heard of estate agents getting into trouble on remote viewings. As she rounded the narrow dogleg bend on the stairs, she swore she saw a shadow pass across the grimy wall. She choked on whatever it was that was constricting her throat. Bile, fear… she didn't know. Instinct told her to get out.

Darting back down into the living room, she ran to the stuck window and raised the poker above her head. She screwed up her eyes and brought it down on the glass over and over, smashing hard at the old panes. Adrenalin and fear fuelled her need to escape as shards of thin glass showered onto the quarry tiles. The brittle glazing bars didn't take much force from the poker before there was a space big enough to climb through.

Shaking, she clambered up onto the ledge and coiled her legs out of the small gap. Remnants of glass cut into her shoulder, but she didn't care. Whoever she'd heard up there was nearly down the stairs. She could hear slow, plodding footsteps on the wooden boards as if they didn't have much urgency, as if they knew she was already terrified.

Claire jumped down off the windowsill onto the soil below. Her heel became trapped between two rocks, so she kicked off her shoes and ran, stumbling, panting, to the safety of her car. Her body didn't feel like her own.

'*Oh God, oh God…*' She yanked the car door open and leapt inside, reaching for the ignition where she knew she'd left the keys. But they were gone.

'No, *no*…!' she cried, covering her face. She searched around frantically – in the ignition again, then on the floor and under the seat. She twisted around to check the back seat, the passenger side footwell…

The keys were gone. And so were her mobile phone and handbag.

CHAPTER SEVENTEEN

It was Maggie who drove to pick her up from the village, with Jason beside her in the camper. She pulled up alongside the kerb and got out, Claire virtually falling into Maggie's arms outside the village shop.

'I'm so sorry, Mags. This is such a lousy start to the week.' She'd charged down to the village store fifteen minutes ago, begging to use the shop owner's phone so someone could fetch her. She'd tried Callum's number first, but there'd been no reply.

'What on earth happened, Claire?' Jason said, prising his sister from Maggie's arms. 'Get in the van and tell us.'

Grateful to be sitting, Claire hugged herself, rocking gently, telling them how scared she'd been without actually explaining what had happened. Her words were muddled and didn't make much sense.

Jason touched her shoulder. There was blood on her blouse.

'Someone was in the house, I swear, though I didn't see them. They locked me inside and stole my keys, bag and phone.'

'God, that's terrible,' Maggie said, gripping her hands. 'We should call the police.'

'No, please… don't,' Claire said. 'Jeff won't be happy if there's a story in the local papers about a viewing gone wrong. It'll be bad for our reputation.'

'But someone stole your stuff,' Maggie said, eyeing Jason. 'You need to report it.'

'I can cancel my cards and my phone's insured. Really, I just want to forget it.'

'We should go back to the cottage,' Jason said. 'At least see about your car.'

Claire nodded tentatively. 'Fine, but I'm not going inside.'

'You don't have to,' Jason replied. 'I will.'

'It's in a bad state,' Maggie said, steering the van onto the overgrown driveway.

'We've had it on our books ages,' Claire replied. 'It reminds me of the old cottage on the farm.' She stopped herself from saying more, though she'd already seen the hurt look on Jason's face, knowing it was a trigger for him. She still wasn't thinking clearly.

'It's similar indeed,' Jason said. 'We spent hours playing up at the farm cottage as kids, do you remember?' Claire knew he was trying to sound light about it.

'I remember!' Maggie chipped in, wrapping a cardigan around Claire. She was shivering. 'We used to make up murder mysteries, scaring ourselves witless.'

The little cottage was built on Trevellin's eastern boundary during the late eighteen hundreds. It was a typical workers' dwelling, common to the area. Surrounded by a thicket of trees, they'd believed their father when he once told them Hansel and Gretel lived there, and it remained their playhouse until he banned them from it when half the roof caved in. It was way beyond any repairs Patrick could tackle. Like the barns on the farm, it had since just sat there, unloved and unneeded, for years.

Claire reckoned it would fetch a good price if sold separately to the farm with an acre or so of land. It was ripe for development. But no one would ever forget that it was the source of Jason's resentment, the catalyst for the argument that drove a wedge between him and their father.

'I thought you said you'd been locked in?' Maggie said, pointing at the front door. It was wide open.

Claire leant forward on the dashboard. 'But... I don't understand.' She saw the look that Jason shot Maggie. 'I promise you, it was locked when I was inside. That's why I smashed the window.'

Jason reached forward and touched his sister's arm. 'We believe you,' he said. 'Wait here while I go and check the place over.' They all got out of the van, though Claire refused to take a single step away from it.

'Be careful,' she called out as Maggie and Jason walked off together. The sight of the cottage made her feel sick and she wasn't sure she'd be able to do another viewing there, not alone anyway.

Claire shielded her eyes from the sun, squinting as Jason showed something to Maggie by the front door. Then they both looked back at Claire. She watched as they went around the side of the cottage where she'd parked her car. It was something Jeff had taught her long ago – not to detract from a property's frontage with an agency vehicle, maximising its kerb appeal. And Galen Cottage needed all the help it could get.

A few minutes later, Jason and Maggie came back into sight. Maggie returned to the camper while Jason went into the cottage. 'Why don't you sit back in the van again? You look pale.'

'I don't need to sit down,' Claire said. 'Sorry, Mags. I didn't mean to snap. The day hasn't got off to a great start.'

Maggie took her by the shoulders. 'It's fine. I'm your oldest friend.'

As kids, they'd trusted each other implicitly, looking out for each other. But as they'd hit their teens, Claire wondered if she'd sensed a tinge of jealousy from Maggie. So when a few of her things had gone missing – a couple of CDs, some money, bits of cheap jewellery – she decided not to say anything. Even though she was convinced Maggie was responsible.

'Thanks, Mags,' Claire said, closing her eyes for a moment. 'I'm just a bit wrung out.'

'Do you remember that time at the circus?' It was obvious she was trying to distract Claire.

'Dad the lion tamer?'

'Yeah. I was so damned jealous that your dad got picked to go in the ring. Mine didn't even go to the show – he was probably pissed and passed out somewhere. Do you remember what you said to me when the lion tamer asked your dad if he had any children in the audience?'

Claire did remember, but kept quiet.

'You whispered, "Put your hand up, Maggie. Pretend it's you."'

'Did I?' She laughed.

'So I stuck my arm in the air and the lion tamer plucked me out of the audience when it should have been you.' Maggie fidgeted with her fingers. 'For those few minutes in the circus ring, I pretended that he was my real dad. It was magical.' The two women stared at each other for a moment. 'So, thanks, Claire. It meant a lot.'

Claire touched her arm. 'Look, Jason's coming back.'

'All seems fine in there,' he said, holding up a big key. 'It was still in the lock. I made sure there was no one lurking inside.' He shot another quick glance at Maggie. 'And we found these on the ground by your car.' He held up her car keys.

'I don't under—'

'The good news is that your handbag is in the boot, along with your phone.'

'But… but…' Claire touched her forehead. That wasn't possible. That wasn't where she left them, was it?

'They shouldn't have sent you to do a viewing out here alone,' Maggie said. 'It's so remote. If you're feeling stressed, things can blow out of proportion and—'

'I'm not stressed,' Claire said, marching barefoot across the drive. She went up to her car, yanking on the handle, but Jason had locked it. Peering through the window, she saw that her big leather bag was now on the passenger seat. Jason had also plugged in her phone to charge.

She leant back against the car for a moment, feeling dizzy, before marching up to the front window, knowing she looked and sounded crazy. Then she beckoned them over, pointing to her shoes lying in the earth beneath the broken window. 'See? I had to smash my way out with a poker. There was an intruder. I was locked in!' She was close to tears now. 'OK,' she said finally, letting out a big sigh. 'You're probably right. Maybe a cat or a bird got trapped in the house, and then I accidentally locked myself inside.'

'It's not that we don't believe you—'

'Just give me my car keys, Jase. Let's go home.'

'I'll drive your car,' he said, picking up her shoes. Claire didn't argue. On the way back she phoned Jeff, staring out of the passenger window, watching as the narrow lanes whipped by. Jeff told her how well his chapel viewing had gone.

'Oh, and did you get my message earlier?' he added.

'What message?' Claire felt the seat belt tighten around her chest.

'Mr Barrett called to cancel moments after you'd left the office. What a time-waster he turned out to be.'

CHAPTER EIGHTEEN

Fireworks and Vodka

Once in a blue moon (whatever one of those is), I'm taken out. My body aches if we walk too far, so my favourite thing is to sit and watch. One time it was night and we lay on our backs, staring up at the stars. We saw the Plough and Little Bear constellations and the pink twinkle of Betelgeuse on Orion's shoulder.

'It's a dying star,' I was told.

'Is it sick, then?' I got worried it might fall from the sky and crush us.

'Just very, very old.' I could smell the booze. It was chilly, so I snuggled up close, praying we could stay like this forever.

Sometimes I get treats when we're out. Lollipops or chocolates or second-hand shoes that are in the shape of someone else's feet. Once, I got given a mouse in a cage, but it died after a few days. I think it wanted to run free, like me.

Today we're meant to be going out. I don't know where to, but I'm still here alone so I've been gently knocking my head against the wall to pass the time. I don't know if it's day or night. I haven't wound my watch in a while.

I lie on the floor, waiting, stripped naked because my clothes feel like electric shocks on my skin. I twirl my hair, just a small strand winding around my finger, staring at the ceiling. Eventually, it works loose and a clump comes away.

Then the doors are rattling and a familiar shadowy figure looms above me. 'You're not ready.'

I curl up, covering my naked body. 'I thought you weren't coming.' I feel around for my clothes.

'Sometimes it's not easy to get away. You know that.'

I nod, apologising, feeling wretched and mean for complaining. 'Where are we going?' I can't wait to breathe the outside air.

'We can go in the car if you want.'

'But what if we die?' I say, remembering last time. I was crying on the back seat, worried we would crash.

'Then we'll walk.'

I pull on my clothes – too-small garments even for my skinny bent body. Then I lie on the floor with my feet sticking up the wall. One foot scrapes back and forth against it. Back and forth. Back and forth. Something is always going back and forth in here.

'It's a special time.'

I'm suddenly still. 'Special?'

'The last day of the millennium.' I don't know what that means, but I'm given a boiled sweet. 'Get something warm on. It's cold out.'

I pull on my coat, zipping up the hood tight around my face like I'm always made to, and we go through the lengthy process of getting outside. I'm led by the arm. The freezing night air burns my lungs and I screw up my eyes as we walk, stumbling along the lane, across fields. We keep going for ages and I wonder if I should scream out. Last time I did that I got gagged with a scarf.

My feet are freezing and soaking from the long icy grass. My teeth are chattering and my cheeks sting from the bitter breeze. I can't help laughing loudly, hysterically, as we come to a stop. I feel so free.

'What do you think?'

'It's amazing. Beautiful!' I want to cry when I see it but can't because my tears are all used up. I sit down on the blue tarpaulin and wrap myself up in the rug. A storm lamp is lit and a picnic of Scotch eggs, Crunchie bars, vodka and bananas is revealed. We're in the middle of a field with the dark skeletons of trees looming around us. 'Thank you, thank you!' I say, grabbing all the food I can. The cold and the wet don't matter any more.

'There's more to come.' I smell the cigarette smoke, and then I'm given the vodka bottle. Before I can even bring it to my lips, our faces are lit up by colourful flashes of crazy light sparkling across the dome of the black sky. I squeal in delight. My mind is flooded with so many memories I can hardly breathe… *toffee apples and woolly gloves… Goose the dog shivering under my bed… the melting mask of the guy… Daddy lighting the touchpapers and Mummy's hot chocolate…*

'Is it Bonfire Night?' I stuff a chocolate bar in my mouth.

'I told you already. It's the new millennium.' Then more vodka. 'It's auspicious.' But I don't know what that means.

'It looks like the fireworks are coming out of the sea,' I say, pointing to the horizon. The reflection in the water makes it doubly good. We lie back on the grass to get a better view.

It goes on forever, like the heavens are raining jewels on me. I suddenly feel so special, the most cherished person in the world. This is all for me! And I hardly realise I'm even doing it as I slowly, oh so slowly, unfurl my legs from the knot of rug and flex my feet. I can smell the alcohol and I know what it does. Even more slowly, I peel the rug from my shoulders, slide myself away a little. The cold air bites at my neck.

'Want a chocolate bar?' I say but get nothing back – just that droopy vodka stare. I stuff the chocolate in my pocket instead. 'More drink?' I hold out the bottle and it's snatched from my hand as fireworks crackle along the coast. 'Pretty, isn't it?' I say, but there's just a mumble in reply now. The empty bottle drops onto the tarpaulin.

Slowly, I ease myself up so I'm sitting, then into a crouching position. I barely breathe, glancing behind me, the way we came. Our footprints look like black stitches sewn across the iced grass. My mouth is dry, and my knees hurt but I spring up, tripping a little as my shoe strap gets caught in the rug.

I run.

My legs don't work properly, and my lungs feel as if I've swallowed a firework. I have no idea where I'm going. I just keep running, stumbling, my arms flailing, my hair caught in my mouth, my heart firing bullets.

Then I'm flat on my face. A hand is around my ankle.

CHAPTER NINETEEN

Everything Nick owned was going into this project. It was his final chance.

'The thing about kitchens,' he said, looking at his watch, 'is that they have to work.' He was finding it hard to explain, especially when other things, other people, were on his mind. 'It's not about just making sure it all fits and wiring up appliances.' Nick paced about, thinking hard. 'You sure you don't need me to stay on-site, Trev?'

The builder folded his arms. 'Mate, if you don't get your arse out of this building, I'm going to kick it all the way to Land's End.' He gave Nick a playful shove on the shoulder.

Trevor had come highly recommended and, over the last couple of months, they'd become something like friends, enjoying the occasional after-work beer together. Nick reckoned he could trust him, but was still uneasy about leaving the project at such a crucial stage. There was hardly any spare cash or time to undo mistakes, and while he reckoned Trev would keep quiet about the basement, it was still a risk.

He shoved his hands in his pockets and scuffed the rubble-covered floor. He nodded in agreement and took one last look around the site that, in a couple of months, would be opening its doors to some of the fiercest reviewers in the trade. He felt anticipation and fear, as well as utter emptiness. Jess had always been by his side.

*

In the car, he switched between radio stations but couldn't find anything decent. He shuffled randomly through playlists, and when the tune blared out he felt like he'd been punched in the guts. He gripped the wheel tightly, driving through the pain. Jess had chosen all these songs for him – her favourites, some old, some new. This was the song playing when they'd had their first kiss. He was sentimental like that. Now he wanted to smash things if he heard it.

Life had to be recalibrated.

He skipped to the next track, trying not to think. He swerved suddenly as a horn blared, narrowly missing a van.

Shit.

He overrode the satnav and, instead of taking the M4 towards Bristol, he left London on the M3, veering off after Basingstoke. He didn't think it would take much longer and it would give him time to think. Think about *her.*

The last time he'd seen her was at Revel. He'd had no idea she was coming in. They'd met once or twice over the years, trying to keep in touch, trying to do the right thing, even though seeing her always filled him with a sense of loss, of what might have been.

That day, towards the end of a busy lunchtime service, one of the waitresses had handed him a note written on a napkin. His first thoughts were that it was from an undercover critic – there'd been a spate the last few weeks – so Nick wiped the sweat off his face and went to table eight as requested. There was only a handful of diners left, mainly business customers, plus a woman sitting alone, straight-backed, hair the colour of apricot glaze. She was staring out of the window.

'Was everything OK with your meal?' Nick said from behind.

She turned around, making him freeze. His heart waited for his mind to catch up.

Her face broke into a broad smile. 'Hey, Nick…' She stood up, those green eyes taking his breath away.

'My *God*. Claire Lucas!' They hugged briefly, awkwardly. He couldn't help the grin. 'It's been ages. Why didn't you tell me you were coming?'

'Because I didn't know, that's why.' They both sat down. 'I was in London for the day. A friend suggested we eat here, but just as I arrived she had to cancel.' Claire swept her hair off her face. 'I couldn't believe it when I spotted your name as chef on the menu. Do you have a few minutes?'

'Of course,' he said, thinking she looked even more beautiful than he remembered.

'And it's Claire *Rodway* now. Did you forget? We're in the Old Stables now, next door to Mum and Dad. You remember it, right? Took years for Callum and me to renovate… Not that we did the actual work ourselves, Callum's far too busy for that but…'

Nick nodded, trying to listen, to take it all in, but all he could manage was to focus on her lips, watch them move around words he didn't want to hear. Of course he knew she was married. He'd received an invite to the wedding but didn't go.

'That's great.' His eyes were drawn to the cluster of freckles on her nose, the small gap between her front teeth that, when she smiled, made him feel eighteen again.

'And Marcus is growing up fast, and baby Amy is a joy.' Then she'd got out her purse and shown him photographs.

'Fantastic,' he replied. 'I'm glad things are good for you, Claire. And I'm pleased you came in.' Nick swallowed. 'Callum is a lucky man.' He couldn't believe he'd just said that.

He noticed Claire's chest rise quickly as she inhaled suddenly. 'Thanks, Nick,' she replied, holding her water glass.

'It's funny you ended up with him.' He clenched a fist under the table. What was wrong with him? 'I was terrified of him, you know,' he said, adding a laugh. 'Didn't he live in that huge house next to the church with his brother?'

Claire laughed, the smile reflecting in her eyes. 'Yes, he did. But Cal's not scary in the least.'

Nick remembered the Rodway boys well – Callum and Michael. They were clever, rugged and good-looking, the whole family commanding a superior status in the village. 'Didn't Michael go on to become some hotshot accountant?'

Claire nodded, smiling, clearly trying to hold back her amusement. 'A banker,' she corrected.

And Callum Rodway, Nick remembered, was the taller, more handsome brother. Much older than their group of friends, he reckoned Callum was probably shaving while he and Claire were still in nappies. 'Didn't he used to babysit in the village?' Nick wished he could just drop the topic. 'I swear my mum used him a couple of times.' The Rodway boys had a reputation for being responsible, and it didn't surprise him that Callum had become a doctor. 'I'm just glad it's worked out well for you, Claire, and that you're still near your parents.' He knew her plans for university had been crushed after what happened that summer. 'So, you're happy?'

Claire stared at him for what seemed like an age. 'Of course.' She didn't ask if he was.

Nick braked at the junction, winding down the window. Whatever happened during the next week, he had to focus on the restaurant, not get sidetracked with things that couldn't be changed. He'd told Trevor he'd call each day for progress reports. 'I can be back on-site in a few hours,' were his parting words, at which Trev had nearly shoved him out of the door. It was the cellar that was concerning him most.

With the end of the journey in sight, Nick skirted Dartmoor, heading towards Bodmin and Wadebridge. From there it was narrow lanes all the way to Trevellin, and with every bend he took, every gateway he pulled into to allow a car to pass, Nick's apprehension about the reunion grew.

Of course he was looking forward to seeing everyone again, but witnessing the happy goings-on of the Rodway family would still sting. He wasn't sure he could stomach too much familial bliss when his had fallen apart so comprehensively.

He passed a sign. Trevellin village was three miles away. His heart thumped as he tried to work out exactly why he was feeling so apprehensive. Then that kiss in the sea was on his mind again – beautiful, silly, perfect; the only time anything physical had ever happened between him and Claire. Given what came afterwards that day, neither of them had ever mentioned it again.

CHAPTER TWENTY

The beach was crowded at the northern end but as they walked further along it became less so. Stripy windbreaks and colourful parasols flapped in the breeze, while kids splashed about in the shallow breakers of a mid-tide.

'I'd forgotten how beautiful it is here,' Maggie said, hitching up her long skirt as a wave broke around her ankles. Patrick's grin as he tried to keep up with everyone was reminiscent of him as a much younger man, Claire thought as she slowed down to wait. She was relieved he'd come back to the farm safely a couple of hours after driving off, grumbling about having forgotten what he'd gone to the village shop to buy. No one had the heart to tell him he'd not set off for the shop in the first place.

She felt sad that he and Jason hadn't acknowledged each other yet – not even a nod – but she knew that having the pair of them on the same beach was a breakthrough. While Patrick's lack of greeting was perhaps due to his mind letting him down, especially with so many faces around, Claire hadn't failed to notice the way he'd glimpsed Jason a couple of times, as if he'd wanted to speak. She wished she could say the same for Jason, who had walked off ahead at a much faster pace.

'Take your shoes off, Granddad!' Amy called out, dancing around with a wig-like spray of wet seaweed in her hand.

'Why would I want to get my toes all covered in sand?' he replied in a silly voice, wiggling his feet. 'I don't want Grandma telling me off for catching a chill.' He ruffled Amy's hair as she skipped past.

Claire caught up with Jason, hoping she might be able to slow him down, get the two men to fall into step. 'Didn't Rain fancy a walk?' she heard him ask Maggie, who was walking alongside. He threw a piece of driftwood and Russ lolloped along the sand to retrieve it. Amy chased after the dog, dragging the seaweed behind her. 'Or Callum or Mum for that matter?' he said, turning to Claire.

'Mum had some errands to run. You'll have to throw that stick a hundred times now, you realise,' Claire said with a laugh, avoiding answering about Callum. She stared up at the expanse of blue sky, trying to put the earlier house viewing behind her. She'd cleaned up her cut and patched it with a plaster, hoping it didn't look too unsightly. Finally unwinding, she planned on changing into her new dress before Nick arrived later.

'Anyway, I think Rain's more interested in getting to know that son of yours,' Maggie said, linking arms with Claire.

Claire checked behind to see if Patrick was any closer to them. He wasn't. He was stooping down to pick up a razor clam shell, showing it to Amy. 'Don't worry, Callum's back at the house. I doubt they'll get up to anything they shouldn't.'

'Apologies in advance if my daughter corrupts your son,' Maggie said with a laugh. 'Rain's a good girl really.'

Claire squeezed Maggie's arm. 'Marcus is pretty inexperienced when it comes to girls. Having her around might do him some good.'

Jason waited for Greta, who was also struggling to keep up, but when he saw she was talking to his father, he veered off, picking out more driftwood from the tideline to throw for Russ. Claire knew he'd only agreed to come to Cornwall for her and their mother's sake.

'Does Rain see her dad often?' Claire asked.

'Rarely. He has his own family. They don't know about her.'

'That's tough for Rain.'

Maggie hesitated, kicking at the sand. 'The more I try to give her a stable life, the more I mess up. She needs a father figure but all I've managed is a string of disastrous relationships.' Maggie let out a sigh. 'Her biological father pays her school fees and she keeps pretty much everything she owns there. School's her real home.' She gripped Claire's arm tighter. 'I feel such a failure.'

'Oh, Maggie, I'm sure you're a great mum. Rain's a lovely girl.'

'She knows I was Peter's bit on the side,' Maggie whispered, pulling closer. 'It's all hush-hush because of who he is. It's hard for a teenager to accept half of her existence has to be kept quiet.'

'Oh, Maggie…'

'It's ironic. Pete was the only man I've ever truly loved. He was also the only man who wasn't prepared to leave his wife for me.'

Claire knew Maggie had always been unlucky with men and wondered if it was because she'd lacked a stable father figure herself. Growing up, the village lads had taken advantage of her vulnerability, earning Maggie a bit of reputation when all she wanted was love. 'That sounds hard. But at least you and Rain have each other.'

'It's harder now she's older,' Maggie replied. 'I always believed that having Rain would somehow make Peter want me, but it actually pushed him away. Initially, he didn't believe she was his daughter, so we did a paternity test. He's scared I'll tell his wife.' She hesitated, taking a deep breath of sea air. 'He's a well-known politician, Claire, and has four kids of his own, one of them younger than Rain. It didn't end well between us.'

'In what way?'

'While I'd never truly wanted to break up their happy family, I did want to get what Rain deserved. I had to secure a good future for her and it turned out Peter didn't… well, let's just say I had to persuade him.'

'Persuade?'

'I'm not blackmailing him, if that's what you think. It was more a case of *strongly suggesting* he pay for Rain's education. Office temping doesn't quite cover the fees.'

A large wave came rolling up the beach, making them sidestep quickly as Claire mulled over what Maggie had just told her. She glanced back. Patrick and Greta were walking arm in arm. 'Dad, your trousers are soaked!' She slowed again so they could catch up.

Patrick waved and grinned. As he approached, he squinted along the beach, shielding his eyes from the sun, watching Jason and Russ way up ahead. She wished she knew what she could do or say to make things better between them.

CHAPTER TWENTY-ONE

The Lighthouse had been just that when they were kids – fully functioning, with a doleful foghorn wailing through the night on dank winter nights. It rose out of the headland like a giant cigarette with its red painted tip, white trunk and tan-coloured base. These days there was an unmanned beacon on the rocks further out to sea and the old building had become a ruin over the years. Three years ago, though, it had been sold off and turned into a bistro and coffee shop, popular with the locals and tourists. With its views of the rugged coastline it was the perfect place to sit and while away a couple of hours.

'This is a fabulous place,' Greta said, breathless, when they were seated, as if every movement was an effort. They'd chosen a table outside. It was breezy but warm, and they all agreed that lunch with a view of the beach where they used to play as kids would be perfect. Claire hoped it might stimulate some memories for Patrick, though she couldn't help noticing how Jason made sure he sat at the opposite end of the table to their father.

'Lenni fell off a ledge and broke her arm down there,' Jason said to Greta, pointing down to a slate shelf halfway along the cliff. Amy gasped, wriggling into the seat beside him.

'God, I remember that,' Claire said. 'Mum went on the warpath because you said that kid pushed her.' She broke apart a freshly baked bread roll. 'She marched straight round to his parents' house.

Do you remember that, Dad?' Claire hoped her father would pick up the conversation with Jason.

'Anyone seen my glasses?' was his reply as he patted his pockets. Claire sighed, looking around for them.

'You'll never believe it, Amy,' Jason continued, despite his father's snub. 'But I told a bit of a white lie. Your Aunty Lenni just slipped and fell. She was always pretending to be something or someone and it was a mountain goat that day. I didn't want Mum to stop her coming down to the rocks with us. Lenni loved it at the beach.'

Amy gasped. 'Mummy, Uncle Jason tells fibs!' She giggled, picking an olive from the terracotta dish, nibbling the flesh to see if she liked it. She pulled a face.

'Don't worry, Amy. I don't tell any lies now.'

Claire tensed, her eyes widening as she felt the burn of Jason's stare on her cheeks. She focused on buttering her bread roll. 'Mum's invited us all for a meal at the farm tonight,' she said. 'I hope you'll come too,' she said to Jason quietly.

'I thought Nick was cooking for us at your place?'

'He will at some point.' Claire felt her cheeks flush. 'Shall I tell Mum you'll be there?' She paused. 'Please, Jase?'

Jason put on his sunglasses, and before he could reply, Patrick excused himself, scraping his chair loudly as he stood up. He'd been chatting to a friend from the village at the next table, but suddenly headed for the toilets. Claire watched him walk away, taking hold of the backs of chairs for support as he went.

'It would help Dad no end,' she said, when he was out of earshot. 'He's gone downhill these last couple of months and—'

'I haven't noticed much of a difference.'

'I'm with Claire on this one,' Maggie said. 'Life's too short, Jase.' Claire appreciated her support, but sensed Jason was bristling.

'Especially when he's about to be a granddad again,' Greta added softly.

'Stuff happened a long time ago, love,' Jason replied. 'Things like that don't just melt away over a family dinner.'

'They were only trying to help, Jase,' Claire said, feeling responsible for the tension.

'I needed Dad's help back then and you know it,' he said just to Claire, drawing down the first inch of his pint. He stared out to sea.

'In that case, come tonight. Even if you don't say a word to him all evening, just be there. Please?' Claire glanced towards the toilets. 'It will help more than you know.'

There was a moment of silence – just long enough for a huge wave to crash on the nearby rocks and a gull to swoop overhead, crying as it circled the lighthouse.

'Help what, Claire?' Jason said quietly, laying his hands flat on the table. 'Your guilt?' He turned to stare out to sea again.

It was nearly three o'clock when they ambled up the drive to Claire's house – laughing, windswept, sandy and salty. Any earlier tension between Claire and Jason had dissolved over lunch and a couple of drinks. But Patrick and Jason still hadn't spoken.

Conversation had skipped between describing life in eighties Cornwall to Greta and comparing it to her childhood in Amsterdam, as well as excited chatter about the twins and their imminent arrival. Amy had sat patiently with her little hands spread on Greta's tummy waiting for the babies to kick, and the rest of the time sitting on her granddad's knee listening to his made-up stories about pirates.

The chatter continued as they ambled up the drive, with Claire failing to notice the extra vehicle tucked behind Maggie's camper. Shona came out to greet them before taking Patrick back down to the farmhouse for his medication.

'Russ, no, get out!' Claire shooed him away from the door before he did his usual trick of shaking and spraying the walls with whatever had stuck to his coat during their walk. She glanced at her watch as they went inside. She still just had time to change. 'Right, who's for a cup of—'

She froze in the kitchen doorway.

Callum was sitting at the old pine table with a mug clamped between his hands. But Claire's eyes were drawn to the person sitting opposite him – someone she recognised, yet someone who looked so completely different to the last time she'd seen him. The smattering of stubble, his hair slightly longer, a distinct tan, the check shirt and jeans…

'Nick…' It was almost an accusation as she croaked out his name. Let down by her voice, Claire was also aware that the rest of her was a let-down too.

'Claire, hi…' In contrast, Nick's voice resonated deeply. He stood, grinning, and came over, holding out his arms for a tentative hug. 'It's so good to see you. You look really well.'

'You too,' she said, glimpsing Callum over Nick's shoulder as they embraced. She closed her eyes for a second, feeling as if she were in the eye of a storm – a safe and calm place. But then she pulled away, self-consciously fiddling with her hair, smoothing down her top. 'We've just been to the old lighthouse. It's a café now.'

But before Nick could reply, the kitchen was filled with noise and chatter as everyone came inside. Russ had found his way in and careered around the kitchen, his claws clicking on the flagstones as he greeted Nick.

'Maggie, Jason, how fantastic to see you both.' Nick hugged them, and Jason introduced Nick to Greta. Claire couldn't help noticing how he stared at her pregnant body a moment too long.

'It's twins, if you're wondering why I'm so massive,' she joked, shaking hands.

Claire busied herself by filling the kettle and setting out a load of mugs. 'Where's Marcus?' she asked Callum. He'd not said a word since they got back.

'Out with Rain visiting his mates in the village. They're plotting something for tonight. A house party in Newquay, I think.'

Claire rolled her eyes. She wanted everyone at her parents' place later and wasn't keen on ferrying teenagers to and from town at all hours.

'Isn't he a bit early?' Callum whispered, eyeing Nick. He slipped his arm around Claire's waist. 'It would have been rude to leave him here alone, but you know I had important things to do today.'

'I thought he was arriving later,' she said quietly. 'I'm sorry. What was so urgent anyway?'

But she never got a reply because Callum pulled away, easing between the group of friends who were all chatting and laughing. She watched as he left by the back door, staring out of the kitchen window as he crunched across the gravel, got into his car and sped off up the drive.

CHAPTER TWENTY-TWO

Rain thought Marcus's friends were as lame as he was, but a night out was a night out. And besides, she'd promised Katie and the girls that by the end of the week she'd have some gossip to report.

'What was up with your mate Alex just now?' Rain asked Marcus, as they walked away from the village back to the Old Stables. 'He was acting really stupid. And what's that disgusting smell?'

'Alex is OK. He was just being awkward,' Marcus said, laughing. 'He's not had much experience around girls.'

Rain choked on her Coke, nearly spitting it down her top. He'd been a complete idiot. But she also kind of understood, though would never say. 'I don't suppose he's had much chance living here.' She gestured around, spreading her arms wide. 'I mean, look at it.'

To their right, the fields dipped down towards the coast. Further along they could see the white blocks of a caravan park where Rain imagined old people with little dogs went for their holidays. 'There's fuck all here.'

'You're very opinionated, aren't you?'

Rain stopped. 'What?' She forced an indignant laugh, even though his comment cut deep.

'All you've done is criticise where I live and moan about my mates.'

'I can't believe I agreed to come on this stupid holiday.'

'My mum went to a lot of trouble to make this week nice for everyone. Show a bit of respect.' Marcus pulled a packet of cigarettes from his pocket. 'Want one?'

Rain's eyes lit up. It was the first decent thing he'd done. She decided to take it as a kind of peace offering. She was stuck with him for a few days, after all. 'Does Mummy know you smoke?' She couldn't help it. Boys like him needed teaching a lesson. 'No weed?'

Marcus stared at her, narrowing his eyes. 'I could get some,' he said, swallowing hard and lighting their cigarettes.

'So, what's all this shit with the oldies getting together about anyway?' Rain asked, as they started off again. She felt comforted by the first draw of smoke. The lane wound between the fields as if it was never going to end.

'Granddad's not well. He's got Alzheimer's.' Marcus drew on the cigarette, trying to stifle a cough. 'Mum wanted to get everyone together, to make it feel like the old days. Apparently, it might help him remember stuff.'

'Don't see how it would.'

'Granddad was like a second father to her friends when they were kids. She thinks it'll help.' He flicked his ash. 'Didn't your dad want to come with you?'

Rain tensed. He might as well have hit her, and her instinct was to hit him back. She clenched her teeth, blinked the tears from her eyes. 'It's the smoke,' she said, running her finger beneath her lashes. 'I don't see my dad much,' she added, hoping it would shut him up.

'Anyway, turns out Nan's going to sell the farm and Mum's all weirded out because they've been there, like, forever.'

Rain hoped the stupid place would burn down with everyone in it. She was so angry, her chest felt as though it had a strap around it. 'Didn't some kid get murdered there?' Maggie had once mentioned something about it. 'Surely that's the real reason they're all here, to find out which one of them did it?'

'That kid,' Marcus said, kicking the ground, 'was Mum's little sister. And she wasn't murdered. She went missing.'

Rain gave a little smile, pleased she'd got to him. 'Was it, like, a really big deal and stuff?'

'Of course it was a big deal. It would be like Amy going missing.'

Rain had barely met his younger sister and wouldn't particularly care if she did disappear, but it made her think. 'That's creepy. Did they find a body and a weapon, you know, like on CSI and stuff?'

'It's not some fucking TV show, for God's sake. It was real life. My mum's life. And no, they never found her body. No one knows what happened to her.'

'But you didn't know the dead kid, right?'

'Of course not. It happened way before I was born. But Mum's told me all about her. She was only thirteen but would be in her thirties now. And they don't really know if she's dead.'

Rain felt herself getting excited as she drew a last lungful of smoke, tossing her butt into the hedge. 'That's so cool,' she said. 'A real-life mystery.'

'For fuck's sake, Rain, just shut up, will you? And don't mention it in front of my mum, right?' Marcus muttered something under his breath, also chucking his cigarette butt into the hedge.

'Do you think it was your mum's fault, then?' she said, pausing. 'That's what my mum said. Or worse, maybe your mum *did* it. Was she jealous of her kid sister?'

Marcus clenched his fists down the side of his legs. 'Don't be stupid. Mum was on the beach with her friends, looking after Lenni. She let her go off to buy an ice cream, but she never came back. Clear now?'

Rain cocked her head slightly. 'So it really *was* your mum's fault? She must feel terrible.' Rain raised her eyebrows. 'Or be a really good liar.' For a second she wondered if she'd gone too far. 'Going to get an ice cream aged thirteen isn't exactly hardcore, is it? I roamed free around London when I was ten.'

Marcus was silent.

'Grown-ups are pretty stupid though. They think that wallowing in self-pity for long enough makes everything better. They never consider actually getting stuff right in the first place.'

'Lenni wasn't like normal kids, apparently,' Marcus went on, not sounding quite so angry.

'What was wrong with her?'

Marcus took out another couple of cigarettes. He lit them both and passed one over. 'She was just kind of "not right" apparently...' He inhaled deeply. 'My grandparents were really protective of her because of that.'

'You mean, like, she was special needs?' Rain didn't really get it. She was just glad Marcus was being generous with his fags.

'Yeah, exactly. And Mum said she was too trusting, couldn't spot danger. She says these days she'd have got a diagnosis, but back then they wrapped her up in cotton wool instead. They were worried something bad would happen.'

'Ironic,' Rain said with a dry laugh. 'Maggie doesn't give a shit where I am. All she cares about is screwing money out of my father to pay for my boarding school so I'm out of her face.'

'They're divorced?'

'Never married.' Rain took a breath. She didn't normally talk about this, let alone to imbecile boys. 'My dad is, like, famous and everything. He's a politician and always on the news. He's got his own family. Maggie used to work for him in some crappy secretary job and so here I am. It's all dirty keep-quiet shit.' Rain felt a glimmer of relief. She'd never told anyone before.

'Sorry to hear that,' Marcus said. She reckoned he meant it.

Rain felt the tears again, so she sucked hard on the second cigarette. 'So,' she continued, composing herself. 'This kid-sister-aunty of yours, why's she got a boy's name?' Rain wanted all the details, though she'd already planned on googling the story later.

'Lenni is short for Eleanor. It's a bit weird.'

Rain laughed. 'I'm queen of weird names. Maggie must have been high when she chose mine.'

'Your mum's cool.' Marcus scuffed the ground as he walked. 'Why don't you call her "Mum"?'

Rain shrugged. 'To piss her off, I guess.' Maggie was always trying to sling a rope between them, connect with her in some way. But she never quite reached her, and Rain wasn't sure she'd grab it even if she did.

Up ahead there was a cluster of barns and houses. They were nearly back at the farm and she hadn't got half as much of this dead kid story out of Marcus as she wanted. 'Let's stop here and watch the sheep for a bit,' she said, going into a gateway and leaning on the wooden bars. The skinny shorn creatures stared at them, chewing, looking dumb. 'Baa-aaaa,' she called out. They just carried on chewing.

Marcus leant next to her, glancing at her. She looked back – making sure she lingered on his eyes, moving her gaze slowly down to his lips. A snog would delay their return, but she didn't want to make the first move. What if he backed off? Besides, she had the whole week. Then her heart sank at the thought of seven days in this place. She needed some excitement.

Her phone vibrated in her back pocket, breaking the moment. 'Katie,' she said. 'I can't hear you, the signal's crap.' She stepped away from the gateway, staring at her phone. 'Can you hear me now?' she asked. 'Good. No, I haven't yet,' she whispered, unable to help the giggle. 'How's France? Oh great. That's just what I want to hear while I'm stuck here. Guess what I can see right now?' She stole a look at Marcus. She knew he was listening. 'Fucking sheep. All I can see is a hundred dozy fucking sheep.'

Marcus spread his arms wide, making a clown-like face. 'Yeah, and don't ask what else I can see,' she continued. He had an OK body, but he was still an idiot. 'Message ya soon, babe. Love you too.' She went back to the gate. 'My best friend is in Cannes for the weekend.' She rested her head on the gate, letting out a long, low moan. One of the sheep bleated a reply.

'So, this Lenni kid,' Rain said. 'They didn't find anything like a limb or a head washed up on the beach, then?'

'You're sick.' Marcus stared at her. 'Mum said the only things found were her ice cream cone, some silver charm thing and a pair of shorts.'

'Her shorts?'

Marcus nodded.

'Were they all ripped and bloody?'

'Fuck's sake, Rain, I didn't ask. Mum gets upset.'

'If I had some amazing family secret like this, *everyone* would know about it.' Rain felt the blush swoop from her cheeks down to her chest.

'And your mum shagging a famous married politician isn't an amazing secret?' He laughed. 'Anyway, Mum prefers we don't talk about it. She says that we can discuss it with her and Dad but no one else.'

'So why are you telling me?' She waited but he didn't reply. 'That smacks of guilt, if you ask me.' A few months ago, she'd had a fascination with stuff like this. Maggie had left a book lying around about old murder cases, detailing how the killers were caught decades later because of forensic advances. She had no idea why her mum was reading it, but Rain had picked it up, hooked from the first page, and gone on to read others like it. 'Maybe that's why your mum doesn't want you telling anyone.'

'You're mental, do you know that?'

'No, I'm serious. Think about it, Marcus.' She brushed her hair slowly off her face. 'A hot summer's day, a bunch of teenagers hanging out and probably getting up to no good, then the little kid they're supposed to be looking after just vanishes. I bet they're all in cahoots to keep quiet.' Rain tipped her head sideways. 'Did the police question them all?'

'I guess,' Marcus said. 'You'd have to ask Mum.' He frowned. 'But don't, OK?'

Rain gave him a look.

'It's why Mum's not happy about Nan selling the farm,' Marcus went on. Rain knew she had a knack of getting people to open up, say or do whatever she wanted. It was something she'd learnt as a little girl, a bonus of Maggie's guilt. 'They once made a pact that someone would always be at the farm in case she came back.'

'I once read something about a mother who made a shrine to her missing son. She lit candles every day, bought him presents and toys, just like he was still there. She became so obsessed, she didn't have a life of her own. She went all weird and twisted until it was like she was dead too.'

'Mum's not like that. She's pretty normal.' He laughed. 'As normal as mums can be.'

'You *say* that.'

'It's true. She's got a good job, she loves Dad, and Nan and Granddad are just regular old folk.'

Rain had to admit that she quite envied Marcus living near his grandparents. She'd never known hers – they'd long since died – and of course access to her father's family was strictly forbidden.

'Anyway, I reckon that's what all this shit's about,' Rain said. 'This reunion.' She folded her arms across her chest, drawing Marcus's eyes to it.

'C'mon, let's get back,' he said, walking off down the lane, this time at a much brisker pace.

CHAPTER TWENTY-THREE

Sweet Sixteen

When it's my birthday, I'm brought cake. I blow out the candles and make a wish.

'You're a big girl now,' I'm told, as if it's time to fly the nest.

'I won't ever leave you,' I say, because I get smiles for that. Anyway, how can I?

We eat the cake and my lips get sticky and my teeth ache.

'I've got you a present.'

I smile and close my eyes, holding out my hands, feeling something cool and smooth in my palms. Then I'm told to look and when I do, I can't help the gasp. 'It's beautiful.' I can hardly speak. 'Is it dead?' I turn the jam-jar around and around, holding it up to the light, letting my eyes soak it up while my brain works it all out.

'Of course it's dead. It's a peacock butterfly. I trapped it myself.'

I place it carefully next to my bed, so it will be the first thing I see when I wake up. Catching things is clever, I think.

CHAPTER TWENTY-FOUR

Claire had a few minutes alone with Jason before Greta came back into the kitchen. 'So, will you come?'

He glanced up from scrubbing his hands. Wherever Callum had sped off to in the car a couple of hours ago had given him a puncture. The recovery service was going to be hours, so Jason had gone out to help.

'For Mum?'

Jason nodded but didn't say anything.

Relieved, Claire handed him a towel, forcing herself not to hug him. He'd hate that. He and their father may have been in proximity on the beach earlier but there was something more intimate about dinner at the farm, something symbolic about setting foot inside the house that Jason had resisted for years.

'I've been wondering if we should tell the police about that message,' she said, but Amy came skipping into the kitchen.

'Mummy, Mummy, will you untangle it?' She held up a Barbie doll with elastic bands knitted into its hair. Claire took it from her daughter and started picking at the tangle.

'Just leave it, will you, Claire?' Jason said, giving her a look before walking out of the room.

The rest of the afternoon was spent at the Old Stables looking at old photographs, selecting the best ones to show to Patrick later. They'd all been in fits of laughter.

'Dad got worn out at the beach,' Claire said, holding up a picture of him, aged thirty-something, standing bare-chested on the same familiar curve of shoreline. His trousers were rolled up to his knees and he was holding a small plastic spade. The photo was black and white, but Claire remembered the spade was pink. 'He's gone for a lie-down. We'll show him these tonight.'

She knelt beside the low table in her living room, spreading out the dozens of pictures she'd borrowed from her mother. They'd been stored in boxes up at the farmhouse and were rarely looked at, let alone arranged into albums. The musty smell coming from them made Claire pensive for a moment, as if their childhood had somehow been preserved. She was bracing herself for photos of Lenni. It never got any easier.

'Here's what I managed to dig out from some of my old stuff back in London,' Nick said, coming back from his car and handing Claire an envelope. She hesitated, their fingers brushing momentarily. 'There aren't very many, I'm afraid.'

Maggie and Jason had also brought a few snaps and they shared them out, laughing at how young and naive they all looked, grateful they didn't have those hairstyles any more. 'These old shots are great,' Maggie said, holding a couple. There was one of her and Claire doing handstands. 'Rain would go crazy to put these on Instagram.'

'Remember how Dad used to stick the Polaroid prints under his armpit to develop when we were really little?' Claire said. 'And count to twenty.' It had seemed like pure magic as a kid. One minute they were in a rock pool or riding the Shetland pony along the sand, and the next they were locked up forever in a photograph.

'Do you remember the sandcastle-building competitions we used to have? Pat could never choose a winner and gave us all a prize.'

'A bag of sweets from the village shop, usually,' Claire replied, watching as Nick flipped through some pictures. His expression didn't change.

'In the winter it was house-of-card building competitions or picture drawing, and sometimes he'd make up those impossible maths games. He was so good at keeping us entertained.' Poor Dad, Claire thought. All these things still locked in his brain, gradually decaying as if they never happened.

She was about to make more tea when Rain and Marcus arrived back. Her heart sank as she smelt cigarette smoke on one or both of them. She decided not to say anything just yet. Marcus knew how she felt about it and she'd have a word with him later. 'What have you two been up to?'

'Just hanging,' Marcus said. 'What's all this?' He eyed the stacks of pictures.

'Oh, seriously cool,' Rain said, taking a bunch of photos from Maggie. 'These are so ancient.'

'Careful,' Jason said with a laugh. 'It wasn't that long ago.'

'Is this you, Claire?' Rain studied a picture.

'Yes, I was only about fifteen. God, my hair looked awful,' she replied.

'No, it's sick. And is that the dead girl?' Rain pointed to the younger child holding on to Claire's waist as if they were doing the conga.

'Rain,' Maggie warned, eyeing her daughter.

'It's OK,' Claire said. 'Yes, that's Lenni, my little sister.'

'Is she definitely dead, then?' Rain flinched when Maggie snatched the photos from her. 'Was she murdered?'

'Rain, that's enough,' Maggie said. 'I'm so sorry, Claire.'

'Marcus has been telling me all about it.'

Marcus squirmed, turning scarlet. Claire didn't want her son to feel that way. 'It's OK. It's fine to talk about it. We don't know what happened to her, Rain. We think that after all this time, she's most likely dead, yes.' She swallowed, aware of how dry her mouth was. 'But we'll never give up hope.'

'Is that why you're all here? To, like, figure out what happened?'

'Rain—'

'Really, Maggie, it's OK.' Jason glanced at his sister and they gave each other a half nod. The silence that followed was broken only by an ambulance screaming down the drive.

'I called your mobile but there was no answer and the landline was engaged,' Shona said, frowning, as they waited in the hospital corridor. She paced about, fiddling with her hair, wringing her hands. 'I was frantic. I couldn't leave Dad like that even for a second, so I thought I'd better just call an ambulance.' Her hands shook as Claire gave her a cup of tea from the machine. Claire remembered that Callum had been organising the golf tournament, the reason the line was engaged. If he hadn't been, he would have gone down to help.

'Mrs Lucas?' A doctor came out of the side room. 'You can come in if you like.' The two women followed her into Patrick's room, not knowing how they would find him.

'You scared the life out of us all, Dad,' Claire said from his bedside. She took his hand. Patrick was sitting up, looking fed up and confused.

'Is he going to be OK?' Shona asked the doctor.

'He'll be fine,' she said. 'He suffered a mild concussion, so considering everything else, we'll keep him in overnight for observations. He has a small cut on his head but no other injuries.'

'Well, I could have told you that before my wife called the bloody ambulance.' Patrick made a move to get out of bed, but Shona gently held him in place with a hand pressed against his shoulder.

While the doctor examined him again, Shona told Claire how she'd found him lying in the yard, dazed, not knowing where he was, how he thought he'd tripped but couldn't be sure. 'To be honest, I thought he was still upstairs resting,' Shona confessed guiltily. 'He must have gone out without me realising.' Claire comforted her, reiterating it wasn't her fault. 'I should keep a much closer eye on him,' Shona went on. 'But the place is so big that it's hard to know where he is all the time.'

'What were you doing, Dad, that made you fall?' Claire asked, turning back to him and stroking his arm. 'Can you remember?'

'There's nothing wrong with me. I'm fine, so just let me go home.' Patrick avoided the question, batting her hand away, though his frustrated expression told another story. His eyes narrowed, as if his brain was processing a thought, a memory he couldn't quite grasp. He sank back into the pillow, dragging his hands down his face, letting out a frustrated sound – something between a sob and a growl. 'I couldn't find her.'

It broke Claire's heart to see him looking so frail in the loose hospital gown. The faded fabric fell away from his shoulder, exposing pale skin that seemed to be only just hanging on to his bones, nothing like the strong and tanned muscles he once had. There was a blood pressure cuff around his arm and a clip with a wire attached to his forefinger. She wondered if the reunion had already been too much for him, stirring up memories he couldn't deal with.

'Mr Lucas, we really do have to keep you in overnight for observation. To be on the safe side.' The doctor held Patrick's medical notes against her chest. Claire and Shona expected another outburst but, instead, he just closed his eyes.

'Can I have a quick word?' Claire said to the doctor. They went into the corridor. 'Do you think this is to do with his Alzheimer's?'

'It's impossible to tell. Alzheimer's can play tricks on patients as well as their carers. He most likely got disorientated and tripped. Something as simple as moving furniture around or changing routines can be upsetting. Has anything unusual happened at home in the last day or two?'

Claire looked away, dropping her head. Then she folded her arms, as if it might protect her from the guilt. 'Maybe.'

'Let's see how he is tomorrow, OK? If there's cause for concern, I'll organise some scans.' She excused herself as her beep sounded and Shona came out into the corridor.

'He's dozing,' she said. 'I'm so worried about him, Claire.' They held hands, each knowing they'd have to face more of this as his illness progressed. They looked back through the open door into his room. He looked so small under the bed covers, flat on his back with his arms down by his sides. His fingers and lips twitched as he played out fragmented dreams, making Claire long for a glimpse into his deteriorating mind.

CHAPTER TWENTY-FIVE

Jason heard the car pull into the drive and went to meet Claire at the back the door. He knew she'd have phoned if things had been serious.

'Dad's doing OK,' she said, dumping her handbag and keys on the table. She touched his arm to reassure him. 'He had a fall and has a mild concussion. But because of everything, they're keeping him in overnight.'

'But Dad doesn't fall,' Jason said. When did he miss him getting old? 'He's really going to be OK?'

Claire stared at him for a moment, then smiled. 'Yeah, he is.'

'But he's grumpy as hell about being kept in, which can only be a good sign,' Shona said as she came inside. She looked wrung out.

'Greta's gone to rest,' Jason told them. 'The twins were trying to kick their way out.' Shona leant against the Aga, which was on all seasons, while Maggie filled the kettle, putting it on the hotplate. 'And Nick went for a walk a while ago.'

'Why don't you show Grandma your new dolls in the play-room?' Claire suggested to Amy, who was listening to everything. She didn't want her to worry about her granddad. Shona agreed and, armed with a mug of tea, she took the little girl's hand and led her out.

'What about tonight?' Claire asked, pulling her hair back off her face. 'Mum's hardly going to feel like having us all up at the farm for supper now, is she?'

'We'll just get a takeaway. No need to make a fuss now all this has happened,' Maggie said.

'Agreed,' Jason echoed, feeling sorry for his sister. 'It's not been the best start to the reunion, has it?' There was a commotion at the back door as Russ scratched at the wood and barked, finally lumbering into the kitchen. The dog thumped his tail against the wall, not knowing who to greet first.

'Russ, settle down,' Callum called out, hanging up the lead. 'How's Patrick?' He gave Claire a quick hug, listening to the update as she told him what had happened. But she trailed off as Nick also arrived back carrying several bags of shopping. Russ was wagging his tail even more furiously, sniffing at the contents.

'Go on, outside,' Claire said, pulling gently on the dog's collar. Once banished, she took the bags from Nick, placing them on the worktop. 'You bought groceries?'

'What a star,' Maggie said loudly, stepping between them to help unpack. 'We were just discussing dinner.'

'I hope I did the right thing,' Nick said. 'I was out for a walk and passed the village shop. They sell everything these days and there's a new butcher's on the corner by the pub. Besides, I didn't think Shona would feel like mass catering.'

'You did absolutely the right thing,' Claire said. 'Thank you.' Jason couldn't help noticing his sister's light touch on Nick's arm, couldn't help noticing Callum watching.

Jason opened the door to the guest room quietly. 'Hey,' he said, seeing Greta was awake. Claire had decorated the Old Stables beautifully, with their room painted in muted blues and greys. The antique sleigh bed used to be in one of the farmhouse bedrooms, he recalled, and was made up with a vintage bedspread embroidered with exotic birds. He dipped his head as he went through the low-beamed doorway. 'Did you manage to sleep?' He'd left the others downstairs discussing Patrick, the logistics of getting the teenagers to Newquay later that evening, and what they would all do tomorrow.

'A little bit.' Greta smiled, hoisting herself up in bed. 'They've been playing games in there.' She spread her palms over her tummy. 'But I feel fine.' She reached her arms out to Jason, who didn't need any encouragement to sprawl on the bed. He updated her on Patrick.

'Poor man,' Greta replied. 'I really like him, you know.' She hesitated, not wanting to seem disloyal. 'But I can see why Shona wants to sell the farm.'

'At least she doesn't have to worry about selling *this* place since Dad *gave* it to Claire and Callum.' Jason hadn't meant to sound quite so bitter, even though he was.

Greta raised her eyebrows. 'Oh, I see. Well, they're very lucky. It's a beautiful home.' She stroked Jason's head as he rested it on her shoulder, knowing what he was thinking. 'But we're better off in London, love. I can't leave my job. We need it. Besides, there'd be no acting work for you here.'

Another blow. Not only did he not get any sort of property handout from his father, but as Greta knew full well, he struggled to get work.

'The old cottage on the farm would have been a good second prize though, right?' He hauled himself up. 'As a holiday place, perhaps? Somewhere for us and the twins to enjoy?' He would never hold a grudge against his sister for being given the Old Stables – it was her and Callum's money and hard work that had renovated the virtually ruined property, after all. But he didn't understand how or why his father would do something like that for Claire and not him. Especially after everything that had happened.

'You've always said that Patrick believes in hard graft.'

'I was ill, and he knew it. And as good as homeless at the time too. He turned his back on me.' Jason flopped back down on the bed again.

'That's the past. It's time to let it go.' Greta pulled him close. 'And we're doing just fine, Jase. We'll have our own family very soon, we have a decent flat, I'm earning enough to—'

'Don't you get it?' Jason hated how bitter he sounded. 'All that is down to *you*. What have I contributed?' He didn't want to take this out on Greta. She didn't deserve it. He swung his legs off the bed, cupping his chin in his hands. 'Look, I'm sorry.' She stroked his shoulders, giving him one of those reassuring looks only her eyes could convey. 'Nick's going to cook for us all tonight up at the farm,' he continued, straightening up. 'Do you feel up to it?'

'Just try and stop me,' she replied, heaving herself off the bed and pressing a kiss on his mouth. She was a good woman. And he was a lucky man.

CHAPTER TWENTY-SIX

Claire boxed up the groceries that Nick had bought while he raided her store cupboards for the extra ingredients he'd need. The little glass jars of spices he picked out rattled as he carried the box out to her car. Even though it was only a couple of hundred yards away, it was easier to drive everything up to the farmhouse.

'I think that's everything,' Nick said, as he put the food on the back seat. Claire leant in the opposite door, looking at him, each of them still for a moment. She was about to reply, but Callum yelled out asking if everyone was ready for him to lock up the house.

'That colour really suits you,' Nick said.

She closed her eyes briefly, half leaning across the back seat, touching the fabric of her new dress. 'Thanks,' she said softly. When she pulled out of the car, an arm clamped tightly around her waist.

'Ace dress, darling.' Callum gave her a tap on the bottom. 'Is it new? And your car's filthy,' he said, pointing to the dirty tailgate as he walked off. Claire brought her hand up to her mouth, her eyes wide as she saw it.

It's nothing… she tried to convince herself, staring at the small symbol scrawled in the grime above the number plate. But her heart still skipped in her chest as she tried to gather herself. It was most likely bored kids scribbling on random cars when she was last parked in town. She was being stupid, seeing things that weren't there. She got into the car and started the engine. Someone opened the passenger door.

'Are you sad, Mummy?' Amy climbed in the front, not bothering with her car seat for the short drive down the track. She'd smeared some play lipstick across her mouth.

'No, darling, I'm not sad.' Claire smiled, marvelling how the sight of her daughter calmed her nerves. But before she drove off, she couldn't help inspecting each of Amy's fingers for dirt.

Trevellin Farm's kitchen was the perfect gathering place for everyone. At nearly forty feet long, with a massive inglenook fireplace and comfy chairs at one end, a pine table capable of seating at least sixteen running up the middle and an Aga the size of a family car, Nick was quite at home preparing a meal in the place he'd spent many happy summers as a child.

He'd already got Amy setting out the cutlery, mats and glasses, which he thought would keep her amused for at least half an hour, the way she was perfecting her folded napkins. Plus, every time she counted how many people there were to set places for, someone either came into the room or went out again, confusing her completely. Claire stepped in to help and, for a few moments, Nick watched her too. She was leaning over the table, the loose cowl of her dress falling away at her neck, exposing an area of paler skin. He turned back to the food.

'Marcus, mate. You have to take the brown stuff off the onions before you chop them.' Nick ruffled the lad's hair, laughing as he ducked away.

'What can I do to help?' Callum said, leaning on the other side of the worktop.

Nick wasn't sure if the offer was genuine – not that there weren't plenty of jobs to do. 'How about you top and tail these green beans?' He handed over several large paper bags. 'Picked fresh today.'

Callum hesitated, his expression unchanging as the two men stared at each other for longer than was comfortable. Then he reached for a knife, drawing the largest one slowly from the block. 'No problem,' he said.

Claire pulled up a stool and sat beside them. She watched as Nick chopped the garlic with frightening speed. 'Cal doesn't usually cook, do you, darling?' she said, touching his arm. 'He prefers the eating part.'

'Indeed,' he replied, handing her the knife. 'Why don't you take over while I go down to the cellar to see what Patrick has in stock?'

When he'd gone, Nick let out the breath he hadn't realised he'd been holding. He was about to say something to Claire, but she lunged for the landline phone as it rang beside her. 'That's great news. Thanks so much for calling,' she said, hanging up a moment later. 'That was the hospital. Dad's doing fine. He's eaten a good meal and was even asking for a bottle of wine.'

'Doesn't surprise me,' Shona said, rolling her eyes and looking relieved.

'Patrick's always been a fighter,' Nick said, as he fried off the lamb in a rainbow of spices. Within seconds, the kitchen was filled with an exotic smell. 'Remember when he got stuck out at sea?'

'Don't remind me,' Shona said, wiping her hands on a tea towel.

'What happened?' Amy asked. She'd climbed up on a stool and was cupping her chin in her hands. 'Was it an adventure?'

'Granddad went out fishing,' Claire said. 'Everyone was here at the farm, just like now, only everyone was little like you. He promised we could cook fresh fish on a fire on the beach. It was so exciting.'

'That sounds fun.' Amy's eyes were wide. 'And I'm *not* little.'

'Granddad went out in the dinghy but didn't come back for ages,' Shona said. 'Do you remember the boat you helped him paint, Nick? It always leaked. Whatever he did, water would seep into the hull. He set out after lunch promising to come back with two dozen mackerel. When teatime came and went, we began to worry.'

Amy gasped as if it was the most exciting story she'd ever heard. 'Why didn't you phone him?'

'Because there weren't any mobile phones in those days,' Claire said, giving her a squeeze. Nick watched them together, ignoring the pain in his heart. There was so much of Claire in the child, but also an undeniable look of Lenni with her little snub nose and dimpled chin.

'We had to call the coastguard,' Shona said, making Amy gasp. 'They sent out a search party.'

'It was Aunty Lenni who eventually spotted him though, Amy,' Claire continued. 'She'd climbed up onto the rocks and saw his flashlight giving out a Morse code SOS. Granddad had taught it to her. She saved his life.'

'That's a big adventure,' Amy said, guzzling down a glass of juice. 'But if Aunty Lenni saved Granddad, why did God let her die?' She kicked her feet against the stool rung.

'Like, duh, because he doesn't exist?' Rain sauntered into the kitchen just in time to hear what Amy said. She flicked back her hair. 'I can't believe they still teach little kids that stuff in school.'

'Mrs Fry says that God could be a woman.' Amy's forehead crinkled with a frown.

'Don't tell me, Mrs Fry's a vegan lesbian too, right?' Rain's reply went over Amy's head as Maggie rang out a very stern warning. 'But what do *you* actually think, Amy?' Rain leant forward on the worktop. 'What do you think God is?'

'I think God is mean to take Aunty Lenni away. She didn't do anything wrong. I think he should put her back because she saved Granddad.'

'Maybe God showed Aunty Lenni where Granddad was,' Shona suggested, trying to restore any faith her granddaughter may have. 'The lifeboat was able to rescue him because of her. His motor had broken down and he'd lost an oar.'

Amy was chewing on her lip and looking very perplexed. 'But Nana, I've never seen God and lots of people say he doesn't exist.' Amy bit on her fingernails, deep in thought. 'And... and... I've never seen Aunty Lenni so maybe she wasn't real either?'

'Oh, Amy,' Claire said, annoyed at Rain for starting this. 'Of course Aunty Lenni was real.'

'You have to admit,' Rain said, helping herself to a raw bean. 'She's kind of got a point.'

CHAPTER TWENTY-SEVEN

Callum was relieved to get out of the kitchen. It was no place for him. And he wasn't keen on being part of the reunion either. He was counting down the days until they all went.

'Hello, Mr Rodway. What's down here?'

Callum stopped as he was going back up the stone cellar staircase, a bottle of Rioja in each hand. The girl was a couple of steps above him, peering down.

'It looks spooky.'

'It's the cellar, Rain. *Patrick's* cellar.' He emphasised that it belonged to his father-in-law in the hope it might give her a hint to get lost.

'Why are you down here, then?' She folded her arms across her chest, blocking his way up as much as he was barricading hers down. Callum felt his heart rate rise. The girl was totally maddening, and he hoped she wasn't giving Marcus a hard time. She was the type who'd be all over an unsuspecting boy like him.

'I'm fetching wine for the meal.'

'But Nick brought some wine back from the shop.'

'Well, I wanted *this* wine, OK?'

'But you said it was Patrick's. Does he know?'

'Patrick won't mind.' Callum forced out a sigh and took a step up. With Rain on the one immediately above, their faces were level.

'But he's in hospital. How do you know he won't mind?'

'Rain, you're a sweet girl.' Callum swallowed, keeping down his annoyance. 'However, I don't feel I have to explain myself to you. Please, let me past.' He made to step around her, but she spread her arms and legs wide. 'Rain… don't do—'

'Will you show me what's down there? I want to see.' She tilted her head to one side so that glossy waves of hair fell across her cheek. The tank top she was wearing hardly covered anything and Callum said a silent prayer for his son. 'Pretty please?'

He sighed again. 'If I do, will you let me go back upstairs?' He was shocked to find himself grinning, placing the bottles on the steps beside Rain's feet. Her toenails were perfectly painted pink, peeking from the crosshatch of her silver sandals. He turned his head sideways, staring at her ankle.

'Do you like it?' Rain giggled, tilting her foot so he could see better.

Callum stared at the tattoo, dreading his son coming home from a drunken night out with something inked across his chest. He swallowed, fighting the urge to touch it, just to see what her smooth young skin felt like. He cursed his stupidity.

'You don't like it, do you?' Rain said.

'No, no, it's not that.' Callum straightened up, clearing his throat. He wondered if Claire had spotted it yet. 'So, if I show you the cellar, you'll come back upstairs with me?'

'Of course, Mr Rodway,' she said with a pout.

The cellar was divided into three chambers, each with a vaulted roof. It smelt musty though not damp, as if the scent of a thousand wines had permeated the bricks.

'It's cool down here.' Rain trailed her fingers across the dusty racks of wine. Patrick was an avid collector.

'It's meant to be cool,' Callum said. 'Cellars remain at the same temperature winter or summer.'

'I mean *cool*, like all this unknown house under here. It'd be great for Halloween parties.' She peeked through into the next chamber. 'How far back does it go? Is there a light? I want to see.'

'It's just more of the same.' Callum knew exactly where the light switch was but couldn't be bothered waiting while Rain checked out the alcohol. 'And just so you know, it's off limits down here.' He suddenly felt very old. She was obviously planning on sneaking back later to steal a bottle or two.

'I want to see,' Rain said, walking off into the next chamber until the darkness swallowed her up. 'How far does it go back?' Her voice sounded dull and far away. Callum knew there was yet another chamber leading off that.

'Come on, let's get back up.' He waited. There was no reply. 'Rain, I'm not leaving you down here alone.' Bloody kids. He swore under his breath. 'Come now, please, Rain or I'll have to lock you in.'

Nothing. No footsteps or shuffling on the dusty bricks, no rattle as she traced a finger over the racks of bottles. No breathing or any other sound. It was as if she'd vanished.

'Rain, where the hell are you?' He went into the first pitch-black chamber and felt for the light switch. When he flicked it on, there was no sign of her. It was just the cellar as normal with Patrick's notebooks and tasting kit set out on a barrel top. He went to the archway of the final chamber. 'Rain, stop messing about now. Where are you?' Again, he felt along the wall for the light switch and flicked it on. Nothing. The bulb must have blown.

Callum edged through into the furthest chamber, taking tentative steps. It was as black as night.

'Gotcha!' Arms suddenly clamped around his shoulders while Rain's giggle rang in his ears.

'Shit! You *stupid* girl! You nearly gave me a heart attack.' Callum tried to shake her off, but she was clinging on to him, laughing hysterically.

'I'm sorry, I couldn't resist.'

He felt her soft hair beneath his chin as she rested her head on his chest. He got a waft of her scent – and not just perfume, his fired-up senses told him.

'Please hold me. I'm really scared of the dark.' Her voice mimicked a little child.

'Then what the hell did you go into a pitch-dark chamber for?' Sweat broke out on his forehead as his arms wound around her back, instinctively comforting her as he would Amy. He noticed the catch of her bra beneath his hands. 'It's OK. I've got you,' he said. She was shaking. 'Come on, let's get back upstairs.' If someone came down, it wouldn't look good – them hugging in the cellar. What was he *thinking*?

'But we didn't do anything wrong,' Rain said, as he led her back to the lit chamber.

No, we didn't, Callum thought, making sure he kept his eyes firmly fixed on his feet as she went up the cellar steps in front of him. Otherwise, her tiny skirt would have been level with his face.

Dinner was perfect. Nick had cooked up a feast, and even Amy, who was usually picky with anything vaguely spicy, was wolfing down a plate of Moroccan lamb tagine. Rain just pushed a few vegetables around her plate, smearing the sauce to the edges.

'You did it all so effortlessly, Nick,' Maggie said. 'If it were left to me, I'd still be in the supermarket turning in circles.'

'It's all about the ingredients. I never go to supermarkets,' Nick replied. 'Seasonal local produce is always best.' He stood and went round the table with one of the wines he'd bought. 'Here, try some of this, Callum.'

Callum put his hand over his glass. 'No… thanks. I've already opened this one,' he said. 'Who's for some of Patrick's Rioja? Just one glass for me because I'm driving.'

'Dad's wine?' Claire said.

'Yes, from the cellar.'

'But Nick chose some wine for this evening, darling.' She didn't want to seem ungrateful. Without Nick's hard work they'd all be eating a sloppy Chinese takeaway.

'Dad won't mind,' Shona said. 'He has tons of the stuff. Best to get rid of it before he drinks it all.'

'I know, but…' Claire didn't press further. She caught Nick's eye and he mouthed *It's OK* followed by a small smile. She allowed him to pour some of his wine into her glass and then he sat down next to her again. When his knee brushed against hers for longer than necessary, Claire pulled away. Whatever these indefinable feelings were, they needed to stop right now.

There was a knock on the door. 'What?' Rain was peering into the mirror. She slammed down her mascara and went to open the door.

'You ready?' Marcus was standing there, hands in pockets. He'd changed out of that grubby tee and put on a white shirt.

'Du-*uh*.' Rain glanced down at her dressing-gowned body.

'How long?'

'An hour.'

'But Dad's leaving in five minutes,' Marcus said, looking pained. 'If you're not in the yard by then, you'll get left behind.' He turned to go but stopped briefly. 'And don't forget your ID.'

Shit, Rain thought on both counts. Her ID wasn't exactly the best fake, and it was only her fast talking and eyelash-batting that had stopped her having it confiscated and cut up last time. The doorman had sent her on her way, telling her to come back in a few years.

She pulled her hair down from its messy ponytailed knot and threw her head forward. With a huge can of hairspray, she messed and ruffled and back-combed until her hair was a big mass of scrunched waves. Then she dug around in her holdall and pulled out her red and black bodycon dress. She stepped into it, wriggling and stretching until the clingy fabric had shaped itself around her. After a smear of lip gloss, she grabbed her bag but froze in the doorway. She went back into the bedroom and stared into the mirror, wondering why the girl looking back at her was a stranger.

'You're so fat, I *hate* you,' she whispered, giving herself a dirty look. She swiped up her huge hoop earrings, hooking them in place as she ran down the stairs. She prayed the tears wouldn't overflow and destroy what little make-up she'd had time to put on.

'What I don't get with girls,' she overheard Marcus saying to his dad, 'is why it takes them hours to get ready, yet when they're in a hurry they can do it in five minutes.'

'It had better be a good night,' she said, scowling.

'Don't expect me to be giving you all a lift back in half an hour if it's not.' Callum took his car keys and the teenagers followed him out. 'Here's some taxi money for later.' He handed Rain forty pounds. 'Put it in your bag. Marcus will only lose it.'

'Cheers, Dad,' Marcus said, climbing into the front of the car. He caught sight of Rain in the wing mirror and rolled his eyes. They picked up two of Marcus's friends along the way, one of whom Rain had met earlier. She still thought he was weird. Twenty minutes later Callum dropped them outside the house Marcus had told him the party was at. It was a residential street not far from the centre of Newquay.

'Another seaside town pretending to be Ibiza,' Rain said dismally, clutching her arms around her. It was cool now the sun had gone down.

Once Callum pulled away, she followed the boys back down the street towards the town. She couldn't help glancing over her shoulder, making sure he hadn't come back to check where they were going. The club was just off the main street and she flashed her ID at the doorman, who barely glanced at it. Inside, the pulsing beat and lights of the place made her feel a little better and the sweet boozy smell of the bar whet her appetite. Marcus leant in to ask what she was drinking.

'Vodka and tonic,' Rain shouted above the music. 'Double.' She watched as he pushed his way closer to the bar, then turned and headed for the dance floor. She reckoned it was as good a night as any to get wasted.

CHAPTER TWENTY-EIGHT

'Uncle Angus, Aunt Jenny,' Claire said, grinning and opening her arms to them the next morning. 'It's so good to see you.'

They'd not been due to arrive until Monday but, hearing that Patrick had been in hospital, they'd changed their plans and come early. She hugged them and led them into the kitchen. 'Mum will be down soon. I don't think she slept too well.'

Claire had stayed the night with her mother at the farm on the pretext that there may be news from the ward. But really it was because she didn't want to leave Shona alone. After Nick's meal last night, they'd sat talking, drinking and reminiscing. Jason had taken Greta back to the Old Stables around ten as she was tired, and Claire asked if they wouldn't mind taking Amy to bed too. Jason had obviously decided to turn in as well as he didn't come back. The sea air always exhausted visitors. Callum, who'd had too much to drink, didn't go back up to the Old Stables until around 2.30 a.m., saying he'd leave the door unlocked for Marcus and his mates. He had a knack of forgetting his keys.

'Any news on Pat today?' Jenny asked, rolling up the sleeves of her blouse. It was a beautiful morning and already getting warm.

'Nothing yet. I'll call the ward after nine.' Claire made breakfast for her aunt and uncle, but she couldn't help feeling a tug of sadness when she looked at Angus. He was a younger, healthier version of her father – his brother. He'd been a big part of her childhood, owning the village garage and petrol station before they'd moved away, and she'd spent many happy days serving at the pumps to earn pocket money in the holidays.

'He's a silly old bugger,' Angus said, tucking into his breakfast. It was his way of showing concern. 'Scaring us all to death like that.'

Shona joined them in the kitchen, holding out her arms fondly to her brother- and sister-in-law. 'A silly bugger indeed,' she said, catching their conversation. 'It's so good to see you both.'

Poor Mum, Claire thought, knowing how much she hated being separated from Patrick. She was as in love with him now as the day they'd met and had often said she couldn't stand it if Patrick was the first to go. She reckoned she'd only be a short way behind him with a broken heart.

'Callum doesn't think discharge is likely to happen on a Sunday as he'll need to see the consultant, who won't be in until tomorrow.' Claire hated seeing her mother's face pale with disappointment. But when she phoned the ward an hour later, the news was not what they'd expected.

'I can't believe you didn't hear all that noise in the night,' Greta said, stretching out in bed. Jason had come back from the bathroom wrapped in a towel from the waist down. Half of him wanted to crawl back between the sheets with his wife – God he loved seeing her pregnant – but the other half wanted to know if there'd been any news about his father. Despite everything, it still mattered.

'With the twins kicking and all that noise in the early hours, I hardly got any sleep.' Greta dropped her head back down on the pillow, closing her eyes.

'What noise?' Jason hadn't heard anything but that wasn't unusual. Once he was asleep, he stayed that way.

'Doors banging, giggling and laughter, then some kind of yelping or shouting. I went to the loo about half past five, but everything was silent by then.'

'Stay in bed and I'll make you some tea,' Jason said, stepping into his jeans. He pulled on a T-shirt and left the bedroom, stopping on the landing to listen. All he could hear was soft snoring coming from Claire and Callum's room, or possibly Marcus's room. He couldn't be sure. He suspected Greta had heard the kids coming back late, most likely a bit drunk, up to silly antics. Marcus's friends were no doubt crashing here for the night. They'd have to get used to that themselves when the twins were teenagers, though he could hardly imagine a time so far in the future.

Russ greeted him with a thumping tail from his bed beside the Aga. Jason filled the kettle and put it on the hotplate, deciding to make Claire and Callum a cup too, knowing Claire would want to get to the hospital as soon as possible. He made toast for Greta because she was always hungry, and poured four mugs of tea, taking the whole lot upstairs on a tray. He put the tray on a chest on the landing, taking two of the mugs with one hand.

He pressed the latch of Claire's bedroom door and gently eased it open. He didn't want to wake them if they were still asleep. As his eyes grew accustomed to the darkness, he stopped in his tracks, forcing himself to remain silent despite his mouth dropping open and the rising gasp in his throat.

When he was able to move again, convinced he wasn't imagining it, he slowly reached into his back pocket and took out his phone, flicked it to silent, before holding it out in front of him with a shaking hand. Then he left the bedroom, closing the door quietly. He put the mugs back on the tray and leant against the wall, not knowing what the hell he should do.

'What do you mean, he's discharged himself?' Shona was suddenly on her feet.

'That's what the ward sister said. Got himself up first thing and told them he was off. She said they couldn't stop him.' Claire felt so sorry for her mother. It was no wonder she wanted to sell the farm.

'So why didn't they call us immediately? Where is he now?'

'Good questions,' Claire said. 'The nurse wasn't particularly helpful and wanted to get me off the phone.' She sighed. 'I suppose this means I'll be driving around looking for him. Knowing Dad, he'll be walking home and getting lost rather than phoning any of us.'

'Dear God, please don't let him walk. It's absolutely miles. Perhaps he called a taxi,' Shona said. '*Stupid* old fool.' She cupped her face in her hands. 'He refuses to carry the mobile phone I bought him months ago.'

'I didn't even know he had a phone,' Claire said, rolling her eyes.

'He told me he lost it,' Shona replied. 'I've searched everywhere, but I think he probably threw it in the sea or something.' She felt guilty for not buying him another one, but knew the same would happen.

Angus drained his mug. 'Don't worry. I'll go out and search for him. You two have had enough on your plates. Call me if he turns up. I'll check in at the hospital too, make sure he's not still wandering around the wards.'

Claire nodded, thanking Angus. As he left, she was distracted by Maggie, who'd come down for breakfast. Her eyes were ringed with last night's make-up and she was wearing an old T-shirt and baggy tracksuit bottoms. Her hair stuck out in sleep-mussed clumps.

'Morning all,' she said, stretching and wincing. 'One too many, I think.' Claire filled her in on the news about Patrick. She'd give it a couple of hours, but would have to call the police if too much time passed.

'Coffee?' she said, handing Maggie a mug.

'Thanks. I reckon that wherever Rain is right now, she'll need a bucketload of this stuff to get her going.' She laughed, wrapping her hands around the mug.

'Isn't she up in her room, then?' Claire noticed the slightly concerned look in Maggie's eyes.

'No, she's not.' Maggie sat down at the table, her shoulders rounded as if there was a weight pressing down. 'She didn't come back last night.'

Jason sat on the bed while Greta ate her toast, crumbs falling onto her bump. 'Quick, feel them kicking.' She took his hand and pressed it against her side. 'It's an elbow or heel.' She pushed the remainder of the slice into her mouth. 'Thanks for this. You're a star.'

'Sorry?' Jason said, suddenly aware that his hand had been placed on Greta's belly. He could feel one of his babies doing cartwheels.

'What's up, Jase? You've been quiet ever since you came back upstairs.'

'Nothing. I'm fine.' He forced a smile. 'I wonder what Claire has planned today.' He sipped his tea. 'There's talk of a beach picnic. Maybe a meal out later.' Jason swept back the curtains, aware he was gabbling. The sun streamed in through the window. 'A beautiful day for a walk, look.'

'Then why didn't you ask her about plans?' Greta said. 'When you took her tea in just now?'

Jason paused, cup halfway to his lips. 'She must have got up early. She wasn't in bed.'

'Maybe she was in the shower.' Greta eyed the two cups of tea going cold on the tray. 'Shall I take them in now?' She made to get out of bed.

'No, no, Callum was still asleep. I think he had… you know, a bit too much to drink last night, judging by the way he was snoring. Best leave it.'

Greta nodded slowly. 'Is your dad still on your mind?' she asked. 'Is that why you seem distant?' She knew him too well.

Jason nodded. 'Yes, yes, you're right. That's it.'

'I know I wasn't a part of your life when you fell out with him, but don't you think now would be a good time to make up, with all this hospital business?'

'You're probably right.' Jason sighed into his mug, grateful for the change of tack. 'But you know what he's like.'

'What *he's* like, or what *you're* like?' Greta put a hand on his shoulder, pressing her fingers into the knotty muscle. 'Do you know how poor we'd be if I held grudges and never made that phone call or sent that email to clients who'd pissed me off? What else is life about, Jase, if not maintaining relationships?'

Jason looked at his wife. She was beautiful, powerful and wise, but then his phone was buzzing in his back pocket so he answered it, relieved to see it was Claire. He listened intently as she told him how their father had walked out of hospital against medical advice.

'Oh, and have you seen Marcus this morning?' she asked, sounding concerned.

'Hang on,' he said, going across the landing to check his room. 'He and his mates are dead to the world,' he told her, almost hearing the relief down the line.

'I don't suppose you've seen Rain, have you?' Claire continued. 'Maggie said she didn't come back last night.'

Jason stared out of the window, watching a lone cloud scudding across a clear sky. 'No, sorry,' he said. 'I haven't.' Before he hung up, he told her that they'd be up to the farmhouse soon, though he couldn't be sure the words came out entirely right.

CHAPTER TWENTY-NINE

'See?' The look of worry on Maggie's face fell away. 'I told you she'd be fine.' She hugged her daughter as she teetered into Trevellin's kitchen on ridiculously high heels. Maggie slipped her arm around her waist as if to show she approved of her behaviour. Rain was still wearing last night's skimpy dress.

'Was it a good party?' Claire asked. She was frying bacon and glanced up.

Rain shrugged but didn't say anything. She came up close to the range, her lips red, almost sore-looking – perhaps the remnants of last night's lipstick.

'Did you stay out all night?' She couldn't help asking, not ready to believe that Maggie would allow it.

'That looks… greasy,' Rain replied, peering into the pan. She went and poured a mug of coffee from the machine and sat silently at the table next to her mother, cupping her chin in her hands.

Claire turned, spatula in hand, trying not to appear wound up, even though she was. 'But where were you all night, Rain?' She knew Marcus would always come home, or phone if he was staying over with a friend. Besides, Callum had given them taxi money. And the thought of Amy staying out all night when she reached Rain's age was abhorrent.

'It's fine, Claire…' Maggie said, giving her a warning look.

She simply couldn't understand why Maggie wasn't concerned where her daughter had been or what she'd been up to. She'd already mocked her for checking with Jason that Marcus had made it back home OK. 'If he's not at home, then he's *somewhere*,' Maggie had said. What she failed to recognise was that in Claire's world that 'somewhere' was exactly the same place Lenni had gone.

'Just at a club,' Rain said. 'Had a few drinks, a dance.' She felt the tears welling and dug her fingernails into her palms to stop them.

'A club? But I thought you were going to a party. And you only just got back now?' For Claire, there was missing time and she wanted it filled.

Rain just stared at the floor.

'She spends a lot of time in London and knows how to look after herself,' Maggie said. 'It's different these days.' As soon as she'd said it, Claire noticed the regretful look on Maggie's face.

'I really don't think it is,' she replied quietly. She turned back to the bacon. 'I don't think it's different at all.'

Callum called out that he wasn't hungry when Greta knocked on his bedroom door to let him know there was breakfast up at the farmhouse, that she and Jason were going up. He hadn't slept well, and last night's wine was banging in his skull. He felt ghastly.

Then he remembered.

'Greta,' he called out again. 'Would you take Amy up to the farm with you?' He was lying on his back in the dark, his arm spread across the empty space where Claire usually was. Greta replied that she would.

There was a pause, then Callum heard his daughter being cajoled into getting dressed. He rolled onto his side and pulled a pillow over his pounding head.

How could he have been so bloody stupid?

The scent on the pillow got to him first. A young, spicy aroma – slightly sweet but still tangy and tempting. Yes, dammit, that was it. *Tempting*. She'd tempted him, and he'd had no choice in the matter, especially with all the alcohol. Any man would have done the same. Then he saw the bangles on his bedside table. She'd left them on top of a novel that he was halfway through reading. *Fuck*.

So where the hell was she now? He'd forbidden her to leave earlier, even though she'd wanted to. He knew she'd just go running off, telling lies – he'd got the measure of her – and he'd needed time to think, to talk to her, for her to calm down. His whole body ached, and his brain throbbed against the inside of his skull.

He threw back the duvet and sat up, feeling giddy and sick. He shuffled into the en-suite bathroom, feeling like an old man – his joints stiff and slow as he caught sight of himself in the mirror. He peed, then turned on the shower as hot as it would go, scalding his skin as he stepped under it. He washed feverishly and then came back into the bedroom wearing a towel around his waist, dripping all over the carpet. He flung back the curtains and opened the window to take away the stench.

He dried himself, dressed, then began to pull the duvet cover off the bed, knocking all the bangles onto the floor. He collected them up and put them in his back pocket. He would dispose of them later. But then he stopped. He would never normally change the bed. That was Claire's job. There was a cup of half-finished coffee on his bedside table. He vaguely remembered bringing it upstairs when he came to bed last night. He'd been so drunk. He took the mug and sloshed the curdled remains over his side of the bedding and the mattress. Then he set to mopping it up, making sure a stain was left, before stripping the bed.

With the washing churning in the machine, Callum sat at the kitchen table. The house was quiet. His nail tracked the grain on the wood as he stared into nowhere, his forehead resting against his fist.

'Dad, have you seen Rain?' Callum glanced up. Marcus stood in the doorway, bleary-eyed and bare-chested– his skinny, white and virtually hairless body a contrast to his bright pyjama bottoms. 'She went off in a strop last night.'

Callum shook his head and Marcus went back upstairs, leaving Callum cradling his head in his arms. He had absolutely no idea what to do.

Nick couldn't resist phoning Trevor for an update, even though it was Sunday. He came down to join the others for breakfast feeling pleased that the renovations were going well. Trevor was polite but had clearly wanted to keep the call short on his day off.

'Morning all,' he said brightly. His meal last night had been a success and, despite Patrick's accident, they'd all had a good evening reminiscing and chatting, digging up stories they'd long forgotten.

But he couldn't fail to notice the worried expression on Claire's face as she passed him a plate of food. 'Thanks,' he said, hoping to catch her eye. He wanted to gently take hold of her hand, sit her down, ask her what was wrong. But he wouldn't do that with everyone present. 'I thought of another one,' he said instead, instantly regretting it. The cold light of day suddenly didn't seem the right time to bring it up, but he wanted to catch Claire's attention.

'Another what?' Maggie's pained voice betrayed her hangover.

'Oh dear, Mags,' Nick said. 'One too many?'

'Don't rub it in,' she replied, popping a couple of pills.

'Another story about Lenni?' Claire asked, sitting down next to Nick with her food.

He paused, knowing he'd have to continue now. They'd been sharing happy memories about Lenni the night before and Claire hadn't seemed to mind; in fact, it was as though she'd wanted to talk about her sister.

'Yes, I remembered it in a dream last night, actually.' He didn't let on that it was Claire who'd featured in his dream, that it had simply reminded him of this other story on waking. 'I'd been to pick Lenni up from school. Your parents asked me to help when you had chicken pox, Claire. I think we were about fourteen. Shona was busy looking after you.'

'We were fifteen,' Claire said. 'I was stuck in bed for days. I thought I was going to die.'

'Lenni was about nine, maybe ten. I was waiting outside the school and all the kids started coming out to their mothers, but there was no Lenni. When the playground was deserted, I went inside. I found her in the cloakroom sitting on a great big central heating pipe and kicking at the floor with bare feet. She just stared up at me with those big eyes of hers.' Nick drank some coffee. Everyone was riveted, as if he was about to reveal what happened the day she went missing.

'Turns out some mean kids had stolen her shoes,' he said, opting for the short version. 'She didn't want to tell on them, so I gave her a piggyback all the way home.' Nick felt the sweat break out on his forehead. The memory burned inside his mind. 'Lenni kept saying "Mummy told me never to go off with anyone except her or Daddy or Claire or Jason." But despite her protests, she was very willing to go off with me.' Nick remembered how she'd bumped along on his back, her breath hot in his ear as she clung around his neck. '"It's OK because you *know* me, Len," I told her on the way back. "It's not as if I'm kidnapping you."'

Everyone stared at him, but no one spoke. He wiped the sweat from his top lip and carried on eating. From now on, he would have to be more careful with what he said.

CHAPTER THIRTY

Claire dashed back up to the Old Stables to change, relieved that Angus had found Patrick still in the hospital grounds. He hadn't seemed particularly disorientated or lost. Just determined and stubborn.

'He's at home now but refusing to rest,' she told Callum. 'Cal, have you been listening to a word I've said?' She closed the wardrobe doors and lay down on the bed next to him. He'd come up for a lie-down, clearly feeling a bit worse for wear like Maggie.

'Sorry, yes, I'm listening. I'm glad Patrick's OK.'

'Why did you change the sheets?' she asked, running her hand over the fresh bedding. 'I only did them on Friday. You never change the sheets.' Claire was puzzled, but smiling. Perhaps he'd finally realised how much she did around here.

'I spilt my drink and didn't want you to have to deal with it. There's a coffee stain on the mattress, I'm afraid. Sorry.' Callum stared out of the window as he spoke.

'Not to worry, love.' She wound her arms around his neck, resting her head on his chest. 'It was fun last night, wasn't it, even if poor Dad couldn't join in?' A good end to a stressful first day, she thought.

Callum remained silent, even when Claire squeezed his hand.

*

Angus offered to look after Patrick's follow-up care and medication, leaving the others free to go for a walk up to the old primary school.

But when Patrick heard of their plans, he insisted on going along too, rebuffing Shona's suggestion to lie down. He refused to miss out on the beach picnic afterwards either.

'Don't think I don't know what Claire's up to,' he'd said to Shona as she followed him about the house while he searched for his sun hat. 'She's done all this for me, you know.' He almost sounded annoyed, but Shona could tell by the twinkle in his eye as he scoured the cloakroom, knew by the raised tone of his voice that he was touched. She hoped, in some small way, that it would help.

'Found it!' Patrick waved the hat in the air. It was hanging by the back door, where he always kept it.

Claire lay on the rug and stared up at the clear blue sky. The sand was warm under her back.

'It was kind of those people at the old school house to let us nose around their home, wasn't it?' she said to Jason. 'Jeff handled the sale about five years ago before it was converted. They've done a really good job.'

'They have,' Jason said. He was massaging Greta's feet as she sat in the deck chair. She didn't think she'd ever get up again if she sat on the sand.

'I reckon it would sell really quickly if they wanted to move.' Claire was conscious that Jason had hardly spoken since Shona and Patrick had arrived at the beach a short while after them. Neither of the men had acknowledged each other.

'No one's taking my home off me, they're not,' Patrick mumbled to himself. He was sitting a few feet away in a deck chair, tuning in and out of what Claire was saying.

'The kindergarten classroom is now a massive kitchen, Mum,' Claire said, trying to keep things light. She was talking for talking's sake. 'And the old book corner is now the utility room.' She offered around the sandwiches she'd hastily packed up. 'Please, do eat them up before they…' But she trailed off, motionless, with the foil-wrapped package held out at arm's length and her mouth slightly open. She stared down to the shore. Nick had taken off his T-shirt and dropped it at the water's edge. He was diving in and out of the waves, not looking much different to how he did that day aged eighteen. Claire felt the hairs on her arm stand up, despite the heat.

This is now, this is now, she said over and over in her head as she felt herself being swept back in time. She gazed along the beach, almost expecting to see Lenni walking off to get ice cream, swallowing down the lump in her throat.

'Well, I'm going for a paddle,' Greta said.

'Good idea,' Patrick said, kicking off his shoes and rolling up his trousers. 'I'll come too.' Greta stood up the way pregnant women do – her belly leading, legs wide apart and her hand leaving the chair at the last moment. She ambled down to the shore with Shona and Patrick.

'To be honest, Jase, I'm finding this all a bit hard,' Claire said, when they were out of earshot. 'And I don't just mean the tension between you and Dad.' She paused, running her fingers through the sand. She was determined not to cry. 'You, Nick and Maggie were in the sea when Lenni…'

'I know,' Jason said, patting her arm. 'Though I wasn't actually in the sea.'

'But you were swimming when Lenni went off, I swear.' She'd gone through the scene a thousand times in her mind since. Had it got distorted over the years? Had she turned it into something it wasn't? She remembered the white foamy waves breaking high from the previous day's storm, carrying the excited friends to shore on body boards, their skin grazing on the sand as they were dumped in the shallows. She'd given Lenni some money, then gone into the sea herself. Claire had told all this to the police. She remembered blushing feverishly when she mentioned that she and Nick were swimming together, skin brushing, lips finally meeting in their one and only kiss.

'I'm certain you were in the sea.' But what if she was wrong and it had messed up the entire investigation?

Jason was shaking his head. 'No, I'd gone for a walk when I should have been there to stop her going off alone.'

'So you'd have stopped her?' While she knew he was trying to lessen her guilt, it felt a lot like blame.

Jason thought a moment, staring up at the sky and squinting. 'No,' he said honestly. 'I felt ridiculously sorry for her most of the time. She was like a butterfly trapped in a jar. I'd have given her the money and sent her off to the shop too.'

'Mum and Dad thought they were doing the right thing, you know. By protecting her so much.'

'I know,' he replied. 'She never seemed quite capable of watching out for herself whereas we always did.'

Jason had a point. As Lenni was growing up, her naivety and gullibility bloomed with her. From talking to strangers, openly telling them her name and where she lived, to handing over her possessions at school when the bullies demanded, Lenni had little concept of mistrust. Once, she'd even run out of the playground, chasing a sick rabbit across the fields wanting to help it. She was gone for hours. Her nature was both beautiful and agonising to watch and, on reflection, Claire and Jason completely understood their parents' hypervigilance.

They sat in silence, chewing it over, watching as Greta, Shona and Patrick walked slowly up and down a short section of beach through the breakers. They'd caught up with Maggie, Angus and Jenny, who were coming back with coffees from the kiosk. Nick was still tirelessly bodysurfing, waiting patiently for the perfect wave – or trying to prove something, Claire wondered. She felt sad Callum hadn't wanted to join them.

'Rain didn't come home last night,' she told Jason. 'And Maggie didn't seem that bothered.'

'Really?' Jason suddenly sat up, brushing sand from his hair.

'Marcus was reluctant to say much. He did tell me that she went a bit weird in a club they went to and she took off on her own. She had their taxi money.'

'Claire…' Jason reluctantly took the sandwich she was offering. 'There's something I should—'

'Thankfully, Marcus had enough money in his account to get some cash from the machine, otherwise the boys would have been stranded.' She rolled her eyes. 'Sorry, what were you going to say?' She bit into a smoked salmon sandwich.

'Nothing,' Jason said, fingering the bread. 'It can wait.' Probably forever, he decided.

'What I don't get is that Maggie didn't seem very concerned about Rain. She sauntered in this morning looking like a dog's dinner, as glum as anything and refusing to say where she'd been all night.'

'OK…' Jason said, cursing his voice for wavering. 'Maybe she was fast asleep on the living room floor at your place. You know, literally just slept wherever she'd fallen. Downstairs.'

'Maybe,' Claire said, waving at Amy who was sitting over with the teenagers.

Jason stuffed the rest of the sandwich into his mouth.

'*Anything* could have happened to her. She went out wearing virtually nothing.'

'Clubs stay open until all hours. She probably met a lad or two, ended up having breakfast in a greasy spoon with them. It's different these days.' Jason's mouth was full and dry. He could hardly speak.

Claire wished everyone would stop saying that. She didn't think it was different at all. She stood up. 'I'm going to join Greta. Coming?' She hoped it would get him walking with Patrick.

'I'll sit this one out, sis,' he said, lying back down on the rug.

*

Claire walked off, keeping Nick in her line of sight as she went. She thought he looked exhausted, though he continued ploughing back out through the waves on the body board, paddling hard against the current so that every strap of muscle stood proud on his back and shoulders. Halfway down to the tideline, Claire stopped. She felt dizzy and dug her toes into the cool wet sand. Something sharp caught against her foot – a razor clam – and she pulled back her wind-whipped hair, staring down the long crescent of beach. The memories swept through her... the coin, fat and full of the promise of an ice cream in the palm of Lenni's hand, her saggy-bottomed swimsuit under her denim shorts, the water quickly seeping through... the creeping tide drenching their stuff as Lenni was about to set off...

Nick had been in the water, that day. She knew that. Though she recalled he'd gone off somewhere shortly after Lenni went for her ice cream, perhaps embarrassed by their kiss. She couldn't be sure. She was certain Jason had been in the water too. But in her mind's eye, she couldn't picture him there at all now. It was as if all the memories had been dislodged by the reunion, stirred up in a freak tide of doubt. Over the years they'd loosened, become malleable, as if taking on the shape of whatever she was told.

She shook her head, not knowing what to believe, and cupped her hands around her mouth. 'Wait for me!' she called out, but her words blew back against the wind.

CHAPTER THIRTY-ONE

Sometime Long Ago

The ceiling, once a measure of my growth, bears down on me daily. I feel like Alice – all gangly-legged and too big for the room. I'm told I won't get much taller, that I'm stunted, like a plant with no light. I stare into the grimy mirror – I'm a wiry, pale creature with a big, bobbing head sprouting thin, ratty hair. I'm nothing like the lovely actresses in the movies I watch. A girl I don't recognise stares back at me, as if one of us is waiting for the other to pounce. I know one of us has given up. Her mouth is blistered and sore and her eyes hang heavy with loneliness. At night, she dreams of what lies beyond the door, but her plans to find out are always dissolved by morning.

Anyway, she tells herself, those pretty actresses always end up dead. Outside is no place for someone like her.

I turn around and around very slowly, looking, checking I'm alone. Sometimes people come, just stand there and watch me. If I stare back, if I blink and rub my eyes, they're gone. But today it's just me and the same four walls. I'm told to be happy, to be grateful. *You're alive, aren't you?*

'I'm alive!' I scream over and over until I cough up blood. But really, the words come out as *Help me...*

Today is a looking-after day, I've decided. Over the years, I've become very good at taking care of my little space. It's the only home I have, after all. Sometimes I ask for things like soap and polish and ornaments to make it more cheerful. My mother always kept a well-run house. 'Ship-shape and Bristol fashion,' she'd say, though no one ever knew what that meant. She'd tell us off for charging about inside with our muddy boots on or not tidying up at the end of the day. My father would mumble an agreement but then, when she wasn't looking, he'd pick me up and swing me round. 'Let's go rock-pooling instead, Lenni,' he'd say. 'Clearing up is boring.' We'd giggle and escape by the back door, leaving my mother to get on with the housework. I'd do anything to help her tidy up now; anything for my dad to take me rock-pooling.

'I wish you'd stay a while,' I say, all excited, clapping my hands when I get a surprise visit later on.

'I've got the weight of the world on my shoulders,' I'm told, and I breathe in the scent of sweat, worry and antiseptic, reminding me of the time I was in hospital. 'Will you rub them for me?'

And so I do, digging my pencil-like fingers into the knots of muscle, causing a symphony of moans.

'Will you ever let me go back home?' I say, kneading hard. Last time I asked this, I didn't get a visit for days and ran out of food. I wish I hadn't mentioned it again because the nice noises turn into a red face, impatient growls and shallow breaths. 'Sorry, sorry,' I say, and the breathing soon steadies as I work my way down.

Anyway, I'm not even sure I have a home, if it ever existed. All that's left is a mysterious family occupying a strange dreamscape in my mind, making me jolt awake at night tangled in a sweaty sheet. It's hard to know what's real any more, though I still have the scar on my left knee from when I fell out of Jason's tree house. And the ring I wear on my right hand was a Christmas present from my uncle and aunt, and my little toe still bends awkwardly from when Claire took me riding and the pony trod on it. Sometimes I get a whiff of Goose the dog after he's been charging along the beach, splashing in rock pools and running through the waves.

His fur stinks of seaweed and the mouldy old cupboard under the stairs. I hang on to these things, checking in with them every day. But this is my real life now, as though everything before was just pretend.

CHAPTER THIRTY-TWO

The teens had made their own beach camp up near the rocks away from the adults. Two of Marcus's friends were attempting to surf – hardly a match for the crowd Rain had hung out with at Bondi last Christmas when her father succumbed to her mother's pressure and coughed up for the trip.

Rain scuffed the sand, wondering how it felt to go through life drilling into someone's conscience for cash. But then she thought about the number of times she'd hammered Maggie for money, demanding designer labels and high-end beauty products to keep up with her rich school friends, many of whom had unlimited credit cards, and reckoned it was the same thing. It was only because of what had happened that she was thinking too much, trying to block it out.

She stretched out her legs. Her whole body hurt, and not just because of all the alcohol she'd drunk last night. She watched Marcus bobbing about in the water, unable to decide if he looked like a drowning newborn foal or a dying octopus. She reckoned, as she weighed everything up, narrowing her eyes behind the cover of her huge Chanel sunglasses, some people needed teaching a lesson. He was as good a place as any to start.

'So, you're actually happy living here?' she asked Marcus a minute later. He was standing dripping wet above her, making her flinch as if she expected him to shake like a dog. She didn't feel like talking to anyone after last night, him included, though she reckoned she ought to act normal. The other girl hanging out with them – Poppy or Pip or something – glanced up from her magazine.

'Yeah, 'course I am,' he replied. His face was cherry-red and his body pure white.

'But it's sooo boring.' Rain lay back on her elbows on the stripy beach towel, tilting her face to the sky. She was wearing her tiny pink and gold bikini and the sun was warm on her skin. Her stomach was flat today, almost concave from losing last night's meal before they'd gone to the club, and skipping breakfast earlier had made a difference. Her belly button bar glinted in the sunlight. Purging was the only control she had, and she wasn't about to give that up for anyone. It felt even more important now.

It was a clear day, with the sky so blue that Rain could almost have believed it was the Med. But the closest civilisation to the farmhouse was the village with its crappy pub and tiny shop selling packet tea and tabloid newspapers. Why, then, was she even considering what it was like for Marcus and his mates to have grown up here, to hang out at the beach in summer and chill by the pub fire playing cards in winter? And what the hell was that feeling inside, she wondered, as though she'd got something pressing down on her heart?

'We like living here,' Poppy-Pip said. 'Our friends are only a bike ride away.' The girl had on a lilac one-piece with shorts that looked as though she'd borrowed them from her grandmother.

'That's so fucking Famous Five.' Rain lay flat on the sand but couldn't get comfortable, so she sat up again. 'Let's go for a swim,' she said to Marcus, feeling something stirring inside. She got to her feet, making sure he got an eyeful of her long, tanned legs. She knew Poppy-Pip wouldn't join them as her nose was stuck between the pages of a history book. 'Will you teach me how to surf?' She adjusted her bikini top, hoping the waves would wash everything away.

Marcus dragged his eyes away from her and grabbed his battered board, lugging it down to the shore. Rain wasn't far behind, but instead of diving straight into the water like Marcus, his chest all puffed out, she took it step by slow, painful step, allowing the chilly breakers to tumble around her ankles, her knees and her thighs before raising her arms high and shrieking that it was too cold. She knew Marcus was watching her every move.

'Come on!' he called out. He hauled himself onto the board, paddling out to where the other surfers waited for the perfect wave. Rain didn't really understand the need to go to all that effort only to be dumped under a load of crashing water and end up with a ton of sand in her hair. But it was a means to an end and, apart from anything, she needed something to text the girls. Something to take her mind off everything.

'Marcus, will you help me?' She pouted, hugging her arms around her chest as he paddled extra hard before allowing himself to be carried to her side on the swell. 'It's *so* freaking cold!' She jumped high to avoid being soaked by a huge wave. Her skin was covered in goose bumps. When she saw him staring at her bikini top again, she forced a laugh through chattering teeth, even though happy was the opposite of how she felt.

'Climb on behind me,' he said, clearing his throat when his voice squeaked. He reached his arms around her tiny waist and hauled her up, but another wave came crashing over them, knocking them both off the board sideways. When they emerged, he grabbed on to her again. Rain squealed as he stood behind her trying to get her on again She wasn't making it easy.

'One, two, three, *jump*!' he called above the noise of the surf, lifting her by the hips as she slid onto the board on her front.

'It's so wobbly. I'm going to fall off again!'

'Lie still and hang on to the sides.' Marcus steadied the board for her. 'Keep your body down the centre line. Slide forward a bit. That's it, now reach out and paddle.'

Rain did as she was told but then the next wave broke and the board rolled sideways, dumping her on top of Marcus. And there they were, underwater, water whooshing in their ears, him grappling with her, her hair billowing everywhere and bubbles churning between them. Marcus dragged her to the surface and they both came up laughing and spluttering. He had her tightly in his arms.

'I'm hopeless,' she said, stringing her arms around his neck and thinking how true this was. 'Maybe we could, you know, hang out later.' She had to do something to take away the pain.

'Hang out?' was all Marcus managed to say as another wave dragged them sideways.

'We could get some vodka. Maybe come down here and light a fire and watch the stars or whatever it is you lot do around here for kicks.' Rain hated that it actually sounded quite nice. And more than anything, that was just what she needed right now.

CHAPTER THIRTY-THREE

Nick towelled himself dry, lying back on the sand. He closed his eyes, exhausted from swimming. He'd wanted to wear himself out until it hurt, until his muscles burned from pain and his heart begged him to stop. Even then he'd carried on, pushing his body to the limits. The water had chilled him to the core but now the sun was breaking through the salty layer on his skin, warming him from the outside in. He felt good. He felt alive. He actually *felt* for the first time in a long while.

A shadow above him eclipsed the sun.

'You realise she's still in love with you, don't you?'

Nick opened his eyes, his forearm shielding him from the glare behind her. Maggie's hair was silhouetted with a crazy candyfloss corona.

'What are you talking about?'

'Claire. She still loves you.'

He screwed up his eyes again. It was safer that way. Maggie sat down next to him, straightening out the rug.

'She always has been, ever since we were teenagers.' She sounded matter-of-fact, as if everyone knew except him. Did this explain the way he'd been acting – the way his body didn't do as he told it when she was around, the way his mouth took his words and muddled them up when she looked him in the eye?

'Is that the conclusion you reached on your walk, Mags?'

'Yes,' she said without hesitation. 'Seeing you two together again made me realise how nothing much ever changes.'

'Firstly, Claire is happily married. Secondly, we never had a "thing" in the past anyway. And thirdly, we've barely had a chance to speak yet, so I don't know how you think you can tell.'

'My point exactly. Since you arrived, you've both avoiding each other. It stands out a mile.'

'And that means she's in love with me?' Nick rolled his eyes, making sure Maggie saw. But he wondered if there was some truth in what she'd said. It did feel as if they'd been skirting around one other, deliberately sidestepping conversations.

'You're a dark horse, Malone,' Maggie said, unrelenting. 'You've barely said a thing about your personal life.'

'That's not entirely true.' Although Nick knew it was. 'I told you I was getting divorced, didn't I?'

'You only told me, no one else, and even then, I had to wring it out of you. Claire asked me if I knew why you'd come without Jess and Isobel.'

Nick flinched, taking a swig from his water bottle. He didn't want to talk about it but knew Maggie too well. She wouldn't let up. 'Jess and I didn't work out, that's all.' He pushed his heels into the hot sand, wondering how much to tell her. 'A lot's happened, Mags.'

'I'm a good listener.'

'The divorce has been bitter,' he said, hoping she wouldn't push further.

'You want to try screwing a married politician.' She patted his thigh with a friendly shove before delving in the cooler bag and taking out a bottle of wine. 'For emergencies,' she said. 'I think this is one. Besides, I couldn't feel any worse.' She cracked the screw top and shook water out of a couple of plastic cups lying on the rug. She poured two measures.

Nick took one. 'Do you ever wonder if your childhood shaped you into…' He hesitated. 'Well, into the wrong shape?'

'Sometimes,' Maggie said thoughtfully. 'Though I'd have been a lot more misshapen without those two.' She stared down at the shore where Patrick was standing in the breakers holding Shona's hand.

'Isobel died.'

'Nick, *shit*.' Maggie gripped his arm. 'Oh God, I'm so sorry…' He saw the tears gathering in her eyes, her hand come up to her mouth. It was all normal, nothing he hadn't seen before. He always tried not to look them directly in the eye, not until the shock had subsided. Then came the sympathy, which always felt a lot like pity.

'It's not been the best couple of years.'

'When? Do you mind me asking what happened?'

Only a couple of people had ever asked him this. Most waited for him to volunteer the information, which he rarely did. But this was Maggie. 'A year and a half ago. No one knows exactly what happened. We probably never will.' It was his stock answer. 'We think it was an accident.'

'What kind of accident?' She was certainly more probing than most.

'She fell down the stairs and hit her head. She was alone at the time,' Nick blew out sharply.

'How utterly awful.'

Nick nodded. If he and Jess had ever discussed it, it always ended in a searing row. She'd either turn grey with sadness, melting into a puddle of grief, blaming him, or she'd take to comprehensively smashing up their home before setting to work on Nick. Once, she'd broken both his nose and wrist on the same day. He'd told the hospital he'd fallen over. Those who'd pushed as deep as Maggie to find out details, those bold enough to tug a bit harder on the unravelling thread of their lives, soon backed off when they realised the sheer depth and danger of Jess's misery. For a tiny person who'd wasted to skeletal proportions, she could certainly wreak destruction.

Even with the wine, Nick's mouth was dry. 'The cause of the accident was inconclusive in the coroner's report. I was the one who found her at the bottom of the stairs. The police eventually ruled out suspicious circumstances.'

'Eventually?' Maggie said, not pressing for an answer when Nick remained silent.

They stared out to sea. Greta and Claire were deep in conversation at the water's edge – Greta standing with her hands settled in the small of her back, and Claire rocking from one foot to another, gesturing with her arms.

Did he love Claire? He watched as she turned to escort Greta back up towards where they were sitting. Facing the sun, there was something ethereal about her, as if the brilliant light had coloured her in with hues not normally visible to the human eye. With Isobel on his mind, it felt wrong to be thinking these things. But he couldn't help it.

CHAPTER THIRTY-FOUR

Callum hated the beach. However hard he tried, sand always got everywhere, and the sea was rarely warm enough to make swimming enjoyable. He couldn't understand why Claire spent so much time down there, either with the kids or friends or simply on her own with a book.

As he sat alone in the kitchen, he wondered if a freezing swim was now exactly what he needed – to feel the surf crashing over him, washing away his thoughts, extinguishing whatever it was that had been ignited. Life was suddenly chaotic, out of control – exactly the way he didn't like it.

Goddam that fucking girl!

The others had gone out while he sat and went over and over what had happened last night. He needed to get it straight, but he couldn't remember it all. What he did know, though, was that Rain was entirely culpable for what had happened. What time had he gone to bed? He needed to get that right. Sometime after midnight, he reckoned. Asking Claire was tantamount to admitting he'd had a skinful (which he had), but the booze was only to numb the dull conversation. Why did they insist on dragging up the past continuously?

Whatever the reasons for Rain setting upon him like she did in the night and what happened next, he was certain it was all because of this stupid reunion – not to mention the pressure he was under at the hospital. A job like his didn't leave room for this kind of thing. He had enough to deal with without teenagers throwing themselves at him.

Callum gathered himself, breathed deeply. He was a good man – a neurosurgeon with a reputation to uphold – and this was just a little blip. Everyone had one from time to time, didn't they? No stupid girl was going to ruin his life, he was certain of that. He had a family and a career. He was solid. Solid as a fucking rock. She'd come into his room uninvited, made him take her clothes off – pretending to be helpless when she was clearly quite the opposite – and then forced herself upon him, refusing to leave. If it came down to it, it was her word against his.

At least the news of Patrick discharging himself had taken the heat off Rain's whereabouts last night. How would he explain being taken advantage of by a teenager? No one would believe him. Not that the girl's irresponsible mother seemed particularly bothered. Maggie was as stupid as her daughter. Always had been.

In fact, the only one he'd ever hit it off with in their group was Claire. From the moment he'd set eyes on her as a kid, he knew there was something about her, something rare and special, something untouchable that he'd… *wanted*. Had to have. Was it so wrong to notice her uniqueness when she was just a child? Back then their age difference had been too great, he knew that. But now, her at nearly forty, him approaching fifty… a decade was nothing.

Goddam! He thumped the kitchen table.

What had actually woken him? Had he even been asleep? He remembered soft skin and hair brushing the length of his naked body, alerting him to either the best dream he'd ever had, or that someone had actually got into his bed.

It certainly hadn't felt anything like Claire.

Where had his wife been anyway? Some rubbish about not wanting to leaving Shona alone at the farm…

Callum forced himself to remember, go over all the details. He'd taken a coffee up to bed to help sober up, but the room was still spinning when Rain had come in. She'd not even knocked, had she? No. Of course she hadn't.

Marcus…?

Seconds later, he'd felt a hand sweeping lightly over his body in the darkness – a hand that couldn't take him quick enough, he decided. A hand whose delicious movements made him feel like the most desirable man in the world. A hand with the gentlest touch ever. Then he'd reached out and gripped her wrist, hearing her slurred voice.

Do you like me…?

He wasn't even sure the words had been real or that she was even there, convincing himself that it could still be a dream, that he wasn't actually doing anything wrong – let alone encouraging her.

You're beautiful…

He felt himself respond to her touch – any man would react the same – and then he remembered the fullness of her lips on his neck, his ear, his mouth. She was so very sweet, her naked body folding lightly over his like the whisper of a silk sheet. He looked up at her, felt soothed by her in a way that Claire could never make him feel, until her young smile, flashing through the darkness, transformed into something else. A shocked look when she realised… but by then it was way too late.

'Russ, come!' Callum yelled. He scraped back the kitchen chair and stood up, whipping the dog's lead from the hook by the door. Russ skidded to his master's side. 'Walk,' he snapped, thinking it would have to be a bloody long one.

CHAPTER THIRTY-FIVE

The conversation had wound back to babies and children, under-standably so with Greta present, but it was the last thing Nick wanted to hear about.

'I'm off in search of mussels to cook later,' he said, getting up off the sand. 'Anyone coming?' He'd briefly hoped Claire would join him. He liked the idea of them scrambling about on the rocks together as they'd done as kids, but she glanced up, declining politely before returning to her chat with Jason and Greta.

'I'd come with you, son,' Patrick said. 'But I'd be a liability.' His eyes flickered with something, as though the hot sun was loosening old memories. Nick couldn't help noticing the look Jason shot his father when he called him son.

His own father lived in Liverpool now with Nick's much older sister. He didn't see them very often. Growing up, his parents had been good to him, but were nowhere near as exciting as Patrick. His father had worked in the council offices and his mother had been a waitress. It was many hours waiting around in the restaurant kitchen for his mother to finish her shift that had sparked his love of food and cooking.

Nick pulled on his T-shirt and started off for the rocky section of beach behind them. The charcoal-coloured slate spotted with barnacles stood out against the fine buff sand. Occasionally, he regretted moving to London, so far away from the coastline that had once made him wonder if his blood was part seawater. So far away from everything he loved.

Nick waved at the teenagers, who'd chosen to sit away from the adults and look after Amy. Earlier, he'd watched as Marcus and several of his friends, plus a rather subdued-looking Rain, had struggled down onto the beach armed with surfboards, a blow-up boat, towels and a cricket bat. He'd stared at Rain too long, he knew that, but he couldn't help it. She was different in every way to Isobel, but his aching heart made him watch her as she spread out her towel.

Nick's feet smarted as the hot rocks dug into his soles. But ignoring the pain was easy compared to the far greater pain in his heart. The day he'd discovered his daughter's body splayed out on the hallway floor was the end of everything good in his life. On top of his and Jess's grief, the police fleetingly considered a ghastly scenario. That someone had even *thought* he'd hurt their daughter was horrendous.

He shook open the plastic bag that he'd brought up from the picnic and pulled some mussels off the rocks. The slate cliffs rose imposing and dark behind, and the shingle path that led to the clifftop track was not far to his left. It seemed less daunting than he remembered, although still not an easy climb. As kids, the shale had made it three steps forward, two back. Everything was simple then. Everything linear – black or white, good or bad. These days, his mind was pickled with bereavement, divorce, financial worries, builders, and all the while trying to remain creative with his cooking. It was nibbling at his sanity, eating away at his brain on a daily basis. He wasn't sure how long it would be before he cracked. He just wanted Isobel back.

'Hey,' a voice called out. Nick glanced up, looking around, not knowing where it was coming from. 'Up here.' Halfway up the shingle track, he spotted Rain. She was waving at him with a small smile, but then her smile dropped away. She'd put on her shorts but was just wearing a bikini top above. He tried not to see Isobel everywhere he looked.

'Careful up there,' Nick called back. 'It's steep.' He held his breath as she slid back down the scree a few feet, lunging for a nearby rock. She missed the handhold and ended up dropping further down on her bottom. In a moment she was standing again, brushing herself down, signalling to Nick with a thumbs up that she was fine.

'Hang on,' he called out, deciding it wasn't safe. 'I'll come and help you.' He left the bag of mussels dangling in a rock pool and started off down to the sand. As he leapt across the rocks, taking the safest but longest way around, a jut of cliff momentarily obscured Rain from view. When he finally got to the bottom of the shingle slope, she was nowhere to be seen. He looked about, calling her name and feeling slightly annoyed that she hadn't waited for him. She'd either got to the top all by herself or abandoned the idea completely and decided to take the long, sensible route along the beach. He thought that was probably the more likely, though something compelled him to go and find her.

CHAPTER THIRTY-SIX

When Claire got back to her parents' house, she discovered a missed call and a message from Jeff. She rarely took her phone to the beach because the signal was patchy. She hoped Jeff wasn't calling her into work again, especially after what had happened at Galen Cottage. She'd decided not to say anything to him about it.

'That's odd.'

'What is, love?' Shona had just come back from the beach and was beating the sand from her sandals on the doorstep. Patrick had insisted on checking on the store of feed for the few goats they owned even though she'd told him they still had plenty. She tolerated these aberrations; little routine errands that made him feel useful when, in reality, Shona had everything under control. But it was having to be in control that was wearing her out.

'Jeff working on a Sunday, that's what…' She trailed off, listening to the message.

Claire hung up, glancing out of the window to see if Patrick was coming back. 'Very odd,' she said slowly, mulling over what she'd just heard. 'Mum, apparently someone's already interested in buying the farm.'

Shona was making tea but stopped. She stared at Claire.

'Some developer is willing to offer full price on condition it's taken off the market immediately.' Claire frowned, pacing about. The details hadn't even gone live. It didn't make sense. 'Have you had a viewing you've not told me about, Mum?' Surely, she wouldn't do that without telling Patrick, or at least her.

Shona shook her head and turned to fill the kettle. Claire could see her cheeks were tinged pink, her jaw tight. 'No viewings. But I did speak to Jeff a couple of days ago,' she said finally. 'It was agreed he'd try some low-level marketing. I didn't want to worry—'

'It was *agreed*?' Claire was shocked. 'Dad doesn't know, does he?' Claire folded her arms tightly, not sure who to feel angrier with – her mother, Jeff, or this mysterious developer. She settled on all three.

'I'm sorry,' Shona said quietly. She put the kettle on the hotplate and sat down, her usually straight back bent and her head in her hands. 'I don't want to let Trevellin go any more than you or Dad, love. It feels as if I'm selling my own child, but I wanted Jeff to see if there was any initial interest. It seems there is.'

'It's more than interest by the sound of it,' Claire said, but then levelled her voice. 'He said this supposed buyer isn't local.' If she'd not taken time off work, she could have checked him out properly herself. 'Jeff's sending out a photographer urgently, to get pictures for this developer, whoever he is. He said if it comes to nothing, the shots can still be used in the brochure.' She'd never heard of anyone making an offer without even viewing a property. Something didn't add up. 'I'll call the office tomorrow. It doesn't sound like Jeff's on top of this.'

'He was just being helpful, love,' Shona said in a quiet voice. 'And I think external pictures only at this stage, don't you?'

Claire frowned. The implication was clear – her mother didn't want Patrick finding out. She sat down next to her, taking her hands, unknotting them gently. 'You know, there's a bungalow with estuary views for sale in Padstow. Dad could still fish and go off on his walks. His friends would be near.'

'A bungalow.' Shona blinked slowly. 'That sounds small and modern.'

'It's been on the market a couple of months. I could take you and Dad up to see it next week, if you like. The owners are lovely and…'

Shona was suddenly in tears – a full-blown, bottled-up meltdown that had clearly been building. Claire pulled her into her arms, not surprised by the depth of her release, but rather that she had one at all. Shona was, as everyone knew, the rock in the Lucas family.

'Oh, Mum,' she said. 'It'll be OK. Dad's getting good treatment now and soon you'll have a lovely new home and…' She trailed off.

Shona sniffed, squeezing Claire's hand in return. 'I don't know what I'll do without you living so close.' She reached across the table for a tissue. 'And I know everyone's thinking what if Lenni—'

'Who the *hell* is that outside taking photos of my property?' Patrick burst in through the back door, brandishing his walking stick back out towards the courtyard. He was red-faced, looking as if he was about to commit murder. He lunged back outside again, tripping on the step which only fuelled his rage. Claire went after him, but he pulled away from her as she tried to calm him.

'Get out of here now or I'll get my shotgun!' Patrick was shaking to the core, every cell in his body on fire. He thumped his stick against the wall, making the young man in the courtyard flinch. 'Go on, be gone with you!' His breaths were shallow and rasping, making his cheeks turn purple with effort. Claire noticed the fleeting confusion on his face, as if for a second he didn't know why he was yelling. She hadn't seen him this mad in a long time.

Shona took hold of his arm, but he yanked himself away from her too. 'Darling, calm down.' He was shaking with anger.

'I'm calling the police!' he shouted, spit frothing in the corners of his mouth. He marched up to the man, who retreated with every step Patrick took. 'Get the hell off my property!' Patrick's eyes bulged as he tried to make his body big and intimidating, like it once was.

'Your blood pressure, darling,' Shona implored, putting her arm around him. Again, he shrugged her off. 'Please, calm down. You'll have a stroke if you carry on like this.'

'Look, you'd better go,' Claire said to the pale-faced man who had a camera slung around his neck. For a moment, he stood completely frozen, wide-eyed and holding Patrick's stare before hurriedly getting into his car. The wheels spun in the gravel as he sped off.

'I bloody well found him up in the woods near the old cottage,' he said, turning back to them, his shoulders heaving up and down. 'He was taking photographs of the house from up there, so I chased him back down.' Patrick seethed through shallow breaths. 'He'd left the gate open and the goats had bloody well got out. How dare he!' He clutched his chest, panting out short breaths. His forehead was covered in sweat.

'Oh, Dad,' Claire said, taking his elbow and guiding him back inside. 'It's fine, it's all absolutely fine.' She silently cursed Jeff as she led her father back inside to his armchair. Gradually, his breathing returned to normal and Claire noticed the frown forming, the dazed look in his eyes as if he was trying to refocus on life. Like he was waking up from a bad dream, not quite sure where he was or what had happened.

'He's gone now, Dad,' Claire said, watching Shona count out his pills. She hated that they were lying to him. He wasn't a child that needed the truth disguising and neither was he anything less than the intelligent man she'd always known. He had a right to know what was going on. 'Look, Dad,' she said, catching Shona's eye. 'That man was a photographer from the agents. He wasn't snooping. He was taking some photographs to send to someone who might be interested in buying the farm.'

Patrick stared first at Claire and then at Shona, as though he had no idea what she was talking about. 'Are we moving?' he asked, quite calmly.

'There's a bungalow,' Claire went on. 'It overlooks the estuary.'

Patrick picked up the newspaper, though she could tell he wasn't really reading it. She noticed his hands were red and chafed, and the skin on his cheeks thin and veined. Seeing him nearly every day, she'd not been aware of him growing old, but truth was, after a lifetime of working on the farm, he'd been this weathered for years.

'I should have bloody thumped him,' Patrick said, glancing at the back door, suddenly remembering again.

The only time Claire ever recalled her father getting violent, exploding like a volcano, was when the detective handling Lenni's case came to give them a three-month update. An update which consisted of absolutely nothing. There were no new leads, no extra evidence, and no fresh witnesses had come forward despite the television appeals. Patrick asked him what the hell they'd been doing, why they weren't finding his daughter.

The detective stated quite calmly that he believed Lenni was most likely dead, that unless new leads came to light it wouldn't be much longer until the investigation was scaled back. It was then that Patrick slowly pulled back his huge right fist and landed a sharp punch right on the detective's nose.

CHAPTER THIRTY-SEVEN

Jason took a long shower. In spite of himself he'd enjoyed being at the beach but, as he rinsed off the sand and salt, he couldn't wash away what he'd seen earlier. He had no idea what to do.

What loomed between him and his father also couldn't be washed away. During the afternoon he'd glanced at Patrick once or twice, watching his actions and movements, listening to what he said, concluding that yes, something intrinsic had changed in him. It was a metamorphosis, as if he was gradually becoming a different person, a man very unlike the one Jason knew as a kid. He screwed up his eyes, allowing the hot water to wash over him. When Shona had told him about the Alzheimer's months ago, Jason had initially felt anything but sympathy.

All things considered, it was easier to stay away from Trevellin.

He put on a shirt his mother had given him on his last birthday when she'd been in London. He'd never ask her to take sides, but as they'd sat in the Fulham café, he admitted to himself that he was looking for clues – maybe even *hoping* for clues – that his father was softening, perhaps even showing remorse. If he was honest, he missed him terribly.

'What you must understand about Dad, darling, is that he firmly believes everyone should graft. Make their own way in life like he did,' Shona had said, but now, with Greta heavily pregnant, he couldn't comprehend how a man could shut out his own son.

'I was ill, Mum. I needed help, and more than just financial.'
From the moment Jason announced, aged eighteen, that he wanted
to be an actor, Patrick's thermostat switched to cool.

'He's old school, love. He thought acting was a cop-out.' Shona
had said this before, and always with a small smile. Jason had been
surprised when she'd once confessed her long-held dream to be on
the stage. But marriage, the farm, a family had put a stop to that.

'Maybe Dad's right,' Jason had said. 'I'm not cut out for it.'

'He was hoping you'd take over the farm one day. He took it as
a personal slight, as if you didn't value everything he'd achieved.
Trevellin was his life and he wanted it to be yours.' Shona sighed,
knowing she was treading a fine line. 'And your dad doesn't
understand mental health. I think deep down he blamed himself
for how you were.'

'It actually felt like the opposite, like he wanted me to be out
of the way and have nothing to do with the farm.' Jason pondered
this for a moment. 'Anyway, let's be honest, Mum. Not long after I
came to London, I got addicted to smack. That's hardly Dad's fault.
I was still grieving and riddled with guilt about what happened
to Lenni. We all handled it differently, and my reaction came out
much later. Understanding and love was what I needed.'

Shona nodded, sipping her drink to cover the quiver of her
lips. But Jason still noticed.

'My life carried on pretty much as normal the morning after
Lenni disappeared,' he continued. 'I *forced* it to carry on as normal,
that's how selfish I was. I put on my uniform and I went to school.
I did my homework and I walked the dog. I hung out with my
mates and got on with growing up. It was my way of coping with
the chaos around me. I went suddenly from the middle child to
being the youngest child.' Jason could see by his mother's expression that she'd never considered that before. 'Then, at college in
London, everything was different. I was surrounded by people like

me – broken people, creative people, desperate people, and people searching for something else in life. They helped me forget, while the drugs took away the pain.'

Jason recalled the day he'd finally plucked up the courage to go back home. It was the second lowest point of his life and he reckoned the only thing that would save him. He was an addict, penniless, and knew if something didn't change, he'd be dead within a year. He'd got on a train without a ticket at Paddington, then hitched from Exeter to Trevellin. His father was in the yard when he tramped down the drive, a dirty canvas pack slung over his back. When Patrick finally recognised his own son, the cold look he gave him made him want to turn around and go right back to the squat.

'Dad,' he said, dropping his bag to the ground as they stared at each other. Jason felt his skin prickling with sweat, the shakes getting worse. He knew he looked dreadful, reflected in his father's expression. Decline happens gradually in your own mirror. Wiping yellowed and dirty fingers down his face, feeling the deep familiar ache in his joints, he pushed his next fix from his mind.

'Your mother's inside,' was all Patrick said. Later, at dinner, Jason broke down. He pushed his plate aside and dropped his head into his hands. He told them everything – about the drugs, his hopeless life, how he couldn't carry on. How he thought he was going to die from the guilt. His mother was beside him, holding him, waiting for assurance from Patrick that everything would be all right, that they'd get help for him, that they'd get through this as a family like they'd always done.

'I want to come home,' Jason had said, sobbing, his pride long gone. 'London's not such a good place for me right now.' He remembered relief exuding from his mother. But there was nothing from his father. 'I can work for you on the farm, Dad. It's what you always wanted, isn't it?' He lifted his face. 'Maybe I can even renovate the old cottage. Make it my own like Claire is doing with the Old Stables. I'll go to the clinic, get healthy again.'

Jason swallowed, hating how desperate he sounded, wondering what else he could do to make the look on his father's face go away.

'We make our own beds,' Patrick said calmly.

'Pat?' Shona said, watching as he continued eating. After three more mouthfuls, he set down his spoon.

'The cottage is too far gone anyway.'

Jason blocked out the rest of the evening, obliterating it entirely with the emergency wrap he'd got tucked in the lining of his coat. When his parents had gone to bed, he retraced his steps up the drive, past Claire's house with lamps shining behind the curtains. She didn't even know he'd been home. The kitchen blinds were open, so he stopped for a moment and watched the scene inside. Callum was sipping on a drink, tapping his phone, while Claire stood at the sink. She'd worn the same expression since Lenni had gone missing – tight, expectant, sad. Not quite her. As if she'd been holding her breath all this time.

Jason pulled up his coat collar, shoved his hands deep in his pockets. He walked on. Hitching got him to the station by 3 a.m. and he slept on a bench until the first train back to London. The squat was freezing but filled with familiar faces, familiar smells and the familiar filth of a life he didn't want any more. He stood in the wrecked kitchen watching the other no-hopers and addicts. Then he turned and left, heading for the homeless shelter. He didn't care how he got it, but there would be change in his life.

In the Fulham café, a tear trickled down Shona's cheek. This was why she didn't come to visit him very often, Jason supposed. Like Patrick, it had become easier not to face the truth.

'Dad doesn't understand about drugs any more than he understands about you asking for help. Seeing you like that, it felt as though he'd lost another child, as if the boy he once knew and loved had gone to the same place as Lenni.' Shona pulled a tissue from her handbag. 'What he didn't realise is that you were the one with a chance of coming back.'

*

Jason wrapped the towel around his waist and went into the bedroom. Greta was already showered and changed, looking beautiful, if anything even larger, as she waited for him to dress. She was lying on her side on the unmade bed reading the newspaper. It was difficult to tell where her pale-blue tunic ended and the pastel duvet cover began. For all he knew, she might have been wearing all of it.

'Are they asleep?' he asked, stroking her belly.

'Thankfully, yes. I hardly dare move.' He didn't think it would be long before she had to take maternity leave, though knowing Greta she'd try to keep working until the end.

He sat on the corner of the bed, cradling his head in his hands. He knew she'd want to go up to the farmhouse soon. She was enjoying the break from London and he didn't want to spoil things for her. 'I'm not sure I can face seeing Dad again today,' he said. His thoughts in the shower had unsettled him. 'I'll walk you up to the farm, but I won't stay. I'll maybe do some job hunting online.' It also meant he wouldn't have to face Claire. He'd promised he'd call the police about the message she'd received, but since this morning the police had been on his mind for other reasons.

Greta sat up. 'I was hopeful things were going OK between you and your dad.'

'Only because he's forgotten much of what's happened, not because he wants to make up.' He reached out and squeezed Greta's leg. 'Which only makes it harder.'

'I was also hoping you'd be able to see a way around this. He's your father, Jase. It's a relationship that deserves healing.' She moved closer. 'Can I be honest? Really honest?'

Jason nodded, bracing himself.

'I think you're being a complete arse. I think you're being selfish and self-indulgent, and not acting like the man I fell in love with.' She swung her feet off the bed and slipped them into a pair of leather loafers that she hated wearing. Greta spent most of her life in heels. 'Your dad's ill, most likely unable to make the first move even if he wanted to. Perhaps your perception of him is really a reflection of yourself, Jason – stubborn, proud and stuck in the past.' She sighed, followed by a big inhalation. 'But I still love you to bits.' She stood up. 'I'm off up to the farmhouse to help out. No need to walk me up, but I do hope you come.' She planted a kiss on her husband's head and went downstairs, leaving Jason turning his phone over and over in his hand, more confused than ever.

CHAPTER THIRTY-EIGHT

'So, when's the big opening?' Claire was scraping seaweed and barnacles off what felt like a never-ending supply of mussels.

'All being well, mid-September.' Nick glanced across at her, his stomach churning at the thought. Things in his life were actually far from being well. 'I'm banking on some pre-opening trade reviews before Christmas. And I've already got a couple of corporate parties booked for December.'

'That's really great, Nick,' Claire said, catching his eye. 'Remember how we used to play restaurants when we were kids? You cooked all kinds of weird stuff over a campfire. I'm not sure all of it was edible.' She sluiced off another batch of mussels. 'Who'd have thought that you'd end up with your own restaurant for real?'

'My speciality was worm and leaf soup with a side of boiled garden snails, wasn't it?'

'You actually used to try to make us eat it.' Claire laughed, looking over at him again. 'Ouch!' She flinched, dropping the knife into the sink.

'Let me see that.' Nick took Claire's hand, gently holding her forefinger under the tap. 'Amy, do you know where Grandma keeps the plasters?' he said over his shoulder.

'Are you a doctor like Daddy?' Amy asked, running up with a little box. She wrinkled her nose at the sight of blood.

'No, I'm not like Daddy,' Nick replied, not taking his eyes off Claire. He dabbed lightly at the wound with kitchen paper, telling her to hold it tightly in place while he unwrapped the plaster. Amy ran off again as he peeled it around the wound.

'Thanks, Nick,' Claire said, but he didn't let go of her finger. When she looked at her hand again, it was enveloped by his. She quickly pulled away. 'I'll… I'll set the table then, seeing as I've made myself useless at the sink.'

The kitchen was suddenly filled with noise and chatter, and Claire was grateful for the reprieve. Shona and Patrick came inside following their evening stroll around the garden, but Patrick was making noises about checking the paddock gates again, wanting to make sure there were no more intruders.

'It's all secure, Pat. There's no need.' Shona didn't want him wandering off again.

Greta arrived next, offering to help with the meal. 'I can't guarantee I won't be more of hindrance, though,' she said, rubbing her bump. 'I've been getting Braxton Hicks contractions all day.'

'You just sit down and relax. It's all under control,' Claire said, but her father thought she was talking to him and he mumbled something about not being a child, about not being mollycoddled.

'I've just had a worrying time with Dad again,' Shona confided to Claire when he was out of the room. 'He got really confused in the garden. He was certain we were out searching for…' She made an expression that Claire knew only too well. She thought back to when he really *had* been scouring the woods and fields, when they'd all filled those early days with frantic and fruitless searches.

Without fail for the first six months, Patrick set off at dawn, taking a pack of supplies with him, tirelessly going over and over old ground. The familiar landscape of the wood, their fields and those of the surrounding farms eventually transformed into a harsh terrain that no one apart from Patrick wanted to set foot on – the land that had taken Lenni, seemingly swallowing her up. Eventually, his searches dwindled to once every couple of days, then maybe only a couple of times a week. Sometimes he'd be out looking when the sun had set, as if Lenni might only reveal herself after dark.

Patrick came back into the kitchen, staring at Greta as if he had no idea who she was. 'You're pregnant,' he said.

'Yes, I am,' Greta replied in her charming way. She smoothed her hands over her bump. 'We're having twins. They'll be born within the next month.'

'We?' Patrick's eyes sparkled with the puzzle, his mind forcing together pieces that wouldn't quite fit. 'One word of advice for you, then. Don't give birth while you're in this house.'

'I'll try not to,' she said with a laugh. 'They're not due just yet.'

'It's not a lucky house for children.'

Greta was about to reply but the back door burst open and Maggie blustered in. 'Has anyone seen Rain?' She was breathless and pink-cheeked. 'Is she with Marcus?'

'Mags, what's wrong? Are you OK?' Claire placed a hand on her arm. 'Marcus is still up at our house in his room, but I know he's alone.'

Maggie came up close to Claire. 'I'm a bit worried.'

'But you said yourself she's always going off, that she can look after herself.'

'I just bumped into that girl they were with earlier, Marcus's friend from the village. The one with glasses.'

'Pip?'

'Yes, Pip. She said that Rain didn't come back up from the beach with them. Apparently, she'd gone off earlier. Alone.'

'I'm sure she'll be fine,' Claire said, despite the small prick of concern she felt.

'If it was three in the morning and I hadn't heard from her, I wouldn't be too concerned. She goes out at night with her sensible head on, if you know what I mean.' Maggie frowned, checking her phone.

'And she doesn't have it on during the day?'

'Not exactly. It's just that… she seemed a bit odd this morning. A bit distracted. Did you notice?'

'She'd been up partying all night, don't forget. She was probably tired.'

'That's not what's bothering me. There's simply nothing for Rain to go off alone for around here. If there was a shopping mall nearby, I'd say she'd have gone there.' Maggie gripped Claire's arm.

'Maybe she's gone for a swim or a walk or taken a bus to Newquay?'

'Rain on a bus? I don't think so.'

'Have you not spotted the good-looking lad who runs the surf shop yet?' Claire said, laughing, but her concern was still growing. 'She's probably having a one-to-one demonstration of all the latest boards as we speak.'

Maggie offered a grateful smile and glanced at her watch. 'I'll give her until nine, then I'm going out to look.'

Claire swallowed and glanced at the kitchen clock. She hadn't realised it was seven-thirty already. The mussels had taken ages to prepare. 'Let's make it sooner,' Claire suggested. 'And I'll come with you.' She gave her a gentle squeeze and then excused herself. She went straight up to the Old Stables and headed for Marcus's room.

'What?' he called out when she knocked on his door. She went in. 'Don't yell, Mum, I'll tidy it tomorrow.' Marcus was lying on his bed texting.

'When did you last see Rain, love?' She leant on the door frame.

Marcus shrugged. 'On the beach this afternoon?' It was more a question than an answer. Claire noticed his cheeks redden. 'She left before us.' His phone buzzed, and he read the message.

'What time was that?'

'Dunno. About three. Maybe five-ish.' He tapped a speedy reply.

'Marcus, would you give me your attention for a moment? Rain's not come back to the farm yet and Maggie's getting worried.'

Marcus laughed. 'You mean *you're* getting worried, Mum.' He looked down at his phone again, finishing his text. 'Actually, I think she said she was going off to the shop.' He narrowed his eyes in thought. 'Yeah, that was it. She said she wanted an ice cream or something.'

'An ice cream?' The room around her suddenly flashed from light to dark. 'Are you sure?'

'Think so,' Marcus said, picking up his phone again when it pinged. 'What's the big deal?'

CHAPTER THIRTY-NINE

Inside Out

'We're going out tomorrow,' I'm told. 'Make sure you wear these.' There's a plastic bag stuffed with clothes that smell funny. Of other places. Of other people. Before I can even ask where we'll be going, I'm alone again.

I peek inside the bag and take out a T-shirt with 'Sale £4.99' written in felt pen on the sticky label. Someone else wrote that. Someone I don't know has given me their felt-pen writing, which is more exciting than the T-shirt itself. I trace my finger over the pound sign, tracking around both nines. It looks like a girl's writing – careful and precise with the dot in exactly the right place. She's underlined the word 'Sale' with a squiggly line.

I pull off the label and grind it into the floor with my foot. I spit on it. I hate the shop girl and I hate the T-shirt with its pink pony. It's babyish and too small but it's clean and new and means I'm going somewhere. Maybe I won't come back. Maybe I'll run away. There's a pair of pale-green shorts and some new socks too, together with a packet of jellied sweets, a hairbrush, some sanitary towels and a shopping list – even more precious than the shop girl's writing on the label.

The items in the bag are listed on the paper. There are also things on the list that weren't for me. My heart skips a beat. The handwriting is large and slopes down to the right... *T-shirt, shorts, socks, sweets...*

Then *stamps, butcher, library, dentist…*

I smooth out the paper. If I collect enough little things like this, maybe the inside will eventually become the same as the outside. I fold up the list carefully and put it in my secrets box – a box that used to contain tea bags. I already have a feather, a leaf, some lollipop sticks and the silver ring pull from a can of Coke. It's already nearly the whole world in there.

The next day I put on my new clothes like I was told. I feel like a baby. Then the noises and the door is unlocked. I haven't bothered to hide behind the chair today. We're going out! It's the day of all exciting days.

'Hello,' I say, dashing up for a hug. But I don't get one. 'Do I look nice?' I stretch out my T-shirt. I would twirl but that would make me sick and then we wouldn't go out.

'Very smart.'

'Can we go to the seaside?'

I get a thoughtful look back. 'We'll have to go in the car.'

'Of course, of course!' I squeal and jump about, even though I hate the car. The stuff in my tummy nearly comes up, but I hold it down. During the short journey I curl up into a ball on the back seat because I have to pretend to be invisible, like I'm not even alive. The engine growls like a horrid monster, making me shake as we swing around bends and go up and down a hill. Tears escape from my screwed-up eyes and my heart nearly stops from being so scared. When we park a few minutes later, I don't want to go to the beach any more. I hate it. I hate the sea and I hate outside! I want to go back.

The breeze blows cool on my neck as the car door opens. 'Come on, get out. It's a beautiful day.' I do as I'm told, unfurling my arms from around my head and sticking my feet out of the door. Blue sky is lashed with grey just like when my dad used to do his watercolour paintings. He'd often set up camp on the clifftop with a little folding stool and wooden case of paints that opened out like a magical kaleidoscope of colour. I know I'll never see those paintings again.

'I'm cold,' I say, shivering.

'Nonsense, the sun is shining.' A hand pulls me out of the car, then drapes a coat over my head and shoulders as I stumble and stagger. 'Get a move on.' There's no one about as we go along a path to the headland, my feet taking tiny fast steps to keep up. Below us is the most deserted beach in the world, big and wide. The wind makes it hard to breathe.

'I want to go back.'

'But I have a surprise,' I'm told and, before I can protest, we are sitting on some rocks and I'm given a pair of huge black binoculars.

'You'll be able to see the whole world with these. Just mind it doesn't see you back.'

I raise them to my eyes slowly, uncertain I even want to see the whole world. Nothing is in focus and all I can make out is the green-blue chop of the sea. It makes me feel sick again.

'There's nothing there,' I say, disappointed, and the binoculars are snatched away.

'Try now.'

And then it *is* like seeing the whole world! One tiny coin-sized piece of it explodes into an entire universe before my eyes.

'What do you spy?'

'I spy a sailboat,' I say. 'And there's a man on board wearing a yellow shirt. He's winding a handle.' I reach a hand out in front of me, trying to touch him in case he can save me, but I can't reach. When I take the binoculars away, he disappears as if he never existed and the boat is just a smudge on the horizon.

'Am I like that boat now?' I ask. 'People only know I exist if they see me with their binoculars?' There's no reply so I pan around, taking a close-up look along the coastline. The rocks leap out at me in furious and fast streaks of slick black and green. A gull flashes past but all I see are the feathers on its wing. Suddenly, it's as though I'm down on the beach, watching the waves dance over the sand as they crash onto the shore. Then I see some people – *three people*! Something inside my heart gets hot, like I've caught fire.

'Look!' I shriek. They've got a kite – a red kite with a bright blue tail made up of a hundred plastic bows. I follow the string back down to the beach, where a boy grips onto the handle, grinning, with his mother beside him. They look so happy. I unhook the binoculars from around my neck, smashing them down on a rock. The vomit goes all down my new T-shirt and I'm dragged back to the car, listening to horrid swear words and being told that I'm ungrateful and selfish. I feel like the stupidest girl alive.

CHAPTER FORTY

Callum switched the headlights to main beam. It wasn't completely dark yet, but he wanted to illuminate the narrow lanes as much as possible. The hedges seemed to be closing in around them, with the matted gorse and weeds obscuring the view of the surrounding fields. 'Stupid bloody girl,' he said under his breath. Claire was staring intently out of the Range Rover windows, peering left then right. 'She'll probably turn up in the dead of night again, waking us all up.'

'Sorry, love?' Claire replied, winding down the window.

'Nothing,' he muttered, swinging the vehicle hard left.

'Try to be a little bit more sympathetic, Cal,' Claire said. 'Maggie's getting really worried.'

There was no doubt in his mind that the girl was a wretched nuisance. He'd planned to work on his research paper tonight and had an early clinic in the morning. The last thing he needed was to be searching for some kid he would never see again after this week. And even that would be too soon, he thought, clenching his teeth.

'Let's drive past the shops at the beach again. I want to have one final check.'

Callum knew there was no point protesting. Nick had also gone out in his car; they'd passed him about ten minutes ago. They'd pulled up alongside each other in the narrow lane, windows wound down, though neither of them had anything to report. Jason and

Marcus were out searching on foot, knocking on doors in the village, checking with Marcus's friends in case they'd seen her.

'Mags, it's me,' Claire said, as they bumped along the lane. The phone signal was patchy. 'No, nothing. Yes, I agree. It's been long enough. And listen, don't worry. I'm sure she'll be fine.' She hung up and turned to Callum. 'Maggie's going to call the police.'

Callum simply nodded and drove to the shops.

Fuck.

It was 10.15 p.m. when a car pulled down the drive to Trevellin. Maggie was watching out of the kitchen window, praying for Rain to return or the police to arrive.

She dashed to the back door, catching sight of the yellow flashes along the side of the car, feeling sick to her stomach at what it meant. When Claire had told her what Marcus had said about Rain going off to the shop, neither of them had mentioned the obvious, the unspeakable. The similarities were already too horrific to contemplate.

A woman, mid-thirties, got out of the car. Her hair was cropped and she was wearing police uniform. She walked up to the house, looking around the courtyard, her face breaking into a cautious smile when she caught sight of Maggie at the door.

'Thank you for coming,' Maggie said, holding the door open.

'I'm PC Steph Wyndham. My colleague has been held up, but he'll be along shortly.' She held out her hand and Maggie shook it lightly, introducing herself.

'Please, come through.' Maggie's voice was fragile and choked. 'I'm really sorry to have to call you out. Knowing Rain, she'll turn up any moment wondering what all the fuss is about.' She attempted a laugh but stopped. The officer was looking around the kitchen, frowning, deep in thought, making a puzzled face as if she knew something. As if Trevellin itself was the keeper of dark secrets.

PC Wyndham put her clipboard and radio on the kitchen table, giving cursory nods to the others present. 'I understand you've reported a missing person? A teenager?'

'Yes, my daughter, Rain. She didn't come back from the beach with the others this afternoon.' Maggie glanced at her watch. 'It's been over six hours. Look, I'm really worried about her. This really isn't like her.' As the evening had worn on, everyone had returned from searching and gathered in the kitchen, with Callum saying he'd been on to the coastguard again. No one had anything to report.

'OK, Maggie. Let's get things rolling. Is there somewhere private we can sit?'

'Feel free to use the snug,' Shona piped up, leading them through. The PC opened her mouth to speak, but then thought better of it. Shona closed the door, leaving them in private.

It was much cooler in the little sitting room and the two women sat side by side on a floral sofa – Maggie perching nervously on the edge. PC Wyndham had her clipboard resting on her knee, pen poised. 'What's your daughter's name, love?'

'Rain,' Maggie replied. 'Rain Carr.'

'That's pretty,' she said, writing it down. 'So, you said she was at the beach this afternoon.'

'Yes, Trevellin Bay. We'd all gone down for a picnic lunch. We're all old friends. We're having a get-together. A reunion. Anyway, the kids – the teenagers – decided to sit up by the rocks away from the adults. I went off for a walk at around two o'clock. I was gone quite a while. That was the last time I saw her. When I came back, she'd already left the beach. I didn't think anything of it at the time.'

'So you didn't see her after your walk?'

'No.'

'How long did you walk for?'

'An hour or two. I'd gone up and down the beach a couple of times, then carried on along the cliff path at the end of the bay, where it runs north past the row of shops.'

'OK.' She wrote everything down. 'And what was Rain wearing?'

Maggie felt like falling into the PC's arms – *anyone's* arms – and sobbing until she was convinced everything would be fine. Instead, she let out a stifled hiccup. 'I know she took her pink bikini with her because I saw it hanging out of her bag, and she wore her denim shorts to go down to the beach. She had on a pale-blue tunic top, I think. It's decorated with sequins and has butterfly sleeves.'

'Will you describe her for me, please?'

'She's beautiful.' Maggie let out a longer sob. 'And this really isn't like her, officer.' This was different to when Rain stayed out late at night. It didn't feel right. 'She's about five feet seven tall. She's got sandy-blonde hair about down to here with lots of highlights and waves.' Maggie indicated around her chest. 'And really bright blue eyes. Like her dad,' she added when the detective stared at her dark ones. 'She's a slim build.' Maggie bit her lip, fighting back tears. 'Too slim, I sometimes think.'

'Any distinguishing marks. Scars or moles?'

'She has a tattoo on her ankle. And her belly button is pierced. I didn't really want her to have either, but she just went ahead and got them done.' Maggie rolled her eyes.

'What's the tattoo of?'

'It's on her left ankle. I feel a bit responsible, to be honest.' Maggie sighed, remembering the first time she'd seen it. Rain had clearly drawn inspiration from the necklace she'd been constantly wearing at the time. 'I can draw it for you, if you like.'

'Yes, that would be helpful in just a moment.' The officer put down her pen. 'Is Rain the rebellious type? Do you think she could have done this on purpose to annoy you or her father?'

'She's feisty, but show me a teenage girl who isn't.' Maggie covered her face, her hands trembling. 'She goes off partying and sometimes stays out all night and it never worries me. I know she'll be safe because she's with her friends. They all look out for each other. But going off on her own and not telling me, that's what bothers me.'

'What do you mean?'

'There's simply nothing to go off *for* around here. She won't have gone fishing or taken a bike ride or anything like that. She hates that kind of thing. Rain was bored of being here already, I know that much.'

'If she was fed up, could she have gone home?'

Maggie shook her head, wondering where it was exactly that Rain considered home to be. 'She has no way of getting there, and besides, she only took a bit of loose change to the beach. Her phone and purse are upstairs in her room. She never normally goes anywhere without them.' She stifled another sob. Breaking down would make it real, and she wasn't sure she could stand that.

Someone was tapping on the sitting room door. When Maggie looked up, another officer in uniform was standing there. He was tall and stooping slightly to avoid hitting his head on the low beams.

'Ah, PC Holt,' the officer said. 'Come and join us. I'm just taking some basics.' She introduced Maggie. 'Is Rain's father here? We'd like to speak to him too.'

'We're not together.' Maggie pressed her hands together in her lap, staring at the carpet for a moment. She felt her cheeks burning.

'Do you think she might have gone to see her father in that case?' the male officer suggested, sitting down.

Maggie shook her head. 'He rarely sees her. We're not married and we've never lived together.' When she was forced into explaining, she always tried to avoid detail.

'I take it you've already called him to check—'

'No.' Maggie looked away for a second. 'It's complicated,' she added, sighing. 'He's a high-profile MP. And he's married to someone else.' There. She'd said it. Now she would just wait for them to put two and two together.

She'd always worried about her dirty little secret getting out, worried even more about kidnapping if it did. Surely, the police would pick up on that possibility too? It might focus Peter's mind if they did.

Her hands shook as she waited but they said nothing. They just sat staring at her. She swallowed. 'What you need to understand is that my daughter, however wild, however stubborn, however hormonal and crazy, would not take off without telling me where she was going, even if it was with her father. And she especially wouldn't go without her purse or phone. She was only wearing beach clothes and not much else. She has no friends around here and it is now going on eleven o'clock at night. I just know that something bad has happened to her. Do you think she's been taken… by someone who maybe knows about her father? Do you think there'll be demands for money?' Maggie swallowed again, staring at the floor.

'Did the others at the beach say where she was going?' PC Holt sat down next to his colleague, ignoring Maggie's question. 'Your friends in the kitchen gave me a brief rundown.'

Maggie closed her eyes and thought. She imagined Rain slipping on her shorts and top at the beach and cheerfully saying goodbye to Marcus and the others. In reality, she saw Rain cursing them for being so boring, cursing the entire week for being so lame, and stomping off on her own. She drew a deep breath, hardly able to get out what Claire had told her. Getting her story right was vital. 'According to Marcus, Claire's son, she… she said she was going off to get an ice cream from the beach shop.' It came out in a breathy rush, as if she was drowning.

'OK,' PC Wyndham said, not knowing the significance. 'Try not to get too worried at this stage. In most cases, missing persons turn up very quickly. But we'll put out all the usual alerts, get it on the system. Meantime, I'd like to speak to a couple of your friends.'

'Of course,' Maggie said. She blew her nose and made to move, but the officer placed a hand on her arm.

'You said you'd draw your daughter's tattoo.' She handed over her notepad and pen.

Maggie stared at the blank page, remembering the moment she'd first spotted it on Rain's ankle a year ago. Her loose trousers had ridden up as she'd sat cross-legged on the floor, the freshly inflamed skin around the simple black design making Maggie's heart pound. Even the cling film protecting it couldn't hide the infection. But it was the design that made Maggie breathless. A course of antibiotics soon cleared up the redness, but the ink was still there to remind Maggie of her guilt forever. She hated what she'd done now, but as a kid her jealousy had burnt deep. Claire had had it all, hadn't she? The happy family, the devoted parents, the beautiful home. And at the time she'd convinced herself it wasn't actually stealing. But then, last year, she'd rediscovered the little pendant hidden away in an old trinket box she'd forgotten about and had taken to wearing it. It had obviously caught Rain's eye.

She handed the notebook back to the officer. 'That's the tattoo,' she said. 'On her left ankle.'

PC Wyndham nodded and showed it to PC Holt. 'We'll get this circulated along with her description,' she said. 'Perhaps we could speak to your friend Claire now?'

Maggie stood, leaving the officers alone for a moment while she went to fetch her. They didn't know of the significance of the ankh symbol – the little silver charm on the pair of necklaces Patrick had bought for his daughters all those years ago; wouldn't know that Lenni's had been found, along with her shorts, in the grass verge after she'd gone missing.

CHAPTER FORTY-ONE

'It's going to be OK, Mum,' Claire said, sitting next to Shona at the kitchen table, even though she was feeling more and more that it wasn't. They all sensed it – a teenage girl had gone to buy ice cream at the beach and she hadn't come back – but no one was ready to say it.

Patrick drummed his fingers on the arm of his chair, in a manner reminiscent of how he'd been in the early days of Lenni's disappearance. Somehow his silence had given him an air of control, even though Claire knew he'd felt as helpless as the rest of them. She wondered if it was the same now or if his mind gave him some protection from reality. For once, she hoped he wasn't completely aware.

'I tell you, this house is cursed,' Patrick muttered, as Maggie emerged from the snug.

'They want to have a word, Claire,' Maggie said quietly. 'If Rain doesn't turn up soon…' She paused, stumbling over the possibility, '…then they'll need to speak to everyone.'

Claire squeezed Maggie's arm as she headed for the snug, but stopped when she heard Callum's voice.

'You don't have to say anything without a solicitor, Claire,' he said.

She swung around. 'I just want to help find Rain. I don't need a solicitor.' She gave him a small smile, hoping he'd return it. He didn't. After their drive around the area earlier, Callum hadn't gone back out searching with the others on foot. She noticed how preoccupied he seemed, but also knew that work was preying on his mind. He didn't have the kind of job that could be cast aside.

She closed the snug door and sat down in the armchair with the two PCs facing her. Perhaps her father was right. Perhaps Trevellin *was* cursed.

'We won't keep you long. If you can just tell us about this afternoon, when you last saw Rain, how she seemed.'

'Of course.' Claire forced herself not to make too much of the similarities that niggled away at her mind. It was too early to read anything into what would most likely turn out to be nothing more than a thoughtless teenager going off in a bad mood.

'It was just a normal afternoon at the beach, really.' She took a deep breath. 'Maggie's daughter, Rain, was hanging out with my son Marcus along with a couple of his mates from the village. She seemed a bit quiet but OK. They sat a little way away from us, like kids do.' Claire paused, trying to ignore the hairs standing up on her arms as today's happenings meshed with those emblazoned on her mind. 'We were all there – eating, chatting and stuff. Maggie went off for a walk and, at one point, Nick went to find some mussels to cook.' Claire walked herself through events as quickly as she could, knowing every second counted. 'We strolled back up to the house about four o'clock, I think, but the kids stayed down a bit longer.'

'Was Rain with your son and his friends when you left the beach?'

'No, no I don't think she was.' Claire frowned, touching her hair. 'I remember waving to Marcus on the way past. He stuck up his hand in return, but I'm not sure I recall seeing Rain.'

'You're not certain?' PC Holt said.

'I wouldn't stake my life on it. You don't think these things will be important at the time.'

'Did all the adults walk back together?' PC Wyndham jotted everything down.

'Nick stayed down on the rocks a bit longer.'

'Was there anyone in the house when you came back?'

'I went back to my house first, the Old Stables.' Claire made a gesture up towards where she lived. 'It's the first house you come to along the drive. But I realised I'd left my handbag and phone down here at Mum and Dad's. I'm always coming and going between the two places.' Claire nodded, confirming to herself that she'd got events right. 'I thought I'd find Callum at home, working, but there was no sign of him. Our dog wasn't around either, so I guessed he'd taken him for a walk. They came back while I was in the shower.'

'Callum is your husband?'

'Yes, sorry.'

'The one who just said you didn't have to say anything without a solicitor?'

'Yes.' Claire felt the flush in her cheeks.

'How well do you know Rain?' the female PC continued.

'I've only met her a couple of times, when she was much younger. Maggie and I were best friends as kids. Maggie was a bit of a tearaway and I was the sensible one. We kind of balanced each other out.' Claire managed a little smile.

'Do you know Rain's father?'

'I've never met him, but I know he's a politician.' She wasn't sure what Maggie had revealed but felt she should be honest with the police. 'He's married, but not to Maggie. His wife doesn't know about Rain.'

Both detectives looked at each other.

'No, it's not like that. This has nothing to do with Rain's father, I'm certain.'

'Let's flip that around, then. Do you think it has anything to do with Maggie? Is she struggling for money, perhaps?'

Claire recoiled at the question. She didn't like what they were implying. 'Maggie's always just got by, but no, of course I don't think she's got anything to do with it. You've seen the state she's in.'

'Then what do you think has happened?' The constable tapped the pen on her lip.

Claire's mind smouldered, reigniting the past. 'In all honesty,' she said, glancing between the two officers, 'I have absolutely no idea.'

Callum stooped to avoid the low beams as he joined his wife and the officers. He knew Claire had noticed his stern look.

'We won't keep you, Mr Rodway, but it would be helpful if you could tell us where and when you last saw Rain,' PC Wyndham said, after introducing herself.

Callum scratched his cheek, frowning. 'I dropped her off with Marcus and a couple of his mates in Newquay for a house party last night at about ten o'clock.' The officer noted it all down while Callum watched, thinking how young she looked, how her cropped hair and flat shoes made her appear almost androgynous.

'And how did they get home afterwards?'

'I gave them forty quid for a taxi,' he said, rolling his eyes. 'Well, I gave it to Rain to take care of because last time Marcus spent it on booze and I ended up having to go out and fetch him at three in the morning.'

'Do you know what time they came back?'

Callum's swallow stuck halfway down his throat as he flicked a look at Claire. 'I don't know for certain. Marcus told me Rain left before them, going off with the taxi money. Thankfully, he was able to get cash out of the machine this time.'

'But do you know how or when Rain came back, Mr Rodway?'

Callum stared at the officer, finally swallowing down the lump. 'No.'

A while later, Claire showed the officers out. 'Maggie's worried sick,' she said quietly at the back door. 'If there are any developments, please let her know as soon as you can.' She remembered how it had nearly killed them as they'd waited for news of Lenni. Minutes turned into hours which turned into days, months and finally years. Now they were counting in decades.

'Mum,' Claire said, when they'd gone. 'Why don't you and Dad go to bed? It's nearly midnight.' Her mother agreed, reluctantly admitting there was nothing more to be done tonight. She coaxed Patrick to do the same. After they'd gone upstairs, Claire went looking for Maggie. She wasn't hard to locate – she just followed the smell of cigarette smoke. She was outside, standing around the corner of the nearest barn, staring up at the pitch-black sky, sucking in hard, blowing out harder still.

'Did the police say anything else?' Claire asked.

Maggie shook her head. 'I'm worried, Claire,' she said, hugging her arms around her body. 'This isn't what Rain does.'

'Maybe she met someone at the club last night and arranged to meet them elsewhere. Perhaps that's why she left the boys. Teenagers aren't exactly known for their honesty.'

'No.' She inhaled again, hand shaking. 'Rain would have told me. She tells me everything like that.'

Claire opened her mouth, then stopped herself. From what she'd seen, she wasn't sure that was entirely true. For a start, it didn't take an expert to notice that Rain had issues with her food. Had she spoken to her mother about that, she wondered? She was about to mention the possibility of kidnapping, the seed sown by the officer about Maggie needing money, but she held back. The police had also mentioned several other scenarios, which she daren't tell Maggie about at this point. The riptides and currents were strong in the area, and the chance of her having had an accident on the rocks or cliffs and falling into the sea were high. With this in mind, they were scaling up the coastguard search at first light.

'I'm worried with you,' Claire said, pulling her close. She felt partly responsible – this week had been her idea, after all. They squeezed each other tightly before going back inside, surprised to see Shona and Patrick downstairs again.

'Help me, will you, love,' Shona said. 'Dad wants to go out searching.' She pulled a weary face. 'For Lenni.'

Claire felt another surge of guilt. What had been intended as a pleasurable and healing week for him had turned into a nightmare. What kind of memories were being stirred up? Not the ones she'd intended, that was for sure. 'Come on, Dad,' she said, gathering what was left of her resolve. 'Let's get you upstairs. It's time for bed.'

'But I need to find her,' he said, squinting as if part of him knew what he was saying wasn't right.

'We'll talk about that in the morning,' Claire said, encouraging him back up. Thankfully, he followed and she guided him upstairs with a hand settled beneath his elbow. He veered off to the wrong bedroom on the landing. 'This way, Dad,' she said.

Her parents' room smelt faintly of her mother's floral perfume, of fresh laundry and of love. Her parents had slept together in this room for as long as she could remember. It was a thick, intense kind of love that filled the house and stuck to all the Lucas kids as they'd grown up. Sometimes, Claire thought, we were loved too much.

'Get into your pyjamas, Dad,' she said, laying them out for him. Her father's watery eyes stared up at her as he sat on the bed. He hated being taken care of, she knew that, but for now he seemed accepting, almost a little relieved. 'Why not say a little prayer for Rain,' Claire suggested, recalling him once saying the same thing to her as she cried herself to sleep a week after Lenni had gone. She fetched a glass of water from the bathroom and, when she returned, her father was in bed, his eyes closed and his thin, dry lips muttering words she could barely make out.

CHAPTER FORTY-TWO

Company

There's someone here. There's someone here! I drop to the floor beside my bed and watch, shaking with anticipation. The little girl is talking, laughing, singing a song. She is in my room. There's someone here, I tell you!

My teeth clamp together and I claw at the foam mattress, putting the pieces in my mouth, waiting for her to see me. I'm way too scared to say hello, just like when I was at school. I haven't seen anyone else in such a long time, I don't know what to say. The only people I see are in the films, and they never talk back.

I want to yell 'Go away' in case she's bad, but I clamp my hand over my mouth, so I keep quiet. Has she come looking for me? Maybe she's here to rescue me, to take me home, to make everything normal again. But then I feel sad. What if she's been captured and put in here too?

The television chatters in the background, the flickering lighting up my little room. A man's voice drones on about nuclear war, about how we will all die if the bomb goes off.

There's a little girl in here. There really, really is!

Why don't you believe me?

My breathing is noisy as I wait and watch – even noisier than the telly or her singing – and I'm scared she'll hear me. My nose is clogged and crusty, as if I've been breathing soil, as if I've been buried alive. And all the while the little girl is chanting. Teasing.

I want her to leave me alone now. Get out!

No, please don't go…

Eventually, I fall asleep on the floor and, when I wake, she's gone.

CHAPTER FORTY-THREE

Nick was the closest to the phone, so he grabbed it, handing it straight to Maggie. 'Hello?' she said, followed by single-syllable responses. She hung up, deflated, turning to the others. 'No news. They have people out making enquiries and will begin a full-scale search in the morning.' Maggie couldn't stand the thought of her daughter out alone in the dark Cornish countryside, possibly lost, possibly hurt. To make matters worse, an onshore wind was getting up, making an overnight storm likely.

'Searching the coast at night would be madness,' Nick said. 'But it's so frustrating not to be doing anything.' He paced about, mirroring how they all felt: utterly helpless.

'Agreed,' Jason said. 'But we're best off trying to get a couple of hours' sleep, then searching again at first light.' They'd all gone back up to The Old Stables, not wanting to disturb Patrick and Shona while they discussed what to do. Angus and Jenny were still at the farmhouse.

'I'm so sorry about this, Claire,' Maggie said, cupping her hands around a mug of sweet tea. Her voice was flat and tired. 'You're all so kind.' She managed a little smile before it fell away. 'And I'm so angry with Rain, yet sick with worry.' She put the mug on the table, dropping her head into her hands.

Claire exchanged glances with Jason then Nick, wondering if they thought it was as serious as she did. 'You should try to get some sleep too,' she said, touching Maggie's back. 'It's only a few hours until dawn.' She looked at her watch, knowing that sleep would be impossible, but any kind of rest was better than nothing.

Jason went upstairs to join Greta, who had already succumbed to exhaustion, and Maggie and Nick reluctantly went back up to the farmhouse. Claire watched from her back door as the pair walked arm in arm, eventually disappearing from the cones of light thrown out from two lanterns standing sentry at her gateway. She stood there a few minutes longer, contemplating the blackness beyond, wondering which part of the night had swallowed up Rain. She gripped the door frame hard, trying to quell the rising tears. Thoughtless teenager or something more sinister – it was all too reminiscent.

After locking the door securely – then unlocking it again in case Rain came back – she decided on a nightcap. It was unlike her, but the only thing that would guarantee an hour or two's sleep. She sat at the kitchen table, unable to prevent her mind from going back to the first night Lenni had gone missing when, shamefully, she'd slept soundly. She'd always hated herself for that, the next morning trying to convince herself she'd been exhausted from dashing about trying to find her baby sister. Or, perhaps, as she now wondered, it was self-protection that had made her sleep that night. The only way to escape the guilt.

Claire sipped the whisky that she'd sloshed into a floral teacup.

'Where *are* you, Rain?' she whispered, tapping a finger on the table as the whisky seared her throat. She knocked back the rest, pouring another shot which didn't do anything to allay the negative thoughts.

Some days, in her mind, Lenni had become someone's new daughter, stolen to order because a couple unable to have children of their own had so much love to offer a trusting little girl like her. Other times she'd been taken out of the country, perhaps by gypsies or kidnapped by a child-trafficking gang. Claire imagined her alive but feral, wasted away with empty, sunken eyes.

She knocked back the second shot of whisky and put the cup in the sink. The most unthinkable scenario, she now realised, was ironically the most desirable. That Lenni was dead. She flicked off the kitchen lights and went upstairs to bed.

Claire woke to the sound of a storm, with rain pelting against the glass. 'Callum,' she whispered. Her husband groaned and rolled over, looping his arm around her waist, pulling her closer as she tried to get out of bed to close the window. It was already starting to get light. 'Cal, no, I have to get dressed. We're going out searching.'

'It's four in the bloody morning,' he moaned, squinting at the clock. 'We've had about two hours' sleep.'

Claire swung her legs out of bed and sat up, bracing herself for what lay ahead. Her mobile phone buzzed on the bedside table. *Are you awake? I'm at the door.* Callum shoved a pillow over his head while Claire slipped on her dressing gown, going downstairs to let Nick in. 'Did Maggie sleep at all?' she asked.

He shook his head. 'We've been up talking for the last hour. She's going to call Rain's father later to see if he's heard anything.'

'About time,' Claire said, closing the door behind him. She couldn't understand why Maggie hadn't called him straight away. Married or not, he had a right to know if his daughter was in danger and Maggie had a right to know if Rain was with him.

Claire filled the kettle. She swilled out a couple of yesterday's mugs, tossing in teabags. 'Nick, does this feel…' She turned away, not managing to finish the sentence, so she stood with her hand on the kettle, head down, waiting for it to boil.

'Familiar?'

Claire poured boiling water into the mugs. 'I don't like it. There are already too many similarities.' She caught his eye as she passed him his tea.

'Losing a child is…' Nick took a sip instead of finishing.

'Is what?' Claire sat down but didn't take her eyes off him. She pulled her robe tighter around her chest.

'It's still raw.' Nick's voice was deep and low, but Claire didn't miss the waver in it. The look on his face told her he hadn't wanted to say anything.

'What's raw, Nick?'

He stared blankly ahead but then, as if the weight of his sadness was too much, his head dropped forward, chin on chest. Claire put a hand on his arm. 'Nick?'

'It's Isobel. She died.'

'Oh, Nick, I'm so very, very sorry.' Claire clasped his hand in hers, hardly able to believe what she was hearing. Hardly able to believe he hadn't told her before now. All the things she felt she ought to say wouldn't come out. 'When?'

'A year and a half ago.'

Claire had assumed that Jess and Isobel were simply unable to make the trip to Cornwall and, for some reason, she hadn't wanted to ask why, perhaps sensing Nick's reticence to talk about his family. 'I can't even begin to contemplate what you've been going through.' She released his hand, allowing him to sip his tea. He looked exhausted, still in yesterday's clothes.

'I may as well be honest, Claire.' He stared at her, as if looking for something of the past, something familiar and safe. 'The coroner's findings were inconclusive, though an accident was stated as a possible cause of death.'

Claire nodded, waiting for him to continue.

'Initially, the police weren't satisfied, especially as some of the injuries didn't quite fit the accident theory. She fell down the stairs, hit her head and suffered a massive intracranial haemorrhage. It was the bruise marks on her upper arms that made them suspect me. I was questioned but never charged.'

'Oh my *God*,' she said, knowing Nick would never hurt anyone, let alone his daughter. 'I don't know what to say.'

'You don't have to say anything. Just believe me.'

'Of course I believe you, Nick.'

'My theory is that she ran downstairs to answer the front door, but tripped at the top.' He shook his head as if he still couldn't believe it. 'A delivery driver had put a card through the letterbox. They'd written down the time of the visit, which pretty much tallied with the estimated time of her death. Isobel was alone at the time. While Jess could prove where she was, I couldn't. It didn't help that a neighbour made a statement saying that I was home, that he'd heard shouting, although he later retracted it as he was uncertain.' Nick took a deep breath, drinking more tea.

'You don't have to talk about it if you don't want.'

Nick shrugged. 'Isobel was home alone most afternoons because Jess and I were too damned busy to be there for her after school. I was working all hours at the restaurant, and then I discovered Jess's affair.' He dragged his hands down his face, sucking in a deep breath. For the first time, Claire noticed the empty space where a ring used to be. 'The same neighbour also told the police he'd heard me yelling a few days before Isobel died, that he saw her running out of the house in tears and that I'd chased after her, grabbing her in a threatening way. True, I did chase after her, but I didn't want to hurt her. She'd fled the house because she heard me yelling at her mother. I'd just found out about the affair. It was her mother she was angry at, not me. Losing Isobel finished Jess and me off.'

'You should have called me, Nick,' she said. Her words echoed between them.

'I'm doing OK. I have the business to focus on and the divorce will be finalised soon. It's all about piecing back together some kind of life.'

Claire didn't think he sounded OK at all.

'I considered calling you for a long time,' he said. Claire's hand itched to take hold of his again, but she didn't. 'In fact, you were the first person I thought of phoning after it had happened. I knew you'd have listened, let me come and stay, given me space to grieve.'

'Of course I would, Nick.' Claire realised how close they were sitting to each other.

'But you have your own life,' he went on, looking around the kitchen. 'And I know it's up to me to make a new one for myself now. Fill the hole that Isobel left with something else.'

Claire took Nick's hand again, despite the nagging voice in her head.

'Or some*one* else,' he added, just as Maggie came through the back door.

CHAPTER FORTY-FOUR

By 9 a.m. everyone except Jason regrouped at the farm after an early search. There was no news to report. Maggie was outside smoking when PC Wyndham telephoned. Shona took the message and hung up, her long fingers still resting on the handset.

'They're going to send some officers up here,' she said quietly, looking worried. 'And she said something about us maybe having to go to the police station too. I don't know how I'm going to convince your father this is normal.'

'Convince me about what?' Patrick was scowling in the doorway.

'Dad, it's Rain. She's still not been found. The police might need some of us to go down to the station,' Claire said.

He went to the window and stared out. 'They want to know which one of us killed her.'

'No, Pat, it's not like that,' Angus said. 'It's just routine. Probably for elimination prints or to take statements.'

Claire was grateful her uncle and aunt were there. They'd moved to Devon a few years ago but had always been a big part of their lives as children. She'd spent some of her school holidays helping Jenny with the boarding kennels she owned behind their bungalow in Trevellin, or working the petrol pumps in Angus's garage if there weren't many dogs to look after. Sometimes Lenni would come and help her feed the dogs. At the end of a long day, they'd go home with the smell of engine oil in their noses and the sound of barking ringing in their ears.

'No, it's not like that at all, Dad,' she added, staring out of the window with him.

When Claire arrived at the police station, she was taken to an interview room located down a grey, lino-clad corridor. She was shown into an equally grey and sparsely furnished room where the two officers from the night before were sitting on one side of a small table. They glanced up from the thick file that sat between them, PC Wyndham beckoning for her to sit down. But Claire's limbs were suddenly heavy and unmovable, her eyes fixed on the stack of papers on the table. The name Eleanor Lucas was printed in an old-fashioned font on a peeling sticky label. Claire swallowed. Her mouth was dry. She looked at the officer, unable to speak.

'Please, sit down.'

Finally, she managed to pull out the chair and lower herself onto it. 'That's my sister's file,' she whispered, hardly daring to hope they'd had news after all these years. Seeing the papers, it was as if Lenni herself was on the table.

'My boss worked on this,' PC Wyndham explained, patting the files. 'I was discussing your friend's daughter with her when I came on shift. I told her where Rain was staying and she remembered the farm and your sister's case.'

Claire tried to recall the many officers and detectives who were in and out that summer. Their faces had melted into a puddle now, just one formless memory who were called the police, rather than individual names.

'I don't understand,' Claire said.

'My boss made us aware of some similarities between the cases.'

Claire held her breath, but her lungs gave way and she made a hiccupping sound instead.

'We wanted to talk to you about your sister, given what's happened,' PC Holt said, sipping from a polystyrene cup. They each had one.

'If you think it will help,' Claire said, unable to ask outright if they thought there was a link to Rain going missing. 'Are you reopening the case?'

'Eleanor went missing from Trevellin Beach aged thirteen,' PC Wyndham said, her finger lightly tracking details in the papers. Neither officer answered Claire's question. 'It says she'd gone off alone to buy an ice cream?'

Claire nodded, feeling the familiar knot of guilt on hearing the words "gone off alone". 'Yes, that's right.'

'You and your brother Jason were looking after Eleanor?'

'Yes.' Her voice was turned down to a whisper as she recalled the grilling she'd received over the following days. It had been so intense she wondered if she was actually guilty of a crime.

Over and over again, she'd told them every shred of information she could recall – from the shade of pink she'd painted Lenni's toenails that morning right down to the length of the first and last kiss she'd shared with Nick in the breakers. *And I remember a green and white plastic bag blowing along the beach as Lenni walked off and someone had a transistor playing Radio 1 and the sea was particularly full of seaweed that day…* None of it had been helpful. Nothing she'd said had led to Lenni being found.

'Rain Carr came to Trevellin with her mother Maggie early on Saturday morning.' Claire was aware of PC Wyndham's voice again. She focused, trying to listen, trying to be helpful. 'She was staying at the farm, the property owned by your parents.'

'Yes.'

The day they tried to accuse one or both of her parents of harming Lenni was the day, deep down, they knew she would never come back. For the police to make such monstrous allegations, the family knew they'd got nothing better to go on. Their leads had run out. Down at the police station, Patrick and Shona were each battered by a flood of questions and accusations – that Lenni had had an accident and they'd hidden her body, that she was a naughty, disruptive child and they wanted rid of her, that Patrick had abused her and Lenni was threatening to tell. As the detectives ripped apart their lives, Shona and Patrick remained stoic and unflinching, knowing they were innocent.

'There's an age gap between the girls,' PC Wyndham said.

'How is that relevant?' Claire asked, touching her forehead. She felt dizzy and lightheaded.

'We're just noting some basic facts.'

'Of course.' Claire wasn't prepared for this reopening of old wounds, though she and the others had already clocked the similarities. They just hadn't wanted to acknowledge them.

'Several witnesses confirmed that Eleanor arrived at the beach shop and bought an ice cream.' The constable was scanning the file as she spoke. 'But then nothing. No more sightings. An ice cream cone was later found with her saliva on it. Its location suggested she'd intended taking the shortcut back to the beach, down the shingle path.'

'Mum always told us not to go that way,' Claire said. 'And I told her a hundred times too. But I don't see how this can help find Rain. Lots of people buy ice cream at the beach. It's surely just a coincidence.'

PC Holt tapped his pen against the edge of the desk in a slow, unpredictable beat. 'Eleanor's shorts were also found,' he said, fixing his eyes on her. 'Denim shorts,' he stated, as if the fabric was significant. 'There were sporadic footprints too, matching the size and type of shoe that Eleanor was wearing. Plastic sandals bought from Woolworths, the records show. The prints led to the area east of the cliff path towards a remote car park.'

'It's a place where couples often go to… you know…' Claire said quietly.

'Those findings suggested she was possibly being carried off, that there was a struggle. Her feet were sometimes on the ground, sometimes not.'

Claire suddenly felt sick. She hadn't known this. She couldn't keep the image of Lenni being grabbed, being dragged off screaming, from her mind. She wondered if her parents had been told and chose to shield her from the truth. 'Why are you telling me this?'

'Sometimes examining old evidence can throw light on new.'

'I just want to know if you're reopening my sister's case,' Claire said, desperate.

'That's not a decision we're making right now,' PC Wyndham said. 'But any cold case can be reopened if new evidence comes to light.'

Claire thought about the implications. What if the same person who'd taken Lenni had also taken Rain? So far, she'd imagined Maggie's daughter going off in a strop and getting into trouble somehow – whether that involved the cliffs, the sea or another person. She'd prayed the coastguard would have found her by now, cut off on a sandbank or stranded on a jut of rock by the tide. But as the hours went by, that was seeming less and less likely.

'There was one thing in the file we hoped you could help us with, Mrs Rodway,' PC Holt said. He sat upright, stretching out his shoulders. 'Rain's mother said that she has a tattoo on her ankle.'

'I don't think Maggie was very happy about it,' Claire said. 'She's not strict in many ways, but I know she didn't like it.'

'Did you ever see the tattoo?'

'No, I didn't. Not properly anyway. I was aware it was there, but I didn't want to stare because Maggie had told me they'd had words about it. A big argument, actually. Why are you asking?' Claire suddenly went cold. What if this was actually for identification purposes and they wanted to check with her first before upsetting Maggie?

PC Wyndham retrieved a piece of paper from another, slimmer file. She slid it across so Claire could see it. 'What do you make of this?'

There was a symbol drawn in Biro as if whoever had done it had gone over and over it until they'd almost scored through the paper. Goose bumps broke out all over her body. 'Yes, it's familiar,' she said, looking away.

The officer then pulled an old, slightly creased colour photograph from Eleanor's file. It was about six by eight inches and had a fold on one corner as if it had been put away carelessly. The image showed a silver charm, about half an inch long, sitting on a pale surface with a ruler beneath it. Claire stared at it, then looked back at the sketch. It was a moment before she breathed properly. 'I don't understand…' she began, though wondered if she did. 'That's Lenni's charm. The one from her necklace. We both had one.'

'That's correct,' PC Holt said. 'And this,' he said, tapping the paper, 'is what Rain has tattooed on her ankle. Maggie drew it for us.'

Claire nodded slowly. 'They're the same.' The officers didn't say anything. Rather they looked at Claire, waiting for her to continue. 'This charm… Mum and Dad gave Lenni and me one each.' She kept her eyes on the photograph. 'They were on silver chains,' she continued. 'But Lenni couldn't stop fiddling with hers and broke it within a day. She was so upset so she carried it around in her pocket instead. I told her she'd end up losing it.' Claire felt the first sting of tears. 'They weren't valuable, but we loved them.' And Lenni had indeed lost her little charm – just not in the way she'd expected. 'I eventually lost my necklace too,' Claire went on. 'I always kept it in my jewellery box, but one day it just vanished. I didn't really look very hard for it, I suppose.'

'So,' PC Holt went on. 'An ankh charm and an ankh tattoo.'

Claire's mouth went dry. She had no idea what they were implying.

'What's it called, Phil?' PC Wyndham asked her colleague.

'It's a hieroglyph,' he replied, tapping the photo again. 'Some Egyptian thing. I went to Sharm El Sheikh diving a couple of years ago. They're all over the place there.'

PC Wyndham arced her head in understanding.

'It says here that Eleanor's charm was found about four inches away from her shorts. In the grass. The shorts were wet from sea water...' His finger tracked down the report, skim-reading the information.

'I don't understand. If you know something, please tell me.' Claire remembered the nasty message and the incident at Galen Cottage, wishing she or Jason had called the police. If she said anything now, they'd wonder why she hadn't mentioned it sooner.

'Apart from the charm, does the symbol have any particular meaning to you or your family?' PC Holt asked, crushing his empty cup and tossing it in the bin. He missed and it spun onto the floor. 'It's also known as the key of life.'

Claire shook her head slowly, but all she could think of was the scrawl she'd spotted etched into the dirt on the back of her car.

CHAPTER FORTY-FIVE

Callum arrived at the police station just after eleven. 'Will this take long? I have a busy clinic.'

'Shouldn't do,' the desk sergeant said without looking up. 'Take a seat.'

He was about to demand they deal with him right away when Nick and Claire were shown back out into the waiting area by a young officer. Claire didn't look great, he thought – grey circles beneath her eyes, her hair all over the place.

'Hey, love,' she said, coming up and giving him a quick squeeze. 'They've just interviewed Nick.' She sighed, sounding worn out. 'He couldn't really tell them much more than they already know. And don't worry, the fingerprinting doesn't take long,' she said, sensing his impatience. 'You'll be back at the hospital in no time.'

'I have a clinic,' he said, glancing at his watch. The more he thought about it, the more he realised it was actually all Claire's fault. While that stupid girl Rain had been nothing but trouble since she'd arrived, the bottom line was that Claire should have been in his bed. She should have been there with him. He took her by the elbow, guiding her over to the window away from Nick. 'Under the circumstances, I think it's best if you send everyone home.' He spoke quietly, glancing back over his shoulder.

'What are you talking about, Cal?' She shrugged out of his grip, frowning and looking up at him. 'I can't possibly tell them to go. They're my friends and family.'

Callum swallowed. He would have to make it clearer. 'Claire, you need to get rid of everyone. Today.'

'Get rid?' Claire said. 'You expect me to send Maggie home without her daughter?'

'Keep your voice down,' Callum replied, folding his arms. 'Look, love, I didn't want to have to tell you this but...' He trailed off, trying to sound calmer. 'Maggie came on to me.' He watched the shock spread over her face. 'I know, I know, I'm as uncomfortable about it as you are. But I have to be honest with you.' He paused as she took it in.

'No, Cal, Maggie would never do that.' Claire's eyes were full of disbelief. 'You must be mistaken. I know she's a bit crazy sometimes, but she'd never do anything to hurt me.'

'I wouldn't have said anything at all if all this other mess hadn't blown up. I would have just let it go.'

'I don't know what to say. Are you sure?' Claire rubbed her temples.

'Maggie's inappropriate behaviour tells me that Rain has most likely done the same and hooked up with some lad, going off with him without bothering to tell anyone. The pair of them have no morals or values. They're as bad as each other. It's all a waste of police time.'

'What do you mean by "came on to you"?' Claire had tears in her eyes.

'The details are unimportant, love. Let's just end this fiasco now.'

'But they're important to me.' Her voice wavered. 'I need to know, Cal.'

'She's always had a thing for me, you know that.'

'No, I didn't.'

'She tried to kiss me. Remember on the first night, I went down to the cellar to get wine? She was on the steps when I came back up. It was dark. When I rejected her, she put her hand on my... you know, down there.'

Claire covered her mouth, a puzzled look on her face. 'She was going down to the cellar? But anyway, she wouldn't do that, Cal. Not Maggie.'

'It's true, love. When I told her no, she threatened to tell you that I'd come on to her instead.'

Claire looked into his eyes as he took her gently by the shoulders, planting a kiss on her forehead.

'Everything will be OK,' he said. 'But let's do the right thing and send everyone home.' He pulled her close again, her head resting against the pounding knot of his heart. A moment later, he was called through by an officer. As he was being led off, Callum glanced back over his shoulder and saw his wife leaving the station with Nick.

'Dr Rodway,' PC Wyndham said with a small sigh. 'I understand your need to get back to the hospital, but this won't take long. And right now, time is of the essence.'

Another officer had already explained that they were taking elimination prints from everyone as a precaution. A young PC took the thumb of his right hand and rolled it over an ink pad. 'I have two operations scheduled this afternoon,' he said, glowering at the mess. 'This stuff had bloody well better come off.'

'Just relax, Dr Rodway,' the officer said. 'Let me do the rolling and pressing.'

Callum's hand stiffened in protest. 'It's *Mr* Rodway.'

'How long have you known Maggie Carr and her daughter, Mr Rodway?' PC Holt asked, while his other hand was being done.

'We've been over this already,' he said. 'I've known Maggie since she was a child, but only met the girl two days ago.'

'You're ten years older than Claire and her friends, is that right?'

'Correct.' Callum failed to see the importance.

'So when Claire was a child of eight or nine, you were a grown man of eighteen.'

'Yes,' Callum replied curtly. 'If you call eighteen being a grown man.'

'Didn't it seem a bit odd?' he went on. 'Hanging out with children?'

'I didn't hang out with children. I knew of Claire and her friends and their families, that's all. I went away to medical school, and when I returned to the area years later, I met Claire in an entirely different context. She was an adult by then.'

'I see. Your wife told me that you used to babysit some of the village children when you were a teenager?'

'Once or twice,' Callum said, feeling a sweat break out on his forehead.

'Who did you babysit?'

Callum shrugged, trying to remember. 'A couple of local kids. Plus Claire and her brother Jason.'

'And Eleanor? Did you ever babysit Eleanor Lucas?'

'Yes, but she was always in bed. I never saw her.'

'Can you tell me why your wife organised this reunion?' PC Wyndham asked.

'Her father is ill,' he replied. 'He was diagnosed with Alzheimer's a few months ago and Claire thought it would be good for him if old friends and family came to stay. She hoped it would help with his memory.'

'And do you think it could help, from a medical point of view?'

'Yes, it's called reminiscence therapy and can be effective for some patients. I have occupational therapists on the brain injury ward who use similar techniques.'

'Such as?'

'Playing a patient's favourite music from the past can be helpful, looking at old photographs, talking about childhood events, remembering their careers, that kind of thing. Family members can help with this too. In fact, it's more effective coming from them.'

'So your wife was quite right in organising the reunion for the benefit of her father's health?'

'Yes, most definitely,' he said. 'I was all for the idea.'

PC Wyndham was silent for a moment before plucking a tissue from a box. She handed it to Callum to wipe his fingers. 'So, tell me, then, Mr Rodway. Why did my desk sergeant just overhear you telling – sorry, *ordering* – your wife to send her friends home immediately?'

Callum called his secretary, telling her to reschedule his first couple of patients.

'We appreciate the extra time you're sparing us,' PC Wyndham said, once they'd gone into the interview room.

'Did I have a choice?' Callum adjusted his tie, laying his ink-stained hands flat on the table in front of him. His back was straight in the uncomfortable plastic chair.

'Not really,' PC Holt said, making Callum want to punch the smug grin straight off his face.

'I'm sure my patients won't mind waiting another hour or so, given that most of them have been waiting months to see me anyway.' He folded his arms. It felt better that way.

'We're trying to build up a picture of the current situation, as well as any links to the past,' PC Wyndham said.

Callum nodded, wondering if this was a good time to ask for a solicitor. But doing that would only drag things out.

'Some of these questions might seem direct, but it's nothing to worry about.' She underlined something with her finger in the stack of papers between them. PC Holt nodded, blank-faced. 'Can you start by telling us where you were when Eleanor Lucas went missing?'

'Eleanor Lucas?' Callum couldn't help the laugh. 'After twenty-one years?' He shook his head. 'Claire and her friends were at the beach. Eleanor went off on her own. That was the last anyone ever saw of her.'

'I asked where *you* were at the time, Mr Rodway.'

'You expect me to remember? I'd be making it up.'

'Let's try a slightly different question, then,' PC Holt said. 'How did you first find out Eleanor had gone missing?'

'I was staying with my mother at the time. She told me. News spread around the village very quickly.'

'You'd come back to Cornwall just a week before Eleanor went missing, is that right?' PC Wyndham glanced down at the file.

'Yes, that's correct.'

'So your memory is actually proving to be quite good, wouldn't you say?'

'If I'm reminded, then yes,' Callum replied. He was a surgeon and refused to be rattled by an idiot cop.

'Why did you return to the southwest?' PC Wyndham continued.

'I was taking up a position at the Royal Cornwall Hospital. I was staying with my mother until I started the job.'

'I see. There are notes in the file indicating that immediately following Eleanor's disappearance, you also went missing. Where did you go for three days without telling anyone, Mr Rodway?'

'And why,' PC Holt added.

'I didn't go missing,' Callum replied, wishing he actually could. 'I went camping and fishing near Penzance. I didn't bother telling anyone where I'd gone. I wanted time alone before I started my new job.'

'It seems you remember many details very clearly, yet you have trouble recalling exactly where you were the day Eleanor disappeared.'

'I was most likely at my mother's house.'

'When did you begin a relationship with your wife?'

'It was later that summer, possibly early autumn. As you can imagine, Claire was in a terrible state. Her sister had gone missing and her friends were all heading off to university or college. She decided to defer her place for a year, but never ended up going. We met, grew closer and things developed. By then our age difference didn't seem so great.' Callum remembered how she'd fallen in love with him in such a short time.

'Can you tell us how Eleanor got on with her parents?'

'I told you, I didn't know her well. But I'd heard that she was an unusual child.' Callum paused. He didn't want to say the wrong thing. 'She was a bit of a loner. People used to say she was a bit slow. I don't think she was allowed much freedom. Shona and Patrick can only be accused of doing one bad thing to their daughter.'

'And what would that be?' PC Wyndham asked.

'They loved her too much,' he replied, thinking he'd leave it at that.

CHAPTER FORTY-SIX

Claire arrived back at the farm to find Maggie sitting at the kitchen table with her head resting on folded arms. Shona was doing her best to comfort her while a young officer that Claire didn't recognise sat beside her.

'Hi,' she said to the officer, dropping her bag and keys onto a chair. 'I'm Claire, Maggie's friend.' She stood behind Maggie, about to put her hands on her shoulders. But she stopped, Callum's words flaring through her mind.

'PC Jenny Watts,' said the young woman, rising a little and offering her hand to shake. Claire reckoned she didn't look much older than Rain. 'I've been assigned as Maggie's family liaison officer. I'm here to keep you updated, try to answer any questions, that kind of thing.'

Maggie blew her nose as Claire sat down beside her. 'Have there been any developments?'

'Not as yet,' PC Watts said. 'But we're doing everything we can.'

'OK,' was all Claire managed to say, almost inaudibly. Her mind burned with questions for both the officer and Maggie, but silence won over in case she said the wrong thing.

'Normally, I'd ask to take a look in Rain's bedroom,' PC Watts said. 'Or maybe we'd go through some of her stuff together, just in case it helped jog a thought about where she might be. But, of course, it's hard with you being away from home…' She trailed off, glancing over to the door.

'We'll find her,' Patrick said, joining them. 'We don't lose hope in this family.' His hands were on his hips as he stood at the window, gazing out.

'Dad,' Claire said. 'How are you feeling?' She wished she could somehow fix him in the present. 'Let me make you a cup of tea.' She hated how patronising she sounded.

'Not too bad, love,' he said. 'But I'll make the tea. You look after…' He stopped and stared at Maggie, squinting, licking his lips as if he could taste what his mind was searching for. 'You look after Maggie there.'

'Thanks, Dad,' Claire replied, watching as he opened half a dozen kitchen cupboards before realising that the mugs were hanging on hooks on the dresser, as they had done forever.

'I just went up to my house,' she told Maggie, sitting opposite. She stared at the empty table between them, trying not to think about what Callum had told her. 'I had to let a couple of officers inside. They wanted a quick look around, so I left them to it. They're coming down here after, said they'll be doing house-to-house enquiries in the village as well as foot searches.'

Claire wasn't sure why a search of her home was necessary, but she wasn't about to question their motives. She didn't like the thought that someone might have been in there, maybe even taken Rain against her will if she'd gone back up there while everyone else was still at the beach. Claire doubted there would be such a police presence here if it hadn't been for what had gone before.

'Mags, did you manage to speak to, you know… Peter?' Claire asked quietly. PC Watts was listening to everything.

Maggie looked up. She'd stopped crying, as if there were simply no more tears left. She cupped a glass, the water inside quivering from her shaking hands. 'No,' she said. 'I left a message. I don't suppose he'll call back.'

'But she's his daughter.' Claire had waited until PC Watts had gone to the toilet, and even then she whispered, leaning across the table.

'It's not that simple, Claire.'

'Mags, you don't think that Peter came and took Rain, do you?'

'God, no,' Maggie replied with certainty. 'He wouldn't want her.'

'If this goes on much longer, I think the police will want to contact him anyway.'

'You really think so?' Maggie's face was tight with worry, as if the long-lasting consequences of the affair had only just occurred to her. For a fleeting moment, Claire wondered if what Callum said was true, that values meant nothing to her.

'I'd be prepared, that's all,' she said, nodding and wondering just how prepared Peter's wife was to have her life blown apart. 'Look, Mags, if Rain doesn't turn up soon, the police will be all over everything.' Claire glanced at the officer as she came back into the room.

But Maggie's attention was suddenly focused on the back door. She stood up, kicking out the chair behind her and gripping the table. 'Is there news?'

'Is there somewhere private we can talk?' PC Wyndham said, coming straight in after knocking on the open door. Her face was blank, giving nothing away.

'Please, use the snug again,' Claire said, wishing she could take back all the thoughts she'd just had. As Maggie left the room, she noticed Patrick's expression. How many times had he and her mum greeted various officers and detectives during the weeks and months after Lenni's disappearance? Too many to count, but each time they'd been buoyed up by the possibility of good news only to have their hopes dashed.

'Christ, I hope she's not come to tell her…' Claire brought her hand to her mouth.

'They do that job in pairs, love,' Patrick replied.

Claire forced the thought from her mind and went around the kitchen, gathering all the mugs and glasses that had been used over the morning. She needed to keep busy. She put them into the big Belfast sink, running a bowl of hot soapy water, and set to washing up. She wondered how many hours her mother had stood at the same sink, washing, rinsing and drying countless plates, cutlery, pots and pans. Shona had been a worker all her life and Claire couldn't think of a time when her mother had ever been idle.

Between them, her parents had saved Trevellin from bankruptcy, their dedication and hard work re-establishing the dairy herd within a couple of years. She recalled how her dad would leave the house before they even got up for school and come back home mid-evening reeking of his beloved cows and the scent of their warm, creamy milk.

'Claire...' Her father's deep voice resonated through the kitchen. She turned, pulling off her rubber gloves in time to see PC Wyndham leaving by the back door. Maggie was standing perfectly still, hands clasped under her chin, looking as if she was the only person left in the entire world.

'What is it, Maggie? Is there news?' Claire went up to her, but Maggie just stood, refusing to move, apart from a small tremor that ran the length of her body.

CHAPTER FORTY-SEVEN

Back When I Remembered

'Hello,' I say next time I'm not alone. 'Am I going home now?' My throat tightens as if a boiled sweet is stuck in there. That happened once and Mummy made me drink hot water to melt it.

There's no reply but I'm given some colouring pens and a pad of paper instead. I like drawing. I also like practising my writing, so I write a letter to Mummy. I know she'll be worried sick about me, while Daddy will be angry, shouting at everyone, shouting at the police if they've been called to find me. But mostly he'll be hating himself for being so careless, for allowing bad things to happen to me. Jason will hide in the barn, chucking his ball against the wall and not wanting to talk to anyone, while Claire will be sad. She was meant to be looking after me.

'Will you give this to my Mummy?' I ask. The letter is snatched from my hand and nothing more is said. I wonder if they think I'm dead, if they've given up on me.

When I'm alone again, I scream as loud as I can. I keep on screaming all day long until my throat bleeds and my eyes don't see properly. Jason used to call me a little firecracker, waiting to explode. He was right, I am about to explode, although when he said it, it just made me even madder, got me hot and sweaty and hating everything. When things went wrong, if Claire or Jason annoyed me or if something got broken and I couldn't fix it, I'd clench my fists and my cheeks would go scarlet. I'd try to hold it in, but sometimes it bled out of me as if I was leaking badness. Mummy would watch me quietly, allowing me to get rid of the rage, then she'd hug me and talk softly to me. Then Daddy would tuck me into bed with one of his stories until the fizzing inside my chest started to go down. They both knew what to do.

Now, alone, I'm standing beside the tiny sink screaming out my unheard anger. I cry and yell, spinning around and around in mini circles like that lion I saw once at the zoo. I jump as high as I can, slamming my feet onto the floor so tingles shoot up my legs. I hurl myself against the wall and drag my nails down the wooden panelling until splinters push up under my nails and crescents of blood appear.

'Help *me*!' I cry a thousand times, pacing the short length of the room until it seems to close in on me, the walls getting closer together with every step. My eyes swell in and out of focus, transforming the dingy space where I now live into the pretty pink of my bedroom, only to vanish again when I scream even louder. My lungs bubble with sadness and despair. Spit froths between my lips.

'Help, please... help... me.' It's just a whisper now. I fall to the floor until it's over, until the anger has leaked to earth. In my head, Daddy tells me a story. His words calm me and send me to sleep. I do this every day.

CHAPTER FORTY-EIGHT

Callum was between patients when PCs Wyndham and Holt came into the consulting room that afternoon, followed by a very flustered nurse. He glared at them. 'This had better be important. I have ward rounds.' He didn't bother standing up or shaking hands. A nerve twitched under his left eye.

'This shouldn't take long, although you might prefer to speak in private.' PC Wyndham looked back at the nurse.

'Thanks, Megan. You can close the door on your way out.' The nurse did as she was told, looking relieved. 'What won't take long?' Callum pushed back in his chair. 'I've already told you everything I know.'

'Are you certain about that?' PC Holt said, sitting in the patients' chair. PC Wyndham perched on the end of the examination couch, her ankles crossed. 'It's slightly unusual, but under the circumstances we made the decision to send a forensics team to both properties earlier today.'

'And that justifies disturbing a busy surgeon?'

'I'll get straight to the point, Mr Rodway. Rain's fingerprints were found in your bedroom. We'd taken known samples from her phone and other belongings.'

Callum's mouth went dry. 'That would make sense. I saw her in there with my wife. They were chatting.'

'And when was that exactly?' PC Wyndham removed a small notepad from her inside pocket, poised to write.

'They arrived early on Saturday morning, so it was... during the afternoon, I think. Yes, it was Saturday afternoon.'

'What time?'

'About three?' Callum felt as though he was asking them, not telling them.

'Rain's fingerprints were found on your bed frame. Your side of the bed, incidentally.'

Callum felt his mouth twisting into an odd shape, as if he'd temporarily lost control of it. 'Again, that makes perfect sense. Claire and Rain were sitting on the bed – *my* side – while they were chatting.'

'As you know, the bed base has a deep, polished board running around it. There were many fingerprints and finger smear marks found all along one side of it, and the angle of them indicates that she may have been trying to push herself off the bed while lying on her front. An odd position for her to be chatting in, don't you think?'

Callum ignored the look on the officer's face. He wasn't fazed. 'I don't know. I only passed the bedroom doorway. I wasn't there the whole time.' He allowed a moment's silence. 'Are we done now? I really need to see my next patient.'

'Of course,' PC Holt said, standing. 'I'm sure your wife will confirm your story.'

Claire searched for her phone and, remembering she'd left it charging in the hallway, slipped it into her back pocket. Everyone had gone up to the Old Stables, having vacated the farmhouse so the officers could look around, take prints, perhaps get an insight into Rain's whereabouts from her belongings. Given that was where she had actually been staying, Claire expected them to take a little longer there.

'How they expect to find anything useful, I don't know,' Patrick grumbled. They'd been discussing reasons why the police were focusing on the two properties so early, concluding that if Rain didn't come back soon, then their investigations would be scaled up and any evidence in the houses might, by that time, have been accidentally destroyed.

After PC Wyndham had left, Maggie had just stood there trembling, looking fragile and unable to talk coherently. In the following few hours, she simply sat where she was told, drank tea when it was made for her, walked up to Claire's house when the others took her, all with the liaison officer glued to her side. Once or twice, Claire wondered if Maggie was about to tell her something, as though she needed to get something out, but when it didn't come, she didn't press her. She didn't understand why Maggie wasn't making a greater effort to contact Rain's father.

Between her childminder and Marcus, Amy was being taken care of. Claire didn't want her upset by the goings-on – the reunion was now far from the fun gathering she'd planned. Shona was making soup in Claire's kitchen, though her heart wasn't in it, evident by the way she slowly stirred the pot, dropping in a few more roughly chopped vegetables she'd found in Claire's fridge.

'Pat,' Shona said, turning towards him. 'Things are done differently these days.' She chopped more carrots – anything to keep busy.

Claire stared at her phone, cursing the missed call. 'Unknown number,' she whispered, her stomach churning.

'They'll leave a message if it's important,' Greta said, passing around yet more cups of tea.

Angus had decided that he and Jenny should go home now that Patrick was feeling more himself. 'Shona doesn't need more mouths to feed,' he said, when Jenny thought they should stay to help. Claire hugged them as they left, feeling terrible that they were leaving under such circumstances. But the police had said they wouldn't be needed for further statements, and Jenny promised to phone later that evening for an update.

As she watched them drive off, Claire's phone pinged with a voice message. She was about to listen to it, but Nick, Jason and Marcus blustered back in, all talking at once. Maggie mustered enough energy to look up, having just left another message at Rain's father's office. He seemed unreachable.

'We just spoke to the lad who works at the surf shop. His name's Blake,' Jason said. 'He told us that he thought he saw a girl like Rain up near the shop on Sunday afternoon. He's already been interviewed by the police.'

'Why didn't they tell us?' Claire said, remembering how any information about Lenni had been fed to her parents on a need-to-know basis.

Maggie stood up, gripping the back of her chair.

'Apparently, Blake saw a girl getting into a car. An old white van, to be precise. It was about 4.30 p.m., he remembers, because he was outside having a smoke and thinking of packing up the surfboards as business was quiet.' Jason took the tea handed to him. 'Though judging by what Blake was smoking just now, I'd question his memory.'

'Is this good news or bad?' Patrick replied. He stared at his son for a moment before turning away, realising what he'd done several moments after the shock registered on Jason's face; his father had actually spoken to him.

'If there's anything significant to report, Maggie will be the first to know,' PC Watts said in a tone that urged them not to speculate.

'But Rain would never get into a van with anyone,' Maggie said quietly. 'Not unless she knew them.' There was silence as everyone digested what that meant. No one dared ask the obvious, whether Blake had seen a struggle.

'That's good, then, Mags,' Claire said. 'They're making progress.' Claire turned her mobile over and over in her hand. 'And perhaps it *was* someone she knew. A friend from school or something. It's a small world.' She stopped. The possibility of Rain bumping into someone familiar in Trevellin when she'd lived most of her life in a boarding school hundreds of miles away was extremely unlikely. Claire's phone pinged another alert, so she ducked out into the hallway to listen to the message.

Claire, it's me. We need to talk urgently. Come to the staff canteen as soon as you can. Text me when you're here. Claire thought the message had ended, but then Callum added, *And keep quiet about it.*

She hung up, puzzled. It almost didn't sound like him. She'd never heard him scared before. She went back into the kitchen, forcing the frown from her face. 'Jeff called,' she said, staring at the floor. 'There's an important contract and he can't find it.' She felt the colour rising in her cheeks. 'I'll have to dash into the office quickly.' She hated lying. 'But I won't be long,' she added, before anyone could say anything. She grabbed her bag and keys, wondering why Callum had sounded so insistent.

CHAPTER FORTY-NINE

Callum walked briskly down the hospital corridor towards the canteen to meet Claire, the nausea rising in his stomach. He couldn't face the sandwich his secretary had fetched him for lunch, could barely keep down the coffee she'd left on his desk.

'Darling,' he said, holding out his arms. She was sitting at a table in the corner of the canteen, the place already filling up with the lunchtime rush. She stood up as soon as she saw him, her hands pressing lightly against his chest as they embraced. The fresh smell of her hair grounded him, making him believe everything was going to be fine.

'What's going on?' she said. 'You sounded really worried.'

'Sit down.'

'Sure, but…' Her face folded with worry.

'Those cops came to see me again.'

'Here at work?'

He nodded. 'I was about to go on ward rounds. It was very unprofessional.'

'It might be worth a complaint.' She reached out, touching his hand.

'Look, I'll get straight to the point.' His mouth went dry. 'It turns out they've found Rain's fingerprints in our bedroom. They were asking me if I knew how they got there.'

'What?'

He paused, allowing her to process the implications. He wasn't about to spell it out, but he also needed to be sparing with the truth. It was for her own good.

'I mean… but… how?'

'Exactly.' He locked on to her eyes. 'It must mean that she was snooping about in there.' He sighed heavily, shaking his head. 'It's horrible, and the last thing Maggie needs to be dealing with under the circumstances, but I want you to check your jewellery box. Don't make a big thing about it. There's bound to be an explanation.'

'I don't understand…' Claire was squinting, frowning, thinking. 'Rain wouldn't steal from us. No way.'

'I know. I don't want to believe it either. But why else would she have been in our bedroom?'

Claire swept her hair off her face. 'For any number of reasons. It doesn't mean she's a thief.' Callum watched as she tried to assimilate the news. She shook her head, biting her lip. He knew her default setting was trust.

He allowed himself another sigh and squeezed her hand. 'Look, it probably wasn't the right thing to do, but I felt I had to say something to protect the silly girl. And even after everything, I felt sorry for Maggie too. Her daughter's gone missing.'

Claire was looking right at him, studying his expression. 'I know, but… after what you said Maggie did to you?'

'They've both clearly got issues, love. I'm not heartless.' Callum tilted his head, touching Claire under her chin. 'And Maggie's not exactly a great maternal influence. Why do you think Amy is such a delight?' He stroked her cheek.

'So what did you tell the police?'

'This is where it gets tricky,' he replied, unable to hide the tension in his voice. 'I said she'd been in our bedroom with you.'

'With me? Why?' Claire recoiled.

'It was a spur of the moment thing. I wanted to make things easier for her. I said I'd seen you both chatting in there on Saturday and that's how her prints must have got in our room.' He watched as Claire absorbed the news. 'It's not going to make a scrap of difference to whether they find her or not, but it might make things easier for Rain if it turns out she has stolen something. The insurance will cover it, so we don't need to make a big song and dance.'

'I'm really not sure that's right, Cal.' Claire was quiet, thoughtful. 'Why didn't you just tell them the truth, that you didn't know why Rain was in our room? What if it does have something to do with her disappearance? I can't believe you lied to the police.'

'Look, I told you. I didn't want to get her into trouble. She was obviously snooping. I thought I was doing the right thing covering for her.'

Claire frowned. 'No, it's not right at all.' She stared up at him. 'Oh God, it's all so awful.' Her voice wavered. 'It's far too much like…' She covered her face, then looked up again, her eyes welling with tears.

'Love, not now. People are staring.' Callum patted her on the shoulder. 'It'll all work out fine, you'll see. I just need you to tell the police that Rain was chatting with you in our bedroom on Saturday afternoon, OK?'

'No, Cal, I can't do it. No way,' she said, pulling a tissue from her bag and blowing her nose. 'I'm sorry.'

'Love,' he replied, taking her by the elbows. 'I honestly don't think we have a choice, not after I stuck my neck out and covered for her. You want to get me into trouble?' He sighed heavily.

'No, of course not. But what if—'

'There are no what ifs, Claire. Tell them you were in our bedroom with Rain on Saturday and it'll all be sorted.'

'I don't know…' Claire felt the grip on her elbows tighten a little. She gave a small nod. 'Maybe you're right.'

Callum stared at her for a second, measuring the depth of her conviction. 'Good girl. I have to get back to work now,' he said, kissing her on the top of her head. 'I'll see you at home later.' Then he turned and strode back to the neurology department, feeling a fraction less distracted.

CHAPTER FIFTY

Nick felt his blood pressure rising, the pulse in his temple ticking, his jaw clenching. 'I already told you I'd contacted the council about this, that we should just proceed. Those were my instructions, Trev.' His heart thumped as he paced around Claire's kitchen. He thought everyone was out, but had he just heard a noise? Was someone back? He didn't want to be overheard, not with everything else going on.

'You didn't need to check with them, Trev. Just continue with the cellar as we agreed.' Nick's throat tightened around the lie. He breathed out heavily, wondering if his lungs might collapse from stress. If he didn't get the basement into a useable, basically habitable state, he didn't know what he'd do. He stepped out into the garden. The sun flared out from behind a cloud, making him squint. He didn't want to get Trevor into trouble, but what choice did he have? Money and time were running out.

'You'll have to trust me on this one. I'll take any flak.' There was a pause as Trevor thought about the implications. Nick could never reveal why he wanted the work done. No one would understand.

'Fine. How much?' he said, knowing when he was beaten. 'Yes, it'll be cash. Just get the job done, Trevor. I want it tanked, wired and hooked up to mains drains with a water supply as soon as possible. And make sure it's fully soundproofed. I'll give you the money when I return.' Then Nick stifled an incredulous laugh. 'How am I supposed to get it to you today? I'm in Cornwall.' A pause. 'Today, then. I'll call you when I'm in London.' And he hung up, red-faced, deflated, angry and absolutely terrified that his plans were falling apart.

✴

'Let me fill you in,' PC Wyndham said to Maggie, pulling out a chair for her in Claire's kitchen. Nick had just left, looking concerned, and Maggie sat down, struggling to hold her head up. It felt as though it had doubled in weight.

'We've managed to speak to several of Rain's friends, but none of them have heard from her since Saturday evening. Katie has been away in France but is back now, confirming that Rain hadn't replied to her most recent texts. She said it was out of character, and she was planning on calling her soon. Phone records confirm all this.'

Maggie nodded, her eyes fixed on nowhere. Until there was good news, she didn't see how she'd be able to carry on.

'More significantly, though, we believe there was a sighting of her at the surf shop yesterday.'

'Yes, I already know,' Maggie said quietly. 'Shouldn't you be widening the search, doing something else?'

'I can assure you that we're doing everything to find your daughter, Maggie.' She touched her arm. 'It's still relatively early days, don't forget.' She paused, but Maggie said nothing. 'Is there any reason why Rain might have gone off with someone outside the surf shop, Maggie? Do either of you know anyone with a white van, a builder or tradesman, perhaps?'

Maggie narrowed her eyes, focusing on the picture PC Wyndham showed her. It was a big van with rusty wheel arches. Her mind was all over the place, trying to work out who they knew with such a vehicle.

'Blake at the surf shop thought it was a Ford Transit, much like this one. From his description, we believe it's an older model, quite battered.'

'She's just a kid,' Maggie said flatly. 'Of course she doesn't know any tradesmen.'

'What about you? Have you had anyone do any work for you who she could have got close to?'

'She's not like that!' Maggie's eyes pooled with tears. Rain wasn't here to defend herself. 'She's a good girl, a good student and has lots of friends. Her own age,' she added.

'I'm just asking if it's at all possible that she could know someone well enough to go off with them. Someone who drives a van like this.'

'No. Definitely not.' The truth was, Maggie didn't know. With Rain away at boarding school much of the year, it felt as if she was answering questions about a stranger.

'OK.' PC Wyndham nodded. 'Then we need to consider she might have met someone who owned a vehicle like this since you arrived, or…' She slowed before continuing. 'Or, if it was indeed Rain that Blake saw, then we have to consider the possibility that she was forced into the van against her will.'

Maggie let out a whimper. They were finally considering kidnapping. 'She'd never go off with a stranger. And she's not really had a chance to meet anyone down here.'

'What about on Saturday night when she went to Newquay? Did she tell you much about the evening?'

'No, and I didn't ask. She was out all night, but that's not uncommon. I trust her to be sensible. If she's in trouble or needs to get home, I know she'll get a cab or call me.' Maggie was defensive, but suddenly felt like the worst kind of mother.

'Does she drink?'

'Sometimes.'

'I have to ask about drugs too, I'm afraid.'

'No!' Maggie said, palms on the table, half standing up. 'She goes to a good school. She is feisty, yes, and strong-willed, yes. She likes a drink and it's not uncommon for her to be out very late or crash at a friend's house. I know she smokes cigarettes sometimes because I smell them on her. She does her schoolwork and she's popular with her friends. She's had boyfriends in the past, but there's no one special right now. I had an affair with her father, an MP, as you know, and apart from paying her school fees, he wants nothing to do with her.'

Maggie was shaking, her eyes fixed across the room. She just wanted to numb herself until they figured it out. Peter's non-responsiveness was starting to get to her and she wasn't sure how much longer she could keep this up. The door opened and Claire was there, looking concerned after hearing Maggie's raised voice.

'OK,' the officer said gently. 'Mrs Rodway, would you mind if I had a word with you in private now?'

Claire swallowed. 'Of course.' She led the way through to Callum's study and shut the door, trying to remember exactly what he had told her to say. And to decide if she should even say it.

CHAPTER FIFTY-ONE

Nick phoned the bank from the car. Nothing, *nothing* would stand in the way of opening Malone's in September. If it meant going over budget and paying off Trevor to work beneath the council's radar on the other project, then so be it. Five grand wasn't going to make much difference in the scheme of things. He had to keep Trevor quiet somehow.

He'd made his excuses to the others, saying he had to dash back to London to sort out a crisis, which wasn't exactly a lie. A disappointed look swept across Claire's face, momentarily replacing the mask of worry. He promised he'd be back in the morning.

Nick parked a couple of streets away from the bank in Exeter, joining the queue inside. He mulled over what had happened in the last twenty-four hours, his mind flooded with a bittersweet mix of memories he knew were best forgotten as he shuffled forward. He recalled the day Lenni disappeared – horror mixed with the elation he'd felt at him and Claire finally kissing. That beautiful timeless moment when they'd stood waist deep in the sea, their bodies pressing against one another, their lips finally meeting.

Decades later, he could still almost feel the chilly swell of the sea buffeting him as he surfed the waves to impress Claire. He recalled her sauntering down to the beach in her red swimsuit, kicking off her flip-flops at the water's edge. Had she known he was watching her? Aged eighteen, it was their last summer together before they went their separate ways, which only heightened the tension.

Claire had tentatively dipped herself little by little into the chilly sea, getting used to the temperature, while he allowed the current to drag him closer. Somehow his hands had found their way around her waist – God, he remembered the surge of courage that took – and, using the current as an excuse, he drew her closer. She was shivering out spasms of laughter as the waves crashed around them, until he silenced her by pressing his mouth firmly over hers. He felt the resonance of her moan as she settled into the kiss. They'd both wanted it for so long. And they'd have had more of it too, if it hadn't been for Lenni.

Claire felt lightheaded as she stood opposite PC Wyndham in Callum's study. She gripped the back of a chair, bracing herself.

'We're still trying to piece together Rain's exact movements, Mrs Rodway. We know that Rain was, at some point, in your bedroom.' She waited for a reply.

Claire took a breath, going back over what Callum had said. She didn't like it one bit, lying to the police, but it was probably easier to do as he'd told her. 'Yes, that's right. We were having a chat in there. On Saturday.' She swallowed.

The officer nodded. 'And what time would you say that was?'

'Four o'clock,' Claire replied. 'Four to half past four,' she added, trying to sound casual. She was a terrible liar but didn't want to get Callum into trouble, not since he'd seen fit to protect Rain. She hadn't had a chance to check her jewellery box yet, but she couldn't imagine Rain stealing from her. Maggie might be rather slack with ground rules, but she'd brought her daughter up not to be a thief, she was sure of that.

'Where did she go in your bedroom, exactly?'

'Exactly?' Claire's heart raced. Callum hadn't mentioned this. 'She… knocked on the bedroom door while I was in there. I called out for her to come in and she sat down. We had a nice chat.'

'Where did she sit?'

Claire felt her cheeks flush. 'On the chair by the window.' Claire nodded, almost believing it herself. 'I'm not sure how this helps find her though.' She just wanted it to end.

'Believe me, Mrs Rodway,' PC Wyndham said. 'It's amazing what we can glean from a few simple questions.'

Claire didn't like the tone of her voice, and it really wasn't fair that Callum had told her to lie. Perhaps she should just come clean now and say she was mistaken, tell the truth.

'Did she go anywhere else in your bedroom?'

'I don't think so. Maybe she had a quick browse in my wardrobe, that kind of thing.' Claire's cheeks felt on fire now as she tried to cover all bases.

'So, she sat on a chair by the window and not on the bed?'

'Yes,' Claire said immediately. She could hardly contradict what she'd already sounded so sure about. 'That's correct.'

'Did she go into your en-suite bathroom?'

'No,' Claire said less convincingly, hoping that was the right thing to say.

'Thank you, Mrs Rodway. You've been most helpful. I'll also need to speak to Marcus about Saturday night. If you could arrange for him to come down to the station this afternoon, that would be helpful.' She smiled, snapping her notebook shut.

'No problem,' Claire said quietly. She didn't like that her son was going to be questioned – it triggered feelings of her ordeal at the same age – but if it helped find Rain, then they would comply. She knew Marcus had nothing to hide.

She watched as the officer drove away before going upstairs to her bedroom, taking the stairs two at a time. She tentatively opened the lid to her jewellery box, concerned she'd find things missing. She didn't have a great many items, but what she did own were of high value, either pieces given to her by Callum on birthdays and anniversaries, or necklaces and bracelets owned by her grandmother. All were priceless in their own right, and irreplaceable should Rain have done the unthinkable.

Claire breathed out a sigh of relief when she saw that everything was still there. Rain had probably just been in their room out of simple curiosity, or perhaps the other bathroom was occupied and she needed the toilet. She didn't believe it warranted Callum lying to the police and telling her to do the same. Her heart was still thumping from the deception.

She sighed when she saw the underpants and socks strewn on the floor beside Callum's side of the bed. She bent down to pick them up to put in the wash, but something caught her eye. With the bunched-up socks and pants in one hand, she reached under the bed with the other. She pulled out a bangle. A cheap, gaudy thing that certainly didn't belong to her. She turned it round and round, staring at it, not recognising it.

Still unnerved by PC Wyndham's visit, Claire went back downstairs to the kitchen, dumping the dirty laundry in the utility room on the way. Then she went to see how Maggie was, but before she could even ask, Maggie was suddenly on her feet, her mouth wide open as she stared at the bangle Claire had forgotten she was holding.

'Where did you get that?' She reached out, snatching it from her.

'It was upstairs in my bedroom. Why?'

Her face was pale and her eyes sore and red-rimmed. 'Are you certain?'

'Of course. I literally just picked it up from under the bed. Maggie, what's wrong? You look like you've seen a—'

She slumped down in the chair again, clutching her hands against her heart, the bangle encased in her fists. 'It belongs to Rain.'

CHAPTER FIFTY-TWO

Marcus jiggled his leg under the table.

'We need to know everything that happened on Saturday night, Marcus, from the moment you left your grandparents' house,' the woman cop said, after introducing herself. He reckoned she was quite fit for someone her age but forced himself not to think about that. He didn't want his cheeks burning beetroot red.

'No problem,' he replied. 'It was, like, we ate dinner at Nan's place and then Dad drove us to Newquay. There was a house party. It was something to do.' He shrugged.

'Whose idea was it to go to Newquay?'

'Mine, I guess. I'd mentioned it to Rain before she arrived.'

'You'd spoken to Rain before her visit?' the male officer said. Marcus couldn't remember his name, thought it might be Hunt or something.

'Yeah, on Messenger.' Marcus watched as he wrote it down. 'When Mum told me about this reunion thing and mentioned that her friend had a teenage daughter, I looked her up. She was easy to find. We chatted a couple of times.'

'How did she feel about the trip to Cornwall?' PC Wyndham asked.

'She was a bit hacked off about it. It's the summer holidays and she didn't want to spend time with her mum and a load of oldies. She told me she goes to a really posh boarding school and she's, like, got really rich friends that do some pretty cool stuff.'

'Such as?'

Marcus thought for a moment. All she'd done since she'd arrived was moan about not wanting to be at Trevellin. He'd been so busy noticing how far removed her life seemed from his, how hot she was, that he'd actually glossed over the fact she was a bit of a shallow bitch. And now he felt bad for thinking that when she could be dead. Marcus picked at his fingers.

'She told me how she gets invited to stay at her friends' parents' villas in Marbella or the south of France. She went to Africa during the last summer holidays. She goes skiing with her friends every January, goes to New York just before Christmas, and goes to loads of parties at massive country houses. She has lots of friends with Chelsea apartments too, and crashes there after they've been clubbing,' Marcus said, almost proudly, as if by knowing Rain some of her glamorous life had rubbed off on him. 'Skimming stones on the beach at Trevellin's hardly a match.' He tried to ignore the pang of jealousy.

'I see,' the officer replied, making a few notes. 'So, when you got to Newquay, what time was it and who was there? We'll need the address.'

Marcus swallowed. He would have to be careful. 'Dad dropped us off at the party, but…' He reddened. 'But no one really wanted to go so we walked into town to go to Spanx instead. That's me, Rain, Alex and Gary. They're my mates and Spanx is a club.' Marcus reckoned they wouldn't know that. 'When we got in there, it was pretty dead. It was still early, about ten thirty, but the drinks were half price until midnight and entry was free.'

'So you didn't actually go to the party?'

Marcus shook his head, staring at the floor.

'Did Rain have any alcohol?' PC Wyndham asked.

'Yeah. She, like, got tanked really fast.'

'Did you all stick together or did you split up?'

Marcus thought carefully about this question. He'd been going over the evening's events and what to say while his mother drove him to the police station. She'd been going on about Nick having to go back to London or something, but he hadn't been listening.

'Rain went straight onto the dance floor, getting close to anyone who even looked at her. But I kept my eye on her,' he added quickly. 'Besides, she'd got the forty-quid taxi money on her and I'd be the one to get it in the neck if she spent it on booze. She was knocking it back fast.'

'Did she dance with any one person in particular? Did you see her swap numbers or details with anyone?' the woman cop asked.

'Don't think so. But she was being a bit, you know… coming on to anyone who looked at her.' Marcus shrugged, thinking she was no worse than most of the girls he knew. 'But she was just having fun. Me and my mates, we like going to clubs but we're not big on the dancing.' Marcus let out a nervous laugh.

'So you three boys were just watching while Rain was partying?'

'Yep. A bit later, Rain came back over and we got more drinks. I said that she'd had enough, but she told me to fu— Well… she didn't listen. She was on double vodkas.'

'We're trying to establish where Rain might have gone after the club closed, Marcus. Even though her mother says it's quite normal for her to stay out all night with her friends, we think that because she's away from home and not with her usual group, it is a little unusual.' The officer was being really nice, Marcus reckoned, and he understood that they wanted to find Rain as quickly as possible, but he couldn't possibly tell them everything.

He carried on. 'At one point, Rain said she felt sick. I wasn't really surprised. It was about 2 a.m., I suppose. I told Gary and Alex that I was taking her outside for some fresh air. I thought that would sober her up and I didn't want her spewing all over the dance floor. We go to Spanx a lot.'

'And was she sick?'

'No,' Marcus said. 'She felt better once we got outside. I took her down this little lane at the back of the club that led down towards the beach. We stood by the railings, listening to the waves.'

Marcus picked at the skin on his thumb. He'd put his arm around Rain's shoulders as they'd walked – staggered, in Rain's case – towards the sea. The air was thrumming with club music and he smelt the greasy tang of kebabs on the salty sea breeze. A bit further on, he'd turned his face towards hers, drawing her in closer, but immediately felt stupid because she pulled away, teetering off down the sloping lane. He remembered how she'd dropped sideways on one ankle in those ridiculously high heels. She hadn't even noticed his feeble advance.

'I told Rain that it was a good time to get a cab home, that we'd all go back together. I didn't want to leave her alone.'

'Very commendable, Marcus. What did she say?'

Bloody hell, the cop was acting like his mum. He smiled weakly, not showing what was really going on inside his head. 'She was, like, waving her arms about and said that she wanted to keep on partying. She was really slurring.' Marcus remembered following Rain down to the railings, feeling the sea breeze on his face. He'd also felt a bit woozy from the drink, but the night air had given him a bit of a wake-up. Though perhaps not enough.

'Nice arse,' he'd said, drawing up beside her, cringing the second he heard his words. He couldn't take his eyes off it, her dress barely covering it. *Shit, shit, shit…* What was even worse was that he actually remembered touching it – maybe even giving it a little smack? Oh God, yes, then he made the wisecrack about being in a club called Spanx and the effect it must have had on him.

'Why don't you come closer?' he'd said, easing his hands around her waist. She felt trim and firm as he pulled her back against him, her bum pressing against him.

'Fucking hell, Marcus,' she said. 'I'm, like, about to puke, you moron.' Something like that. But then she'd giggled and pressed back against him. He felt just how short and tight her dress was as he dropped his hands down around her hips. She wasn't trying to get away. In fact, she reached around and gripped his hips, pumping to the beats vibrating out of the club. It could just have been dancing, Marcus supposed now.

'But you like it, don't you?' he'd said, thankful he'd had the good sense to at least ask.

Marcus cleared his throat, looking up from the floor and meeting the cop's eyes. 'Rain said she wasn't ready to go home.' He pushed his hands through his hair. Just remembering it was making him sweat. A battle was taking place between what was going on in his mind – Rain in that dress, her hands pulling him close – and what was coming out of his mouth. He reckoned he was doing OK.

'Mmm, I do like it,' she'd replied, grinding against him. He could hear the waves spilling up the shore in the inky darkness beyond the railings, could just make out the luminous white of the breakers as the high tide lapped at the sand. 'I *really* like it.'

At this, Marcus slid his hands down her bare legs, allowing one hand to creep back up under her dress. She twisted her head around, so their mouths were close. He didn't want to miss the chance again, so he plunged his lips onto hers, trying to make her mouth open. He couldn't swear she kissed him back, but that was probably because she was so out of it. Her skin was so smooth and... oh, God help him... he thought he was going to die on the spot. He pushed against her, trapping her against the railings. No one was around, no one would see. There were no street lights.

He'd fumbled with the belt of his jeans, one hand still under Rain's dress, but he couldn't undo the buckle properly. He heard his own raspy breath – in and out, in and out – all mixed up with the waves crashing on the beach, which, in turn, got mixed up with the pulsing music, the feeling inside his jeans. He'd been crazy excited.

'Get off me now, you fucking freak,' Rain had yelled, as though she was suddenly stone-cold sober. He felt her hands shove hard against him. 'When I want a little boy dribbling all over me, I'll ask.' She tossed back her hair and wriggled her dress back down over her thighs, glaring at him. She might as well have poked him in the eyes with a screwdriver. It was the worst, the most humiliating moment of his entire life. Marcus had never done it with a girl before. All his mates had. He'd thought she'd wanted it. *What a bitch. What a fucking bitch.*

He watched her stride off, managing her heels perfectly now as she disappeared out of sight.

Marcus cleared his throat. The cops were waiting for him to continue. 'So, she was, like, telling me that she wanted to go to another club, get some more drinks. When I said we should go home, that's when she got stroppy. Next thing I knew, she'd stomped off on her own.' He wanted to screw up his eyes, block out all those images of him grabbing her wrist, yanking her round, the rest of it… but he couldn't. It was all etched on his mind, yet he had to remain blank-faced in front of the cops. 'I tried to stop her, of course. I followed her up to the road to make sure she was safe, but I lost sight of her. I figured she'd be OK. She's eighteen, after all. It was us lot who were stranded because she had our taxi money.'

'That was the last you saw of her that night, Marcus, outside Spanx?'

'Yup,' he said, feeling nauseous. 'I went back inside and hung out with Alex and Gary for a bit in case she came back. Then I got money out from the cash machine and we got a cab home.' Marcus punctuated the end of his story with a nod of his head. He bloody well didn't want to have to think of Rain sodding Carr ever again.

'OK, thank you, Marcus,' PC Wyndham said in a gentle voice that made him want to cry. 'We're trying to track Rain's movements on CCTV. I'm sure what we find will corroborate your story.'

Shit, Marcus thought. He didn't reckon there'd have been any cameras down that alley. They only had them on the main streets, didn't they?

'The other thing you should know, Marcus,' the officer said, 'is that Rain is only fifteen.'

CHAPTER FIFTY-THREE

A sombre mood hung heavy in the farmhouse after another night with no news. It was just Shona and Claire sitting in the kitchen, waiting for developments, waiting for something to happen. Maggie had been taken down to the police station to view CCTV footage following an earlier appeal on local TV news. A woman had called the police to say she'd seen a girl matching Rain's description.

Claire had offered to accompany her, but she'd wanted to go alone. If she was honest, she was relieved – partly because taking Marcus there yesterday had hammered home the gruesome reality of the situation, plus she still couldn't shake off what Callum had said. It was his day off and he'd taken Amy to the cinema after Claire suggested it would do their daughter good to get out of the house, away from the police visits, the whispered discussions, the anxious mood. Jason was out searching again and Nick still hadn't come back from London – some problem with the restaurant, he'd briefly told her yesterday, and she hadn't questioned him. His tone had signalled she shouldn't ask.

The most disastrous reunion in history, she thought, resting her chin in her hands.

'Lots of villagers have joined in the search party that Jason organised,' Shona said. 'He's given out all the flyers Greta made.'

'Everyone's being amazing,' Claire replied. Jason had certainly launched himself into the search to find Rain. His apathy when Lenni went missing had been so noticeable that Claire found herself making excuses for him. 'I think it's guilt,' she'd told Maggie as they'd waited for news of Lenni years ago. 'It's like he's pretending nothing's wrong, as if Lenni will come back from the shop at any moment.'

While the rest of them were slaves to the investigation, their lives consumed by what had happened, Jason carried on as normal. When anyone mentioned Lenni, he changed the subject.

Claire watched her mother put the kettle on for what seemed like the thousandth time in the last three days. She admired her stoicism, her poise, her determination. 'It's almost as if Jason's trying to make up for...' She stopped. There was no point upsetting her. But there was something else troubling her. 'Mum, there was a...' Again, she couldn't finish.

Shona glanced at her before sloshing a dash of boiling water into the pot to warm it. The tea-making was an avoidance ritual, Claire knew, as her mother set out a tray with two cups and saucers, teaspoons, biscuits, a bowl of sugar – even though neither of them took it – and poured milk into a small china jug. She spooned leaves into the pot, filled it up from the kettle and slipped on a knitted cosy. Claire felt like smashing the whole lot onto the floor.

'Let's sit outside,' Shona suggested. 'I think we need the air.' Once they were seated, she poured and passed Claire a rattling cup and saucer.

'Mum—'

'Biscuit, darling?' She offered the plate of shortbread. Claire felt nauseous, holding up her hand. A butterfly fluttered between them and, for a moment, she was mesmerised by the flash of colour. Then she had an overwhelming urge to catch it and keep it safe in a jar, screwing the lid on forever and ever – or to grab it and crush it in her fist. She began to cry.

'Oh, darling.' Shona leant over and rubbed her shoulder. 'Everything's going to turn out fine. They'll find Rain safe and well, I feel sure of it.'

Claire looked up from behind the curtain of her hair, wiping her face on the back of her hand. 'But Mum,' she said, blowing into the tissue her mother gave her. 'How can this have happened twice to the same group of people? We're all being so reserved about it, not mentioning the similarities but… oh God, Mum…'

'What is it?'

'I wasn't going to say anything, but someone left me a phone message on Friday.' She paused. 'One of *those* messages. I told Jason, but stupidly I'd deleted it by then. I was so angry and scared, I didn't think.'

'What did it say?'

'It was horrid.' She took a breath. 'It was a really bad line and hard to tell if the voice was disguised or not.' Claire hiccuped a sob, sipping her tea. 'He said… he said…' This was the bit Claire would never be able to delete, the words that had been replaying over and over in her mind. 'He said, "I know where she is."' Claire stared at her mother, waiting for reassurance, but Shona was silent, blank-faced. 'I'm sorry. I shouldn't have said anything to you, Mum. I should have just told the police and let them deal with it.'

Her mother gave a small nod, stilled by the news.

They'd had many such calls over the years, and all turned out to be hoaxes. Lenni's story was all over the national papers for several months. In the early days, the police took them seriously, followed up as best they could. Once or twice they'd made a token arrest or cautioned the pranksters. Some had called repeatedly, claiming to have news of Lenni, photographs of her in another country, some saying they knew she was dead, that she'd been buried in a shallow grave. The most distressing calls were from those abusing Shona and Patrick for killing her or, at the very least, neglecting her. But over the months and years, as the case grew colder, they'd dwindled almost to nothing.

'Just don't tell your dad,' Shona said, staring into her cup.

Back then, Patrick had been the one to field the calls when they'd come, often at supper time, leaving them with no appetite. Several times the phone had rung in the dead of night and they'd wake, not knowing if it was real or a part of a nightmare.

Then there were the letters and anonymous messages – some from genuine well-wishers, but many from crackpots and despicable people who had no sympathy and too much time on their hands. They received contact from psychics and, on one occasion, someone actually came to the farm claiming to be able to find her with their supernatural powers. Mystical spirit photographs, tarot readings and intricately drawn-up astrological charts arrived in the post, some stating exactly when and where Lenni would be found. One psychic believed that Lenni was being held in a cave. She was so convincing that Shona spent the next three days scouring the coastline for her daughter. Patrick thought she was as mad as the woman herself. But when a letter came saying Lenni's body had been disposed of in a rubbish dump, they made the decision not to open any more. If any slipped through the net, they were disposed of on the fire.

'No, let's not tell Dad,' Claire agreed quietly.

CHAPTER FIFTY-FOUR

Nick stood in the cellar. It was lit by a single bulb in a cage hanging from the beam. He shoved his hands in his jeans pockets, staring around. Work had begun, but it was far from finished. In fact, it was still just a cellar and he wouldn't be happy keeping rats down here yet, let alone anything else. But he refused to allow the council or Trevor to scupper his plans. As things stood, he had no choice.

When he'd viewed the property months ago, it was the vaulted underground space that convinced him it was the property for him. It was mostly dry, spacious and had decent head height – a bonus in what was an otherwise run-down building, although he could see the restaurant had potential. The old Portuguese couple Nick had bought it from clearly didn't anticipate the micro boom about to take place in the area and just wanted a quick sale. No one ate at the grubby place with its grease-stained woodchip paper and maroon-patterned carpet anyway, so Nick made a low offer and the transaction only took three weeks.

Prior to this, life at home had become intolerable. Jess had sunk to a place he didn't recognise and he knew it was over between them. He'd never felt so alone. She needed help, professional help, but he didn't know how to make her take it. She'd shut him out of her life completely; shut *everything* out except alcohol.

That was nearly twelve months ago. Meantime, Nick waited it out while the house they owned together was sold. They'd bought it years ago when Jess fell pregnant with Isobel. They could hardly contain their excitement, everything pointing towards a happy future. But when the house was put up for sale, they lived like strangers. Jess rarely came down from her room, but when she did, she padded about in her dressing gown and bare feet, harvesting leftovers from the fridge, sometimes standing in the garden, her face turned to the sky with a packet of Marlboro in her gown pocket, each cigarette consumed in almost one drag.

'Jess, we need to talk,' he'd said countless times when she shuffled past, her hair a tangled knot and her skin dull. 'Please.' He took her by the shoulders, tried to look into her eyes. She barely had the energy to shrug him off. Back upstairs she went.

'You need help, Jess. Proper help.' Nick sat outside her bedroom. He didn't know what to do. Their daughter had died. Died in this house. Now it was as if Jess wanted them to die too.

'It's your fault she's gone,' she spat one time, whipping open the door. 'You left her alone.'

Nick crumpled from the blow. They'd both agreed it was safe to leave Isobel for a couple of hours after school every afternoon. Other parents did it. The bus dropped her virtually at their front door and she would grab a quick snack before getting on with her homework. Not once did they imagine such a freak accident would occur; not once had Nick imagined that Jess was seeing another man. A married man with a couple of spare afternoons each week.

Nick paced around the cellar, trying to see a future transposed over the past. *Basement*, he thought, preferring to call it that. In his mind, cellars conjured images of damp and mould, spiders and dead rats, along with forgotten, corked bottles of wine and broken old furniture. Rather, this space would represent a second chance, a place to nurture what he'd lost. As he patted the wodge of cash in his inside pocket, he could already envisage things taking shape in the vaulted chambers. Above in the restaurant, no one would suspect his little secret down below, no one would know what he'd done, what he'd had to do in order to survive. That tragedy had forced his hand.

The drive back to Cornwall was a reflective one. Trevor had come for his cash and reassured Nick that he'd keep the council out of the loop. There would be no repercussions and he was committed to finishing the project on time. Nick glanced at the dashboard display as it lit up, immediately taking the call. He was doing eighty in the fast lane.

'Claire?' It was more a question than a greeting. His mouth went dry at the thought of what she might know. She'd always had a knack of reading his thoughts.

'Are you coming back?' she asked, sounding as though she'd been crying.

'On my way now,' he replied. 'Is there news?'

'I'm afraid not. The forensics team have finished and… well, it was weird. They found…' She trailed off and Nick didn't want to press her. 'Maggie went down to the police station to view some CCTV footage of a girl who might be Rain. Someone thought they'd spotted her. We're still waiting to hear.' She cleared her throat. 'How long will you be?'

'Maybe another two, two and a half hours?'

'OK,' she said, but then the line broke up. When it came back, her words made him grip the steering wheel so tightly his knuckles went white. 'Please hurry, Nick.'

In the police station Maggie stared at the blank computer screen, waiting for the film to play. She gripped the sides of the chair, digging her nails into the plastic.

'The images we have are very fleeting and the quality isn't great.' An officer she didn't know tweaked some settings, finally clicking the play button to reveal a grainy Newquay street scene on the monitor. Maggie squinted, leaning in to get a better view of all the people going about their business. There was the usual contingent of regular shoppers along with groups of teenagers and families who were clearly on holiday. Cars queued in one direction only, obscuring some of the people.

'Take a close look here.' The officer pointed to a blonde girl as she came into view from the right-hand side of the screen. He slowed down the frame rate, but this only made her face harder to see. Maggie squinted. 'Her arm is being held by the man beside her,' the officer continued. 'Do you recognise either of them? Take your time. I can play it as many times as you need.'

It was true, Maggie thought. The girl looked as though she was being frogmarched down the street against her will. She couldn't decide which was worse – never seeing her daughter again or witnessing her being abducted by some monster. She leant closer to the screen, her heart pounding. It certainly looked like Rain – she was a slim, fair-haired, attractive, teenage girl, but then so were hundreds of other kids in Newquay. Her hair had fallen over her face a little and, normally, Rain would swish it back, constantly running her fingers through it. But this girl wasn't doing that. Her face seemed taut and blank – perhaps because the man was holding on to her. But it was so difficult to see anything clearly with people and cars getting in the way.

'Can you go back to the start, please?' Maggie watched the footage again. She certainly didn't recognise the man. He was large and looked in his late forties, his belly spilling over his jeans as they passed a gap between two cars.

'Wait. Go back a bit. To when they were just here. Play it at normal speed.' She pointed to the space between the cars. It was the only point at which the girl's entire body came into view. Maggie drew in a breath sharply. She wasn't sure if she was relieved or disappointed. 'It's not my daughter.'

'Are you certain?' The detective stopped the tape when the girl was in full view.

'Look, here,' Maggie said, pointing at her left ankle. 'I know the image isn't totally clear, but there's no tattoo. Rain has one right there. It would show up even at this range.' The detective nodded and made some notes. He asked her again if she was sure about what she'd seen.

'I've never been more positive about anything in my life.'

Maggie was driven back to the farm, where she found Claire sitting outside alone with the remains of a cup of tea on a tray. Some biscuits lay untouched.

'It wasn't Rain.'

When she didn't reply, Maggie sat down beside her in the empty wrought iron chair. 'Claire?' Streaks of watery black ran in wavy lines down her friend's cheeks. 'Oh, Claire…' Maggie reached out and put a hand on her shoulder. It felt, for a fleeting moment, good to be the comforter rather than the comforted, even though she felt her friend tense up.

Claire turned slowly, looking at Maggie, her expression suggesting bad news. She held her breath. 'I'm so sorry the CCTV didn't show anything helpful.' She shrugged away from Maggie's hand. 'I just need to go and freshen up. Excuse me,' she said, hurrying back inside.

Maggie didn't understand. Until now, Claire had been strong, a rock just like her mother, competent and helpful. She'd been exactly what Maggie had needed the last couple of days, helping her through this nightmare. What had changed?

She sat for what seemed like hours. Then, through the heat haze and her thoughts, the summer bugs darting through the air and the birdsong, Maggie became aware of a telephone ringing. Its trill was somehow lost in the expanse of Trevellin's garden. Then she realised the landline handset was beside her on the table. She answered it.

'Hello?' A few moments later, she dropped it onto the grass, unable to move a muscle.

CHAPTER FIFTY-FIVE

Upside-down

I've got a good plan. When the door opens next time, I'm going to watch for that hairy skull and smash it with the kettle. Then I'll run for my life and everything will be normal again. But it's not a very good plan. What if I'm no good at killing? What if I die instead? I'm not very strong and this isn't a made-up adventure story in a book. This is me. My life. My nightmare.

Although I don't really have the nightmares in my sleeps any more. And I've slept a lot of times since I've been here; millions of sleeps, it feels like, though it's probably not that many. No, the nightmares come to me during the day now, when I'm awake – knowing that I'm never going to see my family again or go to school or stroke Goose the dog or splash in the sea or bake a cake with Claire; not being able to choose my own clothes in a shop or ride my bike or play on the farm, even if I was always getting into accidents. Or adventures, as I told Mummy to make her not worry. But this is the worst adventure ever.

They always said that if I stayed good, then nothing bad would ever happen.

I must have been really, really bad, then.

Since then I've tried to be good, even better than good, so I can get out. I've even eaten the food that's brought for me though some of it tastes worse than school dinners. I'd really like a school dinner now and I'd even sit still in history lessons and remember all the battle dates. My teacher called me a fidget. I wouldn't be one of those any more.

I scream and yell for hours, but no one ever hears me.

I fall asleep, and when I wake, I make myself a sandwich. The bread is dry and dusty with green stuff. Before long, I hear familiar sounds – all that clattering and unlocking. Finally, the door swings open. I get ready to pounce, holding the heavy old kettle high above my head. But then those eyes… the way they look at me. I lower the kettle slowly and allow the breeze coming in to wash over my face instead, breathing it in. The hug squeezes the air from me.

'Why are you eating lunch at night?'

'Because I didn't know it was night,' I say, feeling stupid.

It reminds me of what Claire and Jason and I once did. It was just for fun and we called it our upside-down day. I know they only did it to amuse me because I was the youngest, not because they fancied eating pie and mash for breakfast. Mum didn't grumble, but Dad kicked up a fuss because Jason was meant to be helping him clean out the barn. We ate our dinner at eight in the morning and then watched telly and went back to bed. But I never really slept and we were all up after a couple of hours. The plan was to eat porridge for supper and then stay awake all night. Jason liked the idea because it meant he could lounge around all day in his pyjamas and not help Dad.

When we got hungry at midday, Mum made us a tray of treats, telling us it was a midnight feast when really we all knew it was lunch. By midnight, I was a bit confused. Claire said we had to go outside to play. When we ventured into the dark yard, we saw a real live owl hooting in the tree beside the log store. We stopped in our tracks – all dressed up for daytime even though it was night – and listened to the bird's spooky whoo-whoo, all dishy-eyed and wise. He was laughing at us.

'Come on, Len.' Claire dragged me by the sleeve. I was scared because it was so dark, even though I knew Mum was watching me through the window. She never let me out of her sight.

'Do you think there are prowlers about?' I asked, as Jason picked up a big stick.

'No, silly. You're such a baby.'

'Am not. I'm nearly twelve. Practically a teenager.' Everyone at school called me a baby, and that new girl was mean to me because I wore shoes with Velcro fasteners because I couldn't do my laces. She laughed that my skirt wasn't short like theirs. Mum said to ignore them. Dad told me to punch her and taught me how to make a fist. I didn't do either.

'Claire,' I said, as she pushed me on the swing. The night whooshed through my ears. 'Do you think I could swing by myself?'

'You won't be able to,' she said, stepping aside. 'You'll just get your legs tangled again and fall off like last time.' I kicked out my legs like I'd seen other kids do, but it never worked. I slowed down to a wobbling stop. Then Jason called out, so I leapt off.

'Look at this,' he said. I ran to the edge of the pond. 'It's having an upside-down day too.' He was poking a spiky ball with the tip of his stick.

'It's a hedgehog,' Claire said. 'They always have upside-down days. They're nocturnal.' It was all curled up with only its grey-brown spikes showing. Jason rolled it along with the stick.

'Don't,' I said. 'It'll be frightened. It's only a baby.'

A baby, I thought, deciding that's what I needed to do at school when those kids were mean. Curl up into a ball like the hedgehog. Though I didn't have any spikes.

CHAPTER FIFTY-SIX

'Do you remember the bonfires we used to have down here?' Claire said to Nick on the walk she'd pictured taking with him ever since she'd first dreamt up the God-forsaken reunion. She'd needed to get away from the farm for a while.

'I do,' he replied.

'And do you remember how we used to jump over them, saying that if we made it to the other side, our wishes would come true?' Claire's hand briefly brushed against Nick's. Instinctively, she wrapped her arms around herself, hugging her body. 'How do you get over losing a daughter, Nick?'

'You just jump very high and hope you make it to the other side, I guess. Like the bonfire.'

'And did you make it across?' She stopped, turning to face him. The sun was warm on her back and her bare toes curled into the cool sand. She felt a piece of seaweed beneath her foot and toyed with it nervously. They'd stood like this countless times before as teenagers, and each time Claire had prayed that Nick would lean in and kiss her. They'd had their moment long ago, she knew that. But it still added to the churning sadness inside.

'Think I'm stuck mid-leap.'

'You need a hand to pull you across then.'

'And what if there's no one standing on the other side?' he said, drawing her in for a hug. Claire allowed it only briefly before pulling away.

'If I tell you something, will you keep quiet?' she asked, walking on again. Nick nodded. 'Callum told me that Maggie... well, he said that she'd come on to him the other night.'

'OK,' Nick said slowly. 'Tell me more.'

'On the one hand, I don't believe Maggie would do a thing like that, but then I don't get why Callum would tell me such a thing if it wasn't true.' They walked to the water's edge and stood with the sea washing around their ankles. 'Anyway, look, forget I mentioned it. It hardly matters in the scheme of things.' She kicked at the sand, but Nick led them on walking again.

'I think it matters a lot. It's your oldest friend, your husband.'

'Such a cliché,' she said. 'I can hardly ask Maggie about it at a time like this.'

Claire wished she hadn't mentioned it, wondering if he felt uncomfortable, because he quickly changed the subject. 'I'm so sorry to see your dad unwell. He really doesn't seem like himself. When I arrived back from London earlier, I found him in the yard. He had no idea where he was.'

'Oh, not again.' It broke Claire's heart to hear this. She stopped in her tracks.

'What is it?'

'You'll think I'm silly,' she said.

'Try me.' Nick laughed.

'See that little boy over there with the kite? It reminds me of something I saw years ago.' She looked at him, her face serious. 'I once thought I saw Lenni, Nick. In the early days she was everywhere. In the supermarket, on the television, walking down the street...'

'That's only natural.'

'But there was this one time, it was different.' She shook her head, knowing it sounded ridiculous. 'It was about three years after she went missing. I was down here on the beach, heavily pregnant with Marcus at the time. A little boy was flying a red kite.

I remember it so clearly, as if it were yesterday. I was watching it when a glint on the headland caught my eye.' Claire pointed to the rocky jut. 'I thought it was a pair of seals at first. Silly in hindsight because seals would never go that far up onto the land. Anyway, I wanted a better look, so I walked – no, *waddled* – closer. I was very pregnant,' she said with a laugh. 'As I got nearer, I could see that it was actually two people. A man and a girl.'

She felt Nick's warm hands slip around the fists she hadn't realised she'd made. 'They were still a good distance away and the man had his back to me but the girl, oh Nick, I swear it was Lenni up there.'

'Our minds can play cruel tricks. I've seen a thousand Isobel lookalikes since she died.'

'This was more than a lookalike, Nick. I walked as fast as I could towards the headland, calling out her name, but my line of sight became obscured by the rocks at one point. It was so breezy I don't think they heard me calling out, and by the time I'd got closer, they'd gone. There was no way I could climb up in my condition. I called the police and they sent someone out immediately. They found nothing, Nick. Nothing at all.'

'I'm so sorry,' he replied, leading her away from the boy and his kite. They headed back towards the farm, chatting about everything, from Nick's new restaurant to the weather to Claire's job. At the top of the track leading up from the headland, when the dark slate of Trevellin Farm's rooftop came into view, Claire stopped. 'I don't want to go back just yet,' she said. Even though she wanted nothing more than Nick to say the same thing, for them to carry on walking, she needed some time alone. 'I'll see you back at the farm in a bit.'

Nick nodded, and she felt his eyes on her as she walked away from the house. She went through the kissing gate, passing through a couple of paddocks and briskly up the steep hill of the most distant of the farm's fields. This was where they'd always kept the goats, but these days the few animals her parents owned lived in the smaller, more easily accessible paddock near the house. Amy loved to go and feed them handfuls of grass after school and, if she had friends to play, it was the highlight of their afternoon.

She continued on over the crest of the hill where the breeze kicked up, blowing against her face, her hair flying everywhere. The view was stunning. Down below to her right was the array of buildings making up Trevellin Farm, her own house included, and down to her left was the jade-green expanse of fields leading down to the cliffs and the coast. Beyond this, a strip of white-flecked royal-blue sea was visible, and today there was the smudgy-grey outline of a tanker on the horizon. Clouds rolled in from the west.

Claire pressed on down the other side of the hill, the land sloping more gently. After another ten minutes' walk, the grassy pasture turned into granite outcrops and a scrubby woodland. She'd not been out this way for a few months, though she knew her father still tended to the stone walls and stock fences, albeit badly. It was a ritual to him. In his blood to do it. No one could keep him off the land.

As kids they'd played endlessly up here, leaping between the rocks that stuck out from the ground like the elbows or knees of long-buried giants – that's what they'd pretended anyway, as their father worked nearby. Having him close made the monsters in the wood not quite so scary.

Claire continued through the coppice towards the derelict cottage. The mossy stone and rotten timbers of the fallen-out windows soon materialised through the mottled light and, as she stepped out into the clearing where the old building stood, she felt a pang of sadness at how dilapidated it had become. It was in far worse condition than Galen Cottage, although it did look remarkably similar, making her heart race as she was reminded of Saturday's scare. Whoever bought the place, she could only imagine them knocking it down and starting from scratch rather than trying to salvage it. The thought broke her heart.

She walked up to the front door – or rather the place where the front door had once been – and peered inside. Half the roof was missing and many joists were hanging down, covered in the rampant ivy that was strangling the building. She daren't go inside all the way for fear of dislodging something and bringing the whole place down. Inside was the same old broken furniture that had been there when they'd played here as kids, but it was rotten now. It had been their real-life Wendy house, and she and her friends had arranged the old table and chairs and sideboard as if they were a happy family living there. Once or twice the table had been turned upside down, a broom-flagpole erected with a pillow-case tied on the end, and they'd set sail to Africa. Claire's eyes misted with tears.

'Oh God,' she said, covering her mouth, spotting the ancient refrigerator where they'd stored their sandwiches when they'd come out to play for the day. It hadn't done much in the way of chilling their food – the electricity had been cut off long ago – but it made their make-believe house all the more real. Eventually, their father's repeated words about the dangers of the place finally sunk in and they had to play elsewhere, usually climbing on the bales of straw in the barn until Shona declared that off limits too when Lenni fell and badly hurt her ankle. The real dangers in life weren't always the visible or the obvious ones, she thought.

Where did you go, Len-monster?

A twig cracked. Claire's skin prickled with goose bumps.

'Hello?' Had she trodden on something? 'Who's there?' She swung around, expecting to see someone – had Nick come after her? – but there was no one there, just a crow flapping out of a tree above her. She shivered. It was time to go back.

She stopped again. She definitely heard something.

'This is private property,' she called out nervously, bending down to pick up some litter. Someone had been up here recently, she thought, gathering up the discarded food wrappers. Probably kids from the village. When she stood, she felt lightheaded, so she took hold of a tree trunk to steady herself. Looking up, the treetops spun around her as another crow, squawking and beating its wings, escaped the confines of the wood. Claire breathed deeply, gathering herself. 'No one's here,' she said. 'Everything's fine.' But she still walked briskly back to the farm.

CHAPTER FIFTY-SEVEN

Near the Beginning

Everything's dirty and stale and, even though Mummy's not here, I can hear her calling out to me... *Clean your room, Eleanor!*

I pull the wet sheet, yanking it off the mattress. It's not really a mattress at all but a piece of yellow foam chucked on the floor with bits nibbled away as if mice have been chomping on it while I sleep. Sometimes I helped Mummy make up the beds for the boarding guests, so I know what to do. I'm not sure how I will wash the sheet though, in this tiny little house. It's not even a house. Just a stinky room.

I think I'm going to get killed.

I bet Claire got a good telling-off for letting me go off alone to get ice cream. Mummy always warned me that I'd get kidnapped if I kept going off alone. And she was right. I've gone off alone a few times before by accident and Mummy always got scared and angry. But there was one time I went off and I don't even remember because I was too little. Claire does, though, and she used to tell me the story often. I liked hearing it. She would wrap me up in a warm towel after my bath and sit me on her bed. She used to take a comb and gently untangle the mass of my wet hair after a day at the beach. 'Didn't you wash your hair properly, Len-monster? Look, I've found a starfish, an octopus and two crabs in it.'

Then I'd say, 'Tell me the story of when I went off on my own,' and I'd get all snuggly next to her on the bed.

Claire grinned. 'Well, Len-monster, you'd not long learnt to walk. It was summer and you went barefoot everywhere – all around the house, climbing up the stairs and across the soft patch of lawn near the back door. You drove Mum mad with all your walking. But she knew you'd never venture out onto the drive because you didn't have any shoes. You hated walking on the gravel because it hurt your little feet. You did it once and screamed, wailing on the stones with your arms stretched high to be picked up.'

Then Claire tickled my feet and I asked her who saved me.

'I saved you. I came and scooped you up and picked out the gravel from between your toes.'

She was the best big sister.

'Then what?'

'Then Mum took you to town to buy you your first pair of shoes. They were red. You loved them. You walked faster than ever in them.'

I bounced on the bed, waiting for the big finale.

'We were all playing in the garden, Maggie too, and Mum went inside to answer the phone. She came right back out, smiling and chatting. A moment later, she said, "Where's Eleanor?" and she ran around and around the garden peering behind trees and bushes, calling your name until she was screaming.'

I laugh and laugh at this bit.

'Suddenly, we heard a skidding noise further up the drive. Then we heard the crunch of gravel as Mrs Lyons carried you back down to the house with a scowl on her face. "She was halfway to freedom and beyond," she said in her funny Mrs Lyons voice. "Lucky I'm a slow driver. Anyone else and she'd be..."' – and we yelled this together every time she told the story – '"She'd be *splat*!"' Claire and I both clapped our hands together as hard as we could and laughed ourselves senseless. 'That's when Dad first called you Len-monster, when Mum told him what had happened.'

'Raarrr!' I yelled with my claws out, just to prove I was still a monster.

Not really a monster any more, I think, bundling up the stinky sheet and wishing I was halfway to freedom and beyond right now.

CHAPTER FIFTY-EIGHT

Nick was the first to reach Maggie in the garden. He was trying to slow down her sobs with a steadying hand on her shoulder, crouching down beside her, talking softly as she shook and wept. 'Stay calm, Maggie. What's happened? Speak to me…'

Claire also heard the scream and ran outside, dashing up to Maggie, flinging her arms around her. She didn't care what Callum had said any more. Maggie fell forward and flopped down onto her knees in the grass. Claire supported her as she went down. 'Maggie, what *is* it? Please tell us.'

She pointed to the telephone dropped on the grass, sobbing. 'The police have… they've found a pair of denim shorts.' Her words were tissue-paper thin on the breeze. 'And some underwear.'

'Oh God,' Nick said, clenching his fists and closing his eyes.

'What else did they say?' Claire asked. Jason and Callum rushed out, having heard the noise. 'Let's give her some space,' she said, indicating for everyone to step back. 'Did they say the clothing belonged to Rain?'

'They think so, yes. A woman walking her dog found them wrapped up in a carrier bag. She'd heard the story on the news and called the police,' Maggie's lips trembled. 'They said there was blood on the shorts.'

The day had been a scorcher, she'd never forget that. It was emblazoned on her mind as much as the growing panic and fear as she and the others charged up and down the beach. Claire was soon in tears. Nick was silent but diligent in his search and Jason, when he came back from wherever he'd gone off to do, darted about asking people if they'd seen his little sister, tearing across their spread-out towels and picnics, kicking sand over everything.

Twenty minutes later, they assembled back at their own pile of discarded towels and food. The tide had crept up and wet their stuff yet again. 'She's nowhere,' Claire said through choked sobs. 'Please, dear God, don't let me have lost her.' She doubled up, then stood straight again, scanning down the beach.

Then Jason started laughing – almost mockingly, she'd thought – as she'd gone back over things in her mind. 'Listen to yourself, Claire. Lenni walked along the beach, went to the ice cream shop, most likely bumped into a friend, got chatting, got distracted, then went home without coming back to tell you. You know she's away with the fairies most of the time.'

Claire thought about this. Relief washed through her. 'Yes, yes, you're right. I'm being silly.' She touched her temples, frowning, even though she knew that Lenni didn't have any friends. 'Why don't you go back home on the shingle track route with Mags. Nick and I will take the long route past the shops to look again.'

Everyone agreed. She prayed one of them would find Lenni sitting on a log with ice cream dribbling down her chin, loving her new-found freedom and perhaps chatting with someone from her class. All the other kids were allowed out all over the place in the holidays, unlike cooped-up Lenni, and so the novelty of being able to hang out if she'd bumped into anyone would be too great to resist.

'See you back at the farm,' Claire called out, as she and Nick walked off carrying most of their stuff. Maggie and Jason gathered up the remainder of the belongings and headed for the shingle track.

'She will be OK, won't she?' Maggie asked, as they reached the top of the cliff. Even though they took the route regularly, she was out of breath. They continued along the gently rising path heading inland, Maggie walking backwards so she could get a view of the beach below in case the skinny little girl in her too-big swimsuit wandered back to where they'd been sitting. She could clearly see the message that Claire had written in the sand: *Go home Lenni.* They'd also told a lady sitting nearby that if she saw a little girl lost, please tell her to go home.

'She'll be fine,' Jason said, sounding bored. 'I don't know why we're all panicking. The surf's just getting good.' He eyed the sea longingly.

But they were all back at the beach soon enough. Maggie and Jason reached the farm, discovering that Lenni hadn't come home as they'd hoped. Shona, oblivious to Lenni's disappearance at this point, was talking to B & B guests and so they didn't interrupt. The pair sat outside on a wall in the courtyard and, half an hour later, Claire and Nick marched down the drive, their faces expectant, salty and tanned. 'Any sign at the shops?' Maggie called out to them.

'No. Didn't she come home?'

Maggie shook her head.

'God, will you come with me to search down at the beach again,' Claire said, feeling the panic rising.

'Did you ask at the ice cream shop if she'd been in?' Jason said.

'No, but we looked inside and saw she wasn't there,' Nick replied, thinking they should have done. 'I'll go back and check. Look, we'll find her. She's not stupid.'

Everyone was silent as the weight of that sunk in. Lenni *was* stupid. Not because she couldn't do her sums or hum a tune or bake a cake or play board games – no. Lenni was touched with something that no one had ever identified, a cowl of innocence that she'd been born with. Her delightful, trusting nature radiated from her and may as well have been a sign on her head. A sign that told the unscrupulous that she was ripe for the picking. The way she allowed the kids at school to take her belongings, how she offered up her dinner money, or let them ruin her solitary games at playtime, over the years it had made her seem stupid. The more her parents smothered and protected her, the more they tried to keep her safe and out of harm's way, the weaker her defences became. Until she had none left. Lenni would believe absolutely anything anyone told her.

'Rain's not bloody stupid,' Maggie kept saying. 'She wouldn't just go off with anyone.'

'I'm sure she's not,' PC Wyndham replied. Her arrival at the farm, along with PC Holt, had made the group fear bad news, although she'd put their minds at rest immediately. 'There's not much more to report, I'm afraid.'

There was a collective sigh of relief. Clothing likely belonging to Rain may have been found, but as long as there was no body, then there was a strong possibility she was still alive.

'I feel so helpless. She didn't take her phone or purse and that's just not like her.' Maggie was going over everything again and again. She drank whatever anyone put into her hands – water, tea, a bedtime Scotch to help her fitful sleep – but she hadn't eaten more than a few morsels since Sunday afternoon. She kept repeating unhelpful facts, staring blankly at the wall, thinking back to when Rain was a little girl, a toddler, a baby, as if forcing back time in her mind might allow her to relive it all over again, give her a second chance.

'It's actually Marcus I've come to see,' the officer said, making Claire take Callum's fingers as she edged closer to him.

'Not without a lawyer, you don't,' Callum said. 'You've spoken to him once. Marcus hasn't done anything wrong. You're harassing the boy.'

'I'm certainly not implying he has done anything wrong, Mr Rodway. But the nightclub has provided CCTV recordings from the rear of their property. It's a secluded alley and they've had a few concerns in the past, so they installed cameras.'

'He isn't in trouble, is he?' Shona asked.

'Not if he helps us with our enquiries, no.' The PC's tone was kind and calm, unlike Callum who was bristling.

The back door suddenly flung open and a flood of noise and banter spilt into the kitchen. 'Hey, Nan,' Marcus said, eyeing everyone, shoving against Alex with a raucous, incongruous noise that soon faded when they realised the officers were in the room. They stumbled to a stop beside the sink.

'I told you,' Callum reiterated, while glaring at Marcus. 'If you want to speak to my son, then he'll need a solicitor.'

'Cal, I'm sure it'll be fine,' Claire said. 'What about if my husband sits in with you when you talk to him?'

'Dad, what's going on?' Marcus looked at each of his parents, then at the officer, his cheeks pinking up.

'That would be fine,' PC Wyndham said. Callum gave a grudging nod and led the way to the sitting room. Claire patted her son on the shoulder as he passed her, a terrified look on his face.

CHAPTER FIFTY-NINE

Callum sat on the arm of the sofa. It creaked under his weight. Marcus sank down into the cushions beside him. Why couldn't the silly boy just have gone to the house party in the first place, like he'd said?

'No need to look so worried, Marcus.' The PC smiled, trying to put him at ease, but her kindness made him tense up more. 'I just want to go over a few things again, like when you took Rain outside for some fresh air. No trick questions, I promise.'

'You don't have to say anything if you don't want to, son. I can insist we have a lawyer.'

'Mr Rodway, I understand your concern. But this really is just a chat, so we can piece together a timeline.' A smile again, doing nothing to allay Marcus's fears. 'If you can start from when she said she felt sick.'

'Like I said, I took her out the back to get some air. She took a few deep breaths. We stood there and listened to the sea. I asked her if she wanted to go home, but she said no. She wanted to stay out.'

'OK,' PC Wyndham replied, waiting for her colleague to write everything down. 'So where, exactly, were you standing?'

Marcus swallowed. 'After we went outside, we walked down towards the sea. We ended up down by the railings overlooking the beach.'

'And while you were walking down, or when you were down by the railings, did you touch Rain at all?'

'Really!' Callum said. 'What kind of question is that?'

'If you can't remain silent, Mr Rodway, I'll have to ask you to leave.' The officer raised her eyebrows.

Marcus's breath was shallow. 'No, I swear I didn't do anything!' His fists balled up, pressing into the cushions. 'I mean, maybe I put out a hand to steady her or something. She was pissed.' Marcus stared at his feet.

'So you didn't kiss her?'

'Maybe like just a peck. I dunno.'

'Was there any other sexual contact between you?' PC Wyndham pressed on. 'Did Rain tell you to stop?'

'Not really,' he said, trying to swallow. His mouth and throat were so dry.

'Don't say anything else, Marcus.' Callum stood up. 'I'm not happy with you asking these types of questions without my son having a lawyer. It sounds to me like you're blaming him for her disappearance even though he behaved like a responsible teenager by helping the girl.'

'Mr Rodway, please calm down. If you like, we can conduct this interview under more formal conditions down at the police station. I thought it was in Marcus's interests to keep things informal.' She turned back to him. 'Please, Marcus, if you know of any reason why Rain might be upset, then you must tell me.'

Marcus suddenly stood, throwing his hands above his head before dropping them down by his thighs. 'I fancied her, all right? I thought she was leading me on. She was flirting back. She let me do stuff.'

'Oh, for Christ's sake,' Callum said, thumping the sofa arm. 'Marcus, don't say another word.'

'No, Dad, because I didn't do anything wrong.' He stared at his father.

'Carry on, Marcus,' the PC said.

'It was, like, we were holding each other and stuff. It was just me holding her up at first, but then she was, like, pressing against me. I thought she wanted it too.' Tears filled Marcus's eyes. He slumped back down in the chair again.

'I'll ask you again, where were you at this time?'

'He's already told you he didn't do anything.' Callum was red and sweating.

'Mr Rodway, this really is your final warning before I'll be forced to take Marcus in for questioning. Please, let him answer.'

'We were down by the railings by this time. Then…' He looked down at his fingers, knotted in his lap. 'Then we kind of staggered away a bit. There was this brick wall, a little way along.'

'Go on…'

Marcus shrugged.

'Did you have sex with Rain, Marcus?'

'No,' he said, not looking up. 'I didn't.'

'You say you have CCTV footage, so why not look at it and see that my son is telling the truth.' Callum tried to stay calm. The girl was clearly a predator.

Marcus screwed up his eyes.

'Marcus, did you try to get Rain to have sex with you when she didn't want it? Is that why she stayed out all night? Did that make her run away, Marcus? It's important for us to establish if she is missing of her own accord.'

Marcus was shaking his head with increasing urgency. 'No, no, no, no,' he said, getting louder and louder. 'I didn't! No way!'

'I'll ask you a different way then, Marcus,' PC Wyndham said in a kind voice that was at odds with the question. 'Did you sexually assault Rain Carr?'

'Enough!' Callum roared, striding between her and his son.

The officer leant sideways, so she could still see him. 'As you may know, a bag containing some of Rain's clothes has been found. There is blood on the shorts.'

Callum fought back his rage. He would never hit a woman, but right now he felt like taking a swing at this bloody cop. He forced himself to sit down.

'Please, answer the question, Marcus.'

Marcus shook his head, almost imperceptibly. 'No,' he whispered. 'I didn't.'

'How did Rain seem when you saw her the next day? Was she acting normally?'

'She was a bit quiet. Seemed a bit upset about something. But we had a swim together. We even arranged to hang out at the beach that night. Things were cool.' His head couldn't have hung any lower.

PC Wyndham was thoughtful for a moment before getting up to leave. PC Holt followed her. But then she stopped, her hand on the door knob. 'Just to let you know, Mr Rodway, Rain Carr is only fifteen, not eighteen as she'd told your son. We'll show ourselves out.'

Callum slammed the door when they'd left, leaning back against it, cupping his hands over his face, while Marcus dropped his head onto his knees, thanking his lucky stars that he'd always been a loser when it came to girls.

Jason was recounting the news to Greta up at the Old Stables. 'I secured the gates,' he said, still red-faced from dealing with the couple of journalists at the end of the drive. 'They were calling out questions to me. They've already made the link to the past, of course, hoping to get a story.' He went on to tell Greta about the police talking to Marcus again, how Callum was in a rage at the way they were being treated.

'Sounds like they're picking on the poor lad a bit,' she said, adjusting her position on the bed.

'Claire said the police have been trying to get hold of Rain's father. Turns out he's gone away and no one knows where. An odd time to disappear, don't you think?'

'You've been watching too many crime shows,' she said, holding on to her stomach. She winced from the acrobatics taking place inside her, but then her expression turned into one of pain. 'Bloody hell, not again.'

'Love, are you OK?' Jason put his hands over hers. 'What's happening?'

Greta blew out slowly. 'I'm fine, I'm fine. Just a few annoying contractions. That's why I came up to lie down. It's probably nothing.'

'Should we go home? I don't want you having our babies in a hospital you don't know.'

But Greta was already shaking her head. 'No need. I know my body. It's just grumblings.' She sat up straighter. 'Tell me more about what's been going on.'

'Turns out Rain's father, Peter, has been in the news recently about some scandal. Bogus expense claims, apparently. I googled it. Thirty grand or so. He probably did it to pay Maggie off.' Jason rolled his eyes. 'Though he's loaded in his own right.'

Greta shifted again. The kicking was subsiding, but she was convinced that the babies had dropped down a good deal. 'I almost want them to stay in there forever,' she said, stroking her bump. Jason nodded, knowing exactly what she meant.

'It's going to be so weird having a family of our own.' He planted a kiss on the babies. 'I'm going to be super-protective but at the same time I want them to experience everything.'

Greta gave a pensive smile. 'Talking of families, Jase, how do you feel about having a heart to heart with your dad?'

'Maybe,' he said, surprising himself. He stared out of the window, knowing that in a flash, his twins would be at school, working, married, having families of their own, growing old – and at some point along that timeline he would die. How would it feel if his kids weren't speaking to him when that happened? The hairs on his arms stood up. It was unthinkable.

'You might be surprised at the response you get.'

'It's just the unfairness of it all,' he went on as Greta tried to conceal another mini contraction. 'When I was at my lowest point, he rejected me.'

'People react in different ways to a crisis.'

Jason nodded imperceptibly. 'Claire was always the golden girl.'

'Oh, love…' Greta caught her breath. 'Patrick probably felt that you weren't in the right place to take on a property.'

'And he still thinks that, does he? There's another cottage on the farm that's going to ruin. I needed something to focus on back then, and a project would have been good for me.'

'But if you hadn't come back to London, then you wouldn't have met me.'

Jason smiled. 'True. Best thing I ever did then,' he said through a flickering smile, but he still let out a heavy sigh. 'Claire's place must be worth a million quid by now.' Staying here only made him more resentful.

'We have our own home, our own lives, Jase. We don't need handouts.'

If Greta hadn't leant forward, wincing again, he'd have rebutted that by saying that their decent lifestyle was all down to her, not him. 'I want our children to know the happy father I grew up with, not the bitter and resentful man I turned him into,' he said.

'You didn't turn him into anything, Jase,' she replied, sucking in through gritted teeth. 'But I don't want our kids witnessing the same in you. The only way to fix this is… is for you to talk to him. And that's only going to happen if you make the first move.'

Jason knew she was right as he stared at his phone, turning it over and over in his hands, wondering how to break the ice with his father. But first, he had something more important to take care of.

CHAPTER SIXTY

It was just getting light when Claire woke to the sound of banging on the door. She swept back the duvet and swung her legs to the floor, sitting up in a panic. The alarm clock blinked 4.56 a.m. Callum groaned. 'What's going on?' he mumbled, reaching out to her with a flailing arm.

'I think someone's at the door. Did you hear it?' Claire rubbed her eyes, trying to wake up.

'Go back to sleep, love. It was nothing.' He eased her back down into bed.

'Oh God, it *is* the front door,' she said, when the banging started up again. 'Cal?' She looked at him expectantly, but when he didn't make a move, she grabbed her robe and pulled it on, running downstairs. She prayed it wasn't bad news about Rain. Maybe it *was* Rain. In the hall, she pulled back the bolt and unlocked the door. Three uniformed police officers, two men and a woman, stood there with a lit-up squad car in the drive behind them.

'Mrs Rodway?' one of the men said. Claire nodded weakly. She was aware of Callum coming down the stairs, drawing up behind her. 'Are you Mr Callum Rodway?' the officer asked, glancing behind Claire.

'Yes,' he said, taking hold of Claire's shoulders and steering her in-between himself and the police. 'Why are you waking us up at this hour?'

'I am arresting you on suspicion of sexual activity with a child.' You do not have to—'

'*What?*' Claire could hardly speak as she turned to look up at Callum.

'—have to say anything, but it may harm your defence if…'

'No, there's been a mistake,' Claire cried, as the officer continued talking. Her hands were flat on her husband's chest as she looked up into his eyes, imploring him to say something. But he didn't.

The officers eased her out of the way and she didn't hear much else that was said about arrest and evidence and rights because her head was swimming, making her eyes glassy from fear. The thumping of her heart reverberated in her ears. *Why wasn't Callum saying anything?*

'Mum, what's going on?' Marcus was standing at the top of the stairs, groggy-eyed, in his pyjama bottoms. Amy appeared at his side, hugging her brother's leg.

'Daddy!' she squealed.

'It's OK, darling,' Callum said quite calmly. 'There's been a mistake. I just have to go out for a while, but I'll be back very soon.'

'This is ridiculous,' Claire said to the officer, composing herself for her children. 'You can't do this to us. My husband hasn't done anything wrong.'

'I need to get dressed,' Callum said calmly. His face was almost white. He's in shock, Claire thought, desperately wanting to do something but not knowing what.

'My colleagues will have to accompany you,' the female officer said, nodding to them to follow Callum as he went upstairs. Marcus and Amy had their backs pressed to the half-landing wall as they passed, while Claire stayed where she was, completely frozen. Minutes later, he was back in the hallway again wearing jeans and a shirt.

'Call this number,' he said to her. 'Tell John to get down to the police station as soon as possible. I'm not saying a word until he's there. Understand?' He handed Claire a business card.

'Yes, yes, of course,' she said, nodding furiously, her voice on the verge of failing entirely. Surely, she'd wake from this nightmare soon – to the sound of birds singing, the sun creeping through the curtains, everything normal. She tried to hug him before he was led outside to the car, but he didn't respond.

'Cal,' she called out from the doorway. He had a police officer on each side of him guiding him by the arms. 'Cal, please…' He turned in slow motion, about to get into the car. Claire's face was crumpled and questioning as their eyes locked. She couldn't say the words, couldn't bring herself to ask if it was true. Callum turned away, ducking as he got into the police car.

She closed the door and stared at the business card. Then she put it in the pocket of her robe and phoned Nick. It was quicker than dashing up to the farm and waking everyone, but she needed someone to be with her and didn't want to disturb Jason upstairs, knowing how difficult Greta found sleep right now. 'I want Daddy,' Amy sobbed, gripping onto Marcus's legs until Claire told her to be quiet.

'I'm so sorry, my darling,' she said, sandwiching her daughter against Marcus, wrapping her arms around them. 'Mummy's a bit upset, but I promise Daddy will be home soon.' She glanced up at Marcus, who was frowning, urging her to offer a look back that would silently explain what had happened. He wasn't going to be fobbed off.

'Is Dad in trouble?' he asked.

'No, no, of course not. They're being over-cautious because Rain's still missing, love. That's all.' Claire's voice betrayed the truth. She pulled her robe tightly around her. 'Why don't you take Amy upstairs and settle her back into bed? Read her a little story to help her get off again.' She forced a smile.

'Yes, sure,' Marcus said, yawning. When they'd gone, Claire peered out of the kitchen window. Nick was running up the drive from the farmhouse. She hadn't told him details, but by the tone of her voice he knew it was urgent. She opened the back door and, before he was even inside, she'd broken down in tears. Nick took her in his arms, her face pressed against his shoulder. He guided her through into the kitchen.

'They've arrested Callum,' she said. 'Oh God, it was awful.' Then she remembered the business card. 'He wants me to call his solicitor.'

'*Arrested* him? Christ...' He ruffled his hair. 'You're in no fit state to be making phone calls right now,' Nick said, sitting her down. 'It can wait a few minutes. I doubt they'll even have him booked in at the station yet.'

Claire nodded, pulling her sleeves down low over her fists. 'I just don't understand...' The arresting officer's words rang through her head. 'They said they were arresting him on suspicion of...' She couldn't say it. It was too awful, too unreal and so very, very wrong. She hung her head.

'It's important, Claire. The solicitor will need to know.'

'They arrested him on suspicion of having sexual activity with a child.' There, the words were out. Said and done.

Nick blew out a long sigh. 'Fucking hell...' He walked to the window, leaning against the sink and staring out at the line of pink on the horizon. 'Surely, there's no way that's true, is there?' he said, turning to face her.

'No, no of *course* not! He's a good man, a good father. He's a *surgeon*.'

Nick rubbed the stubble on his jaw. 'Do you think they were implying it was... well, to do with Rain?'

Claire shook her head. 'I have no other details. I just don't know what to do, Nick.' Claire hugged her arms around her shoulders, dragging them down her body. She just wanted to escape herself. 'They don't know Callum at all. He's not like that.'

Nick took the business card from between her shaking fingers. 'Let's hope...' He read the name on the card. '...that John Blake doesn't mind being woken up at this hour of the morning, then.'

'He's one of Cal's golfing friends. John and his wife have been here for dinner a few times.' Claire pulled a tissue from the box, blowing her nose as Nick read out the solicitor's number. She was about to hang up when the call was answered by a groggy-sounding man and, five minutes later, she'd told him everything. He promised to get down to the station right away.

'You're both up early.' The lightness of the voice took them by surprise. 'Has there been news?' Greta padded through the kitchen in her robe and slippers. 'The babies were kicking so I thought I'd get up and make tea…' She halted, eyeing them both. 'Oh God, what's happened?'

'Didn't you hear the commotion earlier?' Claire said.

'No. If the babies are still, I sleep like a baby myself. What's been going on?' She pulled out a chair and sat at the table with them.

'Callum's been taken to the police station,' Nick said, trying to make the news not quite so shocking.

'Oh my goodness. Why?' Greta's eyes were wide.

'They arrested him,' Claire said, hoping the more she said it, the less awful it would seem. 'It's ridiculous. He hasn't done anything wrong.' She forced a laugh, trying to make light of it. 'He'll probably be home in time for breakfast.'

'Can I ask why?' Greta asked cautiously.

Nick cut in to save Claire from having to say it. 'It was unfounded rubbish. Something to do with underage sex.'

Greta was silent for a moment, her eyebrows pulling together. 'I see. So surely there's been a mistake?'

'I know,' Claire said, shrugging. 'Of course there has.'

Claire wrapped her hands around the mug of warm, sweet tea Nick had made for her, but all she could think about were Rain's fingerprints in their bedroom, her bangle under their bed, Callum's unusual accusation about Maggie's behaviour, and him asking her to lie to the police. None of it made sense. And none of it had a place in her life.

CHAPTER SIXTY-ONE

When Jason came downstairs, showered and dressed in shorts and a T-shirt, he found Greta sitting awkwardly on the kitchen floor, her bump positioned between her legs, and surrounded by Barbie dolls.

'Make her wear this outfit now,' Amy said, holding out a naked doll and a fistful of tiny clothes.

'Ooh, she'll look beautiful in that, Amy. Nice choice.' Greta attempted to squeeze the doll into an impossibly tight dress.

'Getting in some practice?' He placed his hands on his wife's shoulders, giving them a quick squeeze. Small talk was hard, but keeping things normal in front of Amy was important.

'Jason,' Greta said, looking up at him. He knew her well enough to sense that something was wrong. 'Can you help me up?'

Jason eased her to her feet. 'Are you OK?'

'I'll be back in a minute, Amy love.' Greta made a face at Jason, beckoning him out into the hallway. 'It's Callum,' she whispered, pushing the door closed. 'He's been arrested.'

Jason's eyes flared wide. 'What? Why didn't someone come and wake me?'

'There was no point, there was nothing you could have done. Claire and Nick have gone down to the police station while I look after Amy.' Then she explained why.

'What about Mum? Is she frantic?'

'No one's told her yet. Cal has a solicitor representing him, a good one apparently. Let's hope it's some kind of mistake.'

For a moment, Jason was silent, frozen in thought, but then he shoved his feet into a pair of flip-flops discarded by the back door. 'I need to go up to Mum and Dad's,' he said in a way that belied his anxiety about facing his father.

'Jase, do you think that's wise right now?'

'You don't understand,' he said. 'I *need* to.'

Greta opened her mouth to speak but closed it again. She watched as he strode out of the Old Stables and up towards the farmhouse. Amy grumbled from the other room, complaining that her doll's dress wouldn't go on, so she went back to help. As she lowered herself into a chair, she froze midway, grabbing her stomach.

Oh God, please not now, she thought to herself.

Maggie had finally received a phone call back from Rain's father after he'd heard her increasingly frantic messages. He'd been away for a few days. 'The silly girl has probably run off with some boy. You know what she's like. She'll be back when he gets sick of her or she runs out of money.'

'She's fifteen, Peter. That's a terrible thing to say,' Maggie replied. 'Anyway, she didn't take any money to have it run out.'

'I see where this is going,' Peter said drily. 'How much do you need?'

'For God's sake, I don't want anything from you,' Maggie said. 'Our daughter is missing.' She'd broken down then, realising how little he cared. 'What if someone found out about us and she's been kidnapped? Have you had any demands?'

'No. But you sound as though you're almost expecting that. Or about to make one.'

There was a moment's silence. 'I'd hoped that maybe she'd come to you, that's all.'

'Well, she hasn't,' Peter said curtly. 'Be sure to let me know when she turns up.'

Maggie hung up, mildly heartened that he'd asked to know when she was safe. She needed him to care about her just a little bit. 'She's not with her father,' she said to Shona, who was nearby. 'I should have realised that. If Rain had gone to him, then he'd have phoned me immediately to come and get her. He would never jeopardise his career or his family.'

Maggie had slept fitfully the night before, waking to the sound of someone leaving the house at dawn. She'd glanced at her watch – it was 5.11 a.m. – and gone to the bedroom window. Nick was half walking, half running up the drive towards the Old Stables. Was he going to see Claire? Her brain was too sleepy to think through the implications, though she'd found out why a couple of hours later.

'Jason?' Maggie said, as he came into the farmhouse kitchen looking flustered and wide-eyed. He was the last person she expected to see.

'Darling,' Shona said to her son. The look on his face drew both women close. 'What's wrong?'

'Is there news?' Maggie braced herself.

'There's no easy way to say this,' he said. 'Callum was arrested early this morning. He's been taken to the police station.' He explained what had happened, trying to gloss over the details for Maggie's sake. Shona sat down and Maggie stood silent, stunned, as they listened.

'That's just not possible,' Shona said. 'Callum would never do anything like that. Patrick and I must go down to the station and vouch—'

'But what if he did?' Maggie said quietly, covering her mouth. 'What if he did something to Rain and she ran away or worse, what if he…'

'What if who did what?'

Jason froze. Patrick was standing in the doorway. Whatever the state of his mind, he still commanded a great presence. 'Tell me what's going on.' He eased himself into the fireside chair as if it were the only place he belonged.

'It's Callum, darling,' Shona said, filling him in, having to remind him that Rain was still missing.

'Let the lawyer do his job,' Patrick said, staring at Jason. 'John knows what he's doing.' Then he went quiet for a moment, his stare still fixed on his son. 'Will you give Jason and me a moment, please?'

Shona looked at Maggie, nodding, and beckoned her out before the day's search began once again.

Jason held his father's stare as he went to the armchair on the other side of the fireplace. He sat down. 'Dad,' he said without emotion. It was where Patrick had taught him to play chess. The fire would be roaring, and Jason's left ear and cheek would turn scarlet from the heat and frustration. He'd never won a single game against his father.

'Son,' came the reply.

'How have you been?' Jason asked, knowing he had to start somewhere.

'Apparently, I'm losing my mind.'

Jason gave a tiny smile. 'If it's any consolation, I forgot our wedding anniversary last year.'

'Not me,' Patrick replied proudly. 'I got your mother...' He trailed off. 'A necklace, I think. Yes, it was a necklace.'

Jason nodded, knowing his father would never admit to the full extent of his illness. He was a proud man.

'So where have you been all this time?' Patrick said, as if he'd all but forgotten the long-standing etiquette of their animosity.

Jason gave a small laugh. 'Living in London, building a life for myself. Trying to get over stuff.' He just wanted to get it all out, to spill out all his feelings, to seek answers and settle scores. But he knew things didn't work like that with Patrick.

His father's eyes narrowed as if he was sifting through memories, trying to pick out the correct feelings to accompany them. 'You never understood. Still don't, do you?'

'No, you're right – I don't understand, Dad.' Jason's heart clenched as he considered getting up and leaving. But something made him stay. 'I was penniless, an addict, and I was depressed and suicidal. I couldn't get work, acting or otherwise. I suffered the same as everyone because of what happened to Lenni. My grief may have surfaced years later, but it doesn't make it any less real.'

'And you don't think I've suffered over the years because of her? All the guilt, the worry that I should be doing more for her, the effort and thought it still takes up on a daily basis? What kind of father lets something like that happen to his daughter?'

'No, Dad, none of us were suffering *because* of her. In the end, our suffering came from not having anyone to blame, from not knowing what happened.'

Patrick said nothing, but his eyes misted with tears. Jason felt helpless, angry and as if the wall between them would never be broken down. His father *did* remember why Jason returned to London that day, he could see it in his eyes.

'I needed caring for as much as you cared for Lenni, Dad. That was all.' Realising there was nothing else to say, Jason rose from the saggy old chair and turned to leave.

'Son,' Patrick said, as his hand was on the door. 'I still do care for her,' he said in a weak and shaky voice. 'Like I care for all of you.'

Jason gave a small nod and left. Some things were never meant to change, he thought, walking slowly back to his wife.

CHAPTER SIXTY-TWO

After identifying the clothing as belonging to her daughter, Maggie agreed to do a television appeal. A tearful message from a distraught mother would, the police assured her, create more awareness. And following the phone call with Peter yesterday, she was seriously considering naming him on air as Rain's father. The daughter of a well-known and respected politician would certainly get the camera bulbs flashing, the tabloids picking up the story, and get Rain a national profile. It might be the only way to find her. And to get Peter to take her seriously. A car came to take her to the news conference room in a hotel in town. As she sat in the back, staring at the countryside flashing by, going over and over Callum's arrest in her mind, she didn't think that she had anything left to lose.

'I need you to clarify again, Mr Rodway, why Rain Carr was in your bedroom.' PC Wyndham was perched on the edge of a table along with a detective constable. Callum was seated at another table a few feet away, waiting for his lawyer to arrive. Couldn't Claire bloody well get anything organised?

'Did you have sexual intercourse with Rain Carr, Mr Rodway, with or without her consent?' the detective asked.

Jesus fucking Christ, he thought, sitting stock still. 'No comment until my lawyer arrives.' He knew they would try to wear him down, break his resolve while he was alone. Whatever happened, he wouldn't admit to anything.

'Have you ever had sex with a child before, Mr Rodway?' he said.

'No comment.'

She'd clearly come into his room on purpose that night, drunk and giggling, pretending she thought it was Marcus's room, asking if he was back home yet. Then, when she'd seen he was in bed, she'd started teasing him again, just like she'd done in the cellar – her all over him, him annoyed at having been woken up. Anyway, he'd had far too much to drink and couldn't possibly be held responsible for his actions. Surely that amounted to her actually taking advantage of *him*, not the other way around? Besides, what did she expect, dressed in that ridiculously short dress and all that make-up? If only Claire had been in bed, none of this would have happened. It was absolutely all her fault. And *where* was his bloody lawyer?

Jason went back to the Old Stables feeling as if a scab had been picked off his life. How could his father be so heartless? How could his dead sister command more attention than his own living son, even after all this time? He'd had to get out, get away, before he said something he regretted. One thing was for certain, he would never treat either of his children that way. He would always be there for them, whatever happened.

When he went into the kitchen, Greta was on all fours, panting, sweating, begging for Amy to fetch the telephone.

'Oh God, love. I'm here. What's happening? Are you OK? Tell me what to do.' He crouched down beside her. 'Let's get you into the chair.'

'Noo, I can't fucking move!' she screamed. Amy dropped the phone and covered her ears as Greta roared and growled, rocking back and forth. Her belly hung heavy beneath her. 'The babies...

they're coming,' she wailed, panting and gasping for air. 'Call...
call an ambulance.'

With his hands shaking, Jason dialled 999.

✽

Nick and Claire weren't allowed to see Callum. Claire pleaded
with the officer at the front desk, but there was no way she was
letting them through. 'But he hasn't done anything wrong,' she
said. She felt Nick's hand settle on her arm, trying to calm her.
'They can't just take him away for no reason.' He gently levered
her away from the glass screen before the sergeant got annoyed,
but she refused to move. 'Can I phone him, then?'

'No, sorry,' the officer stated. 'His phone has been taken into
safekeeping.'

'Surely he has rights?'

'He most certainly does, and they will be adhered to strictly.
If you like, you can write a quick note to him. I'll see he gets it.'

'Oh, yes. Yes, OK,' Claire said, rummaging in her bag for a
pen. But the policewoman had already slid a pad and pencil under
the screen. She didn't know what to put so just wrote: *I know you
haven't done anything wrong. I love you. Claire xx.* She knew they'd
read it, hoped they'd recognise her sincerity and let him go. Deep
down though, she knew things didn't work like that.

Together they paced the waiting area until John Blake, a stocky
man in his early fifties, arrived at the station carrying a battered
briefcase. He strode straight up to Claire, taking her upper arms
in his beefy hands, giving them a squeeze as he kissed each of her
cheeks.

'Thanks for coming, John,' she whispered, knowing that if
anyone could help Callum, it was him.

'You must be out of your mind with worry, Claire. Why don't
you go back home? I'll call you when there's news. Let me handle
things now.' John was always matter-of-fact and self-assured.

Claire nodded, feeling slightly better now he was there. And he was right. There was nothing she could do, and she should be with Amy. Her poor daughter had had enough upset for one week. Nick drove them both back to the Old Stables, taking the sharp corners of the tight narrow lanes slowly. Then, when he pulled down the drive, they both stared silently at the ambulance parked outside the house.

Shona didn't think the babies were too imminent, but to be on the safe side she'd gathered lots of towels and pillows, two laundry baskets lined with soft blankets, and a bowl of hot soapy water to keep things hygienic. She'd also fetched cupful of ice for Greta to suck on, and had set Amy to work dabbing at her forehead with a cool flannel.

'Do you feel as though you want to push?' Shona asked between howls.

'No! Yes! It just fucking *hurts*…' Greta screwed up her face in agony as another wave of pain consumed her body. She didn't care who she swore at or if Amy heard. Shona noticed her belly tighten and contract as her body did its work. She stroked her cheek, but her hand was quickly batted away. When the pain subsided, Shona popped some ice in Greta's mouth and leant her forward to massage her back.

'OK, let's take a good look at you, my love,' a paramedic said after they'd knocked and come straight in. There were three of them – two women and a man – and one of the women snapped on surgical gloves, while another set up a portable ultrasound machine. Within seconds, they could hear the *shoo-shoo* of the babies' heartbeats.

'You're about six or seven centimetres dilated,' another said, after examining her. 'So best that we get you straight to hospital. Looks like you're going to be a mum sooner than you'd thought.'

'Ahh… oh *shit*!' Greta screamed. 'Breathe, breathe, you stupid woman,' she said, chastising herself for forgetting everything she'd learnt in childbirth classes. 'I… can't… go… anywhere yet,' she huffed and panted through yet another contraction.

Shona hugged Jason. 'I'm so proud of you,' she whispered in his ear, kissing him on the cheek. 'Now go and look after your beautiful wife and babies.'

Jason nodded, taking hold of Greta's hand as she was helped out to the waiting ambulance by the paramedics. He felt useless, wishing he could take away some of her pain. 'Mum,' he said, stopping and turning in the doorway. 'Dad and I chatted.' He hesitated, caught sight of the expectant look on her face. How could he tell her that Patrick had been as stubborn as ever? 'I think everything will be OK,' he added, feeling a pang of guilt at the sight of his mother's smile.

CHAPTER SIXTY-THREE

Day Eleven

How do you measure time when you can't remember what it feels like? How do you know when to sleep or eat or do stuff if you can't see the sky? The world has gone away, and I don't like it. I just want to go home.

I was given an Enid Blyton book on the first day here, but I'd already had it out from the school library, reading it while lounging in the hammock last summer, rubbing Goose's wet nose with the tips of my fingers as he snoozed beneath me. I know it takes me a day to read it cover to cover, which I've done eleven times so far. Does that mean it's been eleven days now? I'm starving, and my lungs burn from the stale damp air down here. There's no hammock and no sun and the weird fizzy light dangling from the ceiling gives me a headache.

When I was brought here, I was too scared to move, but I'm not scared about that now; not worried that I'll get told off for using the loo bucket in the corner or the sink or the bed or even putting on the clothes left here. They fit as though they were put there just for me. There's even a pair of shoes in my size. If I wore them to school, I'd get teased about the big strap that makes them really babyish.

I run the tap for a drink of water, but it's still sludgy brown. Then I eat some ham, but it makes me retch. It tastes like slime and smells like Goose when he's wet and muddy. Mummy always made my food. Now I'm crying again because thinking of her makes me angry and sad.

I didn't mean to go off alone!

I've yelled a million times for someone to help me, but nothing happens. It's just the hum of the lights and the smell of bad ham. The taste is stuck to the roof of my mouth. For something to do, I stand on the chair and poke at the ceiling. White powdery stuff showers down on me. My heart skips in case this is a way out. I dig dig dig at it with the handle of my plastic fork, but it soon hits something hard. I jab again and again and dig and gouge until it's like snow falling. I can't help laughing.

'It's Christmas!' I cry out, even though I know it can't really be. It wasn't that long ago that I was getting ice cream, was it? I drag down more white bobbles of polystyrene with my nails, clawing and yanking at the ceiling as it rains down on the bed, settling on the blankets. It was put up the other day because I wouldn't stop yelling.

I look around the room. I've made a mess and I'll get told off. I lie down on my bed and fall asleep, dreaming of snowmen made of sand. When I wake, the light's gone off and it's pitch dark. I really wish it *was* Christmas Eve.

'The electricity is broken,' says a voice through the blackness. Spanners, a hammer, pipes and a blow torch are clattered onto the table in torchlight. 'But I'll fix it for you. I'll make it nice for you in here, you'll see.' Then comes the grin, the one that makes me feel safe yet fills my heart with terror. 'It's your new home now.'

CHAPTER SIXTY-FOUR

As soon as the first baby was delivered, Jason went into a state of panic. He was a father. 'Is he OK? Is he breathing?' he said to the midwife at least a dozen times.

'You can see quite clearly he's breathing, Dad,' she said, smiling. 'He certainly has a good pair of lungs.' The baby was wailing about his sudden entry into the world. But Jason felt a stab of worry. Why was he crying? What was wrong with him?

'He's beautiful and healthy,' she said. 'Now just let me sort him out and you can have a cuddle.'

Jason was nervous. What if he didn't do it right? He hadn't quite recovered from cutting the cord – the emotional aspect of severing child from mother as well as the thought that it must hurt had unsettled him. Greta was quiet and resting for the moment, having spent the last hour howling in pain. He did what he'd learnt in childbirth classes – lower back massage, keeping the gas and air handy, letting her grip his hand while breathing steadily along with her, talking to her between contractions and helping her shift into different positions – but Greta was having none of it. She'd sworn at him, hit him, thrown her iced water over him and virtually bitten off his hand. Then, between contractions, she'd pulled him close and sobbed into his shoulder, telling him that she wanted to die, that she couldn't carry on, that she was already a useless mother.

Fifteen minutes later, the second baby was delivered, and Jason immediately saw that it was a little girl. A very quiet, very limp little girl. 'Is she OK? Why isn't she crying?' He darted between Greta's side and the see-through crib where the midwife had laid the baby. She was rubbing her vigorously with a towel, ignoring Jason's concerns.

'Oh God, this can't be happening,' Jason mumbled, his hands pushing through his hair. The assistant midwife had called for help, and within seconds a doctor and another senior midwife were there, crowding around the baby with monitors, tubes and other equipment. Jason had no idea what was going on except that his little girl was still blue and not moving or making a sound.

'What's going on, Jason?' Greta said, trying to hoist herself up in bed so she could see. 'Is she OK?'

'I don't know, love. I don't know what's going on. I don't think she's breath—' Jason checked himself. Their baby would be fine. There was no way he would allow her not to be. 'They're just checking her over, love. Cleaning out her airways.' He'd seen the suction tubes go between her tiny blue lips.

Greta rested back on the pillow. She was exhausted. And then they heard the cry. Softer than the first baby but nonetheless a beautiful, heart-warming cry. It was the most welcome sound in the world. Satisfied with her condition, the doctor went off to another delivery room, leaving the midwife in control again.

'She's absolutely fine now,' she said over her shoulder. 'It just took a moment to get her jump-started.' Ten minutes later, Greta and Jason were holding a baby each, hardly aware that the midwife had picked up Jason's phone and was taking photos of them.

Over the next while, Jason gazed between his son, his daughter and his wife. Where had they all come from? He felt like the luckiest man alive. For the briefest of moments, his happiness was clouded with sadness as he thought he saw a glimmer of Lenni in his daughter's face. Her curious expression – constantly changing as she tried to make sense of the world – glimmered with Lenni's little dimples and serious frown. Then it disappeared, and she was his daughter once again, a perfect little creature in her own right.

'Is there any news about Rain?' Greta whispered to Jason, as the midwife showed her how to latch the baby onto her nipple. They watched as a hungry mouth found its way to the most important place on earth. Greta winced.

'I don't think so.' Jason hadn't heard anything since he'd been in hospital, but then he'd been preoccupied. 'I'll check my phone,' he said, while the midwife showed Greta how to feed two babies at once. She smiled, holding her new family with confidence, as if she'd done it all before.

Jason stared at the screen. He'd had eight missed calls and several texts. He opened a message that had just come in from Claire, reading it three times. He stood, silent for a moment, drinking in the sight of his beautiful new family, before breaking the news to his wife.

CHAPTER SIXTY-FIVE

Day One

I'm sitting on an old plastic stacking chair. I haven't dared move yet in case I get told off. It's earthy warm in here and smells funny. The damp air makes me cough.

After ages of sitting still, I really need the loo. I don't know where it is. Everyone at home will be so worried about me. It's been hours and hours since I went to get my ice cream. I'm jiggling back and forth on the chair. What will happen if I wet myself? When I weed on the floor at school, I got a bad mark. I had to wear someone else's knickers from the lost property cupboard. They were grey and baggy, and everyone laughed.

If I wet the floor now, I'll probably get killed.

I really want to find the loo, but I don't think there is one. It's just one room, and the door out is locked. There's a plastic bucket that's been left beside a foam mattress on the floor, so I use that, sliding off the chair slowly in case something bad happens. As I pee, I look at the mattress. Is that my bed now? There's a stuffed toy owl on it. *Whoo-whoo*, I think as I pull up my sandy swimsuit. I can still taste that yukky ice cream in my mouth.

I don't even know if it's dark outside because there aren't any windows. It feels like I'm underground, but I don't know if I am. I sit back on the chair because I don't want to get told off when the door opens again. I tap my feet and wait. I wait for ages and ages longer. Tappety-tap.

I'm really hungry now. And cold. My swimsuit has dried stiff on me and my skin feels crisp and salty. This place is horrid. I want to get out. It's got old brick walls with a white furry crust. There's just a chair and the mattress on the floor, the bucket and a big metal bowl on a wooden stand. A tap hangs on the wall above it and wobbles when I dare turn it on. The water tastes of soil.

I start to cry. I don't want to be a baby, but I've been here ages now. Hours and hours, though it feels like my whole life. One tear comes and then they all come. I lean forward with my face down on my knees, crying and crying until there's nothing left.

'Help!' I call out, crawling over to the pile of clothes left on the floor, rummaging through them like Mummy does at the jumble sale. I want a jumper and I don't care who knows it! When I find one and put it on, it smells dirty and stale. It has someone's dinner down the front. I get back on the chair. And then I just wait.

CHAPTER SIXTY-SIX

Callum sat facing his lawyer. They'd been allowed fifteen minutes to talk in private. He hadn't liked the way John had lowered his head and sighed grimly when all he'd done was tell him how it had happened. Virtually everything.

'It wasn't like that, John. You know that's not the type of man I am. I'd had a bit too much to drink, I admit. She came into my room uninvited, for God's sake.' Callum didn't like John's blank face either, felt as though he was being judged. 'My first thought was that I was having a bloody good dream.' He laughed raucously, like when the group of them were at the golf club bar, but John's expression remained blank. 'You'd have thought the same if it happened to you, let's be honest.'

John raised his hands to halt him. 'You know she's a minor?'

'Well, I bloody well do now. Fucking little tart. Going around dressed like that. My son thought she was eighteen.'

'But did she tell *you* that?' John didn't wait for an answer. 'To put it bluntly, I imagine the police suspect one of two things. One, that young girls are your thing and you forced her to have sex with you, or at least encouraged it, and then she ran away upset. Or secondly, that you had sex with her and then killed her when she threatened to tell.'

'Killed her?' Callum thumped his fist on the table, half standing up and leaning in towards him. 'For fuck's sake, that's totally ridiculous! I swear I didn't do anything wrong and I certainly haven't bloody murdered the stupid girl. She's a menace. She'd already come on to me inappropriately once before.' His breathing was quick and shallow. Murder? How the hell could this be happening to him?

'She had?'

'Yes. I was in the cellar choosing wine last Saturday evening and she followed me down and started behaving like a provocative little slut.'

'Anyone see this?'

Callum shook his head. 'No,' he said quietly, wondering what the hell had possessed him to tell Claire it was Maggie, not Rain. He'd just wanted a reason to get rid of them both. 'No one saw it at all.'

Shona was alone in the farmhouse, exhausted and awaiting news from Jason about the babies. She'd been looking after Amy, but distracted herself by walking her granddaughter up to the village to play with a school friend. The little girl needed some normality. The other girl's mum, a good friend of Claire, was sympathetic and happy to help out for as long as needed.

The walk had certainly helped clear her head so, on the way back, she decided to take the cliff path rather than the shorter road route home. She found herself gazing along the familiar length of Trevellin beach, remembering Lenni, thinking of all the years that had passed, shocked by how it didn't seem any time at all since they were tearing around trying to find her.

When she got back to the farm, Nick was still there, not realising Shona was within earshot judging by the whispered expletives, pacing and clenched fists. He quickly stopped when he spotted her. Shona thought he looked worn out. 'Sit,' she said, pointing to the chair. 'Let me make you some food.'

'It's been a while since anyone did that for me,' he said, while Shona buttered some bread.

'Then it won't hurt for once, will it?' Claire had briefly hinted to her about his loss, skirting around the horrific details, as well as mentioning his new project in London. She hadn't delved much into any of the friends' lives since they'd been here, but had picked up snippets of conversations, gleaning facts here and there, building up a current picture of the people who'd once played such a large part in Lucas family life. She'd always loved Nick. He'd been a constant member of the usual gang of kids who gathered at the farm, and he'd been good to Claire. *For* Claire.

'The old days were good times, weren't they?' Shona said, grating cheese. She wasn't expecting an answer; rather she was trying to convince herself that things hadn't been all bad.

As it happened, she didn't get any kind of answer because Claire and Maggie burst into the kitchen, spewing out words, talking over each other and not making any sense. Their faces were flushed, their expressions anxious. Shona picked out something about Jason and babies… a boy… a girl, and then she heard mention of Rain.

'Slow down,' Shona instructed. Maggie was clutching her phone to her chest, her knuckles white around it. 'Claire, what on earth's going on?' Shona glanced between the two women.

'Greta's had a boy and a girl. They're all fine. Jason sent me a text. I don't know any more details.' It came out quickly and then Claire fell silent, touching her forehead as she looked across at Maggie.

'That's wonderful news,' Shona replied. But she knew there was more. Maggie had garbled something about Rain. She braced herself for the worst.

'They… they've found her,' she said quietly, as Claire held her. Together they rocked back and forth, Maggie's face pressed against Claire's shoulder. 'Oh God, oh *God…*' she said, ending with a muffled wail. Shona waited for more details, praying that Rain had been found alive but she was too afraid to ask. 'The signal here is so patchy I only just picked up the message from earlier. All they said was that I need to get to the hospital urgently.' She dragged a hand down her face, wiping away her tears.

'I'll drive you,' Nick said. 'And you don't know anything else?'

Maggie shook her head, unable to help more sobs. 'Nothing,' she said. 'She could be on life support, for all I know, or...'

Or worse, they were all thinking.

'I'll come too,' Claire said. 'You can't face this alone. And Mum, we can visit Greta if they let us.'

Clutching her head as if it was about to explode, Maggie allowed Nick to guide her out to Claire's car and they set off for the hospital.

'Will Dad be back soon? Do you think he'll be OK alone for a while?' Claire asked Shona, as they sat together in the back.

Shona sighed, frowning. 'He'll have to be. He was determined to fix the drystone wall up in the top paddock. I left a note reminding him to take his medication, saying we'd be back soon. I didn't mention about Rain. Not until we know for sure.' Claire reached across and squeezed her mother's fingers, remaining silent for the rest of the journey.

CHAPTER SIXTY-SEVEN

Got You Now

The hand comes from behind. The fingers smell like cigarettes and earth. I try to scream but my tongue just presses against bitter-tasting skin. I screw up my eyes, shaking my head and thrashing my arms and stomping my feet, but I'm all scooped up as we lumber across to the other side of the road, stumbling down a bank. My throat makes frog noises and my heart is on fire.

I'm sorry sorry sorry, Claire... I didn't really want an ice cream.

I kick hard, and one leg breaks free, making me hop and stagger as I'm forced down to a parking area with trees all around. I've never been here before; I don't recognise it. Crazy fragments of sunlight and sky and branches shatter in front of my eyes as I flail and struggle. I try to kick harder, but my legs are snapped tightly together again so I can't move. My head is pinned back as I'm dragged towards a van I don't recognise... *Help me!* But my words don't come out.

I can hardly see now because my eyes are all blurry from tears. My feet are lowered down, but my mouth is still clamped shut – a hand strapped around my ice cream lips.

I'll be good, I promise...

The back of the van is opened and that's when I nearly get away. But I'm quickly shoved inside, my face smashing against the spare tyre. I yell out, but my lips are bleeding and my voice is too croaky and scared. The doors are slammed shut before I can see who it is, my screams echoing in the empty space. I feel around, thumping on the wooden panel separating me from the front seats. It's dark in here and I can't see a thing.

I want Claire. Oh God, oh God... I don't want ice cream now.

Suddenly, the engine starts up and then it gets really bumpy. We're driving away. I bang on the metal side of the van, but it hurts my hand. It stinks of petrol and fumes in here and I feel sick.

Help me...

It's useless. No one hears. I don't know where we're going.

Shivering, I lie down, curled up like I do when I can't sleep at night – when I'm too cold in winter or, if it's summer, when it's too light to go to bed. And then my mind starts flying to wonderful places. In this terrible bumping blackness, I see Goose and Claire running towards me with their arms outstretched, trying to save me, screaming my name.

They told me not to go off alone...

The van rumbles along. I'm being knocked and jolted and thrown about as we speed round corners. There's nothing to hold on to except myself. We're going so fast, I feel sick like when I read on long journeys and Mum tells me not to. It doesn't seem real. Nothing seems real.

I really didn't want an ice cream.

I cry, sobbing through snot and tears, eventually falling asleep on the ridged metal floor of the van. It's not really sleep, though. It's fear shutting me down.

When I wake, it's all gone quiet. Am I free now? Are we here? Can I go? Why is this happening?

Then there are footsteps in time with my heart.

The van doors are flung open and the sunlight dazzles me. I can't see a thing apart from a big shadow looming above me. Maybe I'm going to be set free. Maybe it's all a joke.

I promise I won't make a fuss ever again.

Something goes over my head. It smells like a dusty old sack. I am shaking as I'm bundled out, as if I am a puppy about to be thrown in the river. I scream and scream and scream, but I'm still carried away. There is no hand over my mouth, so I keep screaming, keep struggling, but it's useless. We keep going like this forever, although I don't know where to. I pray to God it's home.

We must be going inside somewhere because the pinpricks of light seeping through the cloth suddenly go dark.

'Where are you taking me?' I ask in a deep and calm voice that surprises me. It sounds as if I am asking what's for dinner, wondering if it's my favourite. 'Please don't hurt me.'

No reply.

Wherever we are, it feels cool and damp on my skin now, not warm like outside. I'm shivering. Freezing to my core.

'Where are my shorts?' I ask, suddenly remembering. I must have dropped them. I don't like it that I lost my shorts. I want my shorts! If I'm not taken back soon, then Claire will have lost her swimsuit too and I'll get told off.

Still silence.

We stop, and I'm bent into a hard chair, hands firmly set on my shoulders. They feel warm, resting there for a second. My teacher sometimes does this. It means *Stay sitting down, for heaven's sake, Lenni. Have you got ants in your pants today?*

I daren't move. I know what hands on shoulders mean.

I hear my own breathing inside the sack. It smells like rum and raisin. I have a bit of raisin still stuck between my teeth. Then I hear clattering, like something unlocking, stuff being moved about and shoved. There's a grunt, a wheeze, bad words that make me want to cover my ears. Then I'm pulled up by my arms, though not roughly. I don't struggle.

I'm guided forward, listening to the sound of the chair scraping along too, as if it's being dragged with us. It goes darker and darker and then I hear a door bang and that rattling again. I cough, bending forward as my stomach cramps and clenches. Warm stinky ice cream sick spills down my chin. I can't wipe it away because there's a drawstring around my neck. I'm crying hard again now.

'Help!' I yell, but it comes out as a bubbly retch. It tastes disgusting.

I'm put in the chair again, in the dark, in my sick-smelling bag, and those hands are on my shoulders once more.

Sit still or else.

OK.

Then there's more banging and lifting and metal scraping.

'Will you take me back to the beach now?'

The noises stop, as if it might be a possibility. In a flash, I'm up out of the chair and running – to where, I have no idea as I can't see a thing – but I slam into something hard, falling on my face. My head throbs as I lie, crying, on the floor. 'I have ants in my pants,' I wail. 'Lots and lots of ants.' Then I'm hoisted upside down, like when Daddy carries me to bed on his shoulder as a game. I retch again but this time nothing comes up.

We're going down some steps now and my back scrapes on a wall. I hear keys jangling, like when Mum goes around the house at night locking up. She thinks she's being quiet, but I often hear her; hear her sighing as she peeks around my bedroom door to check on me. I always pretend to be asleep.

Then I'm upright again and I'm really dizzy, staggering and reaching out for something to hold. Except all I find is another hand. So I grab it.

Two warm hands clasping. It makes me feel better. Safer to know it's there.

I'm led on a few steps and bent into the chair again. I wait for the hands to press on my shoulders but this time they don't. I keep perfectly still anyway. No ants for me.

Then there's a bang, a door shutting, and more clattering, though quieter than before. I hear footsteps in reverse, the soft scuff of shoes getting fainter. After that, I just sit and wait and think that if I'm a good girl, I'll be able to go home soon.

But there's only silence. Nothing but me with the sicky bag on my head.

I wish I could take it off.

Do I have to do everything for you, young lady? Mum said this morning. It was my silly beach sandals. The buckles got stuck so she bent down to help me, her hair falling over her eyes as she looked up at me, winking.

Ever so slowly, my hands come up to my throat, untying the stiff knot under my chin. It's slimy from vomit but eventually loosens. I stretch the bag open, looking down to see my legs, all blue and mottled. They don't look like me.

What if I get in trouble for taking it off?

I lift up the front a little, blinking. The light is dim but feels bright after the bag. I slide it off my head, looking around. My plastic shoes are all grubby and it's horrid in here – a scary dark place with a mattress on the floor. There's a table and another chair and stuff I don't recognise. The walls and floor are made of brick and there are cobwebs everywhere. It's really scary and there aren't any windows.

I dash to the door but there's no handle. I thump and scream and yell and cry out for someone to help me. Even after ages and ages and ages and ages and ages, no one comes.

CHAPTER SIXTY-EIGHT

Maggie stared at Rain's lifeless body. She was barely able to step inside the room where her daughter lay. She seemed so small and frail, almost transparent, as if her blood had already drained away. She was lying on a white sheet on her back, arms down by her sides. She was dead still, her thin eyelids pressed closed as if someone had set her face to look angelic – nothing like the feisty girl she knew. A police officer stood at the door, glancing at Maggie sympathetically as she edged past.

A nurse was at the foot of Rain's bed, watching as she approached. From chubby, inquisitive toddler, to cute little girl keen to explore, to a hot-headed and troublesome teen intent on self-destruction, Maggie never believed she'd ever have to face this – a mother's worst nightmare. Rain was a survivor, had always got on with life, somehow dodging trouble around her yet leaving a trail of it in her wake. Or had she got it wrong? Was her daughter way more vulnerable than she'd ever realised?

Maggie covered her face, allowing the first agonising sob to travel up her throat and out into the cup of her hands. She couldn't bear to imagine what vile and ghastly ordeal her daughter must have gone through to end up like this. No one had told her anything yet. She wondered if it was better that way, not knowing the details.

'For fuck's sake!' Rain snapped angrily, suddenly sitting up. Maggie screamed, jumping back as Rain swung her legs out of bed. The nurse was immediately beside her, steadying her, coaxing her back down onto the pillow again.

'You can't go anywhere, my love, you're hooked up to a drip,' the nurse said. 'Lie back and rest,' she continued, trying to settle her.

For a moment, Maggie couldn't move, feeling lightheaded, as though she was going to pass out, but then the relief surged through her.

'Fat fucking chance of that around here,' Rain said, catching sight of her mother. 'Why doesn't everyone just leave me alone?' She hurled her head back against the pillow, curling up her legs.

'Oh, *Rain*...' Maggie lunged for her, wrapping her arms tightly around her. 'You're alive!' She'd never been so relieved to see her daughter so angry. 'Oh, thank God, thank *God*...'

'Of course I'm fucking alive.' She scowled at her mother, though there was something else behind the hard stare – something broken and hurting that gradually took over from the anger. 'I just want to get out of here. Please let me go... I have to ...' Rain trailed off. Her voice changed, became softer, tinged with a sob. She hugged her arms around her body. 'Mum, will you tell them I'm fine, that I just want to go home? I don't have to see the police again, do I?' She was shaking now, her whole body trembling as her eyes rolled back.

'She's in a bit of shock,' the nurse said. 'And very dehydrated.'

'Oh, my *love*,' Maggie said, not failing to notice that she'd called her Mum. She hugged her tightly again and, for once, Rain didn't protest. 'I've been worried sick about you. We all have.' She allowed herself a moment to breathe in the familiar scent of her daughter, pressing her face into her hair. That delicious scent was still there, faintly, but there was something else too, something slightly dirty and almost feral, as if she'd been living wild these last few days. Something earthy about her.

'Mum, tell them I just want to go home.' Rain's voice was thin and weak. 'Please?'

'I think it's best you do as they say,' Maggie said, the nurse nodding in agreement. When she'd arrived at the hospital, PC Wyndham had handed her over to a doctor who had brought her straight to Rain, but before they'd even got inside the room, the doctor's bleep had sounded, and she'd rushed off to an emergency, saying she'd be back as soon as she could. She hadn't told her anything.

'Just take me home, Mum.'

'Stay here a little while longer, love. You need to see the doctor.' Maggie studied her daughter. There was definitely something different about her – the childlike way she curled up in bed, the sad look in her eyes seeping out. 'And you keep calling me Mum,' she said, smiling. 'I like that.' Then she held her at arm's length, tucking a loose strand of hair behind her daughter's ear. Rain looked up at her, as if she wanted to say something, but whatever it was wouldn't come out.

Another nurse came in wheeling an equipment trolley, making chit-chat as she strapped the blood pressure cuff around Rain's arm. Her skin was dirty – patches of grime covering her forearms, with dark stuff under the crescents of her nails. Rain lay there as the machine gripped her arm, allowing these things to be done to her as though she'd given up fighting.

'Remember last Christmas, Mum?' she said, after the nurse had finished. Her voice was flat and quiet. 'I was so excited about you fetching me from school at the end of term, thinking we'd have a lovely time gift shopping together, decorating the tree, just the two of us. But then I got a message from the secretary telling me to go home with Katie for a few days, that you'd gone to Barbados with that guy, Gareth. Next thing I know, we're moving in with him.' She drew up her knees, covering them with the gown. 'So now, for once, would you please just take me home and...' A little sob burst from between her lips which, unusually, weren't daubed in bright lipstick. Instead, they were chapped and dull. '...and just keep me safe.'

318   Samantha Hayes

'Oh, my darling…' Maggie moved closer to hug her, but this time Rain turned away.

'I'll leave you two alone for a moment,' the nurse said. As she opened the door, Maggie caught sight of PC Wyndham along with Shona, Claire and Nick waiting in the corridor. They looked concerned, so she gave them a nod, indicating to give her a moment.

Maggie wanted to explain to Rain how hard it had been for her over the years; how the men in her life had been a compensation for her loneliness and childhood pain; how she'd never truly been happy; how she believed if she kept on running everything would somehow be OK. All she'd ever wanted was for her and Rain to be settled, to feel secure and loved. She knew she'd failed. And she also knew this wasn't the right time to discuss it, especially as PC Wyndham had just come into the room. She touched Maggie on the elbow, giving her a relieved smile.

'How are you feeling now, Rain?' she asked.

Rain pulled the sheet up to her chin, as if she wanted to hide behind it. She was on the verge of tears. Maggie reached out a hand, resting it on the knot of her daughter's fists.

'The police have worked so hard to find you over the last few days,' Maggie said, hoping she would talk, tell her what had happened. Instead, she just gave a small nod, her face turned down to her chest. Her shoulders were shaking. 'Oh, Rain,' Maggie said, glancing at the officer with an apologetic look. 'Maybe talking about it will help?'

Rain twisted the sheet, her thin fingers working the fabric. 'I told them some stuff already. But you won't understand everything. No one will. *Ever.*'

'It's OK, love,' Maggie replied, knowing that forcing anything out of her was usually counter-productive. 'All in good time.' But she couldn't get Callum's arrest out of her head.

'When you're feeling more up to it, Rain, we'll need to take a statement from you,' PC Wyndham said, pausing, hoping to elicit something. But all she managed was a small nod.

'A statement?' Maggie looked between the two of them.

'I want you both to know that we're taking what happened extremely seriously. We'll do everything we can to help you.'

'Just tell me what's going on,' Maggie said, gripping the officer's arm. 'No one's told me anything.' Her voice wavered.

Rain's head jerked up. 'But I haven't done anything wrong,' she half-sobbed, burning crimson. 'It wasn't like that.'

'I know you haven't, Rain. You've suffered a terrible ordeal and we'll do everything in our power to get justice. But we do need to get the facts from you. You won't have to see him.'

'See *who*?' Maggie said, on the verge of tears. She didn't understand – or rather, was it that she didn't *want* to understand?

'As you know, Maggie, we arrested Callum Rodway on suspicion of…'

Maggie suddenly felt dizzy, her chest tightening when she heard his name, hardly able to take in what she was being told. She'd tried to block out the implications of his arrest, but hearing the words direct from PC Wyndham made it painfully real. As she listened, she couldn't stand to think of that bastard – someone they'd all known and trusted for years – doing such a vile thing to her daughter. She knew he'd been arrested, and now her worst suspicions had been confirmed. She needed to stay calm for Rain, but the anger was boiling up inside her. All she wanted to do was find him and punch his disgusting face.

'I shouldn't have gone into his room, Mum, I know that, but I was drunk. I thought it was Marcus's room,' Rain said, curling up even more. 'Then, when I saw *him*, it was just like a part of me, you know…' She pulled a pained expression, struggling to find the right words. 'It was like I wanted to prove I'm attractive, that I'm worth something. He'd already hugged me in the cellar. I guess I wanted him to do that again. It was just nice to be noticed for once.'

'Oh, Rain,' Maggie said, holding her. 'None of this is your fault.' Though, as a mother, she couldn't help feeling it was hers.

'Rain, please trust me when I say we're going to do everything we can to help you,' PC Wyndham said. 'What he did is against the law, and however you felt, whatever you thought the situation was, it was never OK for him to have done this to you. Do you hear me?'

Rain nodded, sniffing. 'Yes,' she whispered.

'You can throw the bastard in jail to rot, as far as I'm concerned,' Maggie said, unable to control herself any longer. She gripped the bar on the side of the bed, her knuckles flashing white. 'No one does this to my daughter and gets away with it,' she spat out. 'No one!'

Then Rain started crying – hot, powerful tears bubbling out of her, purging the pain. 'Oh, Mum, I c-c-couldn't stop him.' She buried her face in the sheet, her knees tucked up under her chin. 'After… after he did it, he wouldn't let me go. I was terrified. I just lay there, trying to pretend it never happened. I was trying to act normal the next day, but all I wanted was to die of shame. I hated myself more than ever. I felt disgusting.' Maggie handed Rain some tissues from a box on the side table. She blew her nose. 'I didn't know what to do or where to go, just that I had to get away. I knew no one would believe me anyway. I'd got some spare clothes in my beach bag, so I ran. It was like a switch flicked inside me.' She wiped her face with a fresh tissue. 'I couldn't face anyone, let alone *him*.'

'It's OK, I understand, darling. I'm here for you. And I *totally* believe you.' Maggie forced herself to calm down for Rain's sake, even though inside she felt far from it.

'I admit, a part of me wanted to scare you, Mum. To show you how I felt, to show you all my pain. I wanted you to give a shit about me for once and come find me.' She was silent for a moment. 'But it's not just about that now…' she whispered, shaking her head, covering her face. 'When I ran away, things got so much worse.' Rain broke down again.

As she listened, Maggie felt her own tears pouring down her cheeks. Part of her wanted to smash up the room – take her hatred of Callum out on whatever was close – while the other part wanted to wrap up Rain in her arms and never let her go. 'Love… *oh God, love*, I'm so sorry…I *do* care about you. So much.' She hugged Rain again. Imagining what she would do to that bastard when she saw him would have to suffice for now.

'Rain, I just need to have a word with your mum for a moment, if that's OK,' PC Wyndham said with a kind look. She gestured towards the door. 'Do you want to come out here a moment, Maggie?'

But Maggie couldn't let go of Rain. She rocked her back and forth, promising everything would be OK, that they would get through this together.

'Maggie?' PC Wyndham repeated, touching her shoulder. 'Please, just a quick word if you wouldn't mind?'

'Sorry,' Maggie replied, prising herself away. She held her daughter's gaze until she left the room, mouthing *I won't be long* at her. She was lightheaded from adrenalin, anger and shock. Minutes ago, she hadn't even known if her daughter was dead or alive.

'Let's go down here,' the officer suggested, leading her down the corridor past Claire, Shona and Nick. They all fussed over her as she walked by, asking so many questions she thought her head was going to explode. She put up her hands to stall them, following PC Wyndham into a quiet doorway alcove.

'Rain will have a thorough medical examination and further checks, which will form part of the case,' the officer said quietly. 'She's the victim of a terrible crime and I just want to reiterate how seriously we're taking this.'

Maggie nodded, sniffing back another round of tears, swallowing down her anger.

'But I do feel there's more to this, as if she's holding something back. I thought I should mention it in case you can throw any light on it.' PC Wyndham paused, but when Maggie remained silent, looking puzzled, she continued. 'Rain had a very brief initial

chat with a psychologist earlier. The clinician suspected there
was something else that Rain wanted to talk about, something
she wasn't ready to let out. While she seems willing to make a
statement concerning the sexual assault, I'm wondering if there's
more to this.'

Maggie remembered the look Rain had given her – a lonely,
terrified look that had cut her to the core. And what had she meant
by *things got so much worse*. 'Yeah, me too,' she said, nodding. 'But
I have no idea what.'

'A woman from the village brought Rain to hospital. She came
across her down on the beach near Trevellin. Apparently, she was
on her knees, hysterical and trying to wash herself in the sea. The
woman asked her if she was OK and, when she clearly wasn't, she
persuaded her to come here.'

'Oh Christ,' Maggie said. 'Thank God she helped her. Rain
must feel so dirty…'

'Before you arrived, I tried to ascertain where she'd been these
past few days. At first, she told me that she'd hitched a lift out of
Cornwall and gone to her best friend Katie's house, that she'd not
been in the area at all. It might explain the van sighting. But then
she switched her story and said that she'd hit her head and lost her
memory, that she had no idea what had happened. Finally, she
told me that she'd been sleeping rough not far away, though she
wouldn't tell us where exactly. Like I said, her story kept changing.'

'None of it makes any sense.' Maggie felt sick.

'She told the psychologist that after what she did, she couldn't
live with herself.'

'Well, she clearly blames herself for what happened.'

'That's an understandable reaction, yes. But in this case, the psychologist said she was referring to something that happened during
the time she was missing, like she wants to talk about it but can't.'

Maggie paused, thinking. She'd seen the sadness in Rain's eyes,
felt something essential had changed. But that was hardly surpris-

ing, given what she'd been through. 'I see,' she replied quietly. 'I'll try to talk to her, but Rain won't ever be pushed.'

'I understand,' PC Wyndham replied. 'Anyway, as you know, we arrested Mr Rodway and he's now been charged with sexual activity with a child. With Rain.' The officer paused. 'It's a very strong case.' She took a breath, hesitating. 'We have photographic evidence.'

'Photographic evidence?' Maggie leant against the wall, her head bent back. 'The bastard took fucking pictures of her?' She banged the wall with her fists as more tears came and the implications sank in. Would he have shared the photographs online?

'Actually, the pictures were taken by a third party. And not in the way you might imagine, if that's any comfort. It strengthens our case enormously.'

Maggie tried to process what she was hearing but couldn't. She touched her forehead, shaking her head, kicking the wall with her foot.

'And just so you know, Mr Rodway has been released on conditional bail.'

'You let him *out*?'

'He's obviously banned from talking to witnesses and being alone with children. And sometime soon, Rain will need to make a video statement for court.'

Maggie was nodding, trying to absorb everything. All she wanted was to block out what he'd done to her daughter, but she didn't know how. And what did it all mean for Claire, the rest of the family? The repercussions felt endless, made her feel sick.

'Your liaison officer will still be in touch, and Rain will receive victim support, plus counselling services are available. And we'll be in close contact, of course, in case there's anything else she wants to tell us about.'

Maggie just kept nodding. It was all too much to take in. She watched as PC Wyndham walked off, going up to Claire and taking her aside. Claire glanced back, giving her a sad smile and, before she disappeared from sight, Maggie managed a small smile back.

With a couple of deep breaths, Maggie took a moment to compose herself before going back into Rain's room, avoiding the knot of people in the corridor. She couldn't face talking to anyone yet. She didn't feel real, praying that she would wake up from this nightmare and that everything would be back to normal – whatever normal was. She closed the door and sat on the bed, watching Rain who was now dozing. She leant forward, kissing her forehead. 'I really, *really* like it when you call me Mum,' she said, curling up beside her.

CHAPTER SIXTY-NINE

'Lucas Baby Number One' Claire read on his ankle tag as she held him. She stared down at the wriggling little bundle, all searching and curious expressions. She didn't know how she managed the smile as Jason took yet another photograph of her and her new nephew. Inside, she was shaking to the core, unable to rid her mind of what PC Wyndham had just told her in the corridor. The disgusting revelation about her husband – *how would she ever be able to call him husband again?* – had shattered her life into a million pieces. Holding this precious new life seemed so at odds with the monstrous crime he'd supposedly committed. She was being so gentle with the baby, yet all she wanted to do was get hold of Callum and rip him to pieces.

Claire peeked at the face of the wrapped-up baby girl cradled in her grandmother's arms, wondering if Shona saw what she saw reflected there – the furrowed and serious brow, the dimpled cheeks, the long fingers – all so reminiscent of Lenni. She turned to Jason, who was sitting right beside her. She drew in a breath, about to speak, but stopped.

'I know,' he said. 'I thought exactly the same thing the moment she was born. Mum saw it too.'

'They're beautiful,' Claire said, forcing another smile. She handed Baby One back to Jason and then prised Baby Two off her grandma. She thought Greta looked remarkable after such a short and sharp labour and wouldn't be surprised if she was back at work in a week. Claire thought how different their lives were, how much she'd always loved country living, the Old Stables, her family, her parents close by, her job, Russ the dog, the cats… Callum had been an integral part of all that and she'd never once considered him not being in her life. But now it was gone, destroyed in an instant by his… God, she didn't even know what to call it, would never understand what he had done.

Her mind flooded with horrible and intrusive thoughts – of him hurting Rain in that way, how terrified she must have been, how she would be feeling now. It was all unthinkable. The man she'd married, trusted for twenty years, was a criminal of the worst kind. She'd never been a violent person, but this had changed all that. Something powerful was rising inside her, something she knew she had to let out.

Shona left the others at the hospital and took a taxi back to Trevellin. She was worried about leaving Patrick alone too long. He wasn't answering the house telephone and she wanted to tell him the good news – about the babies as well as Rain being found. Besides, she was concerned he'd forget to take his medication.

The taxi left a trail of dust as it pulled down Trevellin's long drive. It hadn't rained in several weeks and the ground was hard and cracked – almost as if it was irritated. There was an eerie orange glow to the sun today, perhaps from the fine skim of high cloud shielding the landscape from the summer glare. Shona paid and got out of the car, staring up at the place she'd called home for as long as she could remember.

'I don't really want to sell you,' she said to the old building, not feeling in the least bit stupid. The house had its own character and she wouldn't have been particularly surprised if it had replied.

Inside, she felt another wave of worry when she didn't see Patrick sitting in his chair reading the paper. 'Pat, I'm home…'

she called out, wandering through the downstairs rooms. 'Are you here? I have lots of news.' She went upstairs to look, but he wasn't there either.

'Oh, Pat,' she said, her heart kicking up a gear. How she wished he'd carry the phone she'd bought him, but he was so stubborn, telling her he had no need for it. She went back into the kitchen. His medication was untouched on the counter and the note she'd left was still lying in exactly the same place. She went out into the courtyard, calling for him, listening out for his reply, but she heard nothing apart from the occasional cluck of a hen. Back inside, she saw his hat was missing from the hook in the boot room. His stick wasn't in the umbrella stand either, and his slippers lay discarded on the tiles.

'Oh, *Pat*,' she said again, wringing her hands. He wasn't usually gone this long. Enough was enough. He wouldn't be going anywhere unaccompanied again. She grabbed the phone, dialling Claire's number. 'Darling, it's Mum. Listen, I don't know what to do...'

CHAPTER SEVENTY

Shona heard a noise. She put down her mug of tea. 'Pat, is that you?' She'd spent the last half an hour going back and forth between the farmhouse and the Old Stables looking for him. She'd gone far out into the fields, calling out for him until she went hoarse. 'Oh, thank goodness,' she said, letting out the breath she seemed to have been holding forever, although she couldn't understand why he would knock on his own door. She got up and went to answer it.

But when she opened the door, her heart sank. 'Oh,' she said, unable to hide her disappointment. She glanced beyond the strangely dressed woman standing in front of her, hoping to see her husband. Had this person found him and brought him home? When she couldn't see Patrick anywhere, she looked the girl up and down. She was in a terrible state. Probably homeless or lost.

'I'm not buying anything, sorry,' Shona said. She was about to close the door when she spoke.

'I want to come in.' It was the hopelessness in her voice that prevented Shona going back inside. She squinted at her, her heart stumbling for a second.

'I'm sorry, you can't,' she said, for some reason not truly meaning it. There was something about her.

'Please,' she said in a childlike voice. Her mouth was covered in sores and her clothes were filthy. She looked like a child, even though she wasn't.

'I…' Shona faltered. Was it the pathetic '*Please*' that the girl uttered from crusted, swollen lips?

'I'm hungry,' she said.

Shona looked her up and down again. Some of her teeth were missing and she was pitifully thin. Her clothes were pink and pale green – a T-shirt with a fairy printed on the front, while faded tracksuit bottoms, far too short, clung to bowed legs. Brittle is what she brought to mind, as if she might snap at any moment.

She couldn't be cold-hearted. It wasn't in her nature. But there was something more concerning about her than her dark-ringed eyes, that smell making her feel sick. It was more than just an unwashed odour. It was how Shona imagined death would smell. She glanced around the courtyard for Patrick again. There was no sign of him.

'Where do you live?'

The girl waved her hand towards the fields. 'Over there…'

Travellers, probably, Shona thought. 'I'm so sorry, but you can't stay here. It's private property.'

'Where's Goose?' the girl said, louder. Her screwed-up eyes popped open, making Shona recoil. 'I want Goose!' This time it was a scream. The girl's voice broke and cracked and cut through the heat of the afternoon. She stamped her foot.

'What did you say?' It was Shona's turn to whisper now. Beyond the door, the courtyard seemed to sparkle, as if particles of the past were catching on fire. 'Tell me what you just said.'

'I want Goose.' Her words were automaton-like, dug up and spewed out as if she had malfunctioned. She jumped, slamming her feet onto the ground. Shona could almost hear her bones cracking as she did it over and over.

Goose?

The blood drained from Shona's head. She felt faint. Her hand slipped off the door handle, dangling by her side. 'Goose died a long time ago.'

They stared at each other, a connection in their eyes, something bubbling and simmering.

'Come in,' Shona whispered, opening the door wide. This couldn't possibly be real. Could it?

Very slowly, very tentatively, as if she was coaxing and taming a feral animal, the girl took a step forward. She wore too-big brown leather T-bar shoes like a child would wear to school. They flopped off her bony and bent feet as she took several more steps.

'That's right,' she said. 'Don't be afraid. I won't hurt you.'

Doleful eyes latched on to Shona's as she stepped inside the farmhouse. Her pungent smell grew stronger, but Shona didn't care. There was something about her, something that set her pulse skittering. For the moment, she couldn't think about anything else – not Patrick and where he was, or Jason's new babies or Rain's ordeal or Callum… nothing. She was simply transfixed, *entranced*, by the stranger in her house.

She hardly dared breathe. She'd been waiting for this moment for over two decades. If it wasn't real, it would kill her.

Shona closed the back door and led her into the kitchen. 'Shall I call a doctor?'

'Doctor…' the girl repeated, as her gaze flickered about. She backed away, her fists cracking into tight balls.

There, Shona thought. That look again, as if her eyes were fossilised with secrets. And the way her lips curled, slightly lopsided to the left, and the tinge of red in her tatty, unwashed hair set Shona's heart alight. She focused, forcing herself to stay calm. How many times had she seen what she'd wanted to believe?

'I'll call the doctor. I think you need help,' she said, reaching for the phone, her heart racing as she explained to the receptionist that a sick girl had turned up at her door. She promised to pass the message on. Erica had been the family's doctor for eons and would check her over. 'Would you like to sit down?' Shona asked, not knowing what else to say.

The girl didn't speak but slowly pulled out a chair from under the old pine table. She perched on the edge of the red spotty cushion. A hand went to the table's pitted surface and she ran her dirty fingers over the dents and stains that had accumulated from thousands of family meals.

Shona sat down opposite, watching her. 'Would you like something to eat?'

The girl didn't reply.

Shona knew what she had to do, but what if she was wrong? What if her mind was playing tricks, just like Patrick's did to him every single day? Malicious phone calls were one thing, but if she was mistaken about this, it would finish her off.

The girl's eyes rolled back in their sockets and pinpricks of sweat burst from her skin as if she had a fever. Her breathing was laboured and raspy while her collar bones jutted from beneath her T-shirt.

Shona went around to the other side of the table and tentatively brought a hand towards her. 'Do you mind?' There was no reply, so she placed her palm flat on her forehead. She felt the heat emanating from her. Then, without asking, Shona peeled back the thin layer of hair behind her left ear, leaning down to take a closer look. If it was there, she thought, it would be easy to find. Her fingers trembled as she parted the knotted strands. She held her breath and her heart thumped.

And there it was. About two inches long, the scar zigzagged away from the dirty creases behind the girl's ear down towards her equally grimy neck. It was much paler now and somehow seemed smaller than she remembered.

The clifftop walk, the windy day, then the fall down onto the rocks followed by the guilt at having to confess to the emergency doctor that they'd taken their eye off their daughter. Lenni had been pretending to be a bird but was more upset at not being able to fly than she was about the blood pouring from her head or the stitches she needed. Shona had felt like the worst mother in the world.

'Eleanor,' she whispered, crouching down beside the girl. She wanted to pull her into her arms but was worried she might crush her. Instead, her eyes blurred with tears. She had no idea if she was dreaming or had simply lost her mind. Nothing seemed real.

Silence for a few moments – no words, no joy or confusion, no breath or movement – just the beating of two hearts as they synchronised and fell into an old, familiar rhythm.

The girl tilted her head towards Shona as if it weighed a ton. Her eyes were washed out, vacant and staring, while her brain wrestled with the decision.

Yes or no? Am I Eleanor or not?

'Are you cross?' she whispered.

CHAPTER SEVENTY-ONE

Shona's message sounded urgent and desperate so, instead of calling her back, Claire headed straight back to the farm. She'd had enough of the hospital anyway and drove recklessly along the narrow lanes to Trevellin – her mind on fire from what Callum had done, as well as what she was going to do to him. Seeing the beautiful new babies was completely at odds with how she felt. She didn't think she'd ever felt so emotional, angry or upset.

She pulled into the courtyard and got out of the car, but even before her hand touched the back door knob, she slowed to a stop, sensing something was wrong. She wasn't sure what – perhaps just something in the air, the way the light was today. She knew this place too well, sensed every nuance, every tiny change. Even the chickens seemed to notice it, huddling against the barn wall. It was the silence that got to her most, making her pause before she went inside. She listened – nothing. Nothing except a slow, resonant heartbeat, as if the house itself was waking up from a long, long sleep. Then she went inside.

'Mum?' she called from the boot room. 'I got your message. What's going on? Is Dad back yet?' She dumped her bag on the side table and went through to the kitchen. Her initial feeling was relief. Shona was bending down, fussing over someone sitting in the armchair – her father, she assumed.

But when Shona stood, her worried expression conveyed to Claire that no, her father wasn't home yet. A dishevelled-looking girl sat beside her.

'I don't know where he is,' Shona confirmed, shaking her head.

'Have you been out looking?' Claire's eyes flicked between her mother and the girl in the chair. 'Shall I go up into the fields?'

'Love,' Shona said, ignoring her question. She reached out a hand to her. 'I think you'd better sit down for this.'

'Mum, what is it? Where's Dad? Just tell me what's happened?' Claire wasn't sure she could take anything else today.

'I'm praying Dad will be OK. Just sit down, will you, love? This is important.' Shona pulled out a chair from the table, but Claire remained standing.

'I think we should call someone, Mum. Maybe the police. It's been ages since he went.'

'Actually, I've already called them,' Shona said through a smile Claire didn't recognise. She nodded in return, relieved her mother had taken action, but then found her gaze drawn back to the silent girl. 'Although not for the reasons you think,' Shona added.

Claire sighed, annoyed at the intrusion of this girl's presence, but then she did a double take. What was that she just saw? That look. Goose bumps travelled down her entire body. She didn't want to embarrass the ill-looking visitor, but her being here was disturbing in a way she couldn't quite fathom.

'Darling, something has happened.' Shona's face was alight with wonder, as if she was in some kind of dream. Curiously, Shona got down on her knees in front of the girl and took hold of one of her hands. Claire thought she might kiss it and, when she actually did, she let out a shocked cough.

'Mum?' she said. 'You're scaring me now. What's going on?' Claire drew up to Shona's side, taking hold of her outstretched hand.

'Come here, Claire,' Shona whispered, beckoning her down to where she knelt on the rug. The girl sat blinking, staring straight ahead, her knees pressed together and her lips constantly churning as if they'd never been taught how to be still. She was dirty, thin, unhealthy-looking and the smell coming from her was nauseating. Yet there was something about her, something strangely beautiful and serene, though Claire's stressed and fragile mind couldn't pinpoint exactly what.

She did as Shona said, crouching down tentatively beside her mother. 'Please, Mum, tell me,' she said quietly, staring into the girl's sad eyes. Even before Shona had a chance to reply, the realisation flickered through her, filling her mind with possibilities. Though she hardly dared hope. What if she was wrong? But that *look*…

Claire clasped her mother's hand tighter, listening to the girl's rasping breaths, as if each one was a struggle.

'It's her,' Shona said. 'Darling… She's come home.'

Claire felt as though she was going to pass out. Without taking her eyes off the girl, she knelt down properly at her feet, studying every feature. What her mother was telling her, what she could see for herself, what had happened two decades ago were all at odds in her mind. Her rational side screamed out that this wasn't possible. She didn't know whether to laugh, cry, yell or punch something. Instead, she was perfectly still in case the beautiful moment disappeared.

'Lenni…?' Claire whispered, daring to take hold of one of the girl's thin hands. Shona held the other one and, between them, they formed a triangle, inching closer, drawing in to the daughter, the sister, they never thought they'd see again. Slowly, Claire brought Lenni's hand to her lips, kissing it, breathing in a glimmer of the last two decades.

Claire stared out to sea. The tide lapped at her ankles, soaking her trainers and the bottom of her jeans. She didn't care. The ambulance, with Lenni and several police officers in it, had not long left, but *she had actually been there at Trevellin all along?* Claire could hardly take it in.

Lenni. Eleanor. Len-monster.

She kicked the sand and an arc of watery sludge flew through the air. She did it again and again until her foot ached and a pair of hands came down gently on her shoulders from behind, steadying her.

'I saw her, Nick. I *saw* her.' She covered her face. The whole day was as far from reality as anything could be. Callum, Rain, the twins, Lenni… It somehow compressed the last couple of decades into a fleeting few seconds. They might as well all still be charging around the beach searching for Lenni the day she went missing. And Nick walking alongside her now made it seem as though nothing had changed. Yet everything had.

'It's fucking incredible,' he said, shaking his head. 'I still can't believe it. I mean, how did she seem? Do they know anything… did she say much? Is it really her?' Nick put his arm around her as they stared out to sea. There were so many questions, yet she couldn't answer them all yet.

'It was definitely her. They'll do DNA tests of course but Mum and I know. We saw the scar. Beneath the years of abuse, we still recognised her. She was ill, Nick, very ill. But she was still Lenni. They wouldn't let us go to the hospital with her yet. Something about infection risks and gathering evidence. We can see her again later.'

Nick nodded as the water lapped around their ankles.

'I literally thought I was going to pass out when Mum told me. I felt sick.'

'You've had more stress in a few days than most people have in a lifetime,' Nick said, pulling her closer. They stared at the horizon, watching the sun sink lower. In a few hours, there would be a spectacular sunset. Claire glanced at her watch.

'I should get back,' she said, feeling guilty. She'd told Shona she wouldn't be long, that she'd just needed time to think, to process what had happened. She still had Callum to deal with, after all. 'Plus, I'm worried sick about Dad. He wasn't back when I left.'

Nick agreed, and they walked back, their hands folding naturally together as they headed up the beach.

CHAPTER SEVENTY-TWO

When they got back to the farmhouse, Shona was about to leave with two police officers. 'Darling, they've said she's allowed one visitor at the hospital, so I must go, but I'm desperately worried about Dad. He's still not back.' She looked broken and was on the brink of tears. 'The police are going to look for him now. He needs to be told about Lenni.'

Claire placed a hand on her mother's arm. 'Yes, you go, Mum. I'll help find him. Try not to worry.' She paused, hardly able to believe what she was about to say. 'And tell Lenni I love her. Tell her I'm waiting for her. That I always have done.' She was fighting back the tears too, willing herself to stay strong. On the way back from the beach she'd spotted Callum's car at the Old Stables. Before she looked for her father, there was something else she needed to do.

The house was unusually dark and cool inside, as if it what had happened in it had somehow drained it of warmth and love. She didn't bother calling out his name; she knew the sick bastard was in there somewhere. Feeling oddly calm, her anger having transformed into a strange sense of power, Claire walked slowly through the hallway and into the kitchen. His keys were lying on the counter, as if he'd just come home from work, expecting his evening meal to be ready, plus all the other things he'd taken for granted over the years. None of it had ever bothered her before – she'd always enjoyed being a wife, a mother, his best friend. So she'd believed. She ran a glass of water, drinking it in a few swift gulps, wiping her mouth before going to the living room doorway.

Callum was sitting on the sofa, his head bent forward in his hands, staring at the floor.

Claire thumped her fist on the door, slamming it back against the wall. He didn't look up immediately, but when he did, he couldn't meet her eyes.

'You fucking disgusting piece of shit,' she spat out, her hand smarting. She didn't care. She thumped the door again, almost enjoying the feeling. 'How fucking dare you even set foot in this house after what you did. You shouldn't be near any of us.'

'Claire—'

'Don't give me your bullshit. I don't want to hear it.' She marched up close to him, shoving him on the shoulder. He flinched. 'What were you *thinking*?' She kicked his foot, but he just sat there. 'I've already told the police you made me lie to cover your slimy arse. You make me sick!'

'None of this is what you think,' he said, making to stand up. Claire shoved him again, catching him off balance so he fell back into the chair again.

'What, raping a fifteen-year-old isn't what it sounds like?' She let out a disgusted noise. 'I can't even listen to your pathetic excuses.' Claire spat at him, kicking his leg hard. He stood up, looming over her.

'You don't know what you're talking about, Claire. You're stressed and not thinking straight. We'll sort this out and everything will be normal again. Me, you, the kids – a fresh start.' He went to take her by the shoulders, perhaps even bring her in for a hug, but she shoved him again, her palms thumping flat against his chest.

'Don't fucking touch me, you pervert! I want you out of my life. And don't even think of going near our children ever again, you sick, sick monster.' Claire swung round, shaking, firing on pure adrenalin, and ran upstairs to their bedroom. She yanked open the wardrobe doors, grabbing armfuls of Callum's clothes – clothes she had once pressed and neatly put away. She opened the window and flung them out, hurling bundles of underwear, suits, sweaters, shoes – everything he owned – onto the front lawn.

'Claire, stop. You're not seeing sense right now. We need to pull together as a team—'

'Get out! Now!' she screamed. He was in the doorway – his face pale, his shoulders hunched.

'Claire…' he said, holding out his hands.

'Don't *Claire* me,' she replied, returning from the bathroom with an armful of his toiletries. They all went out of the window too. 'Rain is a *child*. What else have you done over the years that I don't know about?' She shook her head, blowing out a sigh through clenched teeth. Then she pulled two suitcases from the top of the wardrobe and shoved them at Callum. 'Get the fuck out of this house and don't come back. Ever!' The tears were flowing hot and fast now. 'I'll have the rest of your stuff sent on. To hell!' she screamed, lashing out at him again.

Fending off her blows, Callum finally retreated, taking the suitcases with him. When she heard the front door bang shut, the Range Rover roar off, Claire hurled herself onto the bed and sobbed like she'd never done before. Her life had been destroyed in the worst way imaginable, yet a part of it was also about to be rebuilt. She didn't know what to think or do, so she pressed her face into the pillow instead, letting the tears flow.

'Should I phone Mum *now?*' Claire said to Nick for about the tenth time. She'd tried to freshen up before coming back to the farmhouse, but even an hour later, her eyes were still red and sore. 'And should I call the police again about Dad?'

'Drink?' he said, pouring two glasses of wine. 'And no. You shouldn't call anyone. It's too soon.' It was good to see a flicker of hope in Claire's eyes, he thought, even though he could see she'd been sobbing. 'Just take a moment to relax, Claire. You're in a mess.'

They'd not long had a call from a detective about Lenni, but hadn't learnt much more. 'Your sister has been taken to a place of safety,' he'd told her. 'A secure medical facility. She'll be able to have more visitors tomorrow, but for now it's important we collect evidence before it becomes degraded.'

Claire had understood, though she wanted nothing more than to bundle Lenni up, bring her home and never let her out of her sight again. But she was grateful that Shona had at least been allowed to see her. 'Thank you,' she'd said flatly before hanging up. One more day without her. But it would be the longest of them all.

She took the wine gratefully. 'Why, Nick, *why*, after all these years, did she turn up out of the blue? Did someone release her, did she escape?' Her mind was leaping ahead, filling up with questions that didn't yet have answers. 'She was virtually mute when she was here and seemed terrified, so we didn't press her.' She took a mouthful of wine. 'What if she'd *wanted* to disappear?' She covered her face at the possibility, that life here at the farm had become too intolerable.

She stared at the chair where Lenni had sat. It had swallowed her up.

'If someone took her, I swear I'll kill the fucker who did it.' Her voice was wavering. 'I'm so angry. Angrier than I've ever been… about *everything* that's happened.' Shaking, she put down her wine and tugged hard at her wedding ring, pulling it off and tossing it across the table so it skidded onto the floor.

'I'm here for you, Claire. We'll get through this,' Nick said, taking her hand.

She looked at him, about to say something, but she heard a noise outside. She stood, glancing out of the window. 'Oh, thank

God. Jason's back,' she said, watching as the taxi pulled away. She'd phoned him a hundred times, but his battery must have run out. 'And Maggie and Rain are with him too.' She ran to the back door, grabbing onto her brother as he came inside, pulling Maggie and Rain close too. She tried to tell them everything coherently, but it all blurted out in garbled sobs.

For a while, Jason didn't speak. He dropped into his father's chair and sat, stunned, unable to comprehend the end of what had already been the most momentous day of his life. He'd left Greta in hospital sleeping with their babies – each was adorable and healthy, and Greta was glowing, ready to take on motherhood. But this… this was not what he'd expected. It was joy enough to be a father, to have Rain found safe and well, but to learn that Lenni – *were they sure it was her, he'd asked a thousand times* – had somehow come home, alive, was more than he could take in.

'Oh, Claire, that's unbelievable, incredible,' Maggie said, as they hugged. 'I don't know what to say… about anything any more, frankly.' She went over to be with Rain who was sitting in the corner, watching and listening to the goings-on, though quietly indifferent with a fearful look in her eye. Her legs were curled up on the chair and her arms clutched an oversized cardigan around her body – so unlike the Rain any of them knew. She needed her mother more than ever now.

By the time Marcus came back, plans were being made amid a cacophony of speculation and unanswerable questions. Claire had arranged for Amy to stay on and sleep over at her friend's house. Explaining everything to her daughter was not something she could deal with tonight. Besides, Amy had witnessed enough upheaval and drama these last few days, and time with her best friend would do her good. She knew she'd be perfectly safe.

'Mum, that's totally incredible,' Marcus said, wide-eyed. 'It's just, like, amazing.' He didn't know what else to say so he pulled his phone from his pocket and began thumbing the keys.

'I'd keep quiet about it if I were you, mate,' Nick said. 'Don't put anything on Facebook, and I wouldn't text your friends either. Once the story gets out, there'll be no peace.'

Marcus sheepishly stuffed his phone back into his pocket. 'Anyway, where's Dad? I've been trying to call him all afternoon, 'cos he was going to give me a lift later.'

Claire looked away for a moment, breathing in deeply. 'He has some things to take care of, love.' It was a placeholder lie that she hated telling, but it would have to do for now. She had no idea where Callum had gone or what she would tell her children. They had a right to know everything, but how would she explain that their father had been charged with a sexual offence against a child? The police had put Marcus through the mill, grilling and almost accusing him while Callum had looked on, knowing what he'd done.

But any further thoughts were interrupted by the telephone. 'Yes,' Claire said several times after answering. She gripped the worktop, drawing in breath – a breath that was deep enough to signal either a scream or a long sigh of relief. In the end, it escaped as a small gasp. A gasp that said *Nothing more can shock me today*. She hung up and stood perfectly still. 'That was the police,' she said. 'They've found Dad.'

CHAPTER SEVENTY-THREE

Easy As

I'm humming a little tune and my teeth are chattering. I wish I'd put on my cardigan. The water swells around my ankles, then draws out again, sucking me down an inch or two into the sand with every step. I glance behind me to check I'm not leaving a trail of footprints, the wind whipping my hair across my face. With every wave that rolls in, with every footstep washed away, it's as if I never even existed.

Claire watched me like a hawk when I set off, but she isn't any more. It's just her bright green towel left on the sand as she leaps in the surf with Nick. Everyone knows she fancies him.

I'm going to buy ice cream, and no one can stop me!

'Ha ha,' I call out to a dog as it gallops past me in the breakers. 'I'm off on my own like you.' Its owner trails the dog's lead in the water as he plods along.

I'm running! Running like the dog, bounding through the waves in my plastic sandals, water splashing up everywhere. Up ahead on the flat expanse of beach, the sand blows in horizontal streaks as if it's coloured with pastel chalks and someone's smudged their finger through it. The pound coin is hot in my salt-sticky palm.

Rum and raisin or chocolate?

I glance back at the others again for good luck. They are dots in the distance now and my heart picks up speed as I wade knee-deep

in the sea. '*My* sea', I told Claire, as we raced down to the shore
after our picnic. 'My sea and I'm in it first.'

'Stupid Len-monster', she called out and I'd laughed, falling
head first into the waves. 'You'll get a stitch swimming so soon
after eating, silly!' She only said it because Mummy always does.

Why are they always so worried about me? It's not as if I'm
going to die.

There aren't many people on the beach today. It's too windy,
though the holiday season has begun – *swarming with tourists*,
Mummy told me, as if they were insects. They pay her money
to stay at the farm – Trevellin Farm Bed & Breakfast, £18 per
person per night. We get a lot of guests in the summer. There's
that weird man in the lilac bedroom at the moment. He smells
of wet dogs and always has crumbs stuck in his beard. Claire says
he's saving them for later. She also says that he's come away for a
dirty weekend because she found a rude magazine under his pillow
when Mummy made her do his room. Claire gets a pound every
time she makes a bed and wipes around the bathroom.

I wade out of the water and head inland across the ridged sand.

'Where you off to, young lass?'

My heart leaps. *Don't speak to strangers.* I glance sideways at the
man, breathing a sigh of relief.

'To get ice cream,' I tell Mr Headley. He's the headmaster at
my school. My cheeks flush red because he's looking at me in my
swimsuit – *Claire's* swimsuit – and it's a bit big. I clamp my arms
around my chest.

'I'm off to get a breath of fresh air,' he says, as if there might
be one tumbling along the sand.

'I hope you find one,' I say, and begin walking again. But
Mr Headley grabs hold of my arm, making me swing around on
my heel.

'How's your mother?' he asks. There's a glint in his eye.

'She's fine, thank you.' I remember to be polite even though he's hurting me.

'Send her my regards, then.' When he lets go, I run off without looking back until I reach the scratchy grass up on the sandbank. Only then do I turn, panting, hands on knees, looking down at the beach. Mr Headley is nothing more than a speck on the sand.

The marram grass stings my bare legs as I push through. I step over it like a circus pony – big high strides with my skinny legs. Finally, I reach the road. To the right, the track stretches back towards the rocky cliff end of the beach near where the others are. I could have come that way as it would have been quicker, but Claire said not to take the cliff path. It's perfectly safe after a quick scramble up the scree track, which is just plain fun, taking three giant leaps up and sliding back another couple on the slate chips. Your toes go dusty blue.

I look both ways and cross the road. No cars except for the ones parked outside the row of shops opposite. There's the ice cream shop, which is quite famous – people come from all over to buy their Cornish ices. Imagine owning a shop that sold only ice cream. I know what I want to be when I grow up! Then there's the little café that Mummy won't go in because Daddy fell out with the lady. Although Claire says that it's because Daddy *likes* the lady in there, what with her blue spotty dress and pinned-up hair and her thinking she's a movie star even though she just serves tea and scones and has jam on her apron. There's a newsagent shop where Claire and I sometimes come to fetch milk or bread, and then there's the surfers' shop that has giant, colourful boards outside on the pavement, all standing upright in a giant toast rack.

Nigel, the surf shop boy with curly blond hair, is standing in the doorway. He smiles and waves at me. He's smoking a cigarette. 'Where's your big sister?' he asks.

'Down on the beach. I'm getting ice cream.'

'Choose wisely, then.' His long hair blows across his face and gets caught in the tip of his cigarette. 'Fuck,' he says under his breath.

I go inside the ice cream shop, tucking my salty, tangled hair behind my ears. The glass freezer counter stretches the width of the shop and there are a few little round tables in front in case you want to eat your ice cream sitting down. I like to eat mine walking along. It tastes better with every step.

'Hello,' the lady says. 'What can I get for you?'

'Not sure,' I say without looking at her. The tubs are arranged in colour order – from the palest, most delicate lemon sorbet on the left to the deepest double chocolate on the right. In-between is a rainbow of tastes – pink, blue, green, red, yellow, beige, orange. My tongue fizzes at the thought of them all.

'What's that?' I ask, pointing to a bright blue one.

'Bubble-gum heaven,' she says. 'It's new.' She's holding the scoop. Water drips off it.

'Can I have a scoop of that, then,' I say, 'and a scoop of rum and raisin?'

The woman hesitates, pulling a face. 'Are you sure?'

I nod. I have never been more certain of anything.

Someone else comes into the shop. I spin around on my heel a couple of times, waiting for my ice cream.

'Hello, Eleanor,' Mrs Lyons says. 'Fancy seeing you here.'

'Fancy,' I say, proud to be out on my own. Mrs Lyons is Mum's friend. She used to be our cleaner. She's got her two boys with her. They're younger than me, and one of them pokes his tongue out.

'Here you go,' the ice cream lady says. 'That's one pound twenty, please, love.'

My cheeks burn the colour of raspberry ripple. 'But I've only got a pound.' I don't know what to do. 'I thought it cost a pound.'

'Price went up,' the woman says. 'Do you want it or not?'

I hang my head. 'I suppose not,' I say. By the time I go back and pester Claire for more money, it will have melted. Besides, she won't let me walk up here all by myself again.

'Here,' Mrs Lyons says. 'I've got twenty pence.' She gives it to me. It's really shiny.

'Oh, *thank* you,' I say, beaming and handing it to the ice cream lady. She has one hand stuck on her hip, passing me my cone with the other, before turning to serve Mrs Lyons. I leave the shop, whispering a silent prayer.

Outside, there's a car parked with a man sitting in the driver's seat. Two wheels are up on the pavement. The window is down, and his arm is resting on the door. 'Hurry up, Sal,' he yells, as I walk past, making me jump. Mrs Lyons glances around. She scowls and taps her watch, making the man swear under his breath. I walk past, licking my ice cream, and he stares at me long and slow.

'I'm off, then, if you're going to piss about in there,' he yells, before starting the engine, spinning his wheels and driving off towards the cliffs. I watch him go, suddenly shivering even though it's warm. My shorts are soaking, and the ice cream is making me even colder.

'No one will ever know,' I whisper, staring in the direction of the car. It's only a short way along the road, then a few minutes' walk along the clifftop path, then a fun slide down the shingle slope. It'll be much quicker. My mind is made up, so I set off, making sure to keep on the verge. This ice cream is delicious. I feel very grown-up.

The track rises up and it's even windier up here than down on the beach. I walk fast but my wet shorts rub against the insides of my legs, making my skin sore, so I take them off, hopping about as they get caught on my sandals. I nearly drop my ice cream.

A car comes past, hooting at me, slowing down. Red brake lights flash on and off as it pulls to a stop. Then a white light comes on and the car reverses. I stand quite still, frozen. In another second, it's alongside me. It's really old and more like a long van, rusty around the wheels. There's loud music coming from the open window, two people inside.

Suddenly, my ice cream doesn't taste very nice. My shorts are around my ankles.

'You know anywhere we can park up, love? If you know what I mean…' The man is all slurry, as if he's just woken up. He's got stubble and his eyes are droopy. He's not very old. The passenger is a girl. She's pretty and has her bare feet up on the dashboard. Her toenails are painted purple. 'Anywhere, like, private?'

I shrug, licking my lips.

'She's just a kid, Gaz. She won't know,' the girl says, prodding him. 'C'mon, let's go.'

The man stares at me, then puts the car into gear before driving off.

'Sorry,' I call out after they've gone. Really, I'm saying sorry to Claire for taking the cliff route back, but if I double back now and go the beach way, it'll take even longer, and she'll be even more cross. My ice cream cone tastes really horrid now – the bubble-gum flavour has dribbled into the rum and raisin. If I take it back to Claire, then I'll have to eat it in front of her and I'll be sick, but Claire won't like that I wasted her money. I glance around. There's no one here. Guiltily, I chuck the cone and its remaining scoop of softening blue sludge onto the verge.

I pull my shorts off properly and walk on, finally heading across the springy grass towards the scree slope. I weave between the bushes that have sprouted up, all bleached pale like the surfers' hair. They whip and scratch around my ankles as I hum. Just a little tune to stop me feeling scared for being out here all alone.

Then, as easy as anything, a warm hand comes over my mouth from behind. I can't even scream. Can't even breathe.

I twist around to see crazy eyes above me – eyes filled with fear and sadness. A finger goes up to puckered, dry lips, telling me to shush, warning me not to make a sound. I drop my shorts as I'm dragged away.

CHAPTER SEVENTY-FOUR

Eleanor Mary Lucas was dressed in white – a white medical gown beneath a white towelling robe. They'd given her pristine white slippers, and her toes, with their misshapen nails, clawed out from the end. After multiple medical tests and hours of police evidence gathering, she'd finally been allowed to wash with the help of a nurse. But the grime was still ringed around her neck, her wrists, her knuckles. Looking at her, sitting in the vinyl-covered chair beside her bed, it wasn't obvious that Eleanor had spent nearly two thirds of her life locked away. Though it was clear that part of her wasn't there.

'No bother, my love,' the nurse had said of the dirt. 'It'll come off in good time.' Eleanor hadn't known what she'd meant by that. No amount of time was good in her mind. She'd sat bent forward in the bath, watching as the water lapped at her veined and naked body, rippling over skin that looked unfamiliar in the daylight. She wondered who she was, if she was the same person or a new person. A third incarnation of someone she'd forgotten. The nurse, elbow-deep, had encouraged Eleanor to hold the sponge, soap it up, to wash away everything. Her body burned and stung from the bubbles, and then she laughed. She laughed so much she made waves. She wasn't free at all.

Of course there were questions, a lifetime of those, and Eleanor had to have her lawyer present when they were asked. She didn't even know she had a lawyer, she realised, as the words floated around her.

'I don't know,' she said, when they asked if she'd killed him. Her eyeballs felt huge.

Shafts of sunlight sliced between the blind slats. In the brightness, she saw a silhouette of the hammer. The big heavy hammer he'd brought down to fix the pipes with. She hadn't waited to find out if he'd actually died from the blows, but he must have because he hadn't chased after her. And there was all that blood.

I am as bad as bad can be…

He'd given her enough movies to watch over the years. She knew what it was to be evil. She'd told the police about the films, recounted how she thanked her lucky stars that she was safe in there, out of harm's way. She told them about the little gifts and the trips out too – the places he'd taken her when she'd been good. She smiled when she remembered the butterfly in the jar, but they didn't smile – the doctors and the police. They just sat there, swallowing, breathing, unmoving. She spoke about the bits she could remember and then, when they asked her a question about one thing, she'd get sidetracked and tell them all about another. Her mind went everywhere. Like that butterfly set free. If it hadn't already been dead.

'I read books too,' she said in response to *Why do you think he did it?* because she couldn't answer that. When they asked about how he treated her, she told them about the mouse in the cage and how some of her teeth had fallen out. *Did you ever go hungry? Did he hurt you? Did he force himself on you sexually? Did anyone see you when you went out on trips? Why didn't you scream for help?*

'Goose is dead now,' she said, staring at the feet of people she didn't recognise. But they didn't know what that meant, that she was sad because of it.

'Why now, Eleanor? Why didn't you overcome him before?'

They didn't understand. Didn't understand how she could never, and *would* never, hurt him. She couldn't tell them why – that she loved him with all her heart. Then that voice in her head again, ringing noises inside her skull just as the hammer must have rung loud in his: *Fucking kill him! Do it!*

But she hadn't.

Had she?

Those moments of her life, those few seconds, wrapped up in the years (she thought it must have been many, many, many years by now) blurred into what seemed an even longer stretch of time. Her eyes had refused to see the blood; her ears were deaf to the crack of bone and core-deep moans coming from him. Even her skin was numb to the fresh wind tunnelling down to greet her, to tempt her out. Blowing her hair.

And then there was that girl. That beautiful, strange girl. Setting the butterfly free.

Doing what she'd never been able to do all those years.

Where had she come from?

Eleanor stared up at the ceiling to make the tears go back in, then she looked around the hospital room, blinking. She pined for the jaundiced glow of the flickering bulb above her mattress, the tiny fridge that hummed her to sleep, the steady drip of the wobbly tap and the comforting clank of the locks when he came to visit, making her tummy go tight with anticipation. She couldn't bring herself to look out of the hospital window yet, because she knew it was filled with the whole world. And that was way too big for someone like her.

CHAPTER SEVENTY-FIVE

It was Jason who identified Patrick's body. A brief, clinical and impersonal procedure, there were several medical staff flanking him as he gagged at the sight of his father's smashed-up skull. He'd been bludgeoned to death by a hammer. 'That's him,' he said, nodding and cupping his hand over his mouth. He turned and left, rushing to the toilets.

Later, he crossed the street to buy cigarettes – his first in years – darting onto the pavement as a car hooted. How the fuck had the bastard got away with it for so long? Outside the shop, he lit up and inhaled deeply, needing to get rid of the bad taste in his mouth. How in God's name had he hidden her for all these years?

'In plain sight,' the senior detective said, before he left. Jason knew that, eventually, it would all be unravelled – the forensic teams picking apart what had happened up at the old cottage, how their father had kept his youngest daughter alive, barely, in the most horrific conditions. Breaking it to Claire that Lenni had been so close, right under their noses all this time was not going to be easy. He crushed the half-smoked cigarette under his foot and drove slowly back to Trevellin.

Three days later, after Lenni had gradually given more and more detailed descriptions to the police with the help of psychologists, the area around the derelict cottage was still sealed off. Forensic investigators swarmed up and down the hill to do their work, picking apart the remnants of several decades, photographing, bagging, labelling, removing, in order to piece everything back together in a way that might, by some miracle, make sense. The hopelessness was palpable, could be tasted on the sea breeze. It went unspoken that finding sense, of any kind, was unlikely.

Police worked tirelessly in the cottage and around the woodland, white-suited, delving in and out like maggots gorging on rot. The lead investigator informed them it could take weeks to analyse everything, to build a picture.

Bit by bit, the cellar beneath the old cottage on Trevellin Farm's land – the cellar that Patrick had secretly soundproofed, shored up and converted over the years – was taken apart. Once or twice Claire went to watch from behind the twisted, flapping crime scene tape, but it was too much to bear, and she retreated to the farmhouse. From the window, as the forensic teams tramped through the courtyard carrying their findings, she tracked their comings and goings as they stowed the items in an ever-changing convoy of police vehicles. Then curiosity would draw her out. Staring into the back of the van, she saw a museum of individually bagged books, items of clothing, cutlery, DVDs, scraps of paper, rotten food, hair, teeth, excrement, shreds of unidentifiable substances and thousands of other miniscule samples of a secret existence. They'd taken out Patrick's body in a bag at the end of the first day.

She couldn't make any of what she saw fit with the man she knew as her father. If she thought too deeply about it, she threw up.

'I could only manage a quick glance at him,' Jason told Claire, when he'd returned from taking Shona to stay with Angus and Jenny. Their mother had needed to get away, but would return, she promised, when she felt stronger, when Lenni was allowed home. A half-empty bottle of wine sat on the kitchen table between them. 'They'd cleaned him up a bit, but to see him lying there in the morgue, knowing what he'd fucking done…'

Claire held up her hands to signal him to stop. 'I don't want to know,' she said, turning away. He'd already told her the hammer wounds on his head were horrific, the top of his skull caved in.

'It must have been instant,' he added. Silence hung between them, though they were thinking the same thing: how did a frail girl like Lenni wield a hammer against Patrick?

Earlier, Jason had ventured as close to the cottage as he could get. He wanted to see his father's perspective on the many trips he must have made up there, going undetected, delivering supplies, deceiving Claire, Shona, conning the whole family – *everyone* – over the decades. Guilt cut through him that he hadn't been around for most of that time. Would he have picked up on the signs, noticed any strange behaviour to unmask his father? Perhaps that was why he'd preferred to keep Jason at arm's length, refusing to build bridges between them. He didn't want him – a young, fit man with an interest in the cottage – working on the farm for a reason.

Standing as close to the building as he was allowed, breathing in the clean air of the coast mixed with the stench of what had happened, Jason tried to see it through different eyes. Had his father's love for Lenni, his over-protectiveness of her, driven him to extremes? Or was he simply a sick fuck who had abused his youngest child over two decades? Try as he might, he couldn't see it as anything other than the vile act it was. Nothing, but *nothing*, could justify what he'd done. He hoped Patrick rotted in hell. He was glad they'd never made up.

Apart from the bright, flickering police tape and the comings and goings of officers, the place looked pretty much a it had done since they were kids. Ivy had almost completely obscured two sides of the wrecked cottage, and a multitude of creatures and birds had made it their home – including, he reflected, his little sister. Above ground, there was no sign of the twenty-one-year secret it contained; not a hint of what the police had described as a feat of engineering for one man. What was left of the collapsing roof had sunk lower on bowing timbers, pressing down on the cracking stone walls, while the windows were being twisted from their frames. But below, the cellar was protected and intact.

Jason glanced down. Something caught his eye. Something glinting in the grass. He looked around before bending down to pick it up. It was a silver pendant, just a simple one – a sort of cross with a rounded head on a chain. He vaguely recognised it.

Had the police missed it, he wondered? Was it evidence? He knew he should hand it in, but the thought that it might belong to Lenni made him slip it in his pocket. He didn't notice the tiny smear of fresh blood left behind on his fingers.

As Jason turned to go, an officer in a forensic suit emerged from the enclosure carrying equipment. He nodded briefly at Jason. The family had been told they could go inside the cellar when the investigating team had finished, but they'd already agreed they wouldn't. The cottage would be demolished, flattened as if it never existed, and the basement filled in with the rubble. Shona wanted trees, she'd said. Something beautiful for the future owners. She was planning on instructing Jeff to get the 'for sale' board up, to get the entire property advertised at a knock-down price as soon as she was back from Angus and Jenny's and felt able to take on a move.

Jason turned his back and walked away, his fingers clenched around the pendant.

CHAPTER SEVENTY-SIX

Maggie planned on staying in Cornwall for a while longer, to support and be with Claire. There was practical work to be done too, helping prepare for Lenni's return home and all the many other arrangements that had washed up like wreckage after a storm.

Since Rain had come back, she'd tried to keep her close, not wanting to let her out of her sight. Generally, she just lay on her bed or sat at the kitchen table staring at her phone, flicking through Facebook and Instagram, but one morning, when Maggie couldn't find her in the usual places, her heart raced. She ran around the farmhouse, calling out her name, getting more and more frantic as the panic swelled.

'Oh… there you are,' she said breathlessly from the doorway, trying to sound casual. The last thing she wanted was for Rain to feel smothered. 'What are you doing in here?' Lenni's room was the last place she thought she'd find her. 'Are you OK, love?'

Rain was staring out of the window, her back to Maggie, gazing across the fields up towards the woods and the old cottage. She shrugged.

'What are you thinking about?' Maggie went up to her and put an arm around her shoulder.

'Just stuff,' she said, picking up a china elephant from the windowsill. 'Is this hers? Lenni's?'

Maggie nodded. 'Shona kept everything in here just as it always was.'

Rain nodded, a tear rolling down her cheek. 'It's so sad,' she said, sniffing, wrapping her fingers around the little ornament.

'I know…' Maggie said. 'None of us can even begin to imagine what she went through, being trapped all those years.'

Rain slowly turned to face her mother. Her eyes narrowed, flickering in thought. 'I can,' she said. 'You don't have to be locked in a room to feel trapped.' She let out a sigh.

Maggie gave a little nod, trying to understand. She wanted nothing more than to fold her daughter in her arms, beg her forgiveness. But she knew it wasn't that simple. Instead, she gently pulled her closer.

'It's funny, you can feel trapped even though you're not really,' Rain continued. 'Like it's become a habit, as if you can only see that one path, treading it over and over again.' She paused a moment. 'Sometimes, though, all it takes is a shove from someone else to help you find a way out.' She leant forward on the windowsill to get a better view up the hill. 'Or *see* a way out. Locked doors aren't always real ones.'

'OK,' Maggie said slowly. 'Go on…'

'Mum, I've been throwing up,' she said, keeping her eyes fixed out of the window. 'For years. Nothing much stays in me. I've hated myself for so long. It was meant to be an escape, but it's not. After what happened to me with…' She broke off, choking back the sobs as she remembered what he did to her. 'Well, it just keeps me even more imprisoned, even more out of control.' Then the tears began to flow.

'Oh, darling, I get that. I really do. You're so brave.'

'You know,' she went on, 'it took something like this,' and she lifted up the little elephant, running her finger over its broken trunk, 'to make me realise that with a little bit of courage, with a little bit of help from someone in the right place at the right time, we can *all* escape.' She reached into her pocket and pulled out a tissue, blowing her nose, hoping her mum would make the connection. But she didn't. 'It's like I've stepped outside of myself. Like Lenni, I feel set free. It's scary but good.'

'I think you're an amazing and strong young woman and we're going to get through this. Together.' Maggie wrapped her up in her arms, holding her tightly. 'I've been offered a job,' she said after a few moments, feeling the time was right to tell Rain. 'It's at Aunty Rose's hotel in the Cotswolds. Mum's younger sister. It's a beautiful place. If you like it there, we can live in. You'll have your own room. There's a good college nearby too.'

Rain watched her mother for a second, seeing the hope spread across her face. How could she destroy that? Some things were best left unsaid, connections left unmade, she decided. After all, in her own way, her mum had been trapped all this time too. She just hadn't realised it.

'I think I'd like that. A new start,' Rain replied, gently placing the elephant back on the sill. 'They never forget, do they, elephants?'

'Apparently not.'

'I'll never forget either.' She followed Maggie out, taking one last look back at Lenni's room. 'Never, ever,' she said, about to close the door behind her. Instead, she decided to leave it wide open.

'Cup of tea, love?' Maggie said, when they were in the kitchen.

Rain managed a small smile. 'Sure, thanks.'

It was a tiny start, Maggie thought, putting the kettle on. A gesture, a tiny piece of the bridge she knew needed building. Rain was beginning to open up, though she knew there was a long way to go. PC Wyndham's words were still in her head, about something else having happened while Rain was missing. But surely, nothing short of murder could be worse than what she'd already been through?

'Here you go, love,' she said, handing her a mug. Russ came in, wagging his tail and sniffing around Rain. She gave him some fuss.

'Thanks, Mum,' she said, as Russ lay down at her feet. 'I'm sorry I scared you. I know I shouldn't have run away.' Rain bowed her head. 'It was my way of dealing with what happened that Saturday night…' She stroked Russ again. 'Wherever you go, your problems come too. I was running away from myself, not you.'

'I hear you,' Maggie said, thinking how she too had done similar things, running from one man to another, using relationships to plug the massive hole inside her. She felt like the worst mother in the world. It was time for things to change. 'I can't imagine the terror of what you went through with…' She couldn't bring herself to say the bastard's name. She knew if she ever saw him again, she'd kill him. 'But I'm here for you now, my darling. We'll work through it together.'

Rain drank some tea. 'I have a confession,' she said. 'I took that pendant you really love.' She hung her head. 'I saw it lying on your dressing table upstairs here, when I was getting ready to go out the other night. After Marcus told me about Lenni's case, I googled it. Turns out she had a necklace that looked identical to yours. You know I love all that mystery stuff.' Rain paused, waiting for a reaction. 'It's the necklace that inspired my tattoo. You wore it all the time last year. So weird, right?' She hesitated. 'Anyway, I was going to put it back, I swear, but then… Anyway, I must have lost it when I was sleeping rough. I'm so sorry, Mum. You know I don't steal, least of all from you.' Rain cupped the mug in her hands.

'Oh, Rain, that pendant is the least of everything.' Maggie came up to her, crouching down. 'You've been through so much these last few days.'

She looked at Maggie, her unmade-up eyes young and fresh, yet tinged with a deep sadness. 'Yeah,' she whispered. 'You have no idea.'

*

'I can't fucking stand it, Claire,' Maggie said, while Rain was resting. 'I can't stand what he did to her being inside my head, let alone my daughter going through it. And she told me she's always hated herself.' Maggie made a noise halfway between a growl and a scream, blowing smoke out of the back door. The women shared a knowing look, each feeling the same raging hatred towards Callum. 'Things like that don't happen to people like us, Claire. Not fucking *rape*. Not my daughter!' She knocked back the shot of whisky Claire had poured each of them. 'I've been such a crap mother.'

'Me too,' Claire said. 'When you think about it, I allowed my kids to live with a monster.' She prised Maggie's cigarette off her, taking a couple of drags. 'Been a long time since I did that,' she said. 'But fuck it. Everything's different now.'

'Rain was screaming out for help in all kinds of ways, but I didn't see the signs.' Maggie took back her cigarette. 'She got pretty obsessed with Lenni's story; said something about drawing in the dirt on the back of your car. She apologised profusely. And she left her shorts to be found too, again to make everyone worry. As if we weren't worried enough.' Maggie pushed the cigarette butt into a nearby plant pot.

'Ah,' Claire said. 'That explains a lot.'

'I have an apology of my own to make, actually,' Maggie said, as they came back inside. 'When we were kids, I stole your necklace, the one you and Lenni were both given. I was so bloody jealous of you, and that necklace represented everything I didn't have – a loving family and parents that cared, a sister.' It felt good to be honest after all this time, Maggie thought. 'I brought it down with me to return. I was going to leave it in your room, but it disappeared before I had a chance. Turns out Rain took it.'

'Oh, Mags,' Claire said, hugging her. 'It's OK. I don't care about the stupid necklace. *He* gave them to us.' A look swept over her face. She couldn't call him Dad any more. 'He said they were lucky, would keep us safe. Lenni broke hers, so she just kept the charm in her pocket. They found it along with her shorts.'

'For what it's worth, I'm truly sorry.'

'No need. Our friendship has always been stronger than that.' And way stronger than the lies Callum told about Maggie too. 'I'll miss you both when you've gone, you know. Despite being the worst reunion in history, it's been good to see you, Mags.'

'The Cotswolds isn't far. We'll visit often, and you must bring Marcus and Amy to stay.'

'We will. Just the three of us,' she added, locking up the back door.

CHAPTER SEVENTY-SEVEN

'So, there was no cash buyer?' Nick asked Claire. While Maggie was sticking close to Rain – they'd moved into the Old Stables and were upstairs playing with Amy – he was also staying on to support Claire.

'Jeff was vague. Embarrassed at not checking him out properly, I think,' she replied.

'Have you heard how Shona's doing today?' Nick slid a plate of toast in front of her, aware she'd hardly eaten the last few days.

'Angus said she's still in a bad way, barely functioning. She's going to stay on with them for a bit, until Lenni comes home. The doctor gave her some tablets, so she's getting a bit of sleep now at least.' She took a tiny bite of toast, feeling sick. 'Mum's always been a fighter, just got on with things. But this… it's destroyed her. I can't stand it, Nick.'

'Nothing will ever be the same again, you know that. But don't rush yourself.'

Claire nodded, thinking. 'All I know is that we have to get rid of this place as soon as Mum's up to it. The whole lot, including the Old Stables. I can't live here knowing what my sick fuck of a husband did. And knowing how close Lenni was all this time, I just can't take it in. It's almost like I need more proof, something to convince me I'm not going mad. How can the two men I loved most in the world be so evil?' She pushed away the toast, feeling the anger rising again. 'There's something I need to do, Nick, but I can't do it alone. Will you come with me?'

He nodded, following her as she grabbed the keys and marched up the drive. He didn't want to leave her side for a moment. Claire unlocked the house and went straight to her father's study, tensing up as they went in, pausing as if she'd caught a whiff of him, perhaps seeking some kind of explanation. It was all about getting answers now, something to ease the turmoil in her mind, to bridge the gap between what she'd believed about her father and the grim reality.

'Jeff told me he'd seen the damage at Galen Cottage and reported it to the police. The damage *I'd* done.' She paused, running over that morning in her mind. 'I need my job more than ever now, so I didn't tell him it was me. The police went up there to check it out and found a pair of glasses in a case.' Claire sighed, hesitating before dropping down onto the old sofa. It still smelt of *him*.

'How's that significant?'

'The glasses case was labelled with a name and address. My *father's* name and address.'

'Sometimes it's best not to read too much into things, Claire.' Nick could see where this was going.

'It was *him* who scared the living daylights out of me at the viewing.' She leant back against the cushions but sat up again. 'Mum said he'd gone off in a right state that morning, after an argument about selling the farm. He must have got lost and confused.' Claire's hands were shaking as she pulled up Greene & Galloway's website on her phone. 'Look, that's Galen Cottage. It's so similar to the cottage where he'd kept Lenni.' She dropped her head, stifling the sobs.

Nick nodded, checking it out. 'They're very similar. But Patrick wouldn't have taken your bag and phone, surely?'

'At the time, I was convinced someone had. But Jason proved otherwise. I was so scared, maybe I was mistaken. My father wasn't the only one muddled and panicking.'

'You think he was panicking?'

'He would have been if he couldn't find Lenni there. His dementia was getting worse.' Claire leapt up, opening the old cupboard behind her, rummaging through decades of collected belongings – everything from trinkets and sticky whisky bottles, books and papers to old electrical items that Patrick had refused to throw away. It all spilt out onto the floor, her breathing getting faster, her cheeks reddening. 'There must be *something* here that will help explain...' She moved on to another cupboard filled with his watercolour paintings before glancing around the study with wild eyes. Then she targeted her father's bureau, frantically pulling out the drawers and emptying them.

Nick came up to her, putting a hand on her shoulder. 'Claire, stop. You don't even know what you're looking for. It's not helping—'

'I need to do this, Nick,' she said, shrugging away, chucking more accumulated junk onto the floor. Dust motes speckled the air as she searched. She pulled down the desk flap, swiping away pens and pencils, stationery and notebooks – all the stuff the police hadn't taken.

She stopped for a second, staring at the ceiling, thinking. 'The compartment,' she whispered, pulling out a mini drawer at the back of the desk. 'The police wouldn't have known to look here when they'd gone through his belongings. He once showed it to me and Lenni. He told us it was a secret. We thought it was the coolest thing ever. Look...' Claire removed the false bottom beneath where the drawer had been. 'He used to let us stash sweets in here, so Mum wouldn't...' She trailed off as she spotted it. 'Nick?' she said, turning to him.

He reached in and took out the phone.

'Mum was looking for that everywhere. He refused to use it. I didn't even know he had one until recently.'

Nick opened it up and switched on the cheap, pay-as-you-go flip phone. 'It's almost out of battery. We should let the police have it.'

'Give it to me,' she said, swiping if from him. She toggled back through the list of calls made and received, scanning the numbers. 'Look, he called Greene & Galloway several times, see?' Her voice was urgent as she thought back over the dates and times, working it out. 'I think he was the supposed cash buyer, Nick. He would have done anything to stop Mum selling up. He couldn't ever leave because Lenni was locked up here. He had his lucid moments too, don't forget.'

Nick shook his head, raising his eyebrows. 'You're probably right.' He leant in close, peering at the phone screen. 'But stop now, Claire. Don't torture yourself any more.'

'There were other numbers dialled too,' she said, ignoring him. 'Look, these were to my mobile. As well the Old Stables landline. He must have been the one who left that twisted message, probably when he wasn't thinking straight.' She explained about the disturbing voicemail the night Jason and Greta arrived. The timing of the calls fitted. 'It's no coincidence all the silent calls I was getting have stopped now. He probably wasn't thinking straight and misdialling me.' She paced around the study, trampling on her father's belongings.

'Don't overthink this, Claire,' he said, reaching out to stop her. She was shaking. 'Trust me, I speak from experience. Sometimes the only closure is accepting there will be none.' He drew her close, placing a finger over her lips. She only stilled when he pulled her into his arms, holding her tight, stroking her hair. 'I'm going to delay the restaurant opening for a while.' He felt her tense again as she looked up at him. 'I'm not leaving you alone with all this to deal with.'

'No, Nick,' Claire said quietly. 'I won't let you do that. The restaurant is everything you've always wanted.'

'Not quite,' he said, staring into her eyes. 'Anyway, my mind is made up. I'm here for as long as you need. Maybe I'll even move back to Cornwall permanently.' He wanted to get it all out, tell her how he felt about her. But now wasn't the time.

She rested her head against his chest. He was right. Searching for answers that didn't exist was only hurting her more.

'I could easily sell the restaurant, even as it is. It's been stressing me out more than I'd like. I had this crazy idea...' He laughed at his stupidity, wondering how he thought he'd ever have got away with it.

'Go on,' she said.

'When Jess and I split up, I couldn't afford my own place. I've been couch-surfing with mates for months, so I was getting the restaurant basement converted into a living space. It's not entirely legal, I know, and I'd have got shut down if it was discovered, but it seemed like my only option.'

'So much has happened, Nick,' she whispered, looking up at him again, thinking about what he'd been through. 'Too much. But what happened to us?' Their faces were close, each aware of the other's breathing, the feel of their bodies pressed close, the warmth shared. They stayed like that for what seemed like forever, each knowing this wasn't the right time for the kiss that would have been perfect if circumstances had been different. Perhaps if they'd been standing in the sea.

CHAPTER SEVENTY-EIGHT

The day they brought Eleanor home was bright and clear, with a sky so indigo it almost looked as if stars should be visible. Having been back home in London for several weeks, Jason had come back to Cornwall alone for a couple of days. Greta's mother had flown over to help out with the babies.

As they stood outside the farmhouse waiting, an onshore breeze heralding Lenni's arrival, Claire turned her face to the sun. She was filled with anticipation. They'd seen Lenni over the last couple of weeks, of course – the short visits gradually getting longer, stretching from ten minutes to several hours. They'd taken her gifts, were patient with her when she wanted to be alone with the curtains drawn and the lights off, yet listened to her when she was ready to speak. So far, she'd said little about what had happened to her. The psychologist said it was normal, that it might come out in time. For now, it was all about reconnecting, rekindling relationships, building trust.

Occupational therapists and mental health workers had come to the farm too, preparing the family for her return. Everyone had been astounded by her progress, how her inner life force was keeping her going – a wilting seedling finally being given light and water.

Claire took her mother's trembling hand when they saw the car crowning the rise of the drive. Shona was still on medication, still struggling with everything, but was making progress each day.

'You OK?' Nick whispered, leaning close to Claire, taking her other hand. He meshed his fingers between hers as the vehicle came closer. Jason was close by, and Aunt Jenny had come down to offer her support to Shona.

'I think so,' Claire whispered back, not taking her eyes off the car.

'Is she here yet?' Rain came tumbling out of the house, squeezing in next to Jason. She'd decided to stay on in Cornwall a bit longer while Maggie got them settled into Rose's place. Hanging out with Marcus and his mates was doing her good, and she reckoned she might be back next holidays.

'This is it, then,' Jason said, as the car pulled across the gravel into the courtyard. The windows flared with sunlight, obscuring the faces inside.

The front door of the car opened and Sarah, the psychologist who'd been visiting, got out. She removed her sunglasses and forked them onto her head, smiling at the small gathering. Low key was best, she'd told them, so as not to overwhelm Eleanor. A nurse got out of the back of the car and came round, opening the other rear door. For those few moments, it was as if the whole world was holding its breath.

And then Eleanor emerged – a hand on the top of the door, her feet reaching tentatively for the ground. Her eyes were blinking, squinting, darting about.

'Lenni,' Jason said under his breath. Claire squeezed Nick's hand, leading him a step forward as Eleanor stood upright. Outside of the hospital, she seemed so small. The nurse tried to help her, but she shied away. Typical Lenni, Claire thought, desperate to run up to her, to hold her, to never let her go.

'Hello, Lenni,' Claire said across the courtyard.

'Hello,' came a faint whisper back, but it could have been a breath of wind in the trees. She looked at the distance between her and her sister – the little girl she'd allowed to get lost. About twenty feet separated them, each one representing a year of missing time.

'Darling,' Shona said from behind, so weakly she didn't think Eleanor even heard.

Claire took another step forward, Nick beside her. She was aware of the others flanking her, how much it felt like Grandmother's Footsteps, the game they all used to play as kids.

Nineteen years.

'Welcome home, Lenni,' Jason said, his voice wavering at words he never thought he'd get to say.

Lenni's mouth motioned upwards, making a small smile.

In turn, she took a step or two closer to them. Seventeen years.

She was wearing grey linen trousers and a white blouse with flat black pumps on feet that shuffled her closer still. A pale-green cardigan was draped over her shoulders – all her clothes chosen by Claire. Her hair was different too, the brittle strands now untangled and trimmed. It sat a couple of inches above her shoulders in a wispy cut, making her look a little more normal, a little more real.

Claire ventured forward a bit more. Fourteen years. It was only as she got closer that Eleanor's flaking fingernails, her bad teeth, her sallow complexion became apparent. Her unusual gait was only noticeable when she walked.

'It's so good to have you home,' Claire said, inching forward to twelve years.

Lenni glanced down at her feet, as if urging them to work. 'I'm sorry,' she said in that defiant, almost childlike voice. 'Sorry… sorry… sorry…'

'Oh, my darling, don't be sorry.' Shona drew closer but halted. She wasn't sure what to do. Was hugging her OK? Maybe she didn't even want to be hugged.

'You mustn't be sorry, Lenni,' Claire echoed. 'You did nothing wrong.' She gripped Nick's fingers as she crept forward. Eight years to go.

As Lenni stood alone in the middle of the courtyard, her psychologist deliberately holding back, the nurse hovering just in case, Claire noticed that her eyes had latched onto something, or *someone*. She tracked her gaze to where Rain was standing, a little removed from the rest of them.

'Hello again,' Lenni said, a smile lighting up her face. Cheekbones stood proud above her beaming mouth, sore lips framing dark teeth. At this distance, Claire saw the white streaks of sunblock smeared on her skin.

Hello *again*, Claire thought? Did Lenni recognise something of herself in Rain, drawn to someone of a similar age when she'd been taken? The psychologist had warned them about things like that.

'It's hot,' Eleanor said quietly, only taking her eyes off Rain briefly to look up at the sky. 'And so big.' She came closer, the nurse taking hold of her elbow when she wobbled.

Four years.

'Yes, we're having a lovely warm spell,' Claire said, flicking her eyes between Lenni and Rain. What was going on?

'A lovely warm spell,' Eleanor repeated, though it was directed at Rain.

'We should go inside,' the psychologist suggested. No one replied. All eyes were on Eleanor as she moved forward, releasing herself from the nurse's steadying hand. She wanted to be free. Just a couple of years apart now.

'Shall we go to the beach?' Eleanor asked, approaching Rain. She held out a hand to her. 'We can get an ice cream.' The cheeky glimmer of thirteen-year-old Lenni was evident in her grin, though she had no idea how deep her words cut. No one heard the psychologist when she suggested that the beach probably wasn't a good idea, that going inside and resting would be wise.

Shona, Jason and Claire nodded to each other, drawing close to Lenni, opening their arms wide around her like a giant flower blooming. She allowed herself to be embraced, swallowed up, absorbed by their love. And as the years between them diminished absolutely nothing at all, as the vast expanse of missing time ceased to exist, they all turned and headed slowly for the sea.

CHAPTER SEVENTY-NINE

Freedom and Beyond

'She's real, she's real, she's really, *really* real,' I say over and over as I scramble up the steps, glancing back down. My legs hurt and I'm panting, but it gets me thinking – if she's real, then maybe I'm not.

My heart thumps as I emerge into the place where I used to play, making pretend boats, houses and hospitals. She told me not to stop, to get out, but I have to lean against the old refrigerator to get my breath back – the fridge he slides over the trapdoor to the cellar below to keep me safe. *All tucked up*, he said. I catch my breath, the air burning in and out of my lungs. As kids, we never knew about the chamber down below. No one did, apart from Daddy. If I had the strength, I'd shove the fridge back over the hole, sealing him in. But then that girl would be locked in too. If she's even real.

She's real. She's real. She's really, really real!

There's a noise from down below. Has he come back to life? Or maybe it's her. Maybe she's bad and wants to catch me. Or perhaps he's going to lock her up now instead of me. I take a step down again, pausing, but I feel sick so pull myself up again, listening carefully. Then the noise again. Someone moving about down there. A tiny bird flaps out of the chimney, veering away through a glassless window.

I step over all the rubbish and go to the front door, what's left of it. I feel like crying because the whole world is out there and it's really scary. But then I hear her words in my head again – *Get out!* – so I stand in the open doorway, sucking in the fresh woody air. Finally, I step outside, blinking as my eyes grow accustomed to the light, feeling the breeze on my face. Through the canopy of leaves above, I can just make out the sun, see a few clouds scudding along. It feels like summer. But which one?

Then another noise from inside the cottage, someone getting closer.

I try to run but can't. My legs won't have it. I set off through the trees, forcing them to work, grabbing onto the trunks as I make my way down the slope. I stumble, not knowing which direction to go. 'Help!' I cry, but my voice barely works.

Finally, I reach the edge of the woods and the world opens up into the biggest, most colourful painting I've ever seen. It's as if an orchestra is playing. It stretches for a thousand miles left and right and up into the sky too. My mouth opens, and my tongue burns dry from the breeze. I spread my arms wide, throwing back my head. I laugh so loudly that I don't even care if I'm discovered.

Then I see him. A man out walking his dog.

I drop to the ground, my fingers clawing at the moss and dirt and twigs. He's down at the bottom of the field, dangling a lead, calling to his dog as it darts in and out of the hedges. But then the dog stops, standing proud, its nose stuck up and sniffing the air. It glances my way and sniffs again, barking. I'm behind a tree now but that doesn't stop the creature looking right at me and letting out another high-pitched bark.

A dog… a man with a lead… me, alone…

I slap a hand over my mouth, stifling the scream. Please don't hurt me, please don't hurt me… I bite my palm, my whole body shaking, watching him walk away. The dog follows him, giving one last bark in my direction.

If you'd just stayed home, none of this would have happened…

I swing around to where the voice is coming from, but there's no one there.

'Yes, yes, I should have stayed inside…' I whisper, my mind spinning back through what seems like a thousand million years. It's as if I'm there again, standing, waiting, whistling to myself, trying to keep cheerful, but still he didn't come. I glanced at my watch. It was new for my birthday. 'Quarter to eleven,' I said to myself, trying not to feel scared. It was dark and the latest I'd ever been out alone. The village disco finished at ten. 'Come on, Dad,' I said, shuffling from one foot to the other. 'Where are you?' I really needed the loo.

'You getting a lift home, love?' the lady who ran the disco said. She'd been sweeping up, and suddenly the village hall car park was plunged into darkness as she turned off the lights. I heard her locking the door, grumbling to her husband that I was still there, that they couldn't leave me alone.

'Yeah, my dad's coming to fetch me. He's probably been held up.'

'Well, you just wait here for him, then,' the woman said. Her husband, the man who played the disco music, took her by the arm and led her off to their car. He had his hand on her bottom. I watched the red tail lights get smaller as they drove the half a mile down the lane back towards the village. And then I was quite alone, standing outside the village hall in the pitch dark on a Friday night. I wanted to cry, but fought it back. I'd never be allowed out again if I acted like a baby.

My watch said five to eleven. If he wasn't here by the hour, I was going to set off walking. It would take me forever to get to the farm, but I didn't want to wait here alone all night. Mum would have been on time.

'Hello there,' a man's voice called out, making me jump. I didn't see him at first, out there in the darkness, but then I recognised him. 'Bit late to be out alone, isn't it?'

Something wet was licking my hands, scrabbling at my jeans. It was his dog. He called it off, but the dog didn't listen. 'I like dogs,' I said, bending down and stroking it. 'Good girl, Ginny.' I ruffled her shaggy coat and gave her a big hug.

'She likes you,' he said. I laughed at that. 'How are you getting home?'

'Dad's coming. He's late. I think I'm going to walk.' I peered beyond him, through the deserted car park and out into lane. The hall was just outside the village; if I turned left and walked for about a mile and a half, I'd reach the top of our drive.

'It's very dark,' he said. 'Do you have a torch?'

I shook my head.

'Look,' he said. 'Ginny likes a long run last thing at night. How about I walk you home? That way you'll be safe.'

'But what if Dad comes?'

'Then he'll pass us on the way.'

That was true, and he was being kind, I thought, even though I knew his house was in the opposite direction. 'OK, then,' I said, but only because I knew him. I put on my cardigan. It was starting to get chilly.

'How was the disco?' he asked, as we tramped along, the streetlights now behind us.

'Noisy,' I said. I wasn't supposed to have gone to the disco at all. Mum wouldn't have liked it. *While the cat's away*, Dad had said earlier with a grin, but I knew it was only because he wanted to sit in the pub with his friends and he didn't want to leave me home alone.

'You mean I can actually go?' I'd pestered him loads.

'Just this once. But don't tell your mum or I'll be in trouble.'

And so, I didn't. Mum, Jason and Claire had gone to Bristol to look at the university for Claire, and while they were there, Mum was going to buy Jason a new suit for church.

'You're getting all grown up, young lady,' the man said, as we walked. I liked that. No one had ever called me grown up before.

I went on to tell him about the disco, about school, about the animals on our farm, and a moment later, his big sweaty hand was snug around mine.

'Don't mind, do you?' I saw the flash of his grin in the moonlight.

I shook my head. I knew this was the sort of thing grown-ups did. It gave me a funny feeling down low, but we walked on. After all, he came to the farm quite often. Mum always said he had an ulterior motive, whatever that meant.

'You have soft skin, young lady,' he said, slowing to a stop. 'And a pretty young face.' He trailed his finger across my throat. For a second, I was scared. No one had ever done that to me before. He smiled down at me. He was tall. Ginny ran between us, her soft fur brushing against my bare legs. I didn't realise what the other feeling was immediately. It just felt warm and almost nice. When I looked down, I saw his hand was on my chest.

'Don't do that!' It came out automatically, just like Mum had always said it would. 'Please,' I added, because he was a family friend.

'But you like it,' he said. 'I know you do.'

I shook my head and backed away. I didn't like it one bit. 'Sorry,' I said, as if I was telling him he couldn't borrow my pencil sharpener. I started to walk off quickly, but before I knew what was happening, I was on my back on the verge.

It hurt so much. His hand was over my mouth the whole time while his other hand grappled with me down there. He undid his jeans and stuck something between my legs and Ginny began to bark. My vision was blurry. My tears were hot. My breathing was fast but my heartbeat slow. It went on forever – just like a million years – and cut me clean in two pieces.

'Don't fucking tell anyone, right?'

I heard his zipper. I nodded frantically, staring up at him.

'If you do, I'll kill your brother and sister. And then you.'

I shook my head frantically. He was the big boy from the village, the one everyone liked. 'No, I won't tell anyone, Callum. I promise on my life.'

I lay on my back and watched him walk back to the village. His dog ran after him. When I looked at my watch, it said half past eleven. Ten minutes later, the headlights came around the corner and a car slowed to a halt. I heard my father's voice, saw his shocked expression as he stood over me. I couldn't look at him; couldn't stand for him to look at me, for him to know what had happened.

'Oh God, Lenni, *no…*' He was on his knees beside me, his hands searching me for injuries. 'Dear God… I'm so sorry I'm late. Who did this to you?' He touched the blood between my thighs and wept, letting out a big howl.

I stayed silent, just as I'd promised. I didn't want Claire and Jason to be killed.

My father bundled me up and carried me to the car, sobbing into my hair. He told me that he was sorry a thousand times over, that he should never have let me go out, that no one must know about this until he could make arrangements.

I'm good at keeping secrets, I wanted to say, but couldn't speak a word. He banged his fist on the car door, cursing himself for being late, swearing that he would never let this happen again.

'You should have stayed inside the hall,' he said, glaring at me in the driver's mirror. 'Mark my word, I shan't let you out again.' We drove off towards home, my father promising that from now on I would always be safe, that no one would ever know what he'd let happen to me. That no one would be able to do it to me ever again.

Instinct tells me where to go and the house down at the bottom of the field eventually comes into view, taking my breath away.

I take one last look back up towards the woods and the cottage and, like a flash of light – an angel with her blond hair trailing behind – I see that girl running away. She sees me too, and stops for a moment. Her eyes are as wide as mine. Then she urgently waves me on, disappearing into the trees. I only get a glimpse of the tattoo on her ankle, reminding me of something from long ago.

I press on down the hill, only glancing back once to see if she's still there. She isn't. The sight of home getting closer floods me with a puzzle of memories. As I approach the gate, the ground is rough. There used to be sheep in the fields but there aren't any more, just a few goats, and there are chickens pecking in the courtyard now. Up close, it doesn't look so very different to the faded, sepia photograph I've kept safe in my mind. I suddenly feel dizzy, as though I'm going to pass out, as if I'm in the wrong life.

I ease my way through the kissing gate, making the hinges squeak. I stop and go back, doing it again and again just to hear the noise. I close my eyes, remembering, hearing children's voices streaming through my head until I realise that it's my own giggles. I cross the yard, going right up to the house, feeling the warmth of the sun-soaked bricks radiating against my boiling skin. I don't feel very well. I knock on the door, then I knock again. A lady comes, and I'm not scared at all. I know she's nice, even though she's frowning at me.

'I want to come in. I *want* to,' I say over and over again, but she tells me I can't. Even when I point up the hill, showing her where I live, she still shakes her head.

I squint up to the woods again, hoping to see the girl so I can give her another wave. She made me promise that I'd never tell a soul what happened, that she killed my father. She said she'd been hiding in the woods for a couple of days, that she'd seen him coming and going to the cottage, that she knew he had a secret. She followed him down and hit him with the hammer, but only because he tried to hurt her first.

'Everything bad inside me just came out,' she said afterwards, shaking and sobbing. She had blood on her hands. I understood what she meant, except all my bad stuff was still locked up.

'Don't worry,' I said. 'I'm good at keeping secrets.'

I turn back to the woman at the door. It's only when I ask about Goose that something gleams in the lady's eye – a fragile bridge spanning a million years. Finally, she opens the door wide and my mother lets me in.

A LETTER FROM SAMANTHA

Dear Reader,

Thank you so much for choosing *The Reunion*. I really do hope you loved reading it as much as I enjoyed writing it! If you'd like to be kept up to date about my forthcoming books, then you can easily sign up here www.bookouture.com/samantha-hayes to receive all my latest news.

The Reunion is a really special book for me, harking back to my many Cornish holidays as a child. Back then, the summers seemed long, endless and carefree when, for several months each year, we'd stay in a caravan at Harlyn Bay near Padstow.

It was actually the inspiration for my fictional setting of Trevellin – a place I remember as rugged, beautiful and mysterious. I had a special spot on the beach where I would sit and read for hours, lost in the magic of a book. As I wrote *The Reunion*, many of the scenes were scooped from my memories.

The ice cream parlour was a place I loved to go too, trekking the long stretch of beach to the row of shops, picking through all the flavours. And I also remember gathering mussels on the rocks, boiling them up in our caravan for supper. Unlike Lenni, my brother and I were allowed to roam free until we dropped with exhaustion.

Having been back to Cornwall for holidays since with my own children (all now grown up), I knew I wanted to set a book there. Being a mum and a thriller writer, I tapped into every parent's worst nightmare – a child going missing. Years ago, one of my own daughters briefly slipped my hand at a theme park. Just those ten minutes searching for her sent me into a flat spin. But what if those ten minutes turned into ten hours, ten days, ten years or more?

So, taking the theme of childhood friendships blighted by the mysterious disappearance of a young girl, I merged the past with the present and came up with the idea for *The Reunion*. Would you trust your friends if the same thing happened again?

Finally, if you loved my book, I'd be so very grateful if you could write a review online. I genuinely cherish feedback from my readers and, of course, it helps spread the word amongst other readers like yourself! Plus, if you'd like to join me on Facebook or Twitter or email me through my website, it would be wonderful to hear from you. All my details are below.

Meantime, happy reading and I look forward to sharing my next book with you!

Sam x

samanthahayesauthor

@samhayes

www.samanthahayes.co.uk

ACKNOWLEDGEMENTS

Abundant and heartfelt thanks to Jessie Botterill, my lovely editor. It's a pleasure to work with you, and your insight and skill has made this book the very best it can be. I'm truly grateful. Huge thanks also to Kim Nash and Noelle Holten for getting me 'out there' into the hands of my readers – your enthusiasm is infectious! And indeed, much gratitude and many thanks from me to all the fantastic team at Bookouture for your passion, hard work and dedication.

As ever, big love to Oli Munson, agent extraordinaire, for always having my back, and to all the lovely people at A.M. Heath, including Jennifer Custer and Hélène Ferey. Everything you do is truly appreciated.

A special shout-out to Tracy Fenton, her amazing admin team and all the lovely members of THE Book Club on Facebook – your zest for books is inspiring! Huge thanks, too, to all my lovely readers worldwide – I couldn't do this without you.

And of course, much love and thanks to my wonderful family – Ben, Polly and Lucy, Avril and Paul, Graham and Marina, and Joe – for all your support, love, listening ears and cups of tea.

Finally, much love to Debbie, my dear friend, who's always there. *Stop it!!*

73304585R00214

Made in the USA
Middletown, DE
13 May 2018